Dear Reader,

I'm delighted to welco   Bestselling Author Co   celebration of Harlequin's 75 years in publishing, this collection features fan-favorite stories from some of our readers' most cherished authors. Each book also includes a free full-length story by an exciting writer from one of our current programs.

Our company has grown and changed since its inception 75 years ago. Today, Harlequin publishes more than 100 titles a month in 30 countries and 15 languages, with stories for a diverse readership across a range of genres and formats, including hardcover, trade paperback, mass-market paperback, ebook and audiobook.

But our commitment to you, our romance reader, remains the same: in every Harlequin romance, a guaranteed happily-ever-after!

Thank you for coming on this journey with us. And happy reading as we embark on the next 75 years of bringing joy to readers around the world!

Dianne Moggy

Vice-President, Editorial

Harlequin

RaeAnne Thayne finds inspiration in the beautiful northern Utah mountains, where the *New York Times* and *USA TODAY* bestselling author lives with her husband and three children. Her books have won numerous honors, including RITA® Award nominations from Romance Writers of America and a Career Achievement Award from *RT Book Reviews*. RaeAnne loves to hear from readers and can be contacted through her website, raeannethayne.com.

Mona Shroff is obsessed with everything romantic, so she writes romantic stories by night, even though she's an optometrist by day. If she's not writing, she's making chocolate truffles, riding her bike or reading, and she's just as likely to be drinking wine or gin and tonic with friends and family. She's blessed with an amazing daughter and loving son, who have both gone to college. Mona lives in Maryland with her romance-loving husband.

CHANGE OF FORTUNE

NEW YORK TIMES BESTSELLING AUTHOR
RaeAnne THAYNE

Previously published as *Fortune's Woman*

BESTSELLING AUTHOR COLLECTION

 Harlequin®
BESTSELLING
AUTHOR
COLLECTION

Recycling programs
for this product may
not exist in your area.

ISBN-13: 978-1-335-00892-3

Change of Fortune
First published as Fortune's Woman in 2009.
This edition published in 2024.
Copyright © 2009 by Harlequin Enterprises ULC

The Five-Day Reunion
First published in 2022. This edition published in 2024.
Copyright © 2022 by Mona Shroff

 Harlequin Enterprises ULC
22 Adelaide St. West, 41st Floor
Toronto, Ontario M5H 4E3, Canada
www.Harlequin.com

Printed in U.S.A.

CONTENTS

Visit her Author Profile page at Harlequin.com,
or raeannethayne.com, for more titles!

CHANGE OF FORTUNE

RaeAnne Thayne

Chapter 1

What was the punk doing?

Ross Fortune stood beside a canvas awning-covered booth at the art fair of the Red Rock Spring Fling, keeping a careful eye on the rough-looking kid with the eyebrow bolt and the lip ring.

The kid seemed out of place in the booth full of framed Wild West art—photographs of steely-eyed cowboys lined up on a weathered fence, tow-headed toddlers wobbling in giant Tony Lamas, a trio of horses grazing against a stormy sky.

Yeah, he might be jumping to conclusions, but it didn't seem like the sort of artwork that would interest somebody who looked more wannabe rock star than cowboy, with his inky black hair, matching black jeans and T-shirt, and pale skin. But as Ross watched, the kid—who looked on the small side of maybe fourteen or fifteen—thumbed through the selection of unframed prints like they were the most fascinating things in the world.

Ross wouldn't have paid him any attention, except that for the past ten minutes he couldn't help noticing the kid as he moseyed from booth to booth in the gathering twilight, his eyes constantly shifting around. The punk seemed abnormally aware of where the artist-vendor of each booth stood at all times, tracking their movements under dark eyelashes.

Until the Western photographs, he hadn't seemed much interested in whatever wares the artists were selling. Instead, he had all the tell-tale signs of somebody casing the place, looking for something easy to lift.

Okay, Ross was rushing to judgment. But something about the way the kid's gaze never stopped moving set all his alarm bells ringing. Even after the crowds started to abate as everybody headed toward the dance several hundred yards away, the kid continued ambling through the displays, as if he were searching for the perfect mark.

And suddenly he must have found it.

As Ross watched, the kid's gaze sharpened on a pink flowered bag somebody had carelessly left on a folding chair.

He moved to take a step forward, his own attention homing in on the boy, but just at that moment somebody jostled him.

"Sorry," muttered a dark-haired man in a Stetson who looked vaguely familiar. "I was looking for someone and wasn't watching where I was going."

"No problem," Ross answered. But when he looked

back, the kid was gone—and so was the slouchy flow-ered bag.

Adrenaline pumped through him. Finally! Chasing a shoplifter was just what he needed right now.

He had been bored to tears all day and would have left hours ago and headed back to San Antonio if he hadn't been volunteered by his family to help out on security detail for the Spring Fling, which was Red Rock's biggest party of the year.

At least now, maybe he might be able to have a little something to relieve the tedium of the day so he couldn't consider it a complete waste.

He stepped out of the booth and scanned the crowd. He saw his cousin J.R. helping Isabella Mendoza begin to pack away the wares at her textiles booth down the row a ways and he saw the Latino man in the Stetson who had bumped into him standing at a corner of a nearby watercolor booth.

He also spied his despised brother-in-law, Lloyd Fredericks, skulking through the crowd, headed toward a section behind the tents and awnings, away from the public thoroughfare.

No doubt he was up to no good. If Ross wasn't on the hunt for a purse snatcher, he would have taken off after Lloyd, just for the small-minded pleasure of ha-rassing the bastard a little.

He finally spotted the kid near a booth displaying colorful, froufrou dried-flower arrangements. He moved quietly into position behind him, his gaze unwavering.

This had always been his favorite moment when he had been a detective in San Antonio, before he left the job to become a private investigator. He loved that hot surge of energy before he took down a perp, that little thrill that he was about to tip the scales of justice firmly on the side of the victim.

He didn't speak until he was directly behind the boy. "Hey kid," he growled. "Nice purse."

The boy jumped like Ross had shoved a shiv between his ribs. He whirled around and shot him a defiant look out of dark eyes.

"I didn't do nothing. I was just grabbin' this for my friend."

"I'm sure. Come on. Hand it over."

The boy's grip tightened on the bag. "No way. She lost it so I told her I'd help her look for it and that's just what I'm doin'."

"I don't think so. Come on, give."

"You a cop?"

"Used to be." Until the politics and the inequities had become more than he could stomach. He didn't regret leaving the force. He enjoyed being a private investigator, picking his own cases and his own hours. The power of the badge sometimes had its privileges, though, he had to admit. Right now, he would have loved to be able to shove one into this little punk's face.

"If you ain't a cop, then I got nothin' to say to you. Back off."

The kid started to walk away but Ross grabbed his shoulder. "Afraid I'm not going anywhere. Hand over the bag."

The kid uttered a colorful curse and tried to break free. "You got it wrong, man. Let me go."

"Sure. No problem. That way you can just run through the crowd and lift a few more purses on your way through."

"I told you, I didn't steal nothin'. My friend couldn't

remember where she left it. I told her I'd help her look for it so she could buy some more stuff."

"Sure, kid. Whatever you say."

"I ain't lyin'!"

The boy wrestled to get free, and though he was small and slim, he was wiry and much more agile than Ross had given him credit for. To his chagrin, the teenager managed to break the grip on his arm and before Ross could scramble to grab him again, he had darted through the crowd.

Ross repeated the curse the kid had uttered earlier and headed after him. The punk might be fast but Ross had two major advantages—age and experience. He had chased enough desperate criminals through the grime and filth of San Antonio's worst neighborhoods to have no problem keeping up with one teenage boy carrying a bag that stood out like a flowery neon-pink beacon.

He caught up with him just before the boy would have slipped into the shadows on the edges of the art fair.

"Now you've pissed me off," Ross growled as he grabbed the kid again, this time in the unbreakable hold he should have used all along.

If he thought the boy's language was colorful before, that was nothing to the string of curses that erupted now.

"Yeah, yeah," Ross said with a tight grin. "I've heard it all before. I was a cop, remember?"

He knew he probably shouldn't be enjoying this so much. He was out of breath and working up a sweat, trying to keep the boy in place with one arm while he reached into his pocket with the other hand for the flex-cuffs he always carried. He had just fished them out and was starting to shackle the first wrist when a woman's raised voice distracted him.

"Hey! What do you think you're doing? Let go of him right this minute!"

He shifted his gaze from the boy to a woman with light brown hair approaching them—her eyes were wide and he briefly registered a particularly delectable mouth set in sharp, indignant lines.

He thought she looked vaguely familiar but that was nothing unusual in a small town like Red Rock, where everybody looked familiar. Though he didn't spend much time here and much preferred his life in San Antonio, the Fortune side of his family was among the town founders and leaders. Their ranch, the Double Crown, was a huge cattle spread not far from town.

The Spring Fling had become a large community event, and the entire proceeds from the art festival and dance went to benefit the Fortune Foundation, the organization created in memory of his mother's cousin Ryan, that helped disadvantaged young people.

Ross was a Fortune, and even though he was from the black-sheep side, he couldn't seem to escape certain familial obligations such as weddings and funerals.

Or Spring Flings.

He might not know the woman's name, but he knew her type. He could tell just by looking at her that she was the kind of busybody, do-gooder sort who couldn't resist sticking her lovely nose into things that were none of her business.

"Sorry. I can't let him go. I just caught the kid stealing a purse."

If anything, her pretty features tightened further.

"That's ridiculous. He wasn't stealing anything! He was doing me a favor."

Despite her impassioned words, he wasn't releasing the boy, not for a moment. "I'm sure the Red Rock police over at the security trailer can sort it all out. That's where we're heading. You're welcome to come along."

He would be more than happy to let her be somebody else's problem.

"I'm telling you, he didn't do anything wrong."

"Then why did he run from me?"

The slippery kid wriggled more in his hold. "Because you wouldn't listen to me, man. I tried to tell you."

"This is my purse!" the woman exclaimed. "I couldn't remember where I left it so I asked Marcus to help me find it so I could purchase some earrings from a folk artist on the next row over."

Ross studied the pair of them, the boy so wild and belligerent and the soft, blue-eyed woman who looked fragile and feminine in comparison. "Why should I believe you? Maybe you're in on the heist with him. Makes a perfect cover, nice-looking woman working together with a rough kid like him."

She narrowed her gaze, apparently unimpressed with the theory. "I'll tell you why you should believe me. Because my wallet, which is inside the bag, has my driver's license and credit cards in it. If you would stop being so cynical and suspicious for five seconds, I can show them to you."

Okay, he should have thought of that. Maybe two years away from the job had softened him more than he wanted to admit. Still, he wasn't about to let down his guard long enough for her to prove him any more of a fool.

He tossed the purse at her. "Fine. Show me."

Her look would have scorched through metal. She scooped up the purse and pawed through it, then pulled out a brocade wallet, which she unsnapped with sharp, jerky movements and thrust at him.

Sure enough, there was a Texas driver's license with a pretty decent picture of her—a few years younger and with slightly longer hair, but it was definitely her.

Julie Osterman, the name read under her picture. He gazed at it for a full ten seconds before the name registered. He had seen it on an office door at the Foundation, next to his cousin Susan's. And he must have seen her there, as well, which explained why she looked slightly familiar.

"You work for the Fortune Foundation, don't you?"

"Yes. I'm a counselor," she tilted her head and looked more closely at him. "And you're Ross Fortune, aren't you?"

He should have recognized her. Any good cop—and private investigator—ought to be more tuned in to that sort of thing than the average citizen and be able to remember names and faces.

"I don't give a crap who you are," the wriggling teenager in his grip spat out. "Let go of me, man."

He was still holding onto the punk, he realized. Ross eased his grip a little but was reluctant to release him completely.

"Mr. Fortune, you can let go anytime now," Julie Osterman said. "It all happened exactly as he said. He was helping me find my purse, not stealing anything. Thank you so much for your help, Marcus! I'm so relieved you found it. You can go now."

Ross pulled his hand away, surrendering to the inevitable, and Marcus straightened his ratty T-shirt like it was two hundred dollars' worth of cashmere.

"Dude's a psycho," he said to no one in particular but with a fierce glare for Ross. "I tried to tell you, man. You should have listened. Stupid cop-pig."

"Marcus," Julie said. Though the word was calm enough, even Ross recognized the steel behind it.

Marcus didn't apologize, but he didn't offer more insults, either. "I got to fly. See you, Ms. O."

"Bye, Marcus."

He ambled away, exuding affronted attitude with every step.

When he was out of earshot, Julie Osterman turned back to him, her mouth set in those tight lines again. He was so busy wondering if she ever unbent enough to genuinely smile that he nearly missed her words.

"I hope you haven't just undone in five minutes here what has taken me weeks to build with Marcus."

It took him a few more seconds longer than it should have to realize she was wasn't just annoyed, she was fuming.

"What did I do?" he asked in genuine bewilderment.

"Marcus is one of my clients at the Foundation," she said. "He comes from, well, not an easy situation. The adults in his life have consistently betrayed him. He's never had anyone to count on. I've been trying to help him learn to trust me, to count on *me*, by demonstrating that I trust him in return."

"By throwing your purse out there as bait?"

"Marcus has a history of petty theft."

"Just the kind of kid I would send after my purse, then."

She fisted her hands on her hips and the movement

made all her curves deliciously visible beneath her gauzy white shirt. "I wanted him to understand that when I look at him, I see beyond the mistakes he's made in the past to the bright future we're both trying to create for him."

It sounded like a bunch of hooey to him but he decided it might be wise to keep that particular opinion to himself right now, considering she looked like she wanted to skin him, inch by painful inch.

"Instead," she went on in that irritated voice, "you have probably just reinforced to a wounded child that all adults are suspicious and cynical, quick to judge and painfully slow to admit when they're wrong."

"Hey, wait a second here. I had no way of knowing you were trying for some mumbo-jumbo psychobabble experiment. All I saw was a punk lifting a purse. I couldn't just stand there and let him take it."

"Admit it," she snapped. "You jumped to conclusions because he looks a little rough around the edges."

Her hair was light brown, shot through with blond highlights that gleamed in the last few minutes of twilight. With those brilliant blue eyes, high cheekbones and eminently kissable mouth, she was just about the prettiest woman he had seen in a long, long time. The kind of woman a man never got tired of looking at.

Too bad such a nice package had to be covering up one of those save-the-world types who always set his teeth on edge.

"I was a cop for twelve years, ma'am," he retorted. "When I see a kid taking a purse that obviously doesn't belong to him, yeah, I tend to jump to conclusions. That doesn't mean they're usually wrong conclusions."

"But sometimes they are," she doggedly insisted.

"In this case, I made a mistake. See, I'm man enough to admit it. I made a mistake," he repeated. "It happens to the best of us, even ex-cops. But I'm willing to bet, if you asked anybody else in the whole damn art fair, they would have reached the same conclusion."

"You don't know that."

He rolled his eyes. "You're right. I completely overreacted. The next time I see somebody stealing your purse, I'll be sure to just watch him walk on by."

The angry set of her features eased a little and after a moment, she sighed. "I hope I can convince Marcus you were just being an ex-cop."

Despite his own annoyance, he could see she genuinely cared about the boy. He supposed he could see things from her point of view. He had a particular soft spot for anybody who tried to help kids in need, even if they did tend to become zealots about it.

"I can try talking to the kid if that would help," he finally offered, though he wasn't quite sure what compelled him to make the suggestion. Maybe something to do with how her eyes softened when she talked about the punk.

"I appreciate that, but I don't think—"

A woman's frantic scream suddenly ripped through the evening, cutting off whatever Julie Osterman had intended to say.

Julie's heart jumped in her chest as another long scream echoed through the fair. She gasped and instinctively turned toward the source of the sound, somewhere out of their view, away from the public areas and the four long rows of vendor tents.

Before she could even draw a breath to exclaim over

the noise, Ross Fortune was racing in the direction of the sound.

He was all cop now, she couldn't help thinking.

Hard and alert and dangerous.

She was too startled to do more than watch him rush toward the sound for a few seconds. It always managed to astound her when police officers and firefighters raced toward potentially hazardous situations while people like her stood frozen.

She knew a little about Ross Fortune from her friend Susan, his cousin. He had been a police officer in San Antonio but had left the force a few years ago to open his own private investigation company.

He was a trained detective, she reminded herself, and she would probably do wise to just let him, well, *detect*.

But as another scream ripped through the night, past the happy laughter of the carnival rides and the throbbing bass coming from the dance, Julie knew she had to follow him, whether she was comfortable with it or not.

Someone obviously needed help and she couldn't just stand idly by and do nothing.

Ross had a head start on her but she managed to nearly catch up as he darted around the corner of a display of pottery she had admired earlier in the evening.

Probably only ten seconds had elapsed from the instant they heard the first scream, but time seemed to stretch and elongate like the pulled taffy being sold on the midway alongside kettle corn, snow cones and cotton candy.

She ran after Ross and stumbled onto a strange, surreal scene. It was darker back here, away from the lights and noise of the Spring Fling crowd. But Julie could still tell instantly that the woman with the high-pitched scream was someone she recognized from seeing her around town, a blowsy blonde who usually favored miniscule halter tops and five-inch high heels.

She was staring at something a dozen yards away, illuminated by a lone vapor light, high on a power pole. A figure was lying motionless on the ground, faceup, and even from here, Julie could see a dark pool of what she assumed was blood around his head.

A third person stood over the body. It took Julie only a moment to recognize Frannie Fortune Fredericks, a frequent volunteer at the center.

And Ross's sister, she remembered with stunned dismay that she saw reflected in his features.

Frannie was staring at her hands. In the pale moonlight, they shone much darker than the rest of her skin.

"It's her. She killed him!" the other woman cried out stridently. "Can't you see? The bitch killed my Lloyd!"

Her Lloyd? As in Lloyd Fredericks, Frannie's husband? Julie looked closer at the figure on the ground. For the first time, she registered his sandy-blond hair and those handsome, slightly smarmy features, and realized she was indeed staring into the fixed, unblinking stare of Lloyd Fredericks.

This couldn't be happening...

Ross quickly crossed to Lloyd's body and knelt to search for a pulse. Julie knew even before he rose to his feet a moment later that he wouldn't have been able to find one. That sightless gaze said it all.

That was definitely Frannie's husband. And he was definitely dead.

Ross gripped his sister's arm and Julie noticed that he was careful not to touch her blood-covered hands. *How did he possibly have the sense to avoid contami-*

nating evidence under such shocking circumstances? she wondered.

"Frannie? What's going on? What happened?"

His sister's delicate features looked pale, almost bloodless, and she lifted stark eyes to him. "I don't... It's Lloyd, Ross."

"I can see it's Lloyd, honey. What happened to him?"

The screaming woman wobbled closer on her high heels. "She killed him. Look at her! She's got blood all over her. Oh, Lloyd, baby."

She began to wail as if her heart were being ripped out of her cosmetically enhanced chest. Julie would have liked to be a little sympathetic, but she didn't fail to notice the other woman only began the heartrending sobs when a crowd started to gather.

Ross turned to her. "Julie, do you have a phone? Can you call 911?"

"Of course," she answered. While she pulled her phone out of her pocket and started hitting buttons, she heard Ross take charge of the scene, ordering everybody to step back a couple dozen feet. In mere moments, it seemed the place was crawling with people.

The 911 operator had just answered when Julie saw a pair of police officers arrive. They must have been drawn to the commotion from other areas of the Spring Fling.

"This is Julie Osterman," she said to the 911 dispatcher. "I was going to report a...an incident at the Spring Fling but you all are already here."

"What sort of incident?" the dispatcher asked.

Julie was hesitant to use the word *murder,* but how could it be anything else? "I guess a suspicious death. But as I said, your officers are already here."

"Tell me what you know anyway."

The woman took what little information Julie could provide to relay to the officers, who were pushing the crowd even farther back.

When she hung up the phone with the dispatcher, she stood for a moment, not sure what to do, where to go. She disliked this sort of crowd scene, the almost avaricious hunger for information that seemed to seize people when something dramatic and shocking occurred nearby.

She wanted to slip away but it didn't feel quite right, especially when she had been one of the first ones on the scene. She supposed technically she was a witness, though she hadn't seen anything and knew nothing about what had happened.

Julie scanned the crowd, though she didn't know what she was seeking. A familiar face, perhaps, someone who could help her make sense of this shocking development.

In the distance, she saw someone in a black Stetson just on the other side of the edge of light emanating from the art fair. He made no move to come closer to investigate the commotion, which she found curious. But when she looked again, he was gone.

"Oh, Lloyd! My poor Lloyd."

The woman who had alerted them with her screams was nearly hysterical by now, standing just a few feet away from her and gathering more stares from the crowd. Julie watched her for a moment, then sighed and moved toward her.

Though she wanted to slap the woman silly for her hysterics—whether they were feigned or not—she supposed that wasn't a very compassionate attitude. She could at least try to calm her down a little. It was the decent thing to do.

She reached out and took the other woman's hand in hers. "Can I get you something? A drink of water, maybe?"

"Nooooo," she sobbed. "I just want my Lloyd."

Lloyd wasn't going to belong to anyone again—not his pale, stunned-looking wife and not this voluptuous woman who grieved so vociferously for him.

"I'm Julie," she said after a moment. "What's your name?"

"Crystal. Crystal Rivers. Well, that's not my real name."

"Oh. It's not?" she asked, with a perfectly straight face.

"It's my stage name. I'm a dancer. My real name is Christina. Christina Crosby."

"How about if I call you Chris?"

"Christy. That's what people call me."

Julie offered a smile, grateful that their conversation seemed to soothe the woman a bit—or at least distract her from the hysterics. "Okay, Christy. What happened? Can you tell me? All I know is that we heard you scream and came running and found him dead."

"I'll tell you what happened. She killed him. Frannie Fredericks killed my Lloyd."

Chapter 2

Julie frowned as the woman's bitter words seemed to ring through the night air.

She still couldn't quite believe it. She had always liked Frannie. The woman seemed to genuinely care about her volunteer work at the Foundation and she had always been friendly to Julie.

She supposed no one could really see inside the heart of someone else or know how they would respond when provoked, but Frannie had always seemed far too quiet and unassuming for Julie to accept that she had murdered her husband.

"How can you be so certain? Did you see her do it?"

"No. He was already dead when I came looking for him." She sniffled loudly and pulled a bedraggled tissue from her ample cleavage. "We were supposed to meet here and take off to my place after his obligations at the stupid Spring Fling. He didn't even want to come, but Lloyd had business tonight he had to take care of."

Business at the Spring Fling? Who on earth tried to conduct business at a community celebration?

"What kind?" she asked.

"I don't know. Something important. Someone he had to talk to, he said. Maybe Frannie. Maybe he told her he was going to divorce her for me. I don't know. I just know she killed him. Now watch—her brother Ross and the rest of the Fortunes are going to cover it all up. They think they own this whole damn town."

Julie shifted, uncomfortable with the other woman's antagonism. She liked and respected all the Fortunes. Susan Fortune Eldridge was one of her closest friends and she adored Lily Fortune, who was the driving force behind the Fortune Foundation that had been founded in memory of her late husband.

"Ma'am? Are you the one who found the body?"

Julie turned and found Billy Addison, a Red Rock police officer with whom she had a slight acquaintance through the Foundation.

"I did," Crystal waved her scarlet red nails like she was rodeo royalty riding around the arena. "My poor Lloyd. Have you arrested Frannie Fredericks yet?"

"Um, not yet. Let's not jump the gun here, miss. We're going to be taking statements for some time now. I'm going to need to ask you a few questions."

"Anything. I'll tell you whatever you need to know. But I don't know why you need to ask anybody anything. It's plain as my nose job that Frannie did it. Look at her—she's got blood all over her."

She let out a dramatic sob, more for effect than out

of any real emotion, Julie thought, with unaccustomed cynicism.

"Lloyd was going to leave her skinny butt," Crystal said. "She knew it and that must be why she killed him. That's what I was just saying."

"Do you know that for a fact, ma'am?" the officer asked her.

"I know they fought earlier today. On the phone. I was with Lloyd and I heard the terrible things she said to him. She called him a two-faced liar and a cheat and said as how she wasn't going to put up with it anymore."

"How did you hear her side of the conversation?" the officer asked. "Was she on speaker phone?"

Crystal gaped at him. "Um, maybe. I don't remember. Or maybe she was just talking real loud."

Or maybe the conversation never took place, Julie thought. She didn't know what to believe—but she did know she shouldn't be hearing any of this. Any affair between Lloyd Fredericks and Crystal Rivers was not something she wanted to know any more about.

She stepped away to leave the police officer to the interview. Still, Crystal wasn't exactly being unobtrusive. Her words carried to Julie as she walked through the crowd.

"I just know Frannie made my poor Lloyd's life a living hell. And now her brother's going to cover it up. Watch and see if the Fortunes don't all circle the wagons around her. You just watch and see."

The Fortunes *were* a powerful family in Red Rock. But most of the ones she had met through the Foundation were also decent, compassionate people who cared about the community and making it a better place.

The family also had its enemies, though—people

who resented their wealth and power—and Julie had a feeling Crystal wouldn't be the only one who would whisper similar accusations about the Fortunes.

What a terrible way for the Spring Fling to end, she thought as she made her way through the crowd. The event should be a celebration, a chance for everyone in town to gather and help raise money for a worthy cause. Instead, one life had been snuffed out and several others would be changed forever, especially those in Lloyd's family.

Julie knew the Frederickses had a teenage son. Josh, she thought was his name. If she wasn't mistaken, he was friendly with Ricky Farraday Jamison, her boss Linda's son, even though Ricky was a few years younger than Josh.

Had anyone told him yet? she wondered. How terrible for him if he were somehow drawn to the scene by the commotion and the crowd and happened to see his father's body lying there. It was a definite possibility, even though the police were widening the perimeter of the scene, pushing the crowd still farther back.

Perhaps proactive measures were called for. Someone should find the boy first before he could witness such a terrible sight.

Ross Fortune seemed the logical person to find his nephew. She sighed. She really didn't want to talk to him. Their altercation seemed a lifetime ago, but she would still prefer not to have anything more to do with the man.

If she had her preference, she would escape this situation completely and go as far away as possible. It reminded her far too much of another tragic scene, of police lights flashing and yellow crime tape flipping in the wind and the hard, invasive stares of the rapacious crowd.

She had a sudden memory of that terrible day seven years earlier, driving home from work, completely oblivious to the scene she would find at her tidy little house, and the subsequent crime tape and the solemn-eyed police officers and the sudden terrible knowledge that her world had just changed forever.

She didn't think about that day often anymore, but this situation was entirely too familiar. Then again it would have been unusual if the similarities didn't shake loose those memories she tried to keep so carefully contained.

She didn't want Frannie's son to go through the same thing. He needed to be warned, whether she wanted to talk to his uncle again or not. She started through the crowd, keeping an eye out for the tall, gorgeous private investigator.

In the end, he found her.

"Julie! Ms. Osterman!"

She followed the sound of her name and discovered Ross in a nearby vendor booth with his sister and the Red Rock chief of police, Jimmy Caldwell.

Frannie Fortune was slumped in a chair while her brother hovered protectively over her. She looked exactly as Julie imagined *she* had looked that day seven years ago. Frannie's lovely, delicate features were stark and pale and her eyes looked dazed. Numb.

She wanted to hug her, to promise her that sometime in the future this terrible day would be just an awful memory.

"I told you, Jim," Ross said. "I was talking to Ms. Osterman just a row over when we heard a scream. We were the first ones on the scene, weren't we? Besides the other woman."

Julie nodded.

"You're the one who called 911, right?" the police chief asked her.

"Yes. But your officers were on the scene before I could even give the dispatcher any information. Probably only a moment or two after we arrived," she said.

The police chief wrote something in a notebook. "Can you confirm the scene as you saw it? Lloyd was on the ground and Frannie was standing over him."

"Yes." She pointed. "And the other woman—Crystal—was standing over there screaming."

"You didn't see anyone else? Just Frannie and Crystal?"

Julie nodded. "That's right. Just them."

"Frannie? You want to tell me what happened before Ross and Ms. Osterman showed up?"

She lifted her shell-shocked gaze from her blood-stained pants to the police chief. "I don't know. I was looking for... I just... I found him that way. He was just lying there."

"Tell him, Frannie," Ross insisted. "Go ahead and tell Jim you had nothing to do with Lloyd's death."

"I... I didn't."

Jimmy scratched the nape of his neck. "That's not a very convincing claim of innocence, Frannie. Especially when you're the one standing here over your dead husband's body with blood on your hands."

Ross glared at him. "Frannie is not capable of murder. You have to know that. You're crazy if you think she could have done this."

The police chief raised a dark eyebrow that contrasted with his salt-and-pepper hair. "This might not be the best time for you to be calling names, Fortune."

"What else would you call it? My sister did not kill her husband, though she should have done it years ago."

"Appears to be no love lost between the two of you, was there?"

"I hated his miserable, two-timing guts."

"Maybe you need to be the one coming down to the station for questions instead of Frannie here."

"I'll go any place you want me to. But I didn't kill him any more than my sister did. I've got an alibi, re-member? Ms. Osterman here."

"He's right. He was with me," she said.

"Lucky for you. Unfortunately, by the sound of it, Frannie doesn't have that kind of alibi. I'm going to have to ask you to come with me to the station to an-swer some questions, Frannie."

"Come on, Jimmy. You know she couldn't have done this."

"You want to know what I know? The evidence in front of me. That's it. That's what I have to go by, no matter what. You were a cop. You know that. And I'm also quite sure this is going to be a powder keg of a case. I can't afford to let people say I allowed the Fortunes to push me around. I have to follow every procedure to the letter, which means I'm going to have to take her in for questioning. I have no choice here."

Ross glowered at the man but before he could say anything, another officer approached them. He was vi-brating with energy. Julie imagined in a quiet town like Red Rock, this sort of situation was the most excitement the small police force ever saw.

"We found what might be the murder weapon, sir,"

the fresh-faced officer said. "I knew you would want to know right away."

"Thanks, Paul," the chief tried to cut him off before he said more, but the officer didn't take the hint.

"It was shoved under a display table in one of the tents and it's got what appears to be blood on it. I'll have CSU process it the minute they show up. Take a look. What do you think, sir?"

All of them followed the man's pointing finger and Julie could see a large, solid-looking ceramic vase. When she turned back, she saw that Frannie Fredericks had turned even more pale, if that was possible.

"What's the matter?" Ross asked her.

She shook her head and looked back at her blood-stained slacks.

"Do you know anything about that vase?" Jimmy Caldwell asked her, his gray eyes intent on her features.

When Ross's sister clamped her lips together, the police chief leaned in closer. "You have to tell me, Frannie."

She suddenly looked trapped, her gaze flitting between Jimmy Caldwell and her brother.

"Fran?" Ross asked.

"It's mine. I bought it from Reynaldo Velasquez," she finally whispered. "I wanted to put it in the upstairs hallway."

Ross muttered an expletive. "Don't say anything else, Frannie. Not until I get you an attorney. Just keep your mouth shut, okay?"

She blinked at her brother. "Why do I need an attorney? I didn't do anything wrong. I just bought a vase."

"Just don't say anything."

"In that case," the police chief said, "I guess we'll have to continue this conversation at the police station."

"You don't have nearly enough to arrest her. You know you don't."

"Not yet." The police chief's voice was grim.

"Josh. You have to find Josh," Frannie said suddenly. She clutched her brother's arm. "Find him, Ross. Get him away from here."

He looked taken aback by her urgency. "I'll look for him."

"Thank you, Ross. You've always taken care of everything."

He opened his mouth to say something, then clamped it shut again.

"Let's go, Frannie," the police chief's voice wasn't unkind. "I'm sure it will be a relief to you to get away from this crowd."

"Yes," she murmured.

The police chief slipped a huge navy windbreaker over her blood-stained clothing, then wrapped his arm around her shoulders. By all appearances, it looked as if he were consoling the grieving widow but Julie saw the implacable set to his muscles, as if he expected the slight woman to make a break for it any moment.

Ross watched after them, his jaw tight. "This is a fricking nightmare," he growled. "Unbelievable."

"Do you need help finding your nephew? I was coming to find you and suggest you look for him. It would be terrible for him to stumble onto this scene without knowing the…the victim was his father."

He muttered an expletive. "You're right. I should have thought of that before. I should have gone to look for him right away."

"I'll help you," she said. "We can split up. You take the midway and I'll head to the dance."

He blinked at the offer. "Why would you want to do that? You've already been dragged far enough into this."

He wouldn't get any arguments from her on that score. She would much rather be home in her quiet, solitary house than wandering through a crowd looking for a boy whose world was about to change forever.

She shrugged. "You need help."

He eyes widened with astonishment, and she wondered why he found a simple offer of assistance so very shocking.

"Thanks, then," he mumbled.

"No problem. Do you have a picture of Josh?"

"A picture?"

"I can't find him if I don't know what he looks like," she pointed out gently.

"Oh right. Of course."

He pulled his wallet out of his back pocket, and she was more charmed than she had any right to be when he opened an accordion fold in the wallet and slid out a photograph of a smiling young man with dark-blond hair, brown eyes and handsome features.

"I'm almost certain I've seen him around at the Foundation but the picture will help immensely," she said. "I'll be careful with it."

"I have more," Ross answered.

"We should exchange cell phone numbers so we can contact each other if either of us finds him."

"Good idea," he said. He rattled off a number, which she quickly entered into her phone, then she gave him hers in return.

"Now that you mention cell phones, it occurs to me that I should have thought of that first," Ross said. "Let me try to reach Josh on his phone. Maybe I can track him down and meet him somewhere away from here."

She waited while he dialed, impatient at even a few more moments of delay. The longer they waited, the more likely Josh would accidentally stumble onto his father's body and the murder scene.

After a moment, Ross made a face and left a message on the boy's voice mail for him to call him as soon as possible.

"He's not answering. I guess we're back to the original plan. I'll cover the midway and you see if you can find him at the dance."

"Deal. I'll call you if I find him."

"Right back at you. And Ms. Osterman? Thank you."

She flashed him a quick smile, though even that seemed inappropriate under the circumstances. "Julie, please."

He nodded and they each took off in separate directions. She quickly made her way to the dance, though she was forced to virtually ignore several acquaintances on her way, greeting them with only a wave instead of her usual conversation. She would have to explain later and hope they understood.

She expected Ross's call at any moment but to her dismay, her phone still hadn't rung by the time she reached the dance.

Country swing music throbbed from the speakers and the plank-covered dance floor was full. Finding Josh in this throng would be a challenge, especially when she knew him only from a photograph.

She scanned the crowd, looking for familiar faces. Finally, she found two girls she had worked with at the Foundation standing with a larger group.

"Hey, Ms. O." They greeted her with a warmth she found gratifying.

"Hey, Katie. Hi, Jo. I could use your help. I'm trying to find a boy."

"Aren't we all?" Jo said with a roll of eyes heavily framed in mascara.

Julie smiled. "A particular boy, actually. It's kind of serious. Do either of you know Josh Fredericks?"

"Sure," Katie answered promptly. "He's in my algebra class. He's kind of cute, even if he is super smart."

"Have you seen him lately? Tonight?"

"Yeah. It's weird. Usually he doesn't go two inches away from his girlfriend but I saw him by himself earlier, over by the refreshments. I think that was a while ago. Maybe an hour. He might have ditched the place by now."

"Thanks," she answered and headed in the direction they pointed.

She found Josh right where Katie had indicated, standing near the refreshment table as if he were waiting for someone. She recognized him instantly from the picture Ross had provided. He was wearing a Western-cut shirt and a black Stetson, just like half the other men here, and she could see his dark blond hair and brown eyes like his uncle's.

She didn't know whether to feel relief or dismay at finding him. She did not want to have to explain to him why she was searching for him. She quickly texted Ross that she had located his nephew at the dance and waited close by, intending only to keep an eye on him until Ross arrived to handle things.

He looked upset, she thought after a moment of observing him. His color was high and he kept looking toward the door as if waiting for someone to arrive.

Did he already know about his father? No, she couldn't imagine it. Why would he linger here at the dance if he knew his father had just been killed?

After two or three minutes, Josh suddenly looked at his watch, then set down his cup on a nearby tray.

Rats. She was going to have to talk to him, she realized, as he started heading for the door. She waited until he walked out into the much cooler night air before she caught up to him.

"Are you Josh?"

He blinked a little, obviously startled to find a strange older woman talking to him. "Yeah," he said slowly, not bothering to conceal his wariness.

"My name is Julie Osterman. I work at the Fortune Foundation with your mother's cousin Susan."

"Okay." He took a sidestep away from her and she sighed.

"Josh, this is going to sound crazy, I know," she began, "but I need you to stay here for a minute."

"Why?"

She couldn't tell him his father was dead. That job should fall to someone closer to him, someone with whom he had a relationship. "Your uncle is looking for you," she finally answered. "He really needs to talk to you. If you can hang around here for a minute, he should be along any time now."

She hoped.

"What's going on?" His gaze sharpened. "Is it my mom?"

"Your mom isn't hurt. Ross can explain everything when he gets here?"

"No. Tell me now. Is it Lyndsey? She was supposed to meet me here but she never showed and she's not answering her phone. Is she hurt? What's going on?"

"Josh—"

"Tell me!"

She was scrambling for words when a deep male voice spoke from behind her.

"It's your dad, Josh."

Chapter 3

She turned with vast relief to see Ross walking toward them, looking tall and solid and certainly strong enough to help his nephew through this.

The boy's features hardened. "Did he hurt Mom again? If he did, I'll kill him this time, I swear. I warned him I would."

"You might not want to say that too loudly," Ross said grimly. "Your father is dead, Josh."

For all his bravado just seconds before, the teenager's color drained at the words.

"Dead? That's crazy." Even as he spoke, Julie thought she saw something flicker in his brown eyes, something furtive, secretive.

"It's true," Ross said. "I'm sorry, Josh."

The boy gazed at him blankly, as if he wasn't quite sure how to respond.

"What happened?"

Ross cleared his throat. "We don't know for sure yet."

"Did he have a heart attack or a stroke or something? Was he hit by a bus? What?"

Ross sighed. His gaze met Julie's for a moment and she saw indecision there as he must be weighing just how blunt he ought to be with his nephew.

She would have told him to be as honest as possible. Josh would find out all the gory details soon enough. In a town like Red Rock, the rumors would fly faster than crows on carrion. Better for him to hear the news from his family than for them to all dissemble about the situation, which he would probably find condescending and demeaning.

Ross must have reached the same conclusion. "It's too early to say anything with a hundred percent certainty but it looks like he was murdered."

"Murdered?" Josh blinked at both of them. "You're kidding me, right? This is all some kind of a sick joke. People in Red Rock don't get murdered!"

"I'm afraid it's no joke," Julie said, her voice soft with compassion.

"Who did it? Do they have any suspects?"

Ross's gaze met Julie's again with a wordless plea for help and she thought how surreal it was that just an hour ago they were wrangling over her purse, and now he was turning to her to help him through this delicate family situation.

It was hard enough telling Josh his father was dead. How were they supposed to tell Josh that his own mother was the prime suspect?

"They're still investigating," Ross said after a moment.

Josh pulled off his Stetson and raked a hand through

his hair. "This is crazy. I can't believe it," he said again. "Where's my mom? How is she taking this?"

"Uh, that's the other thing I needed to talk to you about," Ross said.

Fear leapt into his dark eyes and he turned to Julie with an accusation in his eyes. "You said my mom wasn't hurt!"

"She's not," Ross assured him. "It's just… Frannie had to go to the police station to answer some questions."

Josh obviously wasn't a stupid boy. He quickly put the pieces together. "*Mom* had to go for questioning? They think *she* killed him?"

"Josh—"

The color that had leached away at the news of his father's death returned in a hot, angry flush. "That's the most ridiculous thing I've ever heard! If she had it in her to kill him, she would have done it years ago."

If Julie hadn't worked with troubled youth on a daily basis for the last five years, she might have found his bitterness shocking. Instead, she found it unutterably sad.

"They're only questioning her. She's not under arrest," Ross said. "I'm sure they'll figure out soon enough that your mom is innocent."

"What about his girlfriend? Are they questioning her? Or his last girlfriend? Or the one before that? I could give them a whole damn list of suspects!"

"I'm sure they'll question as many people as they can," Julie said. Unable to help herself, she laid a comforting hand on the boy's arm. Though by all appearances he despised his father, her heart ached at the pain she knew still waited for him down the road. Losing a parent was traumatic for anyone, no matter what their relationship.

Josh didn't flinch away from her touch, but he remained focused on his mother and her predicament.

"I should go to her," he said after a moment. "She's going to need me."

Ross couldn't seem to look away from that soft, comforting hand Julie placed on his nephew's arm. There was no good reason he could figure out that the sight should put a funny little ache in his chest.

He cleared his throat. "I promise, the police station is no place for you right now, Josh. You have to trust me on this."

He, however, needed to get his butt over there as soon as possible to find out what was happening with the investigation. He was torn between dueling obligations, one to his sister and one to his nephew during this difficult time.

"I'll be eighteen in two weeks, Uncle Ross. I'm not a child anymore."

"I know that. But I've spent most of my adult life in police stations and I can tell you the best place for you is at home. I'll go check on your mother."

"I want to see her."

"She won't be able to talk to you, son. Not if she's being questioned."

"Well, I can at least tell them that I know she couldn't have killed Lloyd," Josh answered.

His loyal defense of his mother struck a chord with Ross. It reminded him far too much of the way he used to stick up for Cindy, making excuses to the other kids when she would stay out all night drinking or would bring a new man around the house or, worse, would entirely forget about them all for a weekend binge.

The difference there was that he had foolishly been trying to protect an illusion, while Josh's efforts were on behalf of an innocent woman.

"Everything's going to be okay. Trust me. She's only being questioned. I'm sure she'll be home in a short time. Why don't you head on home and get some rest? You're going to have a lot to deal with in the coming days."

"I should be with her," Josh said stubbornly.

Julie again reached out to Josh and Ross saw that once more her quiet touch seemed to soothe him. "The absolute best way you can help your mother right now is to give her one less worry. You were the only thing she thought about as they were taking her in for questioning. She insisted that your uncle watch out for you and that's just what he's trying to do. As he said, you have to trust him right now to know what's best, okay?"

Her words seemed to resonate with Josh. He looked between the two of them and then sighed. "I guess."

Ross was astounded and more gratified than he wanted to admit that she would come to his defense like this, especially after their altercation earlier in the evening. That encounter and his own honest mistake over the purse had been a fortuitous meeting, he thought now. He didn't know what he would have done this evening without her.

The thought sparked an idea—a nervy one, sure, but one that would certainly lift a little of the burden from his shoulders.

"Josh, could you hang on here for a second while I talk to Ms. Osterman?"

His nephew looked confused but he nodded and Ross stepped a few paces away where they could speak in relative privacy.

"Look, I do need to get to the police station to see how things are going with Frannie, but I don't want to send Josh to his empty house alone. This is a huge favor to ask when I'm virtually a stranger to you and you've already done so much, but do you think you could stay with him for a while, while I check on my sister?"

As he might have expected, Julie's soft blue eyes widened with astonishment at the request. "But wouldn't you rather have someone in your family stay with him? Your cousin Susan, maybe?"

Susan would come in a heartbeat, he knew, and like Julie, she specialized in troubled adolescents. But he hated to ask the Fortune side of the family for anything. It was an irrational reaction, he knew, but for most of his life his particular branch of the family had always been the needy ones.

He didn't know how many times the Fortunes had bailed Cindy out of one scrape or another, before they had virtually cut ties with her out of frustration that nothing ever seemed to change.

Even though he loved and admired several members of his extended family, Ross preferred to handle things on his own when he could. And when he couldn't, he much preferred asking somebody who wasn't a Fortune for help.

"They're all going to be busy with the last few hours of the Spring Fling. Plus, now they're going to have to deal with damage control after Lloyd's murder."

It was bad public relations for the festival, especially since this was the second time a dead body had been found while the town celebrated. A few years earlier, an unidentified body turned up at the Spring Fling. The town had only just started to heal from that.

Her forehead furrowed for a moment and then she nodded. "In that case, of course. I'll be glad to stay with Josh as long as you need."

For one crazy moment, he longed to feel the soft comfort of her touch on *his* arm, though he knew that was ridiculous.

"Thanks a million. It won't be long. I'm sure I'll be taking Frannie home in just a few hours."

He had been far too optimistic, Ross thought an hour later as he stood in the Red Rock police chief's office.

"Come on, Jimmy. This is a mistake. You have to know that. There's no way on earth Frannie killed Lloyd."

"You were on the job long enough, you know how it works. We just want to talk to her but she's not saying a word. She's shutting us down in every direction. I have to tell you, that makes her look mighty guilty."

A white-coated lab tech pushed open the door. "Chief, I've got those results you put the rush order on."

"Excellent. You're going to have to excuse me, Ross. Why don't you go on home? There's nothing more you can do here tonight."

"I'll stick around. Somebody's going to need to drive Frannie home when you're done with this little farce here."

Jimmy opened his mouth to answer, then closed it again. "I can't make you leave. But if you really want to help your sister, tell her to cooperate with us. The quicker she gives us her side of the story, the quicker we can wrap this up."

Ross had been a cop for a long time, trained to catch subtle nuances in conversation. He didn't miss the way the police chief phrased his words. *Wrap this up* was a far cry from *send her home*.

Something about this whole thing gave him an ominous feeling. He suddenly guessed he was in for a long night.

Chapter 4

Four hours and counting.

From his perch in an empty detective's chair, Ross looked at the clock above the chief's glass-walled office in the Red Rock police station.

He couldn't think the long delay boded well for Frannie. It was now nearly half past midnight and she had been in an interrogation room for hours.

His poor sister. Eighteen years of marriage to Lloyd Fredericks had just about wrung every drop of spirit out of her. She must be sick over this ordeal.

What could be taking so long? Frannie should have been released hours ago. With every tick of the clock, his hopes for a quick resolution trickled a little further away.

When the police chief emerged from the hallway that housed the interview room and headed for his office, Ross rose quickly and intercepted him.

"What's going on, Jimmy? I need info here."

His friend gave him a long, solemn look and Ross's stomach suddenly clenched with nerves. He did not like the implications of that look.

"She's going to be charged, Ross. We have no choice."

He stared at the other man, not willing yet to accept the unthinkable. "Charged with what?"

The chief rolled his eyes. "With jaywalking. Lord, Ross, what the hell do you think, *with what*. With murder!"

This couldn't be happening. Ross balled his fists. "That's bull! This whole thing is bull and you know it! Frannie no more killed Lloyd than I did."

"Are you confessing?"

"I've thought about killing the bastard a thousand times," he answered the chief. "Does that count?"

"Sorry, but if we could prosecute thoughts, I doubt there would be anybody left *outside* the walls of my jail."

"What evidence can you possibly have against Frannie that's not circumstantial?" he asked.

The police chief just shook his head. "You know I can't talk about that, Ross, especially not with the suspect's own brother, even if he is an ex-cop and an old friend. Even if you weren't Frannie's brother, I couldn't tell you anything."

"Come on, throw me a little bone here. It's only been four hours since Lloyd's death. Why the big rush? You haven't even had time to look at any other possibilities! What about Crystal Rivers? She claimed she just stumbled onto the body and found Frannie there, but she doesn't exactly seem like the most upright, stalwart citizen of Red Rock. For all we know, she could have killed him, then waited around for somebody else to find him before circling back and throwing her big drama queen scene."

Jimmy was quiet for a moment, then he motioned toward his office. They walked in, and he shut the door and closed the louvered blinds to conceal their conversation from any other curious eyes that might be watching in the station house.

"Look, I don't know if this is my place, but you and I have been around the block together a few times, from our days at the academy together to our time in the same division in San Antonio. I respect you more than just about any detective on my force and you know I'd hire you here in an instant if you ever decided to come back to the job."

"I appreciate that. Just be straight with me, Jimmy."

"I'll just remind you who calls the shots around here when it comes to prosecutions. Bruce Gibson. That's not helping the situation for Frannie, especially when she's refusing to say anything about what happened."

Ross gazed at the other man as the implications sunk in. Bruce Gibson was the district attorney—and a particularly vindictive one at that. He was the one who chose when charges would be filed and what those charges would entail. Even if the police department wanted to pursue other leads, a district attorney could make the final choice about whether they had enough evidence to go forward with a prosecution.

And he had been one of Lloyd's closest friends, Ross suddenly remembered, had practically grown up at the Frederickses' mansion.

Gibson would be out for blood—and it would be a bonus to the man if he could extract a little of that

blood from the Fortunes. Gibson had made no secret of
the fact that he thought the Fortunes were too wealthy,
too powerful. He was up for a tough re-election battle
in the fall and from all appearances, he seemed to be
making an issue of the fact that he considered himself
a man of the people and wouldn't let somebody's social
status sway prosecutorial decisions.

Added to that, there was no love lost between Ross
and Bruce Gibson. Just a few weeks earlier, he and
Ross had exchanged words over an incident involving
a stable fire on the family ranch and the way the family was choosing to investigate it privately.

What a tangled mess. Any other district attorney
would see how ludicrous this whole thing was.

"Can I see her?" he asked.

Caldwell gave him a long, appraising look, then finally nodded. "It's past normal visiting hours but we
can make an exception in this case. It might take a few
moments, though. She's in central booking."

Perhaps half an hour later, Ross was finally ushered
by the young, fresh-faced police officer he had seen
earlier on the murder scene to a stark white interview
room. Frannie looked up when the door opened and
Ross had to stop from clenching his fists again at the
sight of her in a prison-orange jumpsuit.

Since his sister's ill-fated marriage to Fredericks
years ago, he had seen her disheartened and hurt, he
had seen her hopeless and bleak. But he didn't think he
had ever seen her look so desperately afraid.

The chair scraped as he pulled it out to sit down and
she flinched a little at the noise.

"Hey, Frannie-Banannie."

Her eyes filled up with tears at the childish nickname. "You haven't called me that in years."

He was suddenly sorry for that, sorry that while he had never completely withdrawn from his family, he had enjoyed the distance that came from living twenty miles away in San Antonio. He didn't have to be involved in the day-to-day drama of family affairs, didn't have to watch Frannie slowly become this washed-out version of herself.

"How are you doing, sis?"

She shrugged. "I guess you know they're charging me."

"Yeah. Jim told me. Sounds like Bruce Gibson is on the warpath."

Her mouth tightened but she only looked down at her hands.

"What happened, Frannie?"

"I don't want to talk about it."

"That's what I hear. But you told them you didn't do it, right?"

She didn't answer him. Instead she rubbed the fraying sleeve of the jumpsuit between her thumb and forefinger. "How's Josh?" she asked.

He sighed at her evasive tactic but decided to let it go for now. "He's fine. I sent him back to your house."

"He shouldn't be alone right now. Is someone with him?"

"Julie Osterman is with him."

"Julie? From the Foundation? Why?"

Because I didn't want to ask the family to bail us all out once again, he thought but could never say. "She was with me when…everything happened. I couldn't be in two places at once and I needed help and Julie seemed a good choice since she's a youth counselor and all, like Susan."

"Julie is nice."

Frannie sounded exhausted suddenly, emotionally and physically, and he wanted to gather her up and take care of her.

Those days were gone, though. Try as he might, he couldn't fix everything. He couldn't fix her marriage for the last eighteen years. He couldn't get his young, happy sister back. And he wasn't at all sure he could extricate her from this mess, though he sure as hell was going to try.

"Ross, I need you to do something for me."

"Anything. Whatever you need."

"Take care of Josh for me. Stay with him at the house. I know he's almost eighteen and almost an adult and will probably tell you he doesn't need anyone else but I don't want him on his own right now. Help him through this, okay? He's going to need you."

"Come on, Frannie. Don't worry. You'll be out before we know it and this will all be a memory."

"Just help him. You've always been far more of a father to him than...than Lloyd."

"You don't even need to ask, Fran. Of course I will."

"Thank you." She attempted such a forlorn smile it just about broke his heart. "I can always count on you."

If that were true, she wouldn't be in this calamity. She wouldn't have been married to Lloyd in the first place and she wouldn't be facing murder charges right now, if he had been able to rescue her from the situation years ago, like he'd wanted to.

"We'll get the best attorney we can find for you, okay? Just hang in."

She nodded, though it looked as if it took the last of her energy just to make that small gesture. He had a feeling in another minute, his baby sister was going to fold her arms on the interrogation room table, lay her head down and fall instantly asleep.

"Get some rest, okay?" he advised her. "Everything will seem better in the morning, I promise."

She managed another nod. Ross glanced at the officer who was monitoring the visit, then thought, to hell with this. He pulled his sister into his arms, noting not for the first time that she seemed as fragile and insubstantial as a stained-glass window.

"Thanks, Ross," she mumbled before the guard pulled her away and led her from the room.

The Spring Fling seemed another lifetime ago as Ross drove the streets of Red Rock toward the house where Frannie and Lloyd moved shortly after their marriage.

The security guard at the entrance to their exclusive gated community knew him. His fleshy features turned avid the moment Ross rolled down his window.

"Mr. Fortune. I guess you're here to stay with your sister's boy, huh? You been to the jail to see her?"

The news was probably spreading through town like stink in springtime. "Yeah. Can you let me in?"

"Oh, sure, sure," he said, though he made no move to raise the security arm. "Jail is just no place for a nice lady like Mrs. F. Why, you could have knocked me six ways to Sunday when my cousin Lou called to tell me what had happened at the Spring Fling. Too bad I was here working and missed everything."

Ross gestured to the gate. "Can you let me in, George? I really need to be with my nephew right now."

The guard hit the button with a disappointed kind of look.

"You tell Mrs. F. I'm thinking about her, okay?"

"I'll be sure to do that, George. Thanks."

He quickly rolled his window up and drove through the gate before George decided he wanted to chat a little more.

Lights blazed from every single window of the grand pink stucco McMansion he had always secretly thought of as a big, gaudy wedding cake. There was no trace of his sister's elegant good taste in the house. It was as if Lloyd had stamped out any trace of Frannie.

The interior of the house wasn't any more welcoming. It was cold and formal, white on white with gold accents.

Ross knew of two rooms in the house with a little personality. Josh's bedroom was a typical teenager's room with posters on the wall and clutter and mementos covering every surface.

The other was Frannie's small sitting room that hinted at the little sister he remembered. It was brightly decorated, with local handiworks, vivid textiles and many of Frannie's own photographs on the wall.

Lloyd had a habit of changing the security system all the time so Ross didn't even try to open the door. He rang the doorbell and a moment later, Julie Osterman opened the door, her soft, pretty features looking about as exhausted as Frannie's had been.

"I'm sorry I'm so late," he said. "I never expected things to take this long, that I would have to impose on you until the early hours of the morning."

"No problem." She held the door open for him and he moved past her into the formal foyer. "Josh tried to send me home and insisted he would be okay on his own, but I just didn't feel right about leaving him here alone, under the circumstances."

"I appreciate that."

"He's in the kitchen on the telephone to a friend."

"At this hour? Is it Lyndsey?"

Josh's young girlfriend had been a source of conflict between Josh and his parents, for reasons Ross didn't quite understand.

"I think so, but I can't be certain. I was trying not to eavesdrop."

"How is he?"

She frowned a little as she appeared to give his question serious consideration. Despite his own fatigue, Ross couldn't help noticing the way her mouth pursed a little when she was concentrating, and he had a wild urge to kiss away every line.

He definitely needed sleep if he was harboring inappropriate fantasies about a prickly busybody type like Julie Osterman.

"I can't really tell, to be honest with you," she answered. "I get the impression he's more upset about his mother being detained at the police station than he seems to be about his father's death. Or at least that appears to be where he's focusing his emotions right now. On the other hand, his reaction could just be displacement."

"Want to skip the mumbo jumbo?"

She made a face. "Sorry. I just meant maybe he's not ready—or doesn't want—to face the reality of his father's death right now, so it's easier to place his energy and emotion on his mother's situation."

"Or maybe he just happens to be more upset about

Frannie than he is about Lloyd. The two of them didn't exactly get along."

"So I hear," she answered. "It sounds as if few people did get along with Lloyd Fredericks, besides Crystal and her sort."

"And there were plenty of those."

Her mouth tightened but she refrained from commenting on his bitterness. Lloyd's frequent affairs had been a great source of humiliation for Frannie. "How is your sister?" she asked instead.

"Holding up okay, under the circumstances."

"Do you expect them to keep her overnight for questioning, then?"

He sighed, angry all over again at the most recent turn of events. "Not for questioning. For arraignment. She's being charged."

Her eyes widened with astonishment, then quickly filled with compassion. "Oh, poor Josh. This is going to be so hard on him."

"Yeah, it's a hell of a mess," he answered heavily. "So it looks like I'll be staying here for a while, until we can sort things out."

She touched him, just a quick, almost furtive brush of her hand on his arm, much as she had touched Josh earlier. Through his cotton shirt, he could feel the warmth of her skin and he was astonished at the urge to wrap his arms around her and pull her close and just lean on her for a moment.

"I'm so sorry, Ross."

He cleared his throat and told himself he was nothing but relieved when she pulled her hand away.

"Thanks again for everything you did tonight," he said. "I would have been in a real fix without you."

"I'm glad I could help in some small way."

She smiled gently and he was astonished at how that simple warm expression could ease the tightness in his chest enough that he could breathe just a little easier.

"It's late," she finally said. "Or early, I guess. I'd better go."

"Oh right. I'm sorry again you had to be here so long."

"I'd like to say goodbye to Josh before I leave, if it's all right with you," she said.

"Of course," he answered and followed her into the kitchen.

In his fantasy childhood, the kitchen was always the warmest room in the house, a place scattered with children's backpacks and clumsy artwork on the refrigerator and homemade cookies cooling on a rack on the countertop.

He hadn't known anything like that, except at the occasional friend's house. To his regret, Frannie's kitchen wasn't anything like that image, either. It was as cool and formal as the rest of the house—white cabinets, white tile, stainless-steel appliances. It was like some kind of hospital lab rather than the center of a house.

Josh sat on a white bar stool, his cell phone up to his ear.

"I told you, Lyns," he was saying, "I don't have any more information than I did when we talked an hour ago. I haven't heard anything yet. I'll tell you as soon as I know anything, okay? Meantime, you have to get some rest. You know what—"

Ross wasn't sure what alerted the boy to their presence but before he could complete the sentence, he suddenly swiveled around to face them. Ross was almost

certain he saw secrets flash in his nephew's eyes before
his expression turned guarded again.

"Um, I've got to go, Lyns," he mumbled into the
phone. "My uncle Ross just got here. Yeah. I'll call you
later."

He ended the call, folded his phone and slid it into
his pocket before he uncoiled his lanky frame from the
chair.

"How's my mom? Is she with you?"

Ross sighed. "No. I'm sorry."

"How long can they hold her?"

"For now, as long as they want. She's being charged."

His features suffused with color. "Charged? With
murder?"

Ross nodded, wishing he had other news to offer
his nephew.

"This completely sucks."

That was one word for it, he supposed. A pretty accurate one. "Yeah, it does. But there's nothing we can do
about it tonight. Meanwhile, Ms. Osterman needs to get
on back to her house. She came in to tell you goodbye."

He was proud of the boy for reining in most of his
outrage in order to be polite to Julie.

"Thank you for giving me a ride and staying here
and everything," Josh said to her. "And even though I
told you I didn't need you to stay so late, it was…nice
not to be here by myself and all."

"You're very welcome." She smiled with that gentle
warmth she just seemed to exude, paused for just a moment, then stepped forward and hugged the boy, who
was a good six inches taller than she was.

"Call me if you need to talk, okay?" she said softly.

"Yeah, sure," he mumbled, though Ross was pretty sure Josh looked touched by her concern.

They both walked her to the door and watched her climb into her car. When she drove away, Ross shut the door to Frannie's wedding-cake house and wondered what the hell he was supposed to do next.

He would just have to figure it out, he supposed.

He didn't have any other choice.

This was just about the last place on earth he wanted to be right now.

In fact, given a choice between attending his despised brother-in-law's funeral and wading chest-deep in a manure pit out on the Double Crown, Ross figured he would much rather be standing in cow honey swatting flies away from his face than sitting here in this discreetly decorated funeral home, surrounded by the cloying smell of lilies and carnations and listening to all the weeping and wailing going on over a man most people in town had disliked.

It would be over soon. Already, the eulogies seemed to be dwindling. He could only feel relief. This all seemed the height of hypocrisy. He knew of at least a dozen people here who had openly told him at separate times over the last few days how much they had hated Lloyd. Yet here they were with their funeral game faces, all solemn and sad-eyed.

He glanced over at his nephew, who seemed to be watching the entire proceedings with an odd detachment, as if it was all some kind of mildly interesting play that had no direct bearing on his life.

Josh seemed to be holding up well under the strain of the last five days. Maybe too well. The boy's only intense emotion over anything seemed to be rage at the prosecuting attorney for moving ahead with charges against his mother.

It had been a hellish five days, culminating in this farce. First had come the medical examiner's report read at Frannie's arraignment that Lloyd had been killed with a blunt instrument whose general size and heft matched the large piece of pottery his sister had purchased shortly before the murder. Then reports had begun to trickle out that the heavy vase had several sets of unidentified fingerprints on it—and one very obvious identified set that belonged to his sister.

Added to Crystal's testimony that Lloyd had a heated phone call with Frannie shortly before the murder, things weren't looking good for his sister.

A good attorney with the typical cooperative client might have been able to successfully argue that Frannie's fingerprints would naturally be on the vase since she had purchased it just a short time earlier, and that a hearsay one-sided telephone exchange—no matter how heated—was not proof of murder.

But Frannie was not the typical cooperative client. Despite the high stakes, she refused to confirm or deny her involvement in Lloyd's murder and had chosen instead to remain mum about the entire evening, even to her attorney.

Ross didn't know what the hell she was doing. He had visited twice more since the night of the murder in an effort to convince her to just tell him and the Red Rock police what had happened, but she had shut him out, too. Each time, he had ended up leaving more frustrated than ever.

As a result of her baffling, completely unexpected

obstinacy, she had been charged with second-degree murder and bound over for trial. Even more aggravating, she had been denied bail. Bruce Gibson had argued in court that Frannie was a flight risk because of her wealthy family.

He apparently was laboring under two huge misconceptions: one, that Frannie would ever have it in her to run off and abandon her son and, two, that any of the Fortunes would willingly help her escape, no matter how much they might want to.

In the bail hearing, Bruce had been full of impassioned arguments about the Fortune wealth and power, the entire time with that smirk on his plastic features that Ross wanted to pound off of him.

The judge had apparently been gullible enough to buy into the myth—either that or he was another old golfing buddy of Lloyd's or his father, Cordell. Judge Wilkinson had agreed with Bruce and ordered Frannie held without bail, so now his delicate, fragile sister sat moldering in the county jail, awaiting trial on trumped-up charges that should never have been filed.

And while she was stuck there, he was forced to sit on this rickety little excuse for a chair, listening to a pack of lies about what a great guy Lloyd had been.

Ross didn't buy any of it. He had disliked the man from the day he married Frannie, when she was only eighteen. Even though she had tried to put on a bright face and play the role of a regular bride, Ross had sensed something in her eyes even then that seemed to indicate she wasn't thrilled about the marriage.

He had tried to talk her out of it but she wouldn't listen to him, probably because Cindy had pushed so hard for the marriage.

When Josh showed up several weeks shy of nine months later, Ross had put the pieces of the puzzle together and figured Lloyd had gotten her pregnant. Frannie was just the sort to try doing what she thought was the right thing for her child, even if it absolutely wasn't the right decision for *her*.

In the years since, he had watched her change from a luminous, vivacious girl to a quiet, subdued society matron. She always wore the right thing, said the right thing, but every ounce of joy seemed to have been sucked out of her.

And all because of Lloyd Fredericks, the man who apparently was heading for sainthood any day now, judging by the glowing eulogies delivered at his memorial service.

Ross wondered what all these fusty types would do if he stood up and spoke the truth, that Lloyd was just about the lousiest excuse for a human being he'd ever met—which was really quite a distinction, considering that as an ex-cop, he'd met more than his share.

In his experience, Lloyd was manipulative and dishonest. He cheated, he lied, he stole and, worse, he bullied anybody he considered weaker than himself.

Ross couldn't say any of that, though. He could only sit here and wait until this whole damn thing was over and he could take Josh home.

He glanced around at the crowd, wondering again at the most notable absence—next to Frannie's, of course. Cindy had opted not to come, and he couldn't help wondering where she might be. He would have expected his mother to be sitting right up there on the front row with Lloyd's parents. She loved nothing more than to be the center of attention, and what better place for that than at her son-in-law's memorial service, with all its drama and high emotion?

Cindy had adored her son-in-law, though Ross thought perhaps he'd seen hints that their relationship had cooled, since right around the time Cindy had been injured in a mysterious car accident.

Still, even if she and Lloyd had been openly feuding, which they weren't, he would have thought Cindy would come.

He was still wondering at her absence when the pastor finally wrapped things up a few moments later. With the autopsy completed, Lloyd's parents had elected to cremate his remains, so there would be no interment ceremony.

"Can we go now?" Josh asked him when other people started to file out of the funeral chapel.

Ross would have preferred nothing more than to hustle Josh away from all this artificiality. He knew people likely wanted to pay their respects to Lloyd's son, but he wasn't about to force the kid to stay if he didn't want to be there.

"Your call," he said.

"Let's go, then," Josh said. "I'm ready to get out of here."

As he had expected, at least a dozen people stopped them on their way to the door to wish Josh their condolences. Ross was immensely proud of his nephew for the quiet dignity with which he thanked them each for their sympathy without giving away his own feelings about his father.

They were almost to the door when Ross saw with dismay that Lloyd's mother, Jillian, was heading in their direction. Her Botox-smooth features looked ravaged just now, her eyes red and weepy. Still, fury seemed to push away the grief for now.

"How dare you show your face here!" she hissed to Ross when she was still several feet away.

Chapter 5

Several others at the funeral stopped to watch the unfolding drama and Ross did his best to edge them over to a quieter corner of the chapel, away from the greedy eyes of the crowd.

"My nephew just lost his father," he said calmly. "I'm here for him, Jillian. Surely you can understand that."

She made a scoffing sort of sound. "Your nephew lost his father because of *your sister*! If not for her, none of us would be here. He would still be alive. You have no right to come here. No right whatsoever. This service is for family members. For those of us who… who loved Lloyd. You never even liked him. You probably conspired with your sister to kill him, didn't you?"

It was such a ridiculous thing to say that Ross had no idea how to answer her grief-induced ravings.

"I'm here for Josh," he repeated. "Whatever you might

think about my sister right now, and whatever the circumstances of Lloyd's death, Josh has lost his father. He asked me to come with him today and I couldn't let him down."

Though he *had* let him down, Ross thought. And he had let his sister down, over and over. He hadn't been able to get Frannie out of her lousy marriage. He had tried, dozens of times, until he finally gave up. But maybe he hadn't tried hard enough.

"I want you to leave. Right now." Jillian's features reddened and she looked on the verge of some apoplectic attack.

"We're just leaving, Grandmother," Josh assured her and Ross was proud of his nephew for his calm, sympathetic manner.

At that moment, Lloyd's father stepped up and slipped a supporting arm around his wife's shoulders. "That's not necessary. You don't have to leave, Joshua. Come along, Jillian. The Scofields were looking for you a moment ago."

Cordell gave Ross a quick, apologetic look, then steered his distraught wife away from them. Ross watched after him, his brow furrowed. He hadn't seen Lloyd's father in a few months but the man looked as if he had aged a decade or more. His features were lined and worn and he looked utterly exhausted.

Was all that from Lloyd's death? he wondered. He knew the Fredericks had always doted on their only son and of course his death was bound to hit them hard, but he hadn't expected Cordell to look so devastated.

Maybe Lloyd's death wasn't the only reason the man seemed to have aged overnight. Ross had been hearing rumors even before Lloyd's death that not all was rosy with the Frederickses' financial picture. He had heard a few whispers around town that Cordell and Lloyd had been late on some payments and had completely stopped making others.

It wouldn't have surprised him at all to learn that Lloyd had been the one keeping Fredericks Financial afloat. Maybe Cordell was terrified the whole leaky ship would sink now his son was dead.

He made a mental note to add a little digging into their financial records to the parallel investigation he had started conducting into Lloyd's death.

"Follow the money" had always been a pretty good creed when he'd been a cop and he saw no reason for this situation to be any different.

"Sorry about that, Uncle Ross," Josh said when they finally stepped outside into the warm afternoon, along with others who seemed eager to escape the oppressive funeral chapel. "Grandmother is…distraught."

Poor Josh had a bum deal when it came to grandparents. On the one side, he had Lloyd's stiff society parents. On the other, he had Cindy. She was no better a grandmother than she'd been a mother, alternating between bouts of spoiling her grandson outrageously with flamboyant gifts she couldn't afford, followed by long periods of time when she would ignore him completely.

"Don't worry about it," Ross assured him. "Jillian's reaction is completely understandable."

"It's not. She knows my mom. She's known her for eighteen years, since she married my dad. Grandmother has to know Mom would never kill him."

"It's a rough time right now for everyone, Josh."

"I don't care how upset she is. My mom is innocent!

And then to imply that you were involved, as well. That's just crazy."

Ross sighed but before he could answer, he was surprised to see Julie Osterman slip outside through the doors of the chapel and head in their direction.

She wore a conservative blue jacket and skirt with a silky white shirt and had pulled her hair back into a loose updo, and she looked soft and lovely in the sunshine.

His heart had no business jumping around in his chest just at the sight of her. Ross scowled. It didn't seem right that she should be the single bright spot in what had been a dismal day.

How did she have such a calming presence about her? he wondered. Even some of Josh's tension seemed to ease out of him when she slipped her arm through his and gave a comforting squeeze.

"Hi, Ms. O."

She smiled at him, though it appeared rather solemn. "Hi, Josh. I was hoping to get a chance to talk to you."

"Oh?"

She studied him for a long moment. "I have a dilemma here. Maybe you can help me out. I promised myself I wasn't going to ask you something clichéd like how you're holding up. But then, if I don't ask, how am I supposed to find out how you're doing?"

Josh smiled, the first one Ross had seen on his features all day. "Go ahead and ask. I don't mind."

"All right. How are you doing, under the circumstances?"

He shrugged. "Okay, I guess. Under the circumstances."

"It was a lovely memorial service, as far as these things go."

"I guess." Josh looked down at the asphalt of the parking lot.

"When do you go back to school?" she asked.

"Tomorrow. I've got finals next week and I can't really miss any more school if I want to graduate with my class. Uncle Ross thinks I should study for finals at home."

He and Ross had argued about it several times, in fact. It was just about the only point of contention between them over the last five days.

"I just think he should take as much time as he needs," Ross said. "If he doesn't feel ready, he can probably take a few more days, as long as he gets the assignments from his teachers. There's also the scandal factor. Everybody's going to be talking about a murder at the Spring Fling and I want to make sure he's mentally prepared for that before he goes back to school."

"What do you think, Ms. O.?" Josh asked.

Ross could tell she didn't want to be dragged into the middle of things but Julie only smiled at both of them. "There are arguments to be made for both sides. But I think that you're the only one who can truly know when you're ready. As long as you feel prepared to handle whatever might come along, I'm sure returning to school tomorrow will be fine."

"I think I am," Josh answered. "But I won't know until I'm there, will I?"

Julie opened her mouth to answer but one of Lloyd's elderly aunts approached them before she could say anything.

"Joshua? I've been looking all over for you," she said. "You're not leaving already, are you?"

Josh slanted a look at Ross. "In a minute."

"You can't leave yet. Your great-grandmother is here. She specifically wanted to see you."

Josh looked less than thrilled about being forced to talk with more Fredericks relatives but he nodded and allowed himself to be led away by the other woman, leaving Ross alone with Julie.

"I didn't expect to see you here," he said after a moment.

He didn't add that if he had seen her earlier, it might have made the whole thing a little easier to endure.

She made a face. "I decided I would probably regret it if I didn't come to pay my respects. I know Jillian casually from some committees we've served on together and it seemed the polite thing to do, for her sake alone. But more than that, I wanted to come for Josh. It seemed…right, especially as I feel a little as if I were involved, since you and I were on the scene so quickly after it happened and I was with Josh for those few hours afterward."

"Makes sense. It was nice of you to come."

She studied him for a long moment. "Forgive me if I'm wrong, but I get the impression you're not very thrilled to be here."

His laugh was rough and humorless. "Is it that obvious? I can't wait to leave. We were just on our way out. And just so you don't think I'm rushing him away, Josh is as eager to get out of here as I am."

She frowned. "How is he really doing?"

He gazed toward the door, where Josh was talking politely to an ancient-looking woman in a wheelchair. "Not as peachy as he wants everybody to think. He isn't the same kid he was five days ago."

"That's normal and very much to be expected."

"I get the grieving process. I mean, even though his relationship with his dad wasn't the greatest, of course he's going to be upset that he died a violent death. But something else is going on. I can't quite put my finger on it."

One of the things Ross liked best about Julie Osterman was the way she gazed intently at him when he was speaking. Some women looked like they had their minds on a hundred other things when he talked to them, everything from what they had for breakfast to what they were going to say next. It bugged the heck out of him. But somehow he was certain Julie was focused only on his words.

"I'm sure he's also upset about his mother's arrest."

"True enough. If you want the truth, he acts like Frannie's arrest upsets him more than Lloyd's death. He's furious that his mother has been charged with the murder and that she's being held without bail."

"Have you talked to him about his feelings?"

He rolled his eyes. "I'm a guy, in case it escaped your attention."

"It hasn't," she murmured, an odd note in her voice that sent heat curling through him.

He cleared his throat. "I'm no good at the whole 'let's talk about our feelings' thing. Not that I haven't tried, though. Yesterday I took him out on my boat, thinking he might open up out on the water. Instead, we spent the entire afternoon without saying a word about his mom or about Lloyd or anything. Caught our limit between us, though."

Why he shared that, he wasn't sure and he regretted even opening his mouth. What kind of idiot thought a fishing trip might help a troubled teen? But Julie only gazed at him with admiration in the deep blue of her eyes.

"Brilliant idea. That was probably exactly what he needed, Ross. For things to be as normal as possible for a while. To do something he enjoys in a safe environment where he didn't feel pressured to talk about anything."

"I used to take my brothers when we were kids. I can't say we solved all the world's problems, but we always walked away from the river a little happier, anyway. Or at least we stopped fighting for a few minutes. And sometimes we even caught enough for a few nights' dinners, too."

She smiled at that, as he found he'd hoped she would. "You know, Ross, if you think it might help him cope with his grief, I would be happy to talk to Josh in a more formal capacity down at the Fortune Foundation."

He mulled the offer for a long moment, then he shrugged. "I don't know if he really needs all that."

"I'm not talking long-term psychotherapy here. Just a session or two of grief counseling, maybe, if he wants someone to talk to."

Ross thought of Josh's behavior since Lloyd's death. He had become much more secretive and he seemed to be bottling everything up deep inside. Every day since his father's murder, Josh seemed to become more and more tense and troubled, until Ross worried he would implode.

He had seen good cops take a long, hard journey to nowhere when they tucked everything down inside them. He didn't want to see the same thing happen to Josh.

His nephew wouldn't share what he was going through with Ross, but maybe a few sessions with Julie would help him sort through the tangle of his emotions a little better. He supposed it couldn't hurt.

"If he's willing, I guess there's a chance it might help him," he answered. "You sure you don't mind?"

"Not at all, Ross. I like Josh and I want to do anything I can to help him through this hard time in his life. I would say, from a professional standpoint, it's probably better if he gets some counseling earlier rather than later. Things won't become any easier for him in the next few months, especially if the case against Frannie goes to trial."

"It won't," he vowed. He was working like crazy on his own investigation, trying to make sure that didn't happen. "I can't believe such a miscarriage of justice would be allowed to proceed."

"You were a police officer," she said. "You know that innocence doesn't always guarantee justice."

"True. But I'm not going to let my baby sister go to prison for something she didn't do. You can be damn sure of that."

Her mouth tilted into a soft smile that did crazy things to his insides. "Frannie is lucky to have you," she said softly.

He deliberately clamped down on the fierce urge to see if that mouth could possibly taste as sweet as his imagination conjured up.

"We'll see," he said, his voice a little rough. "If Josh is willing, when is a good time for me to bring him in?"

"I've got some time tomorrow afternoon, if that works. Around four, at my office?"

"I'll talk to Josh and let you know. I don't want to force him to do anything he's uncomfortable about."

"From the little I've learned about your nephew, I

don't think you could force him to do anything he didn't want to do. I'm guessing it's a family trait."

He actually managed a smile, his first one in a long time. He was suddenly enormously grateful for her compassion and her insight. "True enough. Thank you for all your help. I've been baffled about what to do for him."

He didn't add that he felt as if was failing Josh, just as much as he had failed Frannie for the last eighteen years.

"You're doing fine," she answered. "Josh needs love most of all and it's obvious you have plenty of that to give him."

She touched his arm again, as he realized was her habit, and Ross felt the heat of it sing through his system.

He wanted to stay right here all afternoon, to just let her gentle touch soothe away all his ragged edges, all the tangles and turmoil he had been dealing with since Lloyd's murder and Frannie's arrest.

What was it about her that had such a powerful impact on him? She was lovely, yes. He had known lovely women before, though, and none of them exuded the same soft serenity that called to him with such seductive invitation.

"Sorry that took so long. We can leave anytime."

At Josh's approach, Julie quickly dropped her hand from his arm and Ross realized they had been standing there staring at each other for who knows how long.

Josh shifted his gaze between the two of them, as if trying to filter through the currents that must be zinging around.

"Um, no problem," Ross mumbled. "I guess we should go, then."

They said their goodbyes to Julie, and he couldn't help noticing that she looked as rattled as he felt, something that probably shouldn't suddenly make him feel so cheerful.

Julie studied the boy sprawled in the easy chair in her office.

For the past half hour, Josh had been telling her all the reasons he wasn't grieving for his father. He talked about Lloyd Fredericks as if he despised him, but then Julie would see flashes of pain appear out of nowhere in his eyes and she knew the truth of Josh's relationship with his father wasn't so easily defined.

"I'm not glad he's dead. I know I said that right after he was killed, but it's not true. I guess I didn't really want him dead, I just wanted him out of my life and my mom's life. It's weird that he's gone, you know? I keep expecting him to come slamming into the house and start picking on my mom for whatever thing bugged him most that day. Instead, it's only Ross there and he never says much of anything."

"It's natural for you to be conflicted, Josh. You're grieving for your father, or at least for the relationship you might have wanted to share with your father."

Josh shrugged. "I guess."

"Nobody can make that process any easier. We each have to walk our own path when it comes to learning to live with the things we can't have anymore. But one thing I've found that helps me when I'm sad is to focus not on the things that are missing in my life but instead on the many things I'm grateful to have."

"Glass-half-full kind of stuff, huh?"

"Exactly. You're in the middle of a crisis right now and many times it's hard to see beyond that. That's perfectly normal, Josh. But it can help ease a little of that turmoil to remember you've still got your uncle standing by your side. You've still got good friends who can help you through."

"I've got Lyndsey."

Josh had mentioned his girlfriend at least five or six times in their session. Julie hadn't met the girl but it was obvious Josh was enamored of her.

"You've got Lyndsey. Many people in your life care about you and are here to help you get through this."

"I know what I have. Just like I know what I have to protect."

Julie mulled over his statement, finding his choice of words a little unsettling.

"What do you need to protect? And from whom? Your mother? Lyndsey?"

He became inordinately fascinated with the upholstered buttons on the arm of the easy chair, tugging at the closest one. "The people I love. I should have acted sooner. I should have protected my mom from Lloyd a long time ago."

"How would you have done that? Your mother was a grown woman, making her own choices. What could you have done?"

After a long moment, he lifted his shoulders. "I don't know. I should have figured something out."

She pressed him on the point as much as she could before it became obvious he didn't want to talk anymore. He became more closed-mouthed and distant.

Though they technically still had five minutes, she opted to end the session a little earlier.

"Thanks for...this," Josh said. "The talk and stuff. It helped a lot."

She had no idea what she had possibly been able to offer, but she smiled. "I'm glad. Will you come again?"

He hesitated just long enough to make the moment awkward. "I guess," he finally said. "I don't think I really need therapy or anything but I don't mind talking to you."

"Great."

She quickly wrote her cell number on a memo sheet from a dispenser on her desk. "I'm going to give you my mobile number. If you want to talk, I'm here, okay? Anytime."

"Even if I called you at three in the morning?"

She smiled a little at his cynicism, the natural adolescent desire to stretch every boundary to the limit. "Of course. I might be half asleep for a moment at first, but after I wake up a little, I'll be very happy you felt you could bother me at 3:00 a.m."

She wasn't sure he believed her, but at least he didn't openly argue.

Ross was thumbing through a magazine in the reception area when they opened Julie's office door. He rose to his feet and she was struck again by his height and the sheer solid strength of him.

With that tumble of dark hair brushing his collar and those deep brown eyes, he looked brooding and dark and dangerous, though she had come to see that was mostly illusion.

Mostly.

Her insides gave that funny little jolt they seemed to

do whenever she saw him and she fought down a shiver. She had to get control of herself. Every time she was around the man, she forgot all the many reasons she shouldn't be attracted to him.

"Hey, Uncle Ross. I'm going to go see if Ricky is still shooting hoops out back," Josh said.

"Okay. I'll be out in a minute. I'd like to talk to Ms. Osterman."

Josh nodded, picked up his backpack and headed out the door. Josh had been her last appointment of the day and this was Susan's half day, so no other patients waited in the reception area.

She was suddenly acutely aware that she and Ross were alone and she ordered her nerves to settle.

"How did things go in there?" Ross asked.

She sent him a sidelong look as she closed and locked her office door. "Just fine. And that's all I can or will tell you."

"Did he tell you he insisted on going back to school today, over all my well-reasoned objections?"

"He did."

"Am I wrong in thinking he should take more time?"

She studied him, charmed despite all the warnings to herself by his earnest concern for his nephew's well-being. She knew Ross was trying to do the right thing for Josh and she could also tell by the note of uncertainty in his voice that he didn't feel up to the task.

She chose her words carefully, loath to give him any more reason to doubt himself. "I think Josh needs to set his own pace. He's supposed to graduate in two weeks. Right now it's important for him to go through the motions of regaining his life."

"He didn't say much about school today on the way

over here, but I know it couldn't have been easy." His features seemed hard and tight for a moment. "I know how cruel kids can be, how they can talk, especially in small towns."

He spoke as if he had firsthand experience in such things and she had to wonder what cruelty he might have faced as a child. She wanted to ask, but she was quite certain he would brush off the question.

"Josh can handle the whispers around school," she answered. "He's a very strong young man."

"He shouldn't have to go through any of this," he muttered.

"But he does, unfortunately. Whether he should or shouldn't have to face it, this is his reality now."

"I wish I could make it easier for him."

"You are. Just by being there with him, caring for him, you're providing exactly what he needs right now."

He studied her for a long moment, a warm light in his brown eyes that sent those nerves ricocheting around her insides again. She wanted to stay right here in her reception area and just soak up that heat, but she knew it was far too dangerous. Her defenses were entirely too flimsy around Ross Fortune.

"Shall we go find Josh and Ricky?"

Could he hear that slight tremble in her voice? she wondered. Oh, she dearly hoped not.

"Right," he only said, and followed her outside into the warm May sunlight, where Josh was shooting baskets by himself on the hoop hanging in one corner of the parking lot of the Foundation.

"No Ricky?" Ross asked.

"Nope. He must have gone home while I was talking to Ms. O. Left the ball out here, though."

Josh shot a fifteen-foot jumper that swished cleanly through the basket.

"Wow. Great shot," Julie said.

"My turn," Ross said and Josh obliged by passing the ball to him. Ross dribbled a few times and went to the same spot on the half-court painted on the parking lot. He repeated Josh's shot, but his bounced off the rim.

Josh managed what was almost a smile. "Ha. You can never beat me at H-O-R-S-E. At least you haven't been able to in years."

"Never say never, kid." Heedless of his cowboy boots that weren't exactly intended for basketball, Ross rolled up the sleeves of his shirt. "Julie, you in?"

She laughed at the pair of them and the suddenly intent expression in two sets of eyes. "Do I look crazy? This appears to be a grudge match to me."

Her heart warmed when Josh grinned at her, looking very different from the troubled teen she knew him to be. "There's always room for one more."

"You'll wipe the parking lot with me, I'm sure. But why not?"

She decided not to tell them she was the youngest girl in a family of five with four fiercely competitive older brothers. Sometimes the only time she could get any of them to notice her was out on the driveway with the basketball standard her father had nailed above the garage door.

H-O-R-S-E had always been her favorite game and she loved outshooting her brothers, finding innovative shots they couldn't match in the game of elimination.

It had been years since she played basketball with any real intent, though, and she knew she would be more than a little rusty.

The next half hour would live forever in her memory, especially the deepening shock on both Ross's and Josh's features when she was able to keep up with them, shot for shot, in the first five rounds of play.

After five more rounds, Josh and Ross each had earned H and O by missing two shots apiece, while she was still hitting all her shots, despite the handicap of her three-inch heels.

"Just who's wiping the parking lot with whom here?" Ross grumbled. "I'm beginning to think we've been hustled."

"I never said I couldn't play," Julie said with a grin, hitting a one-handed layup. "There was no deception involved whatsoever."

She had to admit, she was having the time of her life. And Josh seemed much lighter of heart than he had been during their session. She still sensed secrets in him, but for a few moments he seemed to be able to set them aside to enjoy the game, which she considered a good sign.

After another half hour, things had evened out a little. She had missed an easy free throw and then a left hook shot that she secretly blamed on Ross for standing too close to her and blasting away all her powers of concentration. But she was still ahead after she pulled off a trick bounce shot that neither Josh nor Ross could emulate.

"I'm starving," Ross said. "What do you say we finish this another night?"

"You're just saying that because you know I'm going to win," Julie said with a taunting smile.

Ross returned it and she considered the game a victory all the way around, especially if it could help him be more lighthearted than she had seen him since they had found his brother-in-law's body.

"Hey, Julie, why don't you come to the house and have dinner with us?" Josh asked suddenly. "We could finish the game there after we eat."

"Dinner?" She glanced at Ross and saw he didn't look exactly thrilled at the invitation. "I don't know," she said slowly.

"Please, Julie. We'd love you to come," Josh pressed her. "You don't have other plans, do you?"

"Not tonight, no," she had to admit.

"Then why not come for dinner? Uncle Ross said he was going to barbecue steaks and there's always an extra we can throw on the grill."

"Well, that's a bit of a problem," she answered. "I'm afraid I'm not really much of a meat eater."

"Really?" Josh said with interest. "Lyndsey is a vegetarian."

"I wouldn't say I'm a vegetarian. I just don't eat a lot of red meat."

"Those are fighting words here in cattle country," Ross drawled.

She laughed. "I know. That's why you won't hear me saying them very loudly. I would prefer if the two of you would just keep it to yourselves."

"Okay, we won't blab your horrible dark secret to everyone—" Josh gave her a mischievous smile "—as long as you have dinner with us."

She was delighted that he felt comfortable enough to tease her. "That sounds suspiciously like blackmail, young man."

"Whatever it takes."

She returned his smile, then shifted her gaze to see

Ross watching both of them out of those brown eyes of his that sometimes revealed nothing.

"I suppose we could throw something else on the grill for you," Ross said. "You eat much fish? We've still got bass from the other day."

If she were wise, she would tell Josh 'thanks but no thanks' for his kind invitation. She already felt too tightly entangled with Ross and his nephew. But the boy was reaching out to her. She couldn't just slap him down, especially if it might help her reach him better and help him through this grief.

"In that case, I would love to have dinner with you, as long as you let me pick up a salad and dessert from the deli on the way over."

"You don't have to do that," Ross said.

She smiled and tossed the basketball at him. "I don't mind. It's a weird rule in my family. The winner always buys the loser's dessert. You can consider the salad just a bonus."

He was still laughing as she climbed into her car and drove away.

Chapter 6

By the time she left the deli with her favorite tomato salad and a Boston cream pie, her stomach jumped with nerves and she could barely concentrate on the drive across town to the Frederickses' luxurious home.

She let out a breath. It was only dinner. This jittery reaction was absurd in the extreme. It was only a simple dinner with a client and his uncle.

Nothing more than that.

Still, she couldn't deny that Ross affected her more than any man had in recent memory. It had been seven years since her husband's death. Seven long, lonely years. She had dated occasionally since then but only on a casual basis. She knew she was the one who always put roadblocks up to avoid things becoming more serious. The time and the person never felt right.

For a long time, she had been too busy trying to glue

together the shattered pieces of her life. Then she had been too wrapped up in her new career as a child and family therapist and the new job at the Fortune Foundation to devote much time or energy to a relationship.

For the past year or so she had begun to think that she was finally in a good place to get serious about a man again, to try again at love. She had dated a few possibilities but nothing had ever come of them.

Ross Fortune was definitely not serious relationship material. Despite the attraction that simmered between them—and she knew she was not misreading those signs—Ross Fortune came with complications she wasn't prepared to deal with. Beyond his current family turmoil, she sensed he was a hard man, not very open to warmth and tenderness.

She tried to picture him being content spending a quiet evening at home with a child on his lap and couldn't quite manage it. But maybe she wasn't being fair to him. Maybe that restlessness she sensed was a result of his brother-in-law's murder and the subsequent fallout from it.

Julie sighed as she approached the Fredericses' large house that gleamed a pale coral in the fading sunlight. That unspoken attraction between them was real and intense, but for now that was all it could remain.

She wasn't sure she could afford to see what might come of it, not when she had the feeling Ross Fortune was the kind of man who could easily break her heart like a handful of twigs.

Josh, she reminded herself.

She was here only because he asked her, because she wanted to think they had formed a connection since his father's death and she wanted to help him sort through his jumbled mix of feelings.

Her own weren't important right now.

The evening was warm and pleasant as she closed her car door. In other neighborhoods, she might have heard the happy sounds of children playing in the last golden twilight hours before bedtime, but the Frederickses lived in Red Rock's most exclusive neighborhood. All she could manage to hear was the whir of air conditioners and a few well-mannered birds tweeting in the treetops.

Her own neighborhood near the elementary school was far different, an eclectic mix of old-timers who had lived in Red Rock forever and some of the new blood that had moved into the town, drawn by the quiet pace and friendly neighbors.

Moving here from Austin a year ago had been good for her, she thought as she rang the doorbell. She had made many new friends, she had a busy social life and she enjoyed a career where she felt she was affecting young lives.

Did she really need to snarl that up by yearning for a man who appeared unavailable?

At just that moment, Ross opened the door and she had to swallow hard. He was wearing Levi's and a navy blue shirt with the sleeves rolled up. He looked casual and relaxed and her traitorous body responded instantly.

She was staring at his mouth. She realized it a half second too late and jerked her gaze up, only to find him watching her with a strange, glittery light in his eyes that struck her as vaguely predatory.

"Hi," she murmured.

"Evening."

"It's a gorgeous one, isn't it?"

He glanced past her to the soft twilight and blinked a little as if he hadn't noticed it before. "You're right. It is. Come in."

She followed him inside. Though his sister had been in custody for less than a week, the grand house already felt a little neglected. A thin layer of dust covered the table in the foyer and several pairs of shoes were lined up by the door, something she was quite sure Frannie wouldn't have allowed.

"Where's Josh?" she asked.

"Holed up in his room, claiming homework. I'll let him know you're here in a minute. Actually, I'm glad to have a chance to talk to you alone first."

Her heart skipped a beat, despite her best efforts to control her reaction. "Oh?"

"About Josh, I mean."

She hoped he didn't notice her flushed features or the disappointment she told herself was ridiculous. "Of course."

"Do you mind coming out back with me? We can talk while I throw the steaks and your fish on the grill."

She nodded and followed him through the house, noticing a few more subtle signs of neglect in the house that weren't present when she was first here nearly a week ago. A few dirty dishes in the sink, a clutter of papers on the edge of the kitchen island, a jacket tossed casually over the back of a chair.

Ross grabbed a covered platter from the refrigerator, then opened the sliding doors to the vast patio that led to an elegantly landscaped pool. In the dusky light, the area looked quiet and restful. While she didn't much care for the style of the rest of the house, Julie very much admired the gardens around Lloyd and Frannie Fredericks's mansion.

She eased into a comfortable glider swing near the grill and watched while Ross transferred the meat from the plate to the grill with the ease of long practice. When he was done, he approached the swing and after a moment sat beside her, much to her dismay.

He was so big, so very masculine, and she was painfully aware of his proximity.

"What did you want to talk about?" she finally asked, hoping he didn't try prodding her again to reveal details about her counseling session with Josh earlier.

"I'm looking for an honest opinion here," he said. "What do you think about Josh's girlfriend?"

Okay, she hadn't been expecting that. "Lyndsey? I haven't met her."

"But Josh has mentioned her, right?"

"Yes. That first night when I stayed here with him while you were at the jail." She didn't want to breach Josh's confidences by mentioning all the times he had brought up her name during their therapy session. "Why do you ask? Don't you like her?"

Ross was quiet for a moment, a push of his boot sending the glider swaying slightly. "I've only met her briefly myself. Can't say whether I like her or not. But I know Frannie was concerned about how serious they seemed to be getting. Now that I've had a chance to take a closer look at the situation firsthand, I've got to admit, it worries me a little, too."

"In what way?"

"To me, it seems like they're together all the time. I mean, *all* the time! When he's not over at her place or she's not here, he's talking to her on the phone or texting her or talking to her online. I don't know how intense things were between them before Lloyd's death but I'm a little worried that he's becoming too wrapped up with her. He's only a kid, with his whole life ahead of him."

"Don't you remember your first love? They can be pretty intense."

"No," he said, his voice blunt. "I never had one."

She stared. "You never had a girlfriend?"

"No. Not in high school, anyway. I was too busy with…things."

"What kind of things? Sports?"

His mouth tightened. "Family stuff."

He didn't seem inclined to add any more, so Julie forced herself to clamp down on her curiosity to press him.

"Well, first love can be crazy for a teenager," she said instead. "Wonderful and terrible at the same time, full of raw emotions and all these fears and hopes and insecurities. I'm sure his emotional bond to Lyndsey is heightened by the chaos elsewhere in his life. She must seem like a sturdy rock he can hang on to."

"She strikes me as the clingy, needy sort, just from the little I've been able to see of her," Ross said.

She could barely think straight, sitting this close to him, but she did her best to rearrange her mind to gain a little clarity. "Well, that might be part of her appeal to him. Lyndsey is somebody who needs him. Look at things from Josh's perspective. His father is dead. His mother is in deep trouble, but not any kind of trouble he can solve for her. Aiding this girl with whatever troubles she's having might make Josh feel less helpless about the rest of the things going on in his world."

He pushed the swing again with his foot. "So you think I ought to let their little romance run its course?"

"Josh is almost eighteen. There's not really much you can do about it."

"I could lock him in his room and feed him only gruel," he muttered.

She laughed. "He's a teenage boy. I imagine he would figure out a way to sneak out and go for pizza."

He was quiet for a long moment. When she glanced over to gauge his expression and try to figure out what he was thinking about, she thought she detected a hint of color on his cheekbones.

"Should I take him to buy condoms, just to be on the safe side?" he asked, without looking at her.

The temperature between them seemed to heat up a dozen degrees and she knew it was not from the barbecue just a few feet away. She cleared her throat. "Maybe that's a conversation you ought to have with his mother."

"I can't discuss my nephew's sex life with my sister while she's in jail!"

She supposed she ought to be flattered that he felt he could discuss such a delicate subject with her, but she couldn't get past the trembling in her stomach just thinking about "Ross" and "condoms" in the same conversation.

"I can't tell you what to do," she said. "You're going to have to make that decision on your own. But I will say that if Josh were my son or in my care, it's certainly a conversation I would have with him, especially if he's becoming as serious with his girlfriend as you seem to believe."

He didn't look very thrilled by the prospect, but he nodded. "I guess I'll do that. Thanks for the advice. I can see why you make a good counselor. You're very easy to talk to."

She smiled. "You're welcome."

He gazed at her and she saw that heat flare in his eyes again. The world seemed to shiver to a stop and the night and the lovely gardens and the soft wind murmuring in the treetops seemed to disappear, leaving just the two of them alone with this powerful tug of attraction between them.

He was inches from kissing her.

Ross could feel the sweet warmth of her breath, could almost taste her on his mouth. He wanted her, with a fierce hunger that seemed to drive all common sense out of his head.

He tried to hang on to all the reasons he shouldn't kiss her. This was *not* supposed to be happening right now.

His life was in total chaos, he had far too many people depending on him and the last thing he needed was to find himself tangled up with someone like Julie Osterman, someone soft and generous and entirely too sweet for a man like him.

One kiss wouldn't hurt anything, though. Only a tiny little taste. He leaned forward and heard a seductive little catch of her breath, felt the brush of her breast against his arm as she shifted slightly closer.

His mouth was just a tantalizing inch away from hers when he suddenly heard the snick of the sliding door.

"Ross?" Josh called out.

Julie jerked away as if Ross had poked her with hot coals from the grill and the glider swayed crazily with the movement.

"Over here," Ross called.

He didn't like the way Josh skidded to a stop, his size-fourteen sneakers thudding against the tile patio, or the way his eyebrows climbed to find them sitting together so cozily on the glider.

He also didn't like the sudden speculative gleam in his nephew's eyes.

"Hi, Julie. I didn't hear you come in."

She was breathing just a hair too quickly, Ross thought. "I only arrived a few moments ago. Your uncle and I were just…we were, um…"

"Julie was helping me with the steaks. And speaking of which, I'd better turn them before they're charred."

He definitely needed to get a grip on this attraction, he thought as he turned the steaks while Julie and Josh set the table out on the patio.

She was a nice woman who was doing him a huge favor by helping him figure out how to handle sudden, unexpected fatherhood. It would be a poor way to repay her by indulging his own whims when he had nothing to offer her in return.

"I think everything's ready," he said a few moments later.

"We're all set here," Julie said from the table, where she sat talking quietly with Josh about school. They had set out candles, he saw, and Frannie's nice china. It was a nice change from the paper plates he and Josh had been using while he was here.

He went inside for the russet potatoes he had thrown in the oven earlier while they were waiting for her to arrive, and he put the tomato salad Julie had brought into a bowl.

"Wow. I'm impressed," Julie exclaimed as he set the

foil packet containing her fish on her plate and opened it for her. The smell of tarragon and lemon escaped.

"Better wait until you taste it before you say that," he warned her.

He knew only two ways to cook fish. Either battered and fried in tons of butter—something he tried not to do too often for obvious health reasons—or grilled in a packet with olive oil, lemon juice and a mix of easy spices.

He knew he shouldn't care so much what she thought but he still found it immensely gratifying when she closed her eyes with sheer delight at the first forkful. "Ross, this is delicious!"

He was becoming like one of the teens she worked with, desperate for her approval. "Glad you like it. How's the steak, Josh?"

His nephew was still studying the two of them with entirely too much interest. "It's good. Same as always."

"Nothing like family to deflate the old ego," Ross said with a wry smile.

"Sorry," Josh amended. "What I meant to say is this is absolutely the best steak I have ever tasted. Every bite melts in my mouth. I think I could eat this every single day for the rest of my life. Is that better?"

Julie laughed and it warmed Ross to see Josh flash her a quick grin before he turned back to his dinner. He didn't know what it was about her, but when she was around, Josh seemed far more relaxed. More like the kid he used to be.

"What are your plans after the summer?" she asked.

Josh shrugged. "I'm not sure right now."

Ross looked up from dressing his potato and frowned. "What do you mean, you're not sure? You've got an academic scholarship to A&M. It's all you could talk about a few weeks ago."

His nephew looked down at his plate. "Yeah, well, things have changed a little since a few weeks ago."

"And in a few *more* weeks, this is all going to seem like a bad dream."

"Is it?" Josh asked quietly and the patio suddenly simmered with tension.

"Yes. You'll see. These ridiculous charges against your mom will be dropped and everything will be back to normal."

"My dad will still be dead."

He had no answer to that stark truth. "You're not giving up a full-ride academic scholarship out of concern for your mother or some kind of misguided guilt over your dad's death."

Josh's color rose and he set his utensils down carefully on his plate. "It's my scholarship, Uncle Ross. If I want to give it up, nobody else can stop me. You keep forgetting I'm not a kid anymore. I'll be eighteen in a week, remember?"

"I haven't forgotten. But I also know that you have opportunities ahead of you and it would be a crime to waste those. I won't let you do it."

"Good luck trying to stop me, if that's what I decide to do," Josh snapped.

Ross opened his mouth to answer just as hotly but Josh's cell phone suddenly bleated a sappy little tune he recognized as being the one Josh had programmed to alert him to Lyndsey's endless phone calls.

He didn't know whether to be annoyed or grateful for the interruption. He had dealt with his own stubborn younger brothers enough to know that yelling wasn't going to accomplish anything but would make Josh dig in his heels.

"Hey," Josh said into the phone. He shifted his body away and pitched his voice several decibels lower. "No. Not the best right now."

Ross's gaze met Julie's and the memory of their conversation earlier—and all his worries—came flooding back. Was it possible Lyndsey was part of the reason Josh was considering giving up his scholarship?

Josh held the phone away from his ear. "Uncle Ross, I'm done with dinner. Do you care if I take this inside, in my room? A friend of mine needs some help with, um, trig homework. I might be a while and I wouldn't want to bore you two with a one-sided conversation."

He and Julie both knew that wasn't true. He wondered if he should call Josh on the lie, but he wasn't eager to add to the tension over college.

"Did you get enough to eat?"

Josh made a face. "Yeah, Mom."

Ross supposed that was just what he sounded like. Not that he had much experience with maternal solicitude. "I guess you can go."

The teen was gone before the words were even out of his mouth. Only after the sliding door closed behind him did Ross suddenly realize his nephew's defection left him alone with Julie.

"You know, lots of parents establish a no-call zone during the dinner hour," Julie said mildly.

He bristled for about ten seconds before he sighed. Hardly anybody had a cell phone twenty years ago, the last time he'd been responsible for a teenager. The whole internet, email, cell phone thing presented entirely new challenges.

"Frannie always insisted he leave it in his room during dinner."

She opened her mouth to say something but quickly closed it again and returned her attention to her plate.

"What were you going to say?" he pressed.

"Nothing."

"You forget, I'm a trained investigator. I know when people are trying to hide things from me."

She gave him a sidelong look, then sighed. "Fine. But feel free to tell me to mind my own business."

"Believe me. I have no problem whatsoever telling people that."

She gave a slight smile, but quickly grew serious. "I was only thinking that a little more consistency with the house rules he's always known might be exactly what Josh needs right now. He's in complete turmoil. He's struggling with his mother's arrest and his father's death. Despite their uneasy relationship, Lloyd was his father and having a parent die isn't easy for anyone. Perhaps a little more constancy in his life will help him feel not quite as fragmented."

"So many things have been ripped from his world right now. It's all chaos. I was just trying to cut him a little slack."

She stood and began clearing the dishes away. "Believe it or not, a little slack might very well be the last thing he needs right now. Rules provide structure and order amid the chaos, Ross."

He could definitely understand that. He had craved that very structure in his younger days and had found it at the Academy. Police work, with its regulations and discipline—its paperwork and routine—had given him guidance and direction at a time he desperately needed some.

Maybe she was right. Maybe Josh craved those same things.

"Here, I'll take those," he said to Julie when she had filled a tray with the remains of their dinner.

After he carried the tray into the kitchen, he returned to the patio to find Julie standing on the edge of the tile, gazing up at the night sky.

It was a clear night, with a bright sprawl of stars. Ross joined her, wondering if he could remember the last time he had taken a chance to stargaze.

"Pretty night," he said, though all he could think about was the lovely woman standing beside him with her face lifted up to the moonlight.

"It is," she murmured. "I can't believe I sometimes get so wrapped up in my life that I forget to enjoy it."

They were quiet for a long time, both lost in their respective thoughts while the sweet scents from Frannie's garden swirled around them.

"Can I ask you something?" Ross finally asked.

If he hadn't been watching her so closely, he might have missed the slight wariness that crept into her expression. "Sure."

"How do you know all this stuff? About grieving and discipline and how to help a kid who's hurting?"

"I'm a trained youth counselor with a master's degree in social work and child and family development."

She was silent for a long moment, the only sound in the night the distant hoot of an owl and the wind sighing in the treetops. "Beyond that," she finally said softly, "I know what it is to be lost and hurting. I've been there."

Her words shivered through him, to the dark and

quiet place he didn't like to acknowledge, that place where he was still ten years old, scared and alone and responsible for his three younger siblings yet again after Cindy ran off with a new boyfriend for a night that turned into another and then another.

He knew lost and hurting. He had been there plenty of times before, but it didn't make him any better at intuitively sensing what was best for Josh.

He pushed those memories aside. It was much easier to focus on the mystery of Julie Osterman than on the past he preferred to forget.

"What are your secrets?" he asked.

"You mean you haven't run a background check on me yet, detective?"

He laughed a little at her arch tone. "I didn't think about it until just this moment. Good idea, though." He studied her for a long moment in the moonlight, noting the color that had crept along the delicate planes of her cheekbones. "If I did, what would I find?"

"Nothing criminal, I can assure you."

"I don't suppose you would have been hired at the Foundation if you had that sort of past."

"Probably not."

"Then what?" He paused. "You lost someone close to you, didn't you?"

She gazed at the moon, sparkling on the swimming pool. "That's a rather obvious guess, detective."

"But true."

Her sigh stirred the air between them.

"Yes. True," she answered. "It's a long, sad story that I'm sure would bore you senseless within minutes."

"I have a pretty high bore quotient. I've been known to sit perfectly motionless on stakeouts for hours."

She glanced at him, then away again. "A simple background check would tell you this in five seconds but I suppose I'll go ahead and spare you the trouble. I lost my husband seven years ago. I'm a widow, detective."

Chapter 7

For several moments, he could only stare at her, speechless.

She was a widow. He would never have guessed that, not in a million years, though he wasn't quite sure why he found the knowledge so astonishing—perhaps because she normally had such a sunny attitude for someone who must have lost her husband at a young age.

"I'm sorry. I shouldn't have pushed you to talk about something you obviously didn't want to discuss, especially after you've done nothing but help Josh and me."

"It's okay, Ross. I wouldn't have told you if I hadn't wanted you to know. I don't talk about it often, only because it was a really dark and difficult time in my past and I don't like to dwell on it. I prefer instead to enjoy the present and look ahead to the future. That's all."

"What happened?" he asked after a long moment.

He sensed it was something traumatic. That might help explain her empathy and understanding of what Josh was dealing with. He braced himself for it but was completely unprepared for her quiet answer.

"He shot himself."

Ross stared, trying to make out her delicate features in the dim moonlight. "Was it a hunting accident?"

The noise she made couldn't be mistaken for a laugh. "No. It was no accident. Chris was…troubled. We were married for five years. The first two were wonderful. He was funny and smart and brilliantly creative. The kind of person who always seems to have a crowd around him.

"After those first two years, we bought a home in Austin," she went on. "I was working at a high school there and Chris was a photographer with an ad agency. Everything seemed so perfect. We were starting to talk about starting a family and then…everything started to change. *He* started to change."

"Drugs? Alcohol?"

"No. Nothing like that. He became moody and withdrawn at times and obsessively jealous, and then he would have periods where he would stay up for days at a time, would shoot roll after roll of film, of nothing really. The pattern on the sofa cushions, a single blade of grass. He once spent six hours straight trying to capture a doorknob in the perfect light. Eventually he was diagnosed as schizophrenic, with a little manic depression thrown in for added fun."

Ross frowned. He knew enough about mental illness to know it couldn't have been an easy road for either of them.

"You stayed with him?"

"He was my husband," she said simply. "I loved him."

"You must have been young."

"We married when I was twenty-four. I didn't feel young at the time but in retrospect, I was a baby. I suppose I must have been young enough, anyway, that I was certain I could fix anything."

"But you couldn't."

"Not this. It was bigger than either of us. That's still so hard for me to admit, even seven years later. For three years, he tried every possible combination of meds but nothing could keep the demons away for long. Finally Chris's condition started a downward spiral and no matter what we tried, we couldn't seem to slow the momentum. On his twenty-eighth birthday, he gave up the fight. He returned home early from work, set his camera on a tripod with an automatic timer, took out a Ruger he had bought illegally on the street a week earlier and shot himself in our bedroom."

Where Julie would be certain to find him, he realized grimly. Ross had seen enough self-inflicted gunshot wounds when he had been a cop to know exactly what kind of scene she must have walked into.

He knew her husband had been mentally ill and couldn't have been thinking clearly, but suddenly Ross was furious at the man for leaving behind such horror and anguish for his pretty, devoted young wife to remember the rest of her life. He hoped she could remember past that traumatic final scene and the three rough years preceding it to the few good ones they had together. "I'm so sorry, Julie."

He wanted to take it away, to make everything all better for her, but here was another person in his life whose pain he couldn't fix.

* * *

The unmistakable sincerity in Ross's voice warmed the small, frozen place inside Julie that would always grieve for the bright, creative light extinguished far too soon.

She lifted her gaze to his. "It was a terrible time in my life. I can't lie about that. The grief was so huge and so awful, I wasn't sure I could survive it. But I endured by hanging on to the things I still had that mattered—my faith, my family, my friends. I also reminded myself every single day, both before his death and in those terrible dark days after, that Chris wasn't responsible for the choices he made. I know he loved me and wouldn't have chosen that course, if he could have seen any other choice in his tormented mind."

He didn't say anything for a long time and she couldn't help wondering what he was thinking.

"Is that why you work with troubled kids?" he finally asked, his voice low. "To make sure none of them feels like that's the only way out for them?"

She sighed. "I suppose that's part of it. I started out working on a suicide hotline in the evenings and realized I was making an impact. It helped me move outside myself at a time I desperately needed that and I discovered I was good at listening. So I left teaching and went back to school to earn a graduate degree."

"Do you miss teaching?" he asked.

"Sometimes. But when I was teaching six different classes, with thirty kids each, I didn't have the chance for the one-on-one interaction I have now. I can always go back to teaching if I want. I still might someday, if that seems the right direction for me. I haven't ruled anything out yet."

"Do you ever wonder if anything you do really makes a difference?"

How in the world had he become so cynical? she wondered. Was it his years as a police officer? Or something before then? It saddened her, whatever the cause.

"I have to give back somehow. I've always thought of it as trying to shine as much light as I can, even if it only illuminates my own path."

He gazed at her, his dark eyes intense, and she was suddenly painfully aware of him, the hard strength of his shoulders beside her, the slight curl of his hair brushing his collar.

"You're a remarkable woman," he said softly. "I'm not sure I've ever known anyone quite like you."

He wanted to kiss her. She sensed it clearly again, as she had earlier in the evening. She could see the desire kindle in his eyes, the intention there.

This time he wouldn't stop—and she didn't want him to. She wanted to know if his kiss could possibly be as good as she imagined it. Anticipation fluttered through her, like the soft, fragile wings of a butterfly, and she caught her breath as he moved closer, surrounding her with his heat and his strength.

The night seemed magical. The vast glitter of stars and the breeze murmuring through the trees and the sweet scents of his sister's flower garden. Everything combined to make this moment seem unreal.

She closed her eyes as his mouth found hers, her heart pounding, her breath caught in her throat. His kiss was gentle at first, as slow and easy as the little creek running through her yard on a hot August afternoon. She leaned into it, into him, wondering how it was possible for him to make her feel shattered with just a kiss.

She was vaguely aware of the slide of his arms around her, pulling her closer. She again had that vague sensation of being surrounded by him, encircled. It wasn't unpleasant. Far from it. She wanted to savor every moment, burn it all into her mind.

He deepened the kiss, his mouth a little more urgent. Some insistent warning voice in her head urged her to pull away and return to the safety of the other side of the patio, away from this temptation to lose her common sense—*herself*—but she decided to ignore it. Instead, she curled her arms around his neck and surrendered to the moment.

She had dated a few men in the seven years since Chris's suicide. A history teacher at the high school, a fellow grad student, an investment banker she met at the gym.

All of them had been perfectly nice, attractive men. So why hadn't their kisses made her blood churn, the lassitude seep into her muscles? She supposed it was a good thing he was supporting her weight with his arms around her because she wasn't at all sure she could stand on her own.

In seven years, she hadn't realized how truly much she had missed a man's touch until just this moment. Everything feminine inside her just seemed to give a deep, heartfelt sigh of welcome.

They kissed for a long time there in the moonlight. She learned the taste of him, of the wine they'd had with dinner and some sort of enticing mint and another essence she guessed was pure Ross. She learned his hair was soft and thick under her fingers and that he went a little crazy when she nipped gently on his bottom lip.

His tongue swept through her mouth, unfurling a

wild hunger for more and she tightened her arms around him, her hands gripping him closely.

She didn't know how long the kiss lasted. It could have been hours, for all the awareness she had of time passing. She only knew that in Ross's arms, she felt safe and desirable, a heady combination.

They might have stayed there all night, but eventually some little spark of consciousness filtered through the soft hunger.

This was dangerous. Too dangerous. His nephew could come outside to the patio at any moment and discover them in a heated embrace.

Although Josh was almost eighteen, certainly old enough to understand about sexual attraction, she had a strong feeling Ross wouldn't be thrilled if his nephew caught them kissing.

She wasn't sure how, but she managed to summon the energy and sheer strength of will to pull her hands away and step back enough to allow room for her lungs to take in a full breath.

The kick of oxygen to her system pushed away some of the fuzzy, hormone-induced cobwebs in her brain but for perhaps an entire sixty seconds she could only stare at him, feeling raw and off balance. Her thoughts were a wild snarl in her head and she couldn't seem to untwist them.

An awkward silence seethed around them, replacing the seductive attraction with something taut and clumsy. She struggled for something to say but couldn't think of anything that didn't sound silly and girlish.

Ross was the first one to break the silence. "I swear, that wasn't on the agenda for the evening," he finally said.

His hair was a little tousled from her fingers and he

looked rumpled and rough around the edges and rather dismayed at their kiss.

She found the entire package absolutely irresistible.

"I believe you."

"I'm not… I didn't intend—"

He raked a hand through his hair, messing it up even more. A muscle worked in his jaw and he seemed so uncomfortable that she finally took pity on him.

"Ross, don't worry. I'm not going to rush out and start looking at bridal books just because you kissed me."

His eyes widened with obvious panic at simply the word "bridal." Under other circumstances, Julie might have laughed but it was all rather humiliating in the moment. She was still reeling from the most sensuous kiss she thought she had ever experienced and he just looked at her with that stunned, slightly dazed look, as if she had just stripped down and started pole dancing around the patio umbrella.

"If I could take back the last ten minutes, I would," he said.

She refused to acknowledge the sharp sting of his words. "Don't give it another thought."

"Like that's possible," he muttered.

At least the kiss left him just as off balance as it had her. She found some small comfort that he hadn't been completely unaffected by it, though she still wasn't thrilled that he seemed so aghast.

"Look," he said after another long, awkward moment. "I'm very attracted to you. I guess that's pretty obvious by now and I'd be lying if I tried to pretend otherwise. But this is not a really good time for me to be…distracted."

She wasn't sure she'd ever been called a distraction before and she didn't quite know how to react. At least he had prefaced it by admitting he was attracted to her.

"Right now my focus has to be my family," he said. "Frannie, Josh. They need me and I can't afford to let my attention be diverted by anything, especially not, well, something as complicated as a relationship."

Just because of his family? she wondered. Somehow she doubted it. While she was quite certain he wasn't using his difficult situation as an excuse, she had a feeling even if his family wasn't having such a hard time right now, Ross wouldn't be quick to jump into any involvement with her.

He struck her as a man who shied away from anything deeper or more meaningful than a quick fling.

"I understand," she murmured.

"Do you?" His eyes were murky with regret in the moonlight. Because he had kissed her? she wondered. Or because he was determined not to repeat it?

"You've been thrust into a tough role here with Josh, trying to do the right thing for him at the same time you're deeply worried about your sister. I can see why you want to keep the rest of your life as uncomplicated as possible."

He frowned, shoving his hands in his pockets. "Tell me I haven't jeopardized your willingness to help with Josh?"

She certainly wouldn't be able to quickly forget the magic and heat they had shared. But that didn't mean she couldn't move on from here.

"It was just a kiss, Ross! Of course I'm still willing to help with Josh, if he's interested in more sessions. That's a completely separate issue. I would still want to help him any way I could, even if you and I had just gotten naked and rolled around on the living room carpet for the last two hours."

She wasn't quite sure if it was her imagination but his eyes seemed to glaze slightly and he made a sound that might have been a groan. Julie regretted her flippancy. The last thing she needed right now was that particular image in her head, not with the unfulfilled desire still pulsing through her insides.

Ross drew in a ragged breath. "I'm glad for that, at least. Josh responds to you. I don't want to lose that because I overstepped."

She held a hand up. "Ross, stop. Let it go. It was just a kiss. Just a momentary impulse that doesn't mean anything. You're attracted to me, I'm attracted right back at you, obviously, but that's all it is."

To her amazement, he opened his mouth as if he wanted to disagree—which she decided would make Ross Fortune just about the most contrary man she had ever met, if he intended to argue both sides of the issue.

She decided not to put the matter to the test. "I'd better go," she said. "It's been a long day and I have paperwork to finish tonight."

He still looked as if he had more to say but he only nodded. "Thanks for coming. I'm sorry again that Josh ditched on you. I'll have a talk with him about keeping the cell phone away from the dinner table."

"Excellent idea."

"Let me just go call him down to say goodbye to you."

"That's really not necessary."

Right now she just wanted to leave so that she could

try to put a little distance between them in an effort to regain both her dignity and a little perspective.

"It *is* necessary," he said. "Josh is the one who invited you to dinner with us and then he just abandoned you for a phone call, which I should never have let him get away with. The least he can do is come down to tell you goodbye."

She didn't want to argue, she only wanted to leave, but she decided to give in with good grace. He was right, Josh needed to hold onto civility and manners, even if his life had been turned upside down.

She waited in the ornate foyer of the Frederickses' home while Ross hurried up the stairs to his nephew's room. A moment later, he returned with Josh, who rubbed the back of his neck and looked embarrassed.

"Sorry about leaving, Julie. It was way rude of me and I shouldn't have done it. I wasn't thinking about what bad manners it was, I was just... I needed to talk to my friend."

"I understand. Next time, maybe you could wait until we've all finished eating to take your phone call."

"I'll try to remember to do that. Thanks for coming to dinner and for...everything else today."

"You're welcome. I enjoyed it." *Some parts more than others*, she added silently to herself, and she forced herself not to look at Ross even as she felt a blush steal over her cheeks.

"We never did get to finish playing H-O-R-S-E."

"We'll have to schedule a rematch next time we have a session. If you think you want another one, anyway."

He shrugged. "I guess. You're pretty easy to talk to."

"Thanks." She smiled. "How about Tuesday after school?"

"That should work, I think."

"I'll see you then. Be sure to bring your game for afterward. You wouldn't want me to whip your butt on the court again."

He laughed. "I'll see if I can find it," he said. "See you later."

He headed up the stairs again, leaving her alone with Ross. He looked rough-edged and darkly handsome amid the pale, elegant furnishings of the house and she had a tough time not stepping forward and tasting that hard mouth one last time.

"Thanks again for dinner, Ross," she forced herself to say. "It was delicious."

"You're welcome."

They exchanged one more awkward, tentative smile, then she opened the door and walked out into the Texas night.

As she hurried to her car, she couldn't help wondering how one kiss had managed to sear away seven years of restraint.

Ross stood on his sister's veranda and watched Julie drive away in a sensible silver sedan.

He still felt as if he'd been tied feetfirst to the back end of a mule and dragged through cactus for a few dozen miles.

That kiss. Damn it, he didn't need this right now. He had never known anything like it, that wild fire in his blood that still seemed to sizzle and burn.

He had wanted to make love to her, right there on Frannie's Italian tile patio table. Even now, he could remember the sweet, luscious taste of her, the smell of her, like juicy peaches ripened by the sun that he couldn't wait to sink his teeth into.

What was he supposed to do with a woman like Julie Osterman? She was far too sweet, far too centered for someone like him.

She had lost a husband.

Just thinking about it made his heart ache. He could picture her—younger, even more idealistic, certain she could fix everything wrong in the world. And then to come up against such a tough, thorny thing as mental illness in someone she loved. It would have broken a woman who wasn't as strong as Julie.

She was a lovely, courageous, compassionate woman.

And not for him.

Ross gazed out at the night. What the hell did a man like him have to offer someone like her? She needed softness, romance, tenderness, especially after the pain she had been forced to endure.

He didn't know if he was capable of any of those things. He was cynical and rough, more used to frozen pizza than candlelight dinners. He liked his life on his own and wasn't sure he had room inside it for a woman like Julie.

He couldn't let himself kiss her again, especially not after he'd told her what a mistake it had been. As much as he might want to hold her in his arms, it wouldn't be fair to her to give her any ideas that he might be open to starting something with her, not when he would only end up hurting and disillusioning her.

Like he did everybody else.

He let out a breath, wishing for a good, stiff drink. He needed something to push back the regret that he wouldn't have the chance to taste that delectable mouth again, to hear her soft little sigh of arousal, to feel her curves pressing against him. Frannie and Lloyd had a well-stocked liquor cabinet but he wasn't sure it was a good idea for Josh to see him turning to alcohol to escape the weight of his obligations.

He heard the creak of the door behind him and Ross turned to see his nephew standing in the lighted doorway, studying him with concern in his eyes.

"Everything okay?" Josh asked.

"Sure. Why wouldn't it be?"

His nephew shrugged. "I don't know. You've just been standing out here without moving for at least half an hour. My bedroom window has a perfect view of the front door and I watched you while I was on the phone."

"Oh, right. Your study session."

Josh flashed him a quick, rueful grin but it faded quickly and those secrets took its place. He definitely needed to figure out what was going on with the kid.

"So what's up?" Josh asked. "Is something wrong?"

"No. I was just…thinking."

"About my dad's murder and the case against my mom?"

That was exactly what he *should* have been thinking about out here. The boy's words were a harsh reminder of yet another reason he needed to stay away from Julie—the most important one.

She distracted him at a time when he could least afford the inattention. He had a job to do—clearing his sister. It was quite possibly the most important case of his career, the one he had the most stake in, and he needed to focus.

"There are still a lot of inconsistencies," Ross said instead of answering his nephew directly. "The whole thing is making me crazy, if you want to know the truth. If your mom would only try to defend herself, things would go much easier for her. We just need to hear her side of the story."

Josh leaned against the pillar, his arms crossed over his chest. "Why do you think she's not talking?"

The question was just a little too casual. He searched Josh's features but his face was in shadows and Ross couldn't quite read him.

"It's a good question," he said. "One I sure wish I could answer. Why do *you* think she's staying quiet?"

Josh turned to look out at the quiet road in front of his house and Ross couldn't help wondering if he was avoiding his gaze. "I don't know. Maybe she's blocked out what happened. Lyndsey said that can happen to people when they've been through a traumatic event or something."

What the hell did a sixteen-year-old girl know about disassociation? Ross frowned. "Maybe that's what happened. I don't know. But even if that's the case, I would still like to hear her say so. At this point, I'd like to hear anything—that she can't remember what happened or she's not sure or aliens abducted her and sucked out her memory with their proton beams. Anything at all. I wish she could see that her silence is as good as a confession."

"She didn't do it, though," Josh muttered. "You and I both *know* she didn't. I hate thinking of her in jail."

His voice broke a little on the last word but he quickly cleared his throat, embarrassed, and straightened from the pillar.

Ross rested an awkward hand on Josh's shoulder, wishing he was better at this whole parenting thing. "Your loyalty means the world to her, I know."

To his dismay, instead of taking his words as praise, as Ross intended, Josh seemed even more upset by them. He looked as if Ross had shoved a fist in his solar plexus.

"I'm going to bed," he said after a moment, his voice strangled and tight. "I'll see you later."

"'Night," Ross said and watched with concern as Josh went back inside the house.

These sessions with Julie were a good idea, he decided. He just hoped she could get to the bottom of the kid's odd behavior.

Chapter 8

"I appreciate you coming out here, son. I know you're busy and I hope it didn't mess up your schedule too much."

As Ross shook his uncle William's hand in the foyer of the Double Crown, he thought how much he respected him. His mother's brother was as unlike Cindy as he imagined two people who came from the same womb could possibly be.

William had always struck him as decent and honorable. Though Ross hadn't known him well growing up because William and his wife and five sons lived in Los Angeles and their respective spheres rarely intersected, his uncle had invariably been kind to him and his brothers and sister when they did.

His wife Molly had died a year ago, and William had temporarily moved from California to Texas and the family ranch just a few months earlier after a string of mysterious incidents threatened the family's security.

Ross thought of the word he had used the night of the dinner with Julie that had upset Josh so much—*loyalty.* William typified family loyalty. His uncle invariably thought first about the Fortunes and what was in the family's best interest, and Ross had to respect him all the more for it.

"Not a problem," he said now. "I'm staying in Red Rock with Josh anyway so it wasn't any trouble to come out here to the Double Crown."

Before William could answer him, Lily—William and Cindy's cousin by marriage—walked down the stairs.

At sixty-three, she was still lovely from her Apache and Spanish heritage, with high cheekbones, tilt-tipped eyes framed by thick lashes and a wide, sultry mouth.

She was also one of his favorite Fortunes. He would have loved having a mother as warm and caring and maternal as Lily Fortune.

"Ross, my dear. You don't come to the Double Crown enough," she said, gripping his hands and squeezing them tightly.

"Sorry about that. I've been pretty busy lately."

"You've got your hands full right now, don't you? How is Frannie?"

He frowned. He had seen Frannie that morning at the jail—just another frustrating visit. How had he never guessed that such obstinance lurked inside his delicate sister? He had asked, begged and finally pleaded with her to tell him what had happened the night of Lloyd's death, but she remained stubbornly silent.

"I can't talk about it."

That was her only response, every single time he

pushed her. Finally she had told him she would tell the guards she wouldn't take any more visits from him if he didn't stop haranguing her about it.

"She doesn't belong in prison. That's for damn sure."

He heard his own language and winced. "Sorry, Lily. For darn sure, I meant."

She rolled her eyes. "If a little colorful language ever sent me into a swoon, I wouldn't be much good on a working ranch, would I?"

Ross grinned. "I suppose not."

"For what it's worth, I completely agree with you. I can't believe that pip-squeak Bruce Gibson was able to get his way and have her held without bail. It's an outrage, that's what it is."

"I couldn't agree more," William put in. "Any word on appealing the judge's decision on bail?"

"The lawyers are working on it." Like everything else, they were in wait-and-see mode.

"Whatever you need, Ross," William said, his expression solemn and sincere. "The family is behind you a hundred percent on this. We can hire different attorneys to argue for a change of venue if that would help."

"I don't know what's going to help at this point. I just need to figure out who really killed Lloyd so I can get her out of there."

"Whatever you need," William repeated. "Just say the word and we'll do anything it takes to help you."

"Thanks, Uncle William. I appreciate that."

He did, though it wasn't an easy thing for him to admit. As much as he respected his Fortune relatives, they had all come to his immediate family's rescue far more often than he could ever find comfortable. Cindy would have sucked the Fortune financial well dry if she could have found a way.

"Come on back to the kitchen, why don't you?" Lily said after a moment. "Rosita made cinnamon rolls this morning and I'm sure there are a few left."

His stomach rumbled, reminding him that breakfast had been coffee and a slice of burnt toast made from one of the last pieces of bread at the house. They were just about out of food. If he didn't want his nephew to starve, he was going to have to schedule a trip to the grocery store soon, as much as he heartily disliked the task.

He couldn't help comparing the big, warm kitchen at the Double Crown with Frannie's elegant, spare kitchen. *This* was the kitchen of his childhood dreams, something he didn't think was a coincidence. On his few trips to the Double Crown as a kid, this place had seemed like heaven on earth, from the horses to the swimming hole to the big rope swing in the barn that sent anyone brave enough for it sailing through the air into soft, clean-smelling hay.

Given a choice, he would much rather slide up to this table, with its scarred top and acres of mismatched chairs, than Frannie's perfect designer set.

Rosita, Lily's longtime friend and housekeeper, bustled around in the kitchen in an old-fashioned ruffled apron. She beamed when she saw Ross and ordered him to sit.

"You are too skinny. You need to come eat in my kitchen more often."

He raised an eyebrow. Only someone as comfortably round as Rosita could ever call him skinny. "If those cinnamon rolls taste as good as they smell, I might just have to kidnap you and take you back to Frannie's mausoleum to cook for Josh and me. We're getting a little tired of ordering pizza."

"You know you and Josh are welcome here anytime," Lily said.

"I wasn't hinting for an invitation," Ross said, embarrassed that his words might have been construed that way.

Lily smiled and squeezed his arm. It took him a moment to realize why the gesture seemed familiar. Julie had the same kind of mannerisms, that almost unconscious way of reinforcing her words with a physical touch.

He had come to crave those casual little brushes of her hands on him, though he would rather be hog-tied and left in a bull paddock than admit it.

They spoke of family news for a few moments while he savored divine mouthfuls of the gooey, yeasty cinnamon rolls. William caught him up on the upcoming wedding of his son Darr to Bethany Burdett, a receptionist at the Fortune Foundation, then Lily shared news about her family.

Ross had never quite figured out his place on the Fortune family tree. Sure, he shared the surname since Cindy had never bothered to change her name through any of her three marriages and had made sure each of her children carried it, as well. But he never quite felt a part of the family.

Cindy had been estranged from her siblings for years. Until Frannie's marriage to Lloyd eighteen years ago gave her more of an excuse, Cindy only popped into Red Rock once in a while, usually to hit somebody in her family up for money.

How many times had his uncle William and aunt

Molly bailed Cindy out of some scrape or another? Even Lily and her late husband Ryan had taken a turn.

Ross felt keenly obligated to them all for it—which was exactly why he was here listening to family gossip he didn't really care about and enjoying Rosita's exquisite cinnamon rolls.

"I guess you know the reason we asked you here," William finally said when there was a lull in the conversation. "We're just looking for an update on your investigation."

"Which one?" Ross muttered ruefully, taking a sip of coffee. Right now he felt as if he were spinning three or four dozen plates and was quite sure each one was ready to crash to the ground.

"Finding out the truth behind whoever killed Lloyd has to be your priority right now, for Frannie and Josh's sake. We completely understand that." William paused, his expression serious. "But I hope you understand that my priority right now is keeping the rest of the family safe."

His gaze flickered briefly to Lily just long enough for Ross to wonder if something were going on between the two of them. *William and Lily?* As stunning as he found the idea, it made an odd sort of sense. They each had lost—and mourned—their respective spouses and they were both heavily involved with the Fortune Foundation.

He hadn't heard anything from any other family members about a burgeoning romance between the two of them, but maybe it was still in the early stages.

He had enough genuine mysteries to solve, he reminded himself. He didn't need to concern himself with

any hypothetical romance between Lily and William—
and it was none of his business anyway.

"Have you discovered anything new about the fires
here and at Red or the mysterious notes we've received?" William asked.

In January, a fire nearly destroyed the local res-
taurant owned by good friends of the Fortunes, the
Mendozas. At that same time, William and his brother
Patrick each received a mysterious note that said simply
"One of the Fortunes is not who you think."

Just a month later, another fire had destroyed a barn
at the Double Crown, killing a favorite horse, and Lily
had received a note of her own that read "This one
wasn't an accident, either."

Ross had been brought in after that, when the family realized all these seemingly random events were
connected.

He hadn't been very successful, though, much to
his chagrin, both professionally and personally. Then
in April, the mystery deepened and became even more
sinister when his mother wrecked her car after a visit
with Frannie and the Red Rock police discovered that
her brakes had been tampered with.

Ross still couldn't completely convince himself
Cindy hadn't done it herself for attention. That was a
pretty pitiful suspicion for a son to have about his own
mother, but he had learned during his forty years on the
planet not to put much past her. Still, he was investigating the brake-tampering incident as part of the pattern.

"I'll be honest with you, Uncle William," he said
now. "I'm hitting a wall. The private lab I sent the let-
ters to was unable to find any legible fingerprints on either the notepaper itself or the envelopes used, and they

were both very generic items that could have been purchased anywhere. Nothing distinctive at all that might help us identify who purchased them and sent them. The lab was able to collect a small amount of DNA from whoever licked the envelopes, but it's not in any of the databanks we can access."

"Which means what, exactly?" Lily asked.

He gave them both an apologetic look. "Until we have a suspect to compare the sample to, DNA doesn't do us much good."

"Where do you suggest we go from here?" William asked, his expression troubled. He slanted a look at Lily and the obvious worry in his eyes made Ross wonder again at their relationship.

"I've still got some leads I'm following on Cindy's brakes and the accelerant used in both fires. But I'll be honest, right now my focus has to be on Frannie."

"That's just as it should be," Lily assured him, her features sympathetic. "I worry so for her. She's such a quiet soul, one who certainly doesn't belong in jail. I hate that she has to go through this."

"What about Josh?" William asked. "In a way, he's lost both a mother and a father, hasn't he?"

"Only temporarily, until I can clear Frannie and get her home where she belongs." He spoke the words in a vow.

Lily touched his arm again, her hands cool and soft. "You're such a good brother, Ross. You always have been. I don't know what would have happened to Frannie or your brothers if not for you."

William made a face. "It was an outrage what you children had to endure. The rest of us should never have allowed it. It's one of my greatest regrets in life that we didn't realize just how bad things were and didn't sue for custody of all of you."

How different his life might have turned out, if that had happened. He might have grown up in California with William and Molly and their sons or here on the ranch with Ryan and his first wife. He might have had breakfast every morning in this big, comfortable kitchen, instead of in whatever dingy apartment Cindy found for them.

"I wish I could say my sister ever outgrew her irresponsibility," William went on, "but she's as flighty and self-destructive at seventy as she was when she was a girl. I'm only sorry she dragged the four of you with her."

The last thing Ross wanted to talk about right now was his mother and the chaos of his childhood and all the might-have-beens that seemed more painful in retrospect. He quickly changed the subject.

"I'll admit, I'm worried about how this is all affecting Josh. He went back to school last week but he won't talk about how things are going. I know how kids can talk and I'm sure a scandal like this is the hot topic at Red Rock High School."

As he hoped, the diversionary tactic did the trick. Lily's eyes grew soft with concern, as they did whenever she heard about a child or youth in need.

"Have you thought about grief counseling for him?" she asked. "Perhaps someone at the Foundation might be able to see him. Julie Osterman, for instance, specializes in helping teens who have suffered loss."

Okay, maybe changing the subject hadn't been the greatest idea. He didn't want to talk about Julie any more than he wanted to discuss Cindy.

He certainly hadn't been able to stop thinking about

her since their dinner and the heated kiss they had shared nearly a week before. He had tried everything to get the blasted woman out of his system. He had worked like a maniac tracking down leads in Frannie's case, had taken Josh out fishing three more times, had swum so many laps in his sister's pool he thought he might just grow fins.

But he still dreamed of Julie every night and thoughts of her had a devious way of slithering into his mind at the most inconvenient time. Like, oh, just about every other minute.

"He's actually seeing Julie," Ross admitted. "He's been to a few sessions now. I can't say if they're helping yet."

"Julie is wonderful," Lily exclaimed. "Don't you just love her?"

Ross nearly choked on his coffee. "Um, she seems nice enough." Somehow he managed not to choke on the understatement, as well. "Josh likes her and that's the important thing."

"Julie is the perfect one to help him," Lily said. "She understands what it is to lose someone she loved."

"Yeah," Ross said, his voice gruff. "She told me about her husband."

Lily blinked a little at that. "Did she?"

Ross fiddled with his cup. "Yeah."

"What happened?" William asked. "I had no idea she was even married."

Lily touched his hand. "I'll tell you later," she said, then turned back to Ross. "I can't tell you how pleased and relieved I am that Josh is talking to someone. I've been so worried for him, especially since the last words between Josh and Lloyd were so harsh."

Ross frowned. "Harsh? Why do you say that?"

Lily shifted in her chair, looking as if she wished she hadn't said anything. "They were fighting, maybe a half hour before Lloyd was found dead. I'm sorry. I assumed you knew."

Fighting? Josh and Lloyd? This was the first he had heard anything about Josh even seeing his father the night of Lloyd's death. His nephew had never said a word about it.

Why hadn't he? Ross wondered.

"Did you hear them?" he asked.

"It wasn't my intention to eavesdrop. You have to understand that. But I left the dance for a moment and returned to the art booths, hoping to catch one of the vendors who was selling a particularly lovely plein air painting I had my eye on. I had talked myself out of it then decided at the last moment that it would be stunning in one of the guest bedrooms here. It *was* perfect, by the way. Would you like to see it?"

Lily was stalling, which wasn't at all like her.

"What did you hear?" he asked.

She sighed. "I was taking the painting to my car when I heard raised voices. I would have walked past, but then I recognized Josh's voice. They were some distance away, behind the exhibits, and I'm sure they didn't see me. I'm not sure they would have noticed anyway. They both sounded so furious."

His gut clenched. Why hadn't Josh mentioned any fight with his father? In the nearly two weeks since the murder, his nephew hadn't said a single word about any altercation. Why the hell not?

"Could you hear what they were saying?" Ross asked, unable to keep the harsh urgency out of his voice.

Lily glanced at William then back at Ross. "Not clearly. I'm sorry, Ross. They were some distance away from me. And though their voices were raised, I couldn't hear everything. Lloyd was mostly yelling at poor Josh about something or other. I heard him call him a careless idiot at one point and he said something else about Josh ruining his life."

"Did you hear Josh's response?" he asked. It suddenly seemed vitally important, for reasons Ross wasn't prepared to analyze.

Again Lily looked at William as if seeking moral support. His uncle looked as concerned as Ross was and he was quite certain this was the first his uncle had heard about an altercation between them, as well.

"He's just a boy," she said. "He didn't mean anything."

"What did he say, Lily?" William picked up her hand and curled his fingers around it. "Tell us."

She sighed. "He said he wouldn't let Lloyd get away with it. Whatever *it* might have been. I couldn't hear that part. And then he said something about how he— Josh—would stop Lloyd, no matter what it took."

The coffee and cinnamon rolls seemed to congeal in Ross's stomach. "Have you told anyone else about this?"

"No." She frowned, suddenly pensive. "But I think Frannie heard their argument, too. In fact, I'm almost certain of it. I saw her just a few moments later and she looked white and didn't even say hello, which was not at all like her."

What else had his family not bothered to tell him? His first instinct was to drive to the high school, yank Josh out of his chemistry final and rip into him for keeping these kinds of secrets.

What had Josh and his father been fighting about? And more importantly, why the hell hadn't Josh told him?

"I'm sorry, Ross. I can see you're upset. I would have told you earlier but I just assumed Josh or Frannie must have mentioned it to you."

"No," he said grimly. "Both of them are apparently keeping their mouths shut about any number of things. But I intend to find out what."

He had learned after more than a decade on the police force and two more years as a private investigator that sometimes he just needed to give his subconscious time and space to chew on things, to sort through all the pieces of a case and help him put them back together in the right order.

Sometimes mundane tasks helped the process, so Ross decided to stop at the grocery store on the way back from the Double Crown.

The wheels were spinning a hundred miles an hour as he pushed the cart through the cereal aisle, trying to remember which were Josh's favorites.

He disliked grocery shopping. Always had. He had a service in San Antonio that delivered the same things to him every week. Milk, eggs, cheese, a variety of frozen dinners. He still had to make the occasional trip to the store but most of the basics were covered by the delivery service.

Yeah, it made him feel like a pathetic old bachelor once in a while, but he figured it was all about time management. Why waste time with a task he disliked when he could pay someone else to take care of it?

He knew why shopping bothered him. He didn't need

counseling to figure it out. It was a silly reaction, he knew, but somehow grocery shopping reminded him far too much of those frequent times when Cindy would take off when they were kids—of being nine years old again, pushing five-year-old Frannie in a shopping cart and nagging his six-and seven-year-old brothers to stay with them while he roamed through the aisle trying to figure out what they could afford from the emergency stash he always tried to stockpile with money he stole out of his mother's purse for just these moments.

He pushed back the image as he mechanically moved through the store, trying to remember what kind of food he liked when he was eighteen.

He passed the pharmacy at the front of the store and suddenly saw Jillian Fredericks standing at the counter.

Damn. He was in no mood for a confrontation with the woman right here in the middle of the Piggly Wiggly, for her sake or his own. She had been through enough and he didn't want to dredge up any more pain for her.

Sidestepping to a different aisle was simply the humane, decent thing to do, he told himself, though slinking through the store made him feel even more like that nine-year-old of his memory.

He was so intent on avoiding Jillian that he didn't notice anybody else in the aisle until someone called his name.

"Ross. Hello! How are you?"

He lifted his gaze from the detergent bottles and found Julie Osterman standing just across the aisle from him.

To his eternal chagrin, his heart did a crazy little tap dance at the sight of her.

She glanced at the few items in his cart. "Please tell me you and Josh are eating something besides cold cereal and potato chips."

He felt his face heat. "We had steak the other night with you. And we've gone to Red a few times. Tonight we're ordering pizza."

She didn't roll her eyes but he could tell she wanted to. Instead, she gave a rueful smile. "I won't nag."

He didn't want to think about the way her concern for their diet sent a traitorous warmth uncurling through him. "But you'd like to."

She opened her mouth to answer, but sighed instead. "Just remember, he's right in the middle of finals. A balanced meal here or there won't hurt."

"I'll have Mel down at the pizza parlor throw on extra vegetables, how about that?"

"Sounds perfect." She smiled, her lovely blue eyes bright and amused, and he suddenly couldn't think about anything but the heat and wonder of that blasted kiss. "You're not working today?" he asked.

"It's my afternoon off. Usually I try to catch up on my reports at home where it's quiet but I've been putting off grocery shopping and I decided to check that task off my list this afternoon."

"It's a pain in the neck, isn't it?"

She looked surprised. "I kind of like shopping. All those possibilities in front of me. I can walk out of the store with the makings of a gourmet supper or I can just run in for a glazed doughnut that's lousy for me but tastes divine. It all depends on my mood."

"Must be a girl thing."

She laughed and he realized how much brighter the world suddenly seemed than when he walked into the store. It was an uncomfortable discovery, that she could affect his entire mood just with her presence.

"How's Josh doing today?"

"That seems to be the question of the day. I wish I could tell people some answer other than 'fine.' He doesn't talk much to me about it."

He hadn't pushed the boy, but after his conversation with Lily, he was beginning to think that had been a mistake.

"That's completely normal, Ross," she answered. "Most seventeen-year-old boys would much prefer going outside and shooting hoops to sitting around discussing their emotional mood of the moment."

"I think it's probably fair to say most forty-year-old men aren't much different."

She laughed softly and he was suddenly consumed with the desire to taste that delectable mouth again, right there beside the fabric softeners. He even leaned forward slightly, then caught himself and jerked back.

Josh, he reminded himself. Focus on Josh. The conversation with Lily came back to him. Had Josh told Julie about his fight with his father the night of his death?

"Josh talks to you, though, right? I mean, you've had two sessions with him now."

"Yes," she said, somewhat warily.

"Did he mention anything about talking to his father the night of the Spring Fling?" he asked.

She sighed. "You know I can't tell you anything about my conversations with him, Ross. They're confidential. Right now Josh is still willing to talk to me and I don't want to do anything to jeopardize the trust he has in me. I'm sorry."

Sometimes he really hated when people were decent and honorable.

That didn't mean he always had to play by the same rules. A good investigator could read as much in what a person *didn't* say—in her body language and her facial expressions—as in her words. He had learned that sometimes offering information of his own could elicit the reaction he needed to verify his suspicions.

"I had an interesting conversation with someone today who said she overheard Josh and his father in a bitter argument shortly before Lloyd's death," he said with studied casualness. "I was just going to ask if he had said anything to you about it."

Julie was pretty adept at hiding her reaction to his words—but not quite good enough. He didn't miss how her eyes widened with surprise and the ever-so-slight way her lips parted just for an instant.

So Josh *hadn't* mentioned the fight to Julie in their sessions. *Why not?* he wondered, concerned all over again at what other secrets his nephew might be keeping.

"Do you think that's pertinent to investigating what might have happened that night?" she asked.

He shrugged. "I can't say. I just find it surprising that Josh hasn't bothered to mention it. He never even told me he saw his father at the Spring Fling. Even though he claimed to hate Lloyd, I imagine it's got to be tough on any kid to know the last words he had with his old man were angry ones."

Not that he would know. His own father had left Cindy when Ross was less than a year old. Riley Randolph hadn't exactly been the fatherly type. Big surprise there, that Cindy would pick that kind of husband.

"If you're trying to get me to divulge anything from our therapy sessions," Julie said with a frown, "I'm afraid I can't help you."

Sweetheart, you already have, he thought. While he wouldn't exactly call her transparent, she was far too open a person to keep all her reactions concealed.

"I just wanted to pass on information," he said, which wasn't completely a lie. "Thought it might help you to have a little more background on that night when you're talking to Josh. You could ask him in the next session why they fought."

And why he hasn't bothered to tell anyone, he added silently.

"Thank you, Ross. I appreciate the information, then."

They lapsed into silence and Ross thought he probably ought to be moving his cart along, but he was suddenly loath to leave. He searched for some excuse to prolong their conversation, even as some part of his mind was fully aware of how pathetic it was that he was so conflicted over her.

He told himself every time he was with her that he needed to keep his distance. But then the next time he saw her, he was drawn to her all over again.

He knew he shouldn't find it such a consolation that she didn't seem in a hurry to leave his company, either.

"Josh told me it is his eighteenth birthday this weekend. What are his plans?" she asked.

He seized on the question. "Actually, I'm glad you brought that up. While I have you here, I could use some advice."

"Sure."

"We have to do something to celebrate his birthday.

I mean, a kid only turns eighteen once. But I'm wondering if you've got any suggestions about what might be appropriate. Before everything happened, Frannie had talked about throwing a big party for him, but that doesn't seem right now, given the circumstances."

"That's a really good question." Her brow furrowed. "What would make Josh happiest? What might help him forget for a few hours all that's happened in his world?"

"I think he got a kick out of going out to the lake last week. We could do that again." He paused. "And he has that girlfriend, Lyndsey. Maybe I could have a barbecue that night and invite her and a few of his other friends."

"That sounds like a wonderful idea, Ross. See, you're better at this whole parenthood thing than you give yourself credit for."

He wasn't, though. He had sucked at it when he was a kid forced to take care of his younger siblings and he didn't feel any more capable now.

"Will you help me?"

The question came out of nowhere, surprising him as much as it did her.

"Help you how?" she asked, that wariness in her eyes again.

So much for keeping his distance from her. Ross sighed. But now that he had asked her, it made sense. He really *could* use help. It would certainly be easier on his self-control if that help came from someone else, but it was too late to back down now.

"I'm not sure I can handle throwing a teenage party by myself, even a little one," he admitted. "Sure, I can grill steaks and maybe some burgers but other than that, I wouldn't know where to start."

He thought he caught a flash of reluctance in her eyes

and he felt foolish for asking. He had already dragged her into their lives too much.

"Never mind," he said. "I'll just get some pop and open a few bags of chips. We should be fine."

She let out a long breath. "I can help you. I don't have any plans Saturday. Why don't you take care of the grill and I'll handle all the other details? The side dishes, the chips, the cake and ice cream."

"Are you sure?"

"No problem." She smiled, with no trace of that hesitation he thought he had seen and he wondered if he had been mistaken. "It will be fun."

Fun. Right.

She was an idiot.

Julie sat in her car in the parking lot of the grocery store for several moments after she had loaded her groceries into the trunk of her car.

She had absolutely no willpower when it came to Ross Fortune. Since that stunning kiss they had shared the week before, she had promised herself she would do her best to return things to a casual friendship.

For the sake of her psyche, she had no other choice. It was painfully obvious he wasn't available for anything else. He had made it quite clear that he only wanted her help with Josh, not for anything else.

She was happy to help with Josh. But she wasn't at all certain she could continue to do so when she was beginning to entertain all sorts of inappropriate thoughts about the teen's uncle.

She couldn't afford to let herself care for Ross, not when they obviously wanted far different things from life.

A woman came out of the store and pushed her cart

to the minivan beside Julie's car. She had a preschool-aged boy hanging off her cart and a curly-haired baby in the cart. The baby was perhaps nine months old, in a pink outfit with bright flowers.

The boy said something to his mother that Julie couldn't hear but the mother laughed and kissed the child on the nose before she picked up the baby to settle her in her car seat.

As she watched them, Julie's heart turned over.

That was what she wanted. She was ready for children of her own, for a family. Seven years had passed since Chris's death and in all the ways that mattered, she had been alone for the last few years of their marriage before that.

She was tired of it. She was ready to move forward with her life. She had even talked to Linda Jamison, the Foundation director, about adopting an older child as a single mother. She had so much love inside her and she wanted somewhere to give it beyond her clients.

Allowing herself to become any more entangled with a man like Ross Fortune would jeopardize all that progress she had made these past seven years toward healing and peace. She sensed it with a certainty she couldn't deny.

Oh, they might have a brief affair that would probably be intense and passionate and wonderful while it lasted.

But Julie knew she would end up more alone than ever. Alone and heartbroken.

The mother beside her finished loading her groceries and her children and backed out of the parking lot. Julie watched them go with renewed determination.

She would help Ross with Josh's birthday party and

that would be the end of it. If he asked for her help with his nephew again, she would politely tell him she was only available in a professional capacity for more counseling sessions.

It would hurt, she knew. She was already coming to care for him and Josh too much. But she didn't see she had any other choice.

She'd already lost too much to risk her heart again.

Chapter 9

Two days later, she was working on paperwork in her office when Susan Fortune Eldridge poked her head in the doorway.

"Hey," her friend and coworker exclaimed. "I haven't talked to you in ages. It seems like we're always running in different directions. How are things?"

"Good," Julie answered. "Busy, as usual. How about you?"

"Great. Wonderful, really. Listen, Ethan and I are throwing an impromptu dinner party this weekend. We thought maybe you could bring Sean or whatever is the name of that art teacher you're seeing."

Julie couldn't help but laugh. "I would certainly do that, but I'm not sure his fiancée would appreciate it."

Susan's green eyes opened wide and she moved fully into Julie's office and sat in the easy chair her clients usually took. "Fiancée? When did that happen?"

"A few weeks ago, from what I understand. I bumped into him the other day at the library and he told me about it. He started seeing her not long after we stopped dating, around New Year's."

Susan made a face. "Some friend I am. You broke up with someone five months ago and I'm only just hearing about it? Why didn't I know?"

"We didn't really break up. We just mutually decided that while we enjoyed each other's company, we didn't have that sizzle. We only dated a few times anyway. It was never anything serious."

Unfortunately, their brief relationship had coincided with the holiday party season and Sean had escorted her to several parties around town that Susan and her veterinarian husband Ethan had also attended. Julie could completely understand why she might have been under the impression they were more serious than they were.

"Well, bring whoever you're seeing now," Susan said. "It's obviously been too long since we socialized outside the office, since I apparently have no idea what's going on in your life."

Julie had a quick mental image of the heated kiss with Ross that she couldn't get out of her head. She had a feeling Susan would probably misunderstand if she mentioned that particular encounter.

"When is your party?" she asked.

"Tomorrow night. Around seven."

She winced. "I'm sorry, Susan, but I already have plans tomorrow."

"Oh? Hot date? Tell me all!"

"Nothing to tell, I'm afraid. Um, I told your cousin Ross I would help him throw a small party for Josh's eighteenth birthday."

"I completely forgot Josh's birthday was coming up." She paused, an expression of concern on her petite features. "So tell me. How is Ross doing?"

"Fine, as far as I can tell. Why do you ask? Usually everyone seems to be most concerned with Frannie or Josh."

"I've been worrying about him. I've tried to call a few times to check on him and Josh and always get voice mail. We've been playing phone tag. I was planning on making time this weekend to go to the house to see how things are with them. This can't be an easy situation for Ross."

She frowned. "What can't?"

"The instant parenting thing landing in his lap so abruptly. I've always had the impression he wanted nothing to do with kids and parenting after his lousy childhood. He probably figured he did his share while practically raising his brothers and sister."

Julie suddenly realized how little she knew about Ross's past. She knew he had been a cop in San Antonio but his life before then was a mystery. "Where were his parents?"

"I don't know about his dad. I think he took off when Ross was just a baby. I don't know about him or the other fathers."

"Other...fathers?"

"Frannie's his half sister and he has two half brothers, Cooper and Flint. They all have different fathers, except the middle boys. None of the men stuck around for long, except Frannie's dad, I guess, who might have if he hadn't died first."

"How sad!"

"Yes, well, my aunt Cindy certainly knows how to pick them."

"That's Ross's mother?"

"She's the woman who gave birth to him, anyway," Susan answered. "Calling her a mother might be a bit of a stretch. She was sister to my father, Leonard, as well as Patrick and William."

Julie frowned. "I'm not sure I've met her."

"Believe me, you would remember if you had. Cindy is a real piece of work, let me tell you. She wears tons of makeup and still dresses like a hootchie-kootchie dancer, which I've heard rumors she was, in between stints as a showgirl in Vegas."

"Wow."

"Right. She's seventy years old and still dresses in tight pants and halter tops."

"Sounds like an interesting character," she said faintly.

"*Interesting* is one word for it. From family gossip, I've heard she ran off to Vegas to be a dancer when she was barely eighteen. She had a long string of lousy relationships and three marriages. During that time, she gave birth to Ross and his siblings but I don't think she had much to do with raising them. She was too busy shaking her booty in one club or another."

Julie tried to imagine Ross growing up under those circumstances and couldn't. No wonder he seemed so hard and cynical if that was the only example of a family he had.

"Ross was the oldest," Susan went on. "Frannie told me once that he was always the one who fixed her hair, packed her lunch and sent her off to school. Cindy was always either entertaining company or too tired from working into the night. He kept that family together, dysfunctional as it was."

Julie thought of her own family, warm and loving and completely supportive of whatever she had ever tried to do. During those dark and terrible times during Chris's illness and then after his suicide, she had moved back home with her parents in Austin and they had enfolded her with loving arms of support and comfort.

Her four brothers might drive her crazy sometimes with their overprotectiveness but she adored them all.

What must Ross's childhood have been like? She tried to picture a younger version of the hard, implacable man she knew trying to fix his little sister's hair and the image just about broke her heart.

"I've always wanted to see him happy," Susan went on. "Settled, you know, with a home and family. I don't know if I'd say he's really happy, but he seems content with his bachelor life. It's terribly sad, really, when you think about it. I wonder what scars he still carries from such an unstable childhood."

Julie knew it was ridiculous to feel this sudden urge to cry. She fought back the tears and hoped Susan didn't notice her reaction.

"I've worried that his temporary guardianship of Josh—again, someone else's child he's suddenly responsible for—must in a sense feel like he's reliving his own childhood," Susan said. "I've been worried about his head and wanted to make sure he's in an okay place about the whole thing."

"I had no idea," Julie said. "Ross never said anything."

Susan gave her a curious look, which quickly turned speculative. "Why would he have told you? I wasn't under the impression you knew Ross well, other than in your capacity as Josh's grief counselor."

Her eyes suddenly widened. "Which begs the question—why, again, are you helping with Josh's party? That seems above and beyond the call of duty, no matter how wonderful a counselor you are."

Julie ordered herself not to blush. "Ross asked for my help. I couldn't say no."

Her friend was quiet for a long moment, then she tilted her head, giving Julie a searching look. "Is there something between you and my cousin?"

Did a heated kiss and a fierce attraction she couldn't seem to shove out of her head count as something? Her face felt hot and she couldn't meet Susan's gaze.

"We've become friends, I guess you could say."

"Only friends?"

"I don't think he's available for anything else right now."

She regretted the words as soon as she said them. As a psychologist, Susan was an expert at analyzing people's words, sifting through layers of nuances and meaning to help her have better clarity into their psyches. Julie realized too late how her words must have sounded— and she heard the echo of the ruefulness in her voice.

"If he were?" Susan asked, studying her closely.

She let out a breath. "Since that's a rhetorical question, I don't really have to answer it, do I?"

Susan was silent for a long time. When she finally spoke, her eyes were soft with concern. "I love Ross, Julie. If I could pick anyone in the world for him, she would be someone exactly like you. Someone nurturing and caring and generous. Someone who could help him heal."

Since Julie was also trained to listen carefully to her clients and parse through their words, she didn't miss how Susan had phrased her comment. "Someone exactly like me, but not me?"

"I love Ross," Susan repeated. "But I love you, too. You've been through so much pain. I ache just thinking about what you've had to survive. You deserve a man whose heart is healthy and strong, someone who is free to love you without reservation."

"And you don't think that's Ross."

Susan's silence was a harsh answer. Julie reminded herself she had known. Hadn't she promised herself she would give him one more night for Josh's birthday party and then try to extricate herself from his life so she could move forward?

Still, she couldn't deny the spasm of pain and regret twisting through her at having her own convictions reinforced.

"Then it's a good thing Ross and I are only friends, isn't it?" she said briskly. "I'm only helping him with a birthday party, Sus. That's all."

"Sure." Susan forced a smile. "Well, I'm sorry you can't come to our dinner party. We'll do it another time, then. Give Josh a big birthday kiss for me, okay? And tell Ross I'll keep trying to reach him."

Unexpectedly, Susan hugged her on the way out the door. She hugged her back, then returned to work, trying her best to shake the discontent pulling at her mood like heavy, intractable weights.

Ross pulled into the circular driveway in front of Frannie's house, fighting off the bleak mood that settled over him as he looked at it. There was no reason such a silly froth of a house should seem so ominous, but he had begun to dread coming back here each night.

Josh wasn't home. The boy's aging sports car wasn't in the driveway and Ross knew damn well he shouldn't have this vague feeling of relief that he didn't have to deal with his nephew right now.

He was going to have to talk to him sometime. A serious, blunt conversation between the two of them was long overdue. Ross rubbed his temples as the implication of all he had learned over the last two days centered there in a pounding headache that slithered down his spine to his tight shoulders until it became a cold, greasy ball in his gut.

He still didn't want to believe any of it, but it was becoming increasingly difficult to keep an open mind.

After his talk with Lily and William at the Double Crown, he had spent two days tracking down leads, trying to find anyone else who might have heard Josh fighting with his father and who might be able to shed more light on the content of their conversation. He wanted to be prepared with as much information as possible before he faced his nephew with what he had learned.

He finally found a potter whose stall had been not far from the scene of the argument. Reynaldo Velasquez had indeed heard the fight. He had recounted it much as Lily had—that he couldn't hear many of the words but he had heard raised voices, had heard Lloyd yelling at his son and then had heard Josh say he would stop him, no matter what it took.

And, more chilling than that confirmation, Reynaldo had added that he had been surprised to hear such harsh words coming from Josh. He'd seemed like a nice kid, the artist said, when he had come to his booth to pick up the large vase his mother had purchased earlier in the evening.

Ross closed his eyes, his hands tight on the steering wheel. Even now, remembering the conversation, his stomach felt slick with nausea. As far as he could tell, Josh had been the last one in possession of the vase.

Josh. Not Frannie.

Josh had fought with his father in front of witnesses. Josh had a rocky relationship with his father. Josh was a hotheaded teenager.

And most damning of all was Josh's behavior since his father's death. The furtive conversations, the obfuscations. Ross had sensed he was hiding something. He supposed it made him a pretty damn lousy investigator that he hadn't once suspected his nephew was capable of killing his own father.

Despite the witnesses and Josh's own dishonesty by omission in not saying anything about the fight with Lloyd, Ross still couldn't make himself believe it, any more than he had been able to contemplate the ridiculous notion that Frannie might have killed Lloyd.

Josh was a good kid. Yeah, he had a temper and his relationship with Lloyd was tense and strained and had been for some time now. But Ross couldn't accept that Josh might be able to commit patricide. And he absolutely couldn't see the boy he knew standing by and saying nothing while his own mother took the fall for it.

Ross would have to talk to him about what he had learned, no matter how difficult the conversation. He would have to walk a fine line between seeking the vital information he needed to put these pieces of the puzzle together without sounding accusatory. It would take every ounce of his investigative skills.

He didn't want to ruin Josh's birthday, but he had no choice. Josh would legally be an adult in just a few hours. Perhaps it was past time Ross started treating him like one.

With a sigh, he let himself into the house. The empty foyer echoed with every sound he made, from the clink of his keys on the polished white table to the scrape of his boots on the tile floor.

He hated it here. He found the entire place depressing. He had never liked it, even when Frannie was here, but without her, the house seemed lifeless and cold.

He had a sudden, irrational, very Cindy-like desire to walk away from everything here, to escape back to his apartment in San Antonio where he had no responsibilities except to his agency clients. Where he was free to come and go at will, without this nagging worry for those he loved.

Ashamed of himself for indulging the impulse to flee, even for a moment, he walked through the house to the kitchen and flipped on the light switch.

The first thing he saw was a note from Josh on the memo board above the small kitchen desk that Frannie had always kept meticulously organized. It was written in Josh's careless scrawl on the back of a takeout menu for the pizza parlor.

Helping a friend. Don't wait up.

Ross frowned. Helping which friend do what, where? The kid was a few hours away from eighteen and now thought he could come and go as he pleased without any more explanation than one terse, say-nothing note?

Fighting down that instinctive relief again that he could put off the coming interrogation for a while longer, he pulled out his cell phone and hit Josh's number. The phone rang four times then went to voice mail.

Ross sighed. "Call me," he said after the beep, not unaware of the terseness of his own message.

He thought about dinner, but he didn't have much of an appetite anyway, he decided. A better expenditure of time would be to enter the field notes from his interview with Reynaldo into his case file.

He headed down the hall to the guest room he had taken over for his use since coming to stay at the house. Compared to the rest of the house, this room was simply decorated, with a double pine bed, dresser and a comfortable desk. He figured Lloyd hadn't bothered to come into it enough to insist on more of his atrocious taste.

Ross set his laptop case on the bed and pulled out the digital recorder and the small notebook he used on field interviews.

An hour later, he finished logging in his work for the day. Since the notebook was nearly full, he opened the desk drawer to find a new one and his gut suddenly clenched.

Something wasn't right.

He had a strict system of organization with his case files. He kept the field notebooks he used in numbered order, meticulously dated and filed so he could easily double-check information on any case when needed. No matter what else was going on, he always took the time to refile them in order.

The notebook on top of the stack was *not* the most recent. He frowned and flipped through the half-dozen books he had filled with various casework in the days since coming to stay with Josh.

None of them was in order, the way he was absolutely certain he had left them just that morning.

He stared at the stack as that greasy ball in his gut seemed to take a few more rotations. He might be haphazard and casual about some things—his clothing came to mind and, yeah, he needed a haircut—but not about work. Never about his cases and the interviews.

He couldn't afford to be careless as a private investigator. He had to be able to find information quickly and reliably. And while the computer was a great backup for storing data, he still depended on his own handwritten field notes.

Someone had rifled through his notes. He should have locked them up, but the thought had never even occurred to him.

His mind sorted through other possibilities. He wanted to think maybe he had just been sloppy the last time he was in here. That would be a much more palatable option than what he was beginning to suspect, but he couldn't lie to himself.

He knew without a doubt that he hadn't left his notebooks like this. Which meant someone else had rifled through them.

He only had one suspect and it was the very one he didn't want to believe capable of it. Josh. Who else could it have been? The boy had access to the notebooks and plenty of opportunity when Ross wasn't here. He never bothered to lock the desk drawer. That heedlessness on his part had obviously been a mistake, but Ross had never considered it, had never believed for a moment it might even be necessary.

But motive. Why would Josh want to know what

Ross was digging into, unless he had reason to want that information to stay buried?

It was another good question. He now had several for his nephew—if only he could find the kid.

By 8:00 p.m., he still hadn't reached Josh.

Ross paced the living room of Frannie's house, not sure whether to be angry or worried about his nephew, especially when all his calls started going directly to voice mail.

He had been through this waiting game enough with his brothers. He couldn't count the number of nights he had sat up stewing while he waited for either Flint or Cooper to come home, hours later than they were supposed to. Of course, this was a little different situation, since he had never been preparing to question his brothers about a murder.

When his cell phone rang at eight-thirty, he lunged for it.

"Yeah?" he growled.

A slight pause met him then he heard Julie Osterman's voice. "Ross? Is that you?"

His hopes that he might be able to clear everything up quickly with Josh and get the kid home faded.

"Oh. Hi."

A slight pause met his response. "That's a bit of a disheartening reaction," Julie said, her voice suddenly tight. "I just needed to ask a question about tomorrow but I can call back later. Or not."

He cursed under his breath. "Sorry. It's not you, I swear. I'm always glad to talk to you." He probably shouldn't have said that, even though it wasn't a lie. "I was just hoping you were Josh."

She picked up his concern right away. "Josh? Is something wrong? What's going on? Where is he?"

"No idea. He's not answering his cell. He left a note saying he was helping a friend and that I wasn't to wait up."

"But of course you will."

"Oh, undoubtedly," he said grimly. "I have a few words to say to my nephew."

"When did you see him last?"

"This morning at breakfast. Everything seemed okay. Nothing out of the ordinary. He left for school to take his last final. We talked about the kids he had invited tomorrow and what movie they planned to watch after dinner. Nothing unusual."

"He didn't say anything about going anywhere after school?"

"Not a word."

But then Ross had kept secrets of his own. He hadn't mentioned anything about the direction he was taking in the investigation because he had wanted to be more certain of his information before confronting Josh about the fight with his father. "He took a call, said something about being on his way, then took off for school."

"Are you sure he went to school?"

"No. But the school's long closed. Unless I drag the principal in from home to go through the attendance records, I'm out of luck."

"What about his other friends? Did you try Lyndsey's cell phone?"

"I don't have her number. I called her home, though, and got no answer."

"What about Ricky or one of his extended cousins?"

"Good idea. I was planning to give him a little longer before I hit the phones."

He didn't tell Julie he would have done that before, but he had still been holding out the vague hope that Josh would walk through the door on his own.

She was quiet for a long moment. "You know, Ross, it's a natural human reaction when life becomes too stressful to seek escape. Perhaps he just needed a little time away from things here in Red Rock."

He hated to ask, in light of her own firsthand experience with suicide, but he had to know her professional opinion. "You're right. Things have been tough for him lately. You don't think he would do anything rash, do you?"

She was silent for a moment and he knew she guessed what he meant. "I couldn't say definitely, but in our two sessions, I didn't get any vibe like that from him, Ross. He wouldn't have any reason to, would he?"

A guilty conscience, maybe? Ross thought of those disordered notebooks and what he had learned the last two days. He hoped Josh didn't feel hopeless or cornered enough to do something drastic.

"I'm going to go look for him," he said suddenly. "I can't just sit here."

Chapter 10

Julie heard the desperate determination in Ross's voice and she ached for him, especially in light of her conversation with his cousin earlier in the day. He was a man who took his responsibilities seriously and right now he had far too many.

"I'll come with you," she said. "I can be there in fifteen minutes."

"You don't have to do that," he exclaimed, not bothering to hide his surprise that she would make the offer.

"I know I don't. But a second pair of eyes wouldn't hurt, don't you agree? And I have a few advantages."

"What are those?"

"From my clients at the Foundation, I happen to know the location of many of the local teen hangouts. I also have connections among the different teen groups, from the jocks to the druggies to the cowboys to the hackers. I can help you, Ross, if you let me."

She kept her fingers crossed even as she went to her closet and pulled out a jacket and sturdy walking shoes.

Silence met her assurances as he hesitated and she was certain he would refuse her offer of help. Ross was a man who liked to do things on his own, she was learning. He hated depending on anyone else for anything, even for assistance he might desperately need.

She was bracing to tell him she would go on her own looking for Josh when he surprised her.

"All right," he answered. "I probably *could* use your help, especially given your connections to the local teen scene. But stay at your place and I'll come pick you up."

Julie quickly changed out of her lounge-around-the-house sweats into jeans and a tailored blue shirt and sweater and pulled her hair into a ponytail.

While she waited, she went to work gathering a few provisions and compiling lists of any possible friends she might have ever heard Josh mention and several potential places they could look.

When Ross pulled into her driveway exactly sixteen minutes later, she was ready. She opened the door to her house before he could walk up the steps.

He drove a white SUV hybrid that she imagined was perfect for a private investigator—bland enough to be inconspicuous but sturdy enough to be taken seriously.

She opened the door to the backseat and set the large wicker basket inside before she opened the front passenger door and climbed inside.

In the pale glow from the dome light, she could see baffled consternation on his rugged features. "What's all this?" he asked, gesturing to the basket.

She shrugged, feeling slightly foolish. "A few supplies. A Thermos of coffee, some soda, a few snacks, sandwiches. I didn't know what might come in handy so I packed a little of everything."

He glanced at the overflowing basket in the backseat and then back at her as if he didn't quite know what to make of her. "We're not heading out on a cross-country trek here. We're only driving around town looking for one kid."

"It doesn't hurt to be prepared, does it? You never know what might come in handy." She swiveled in the front seat and reached back to pull a flowered tin off the top of the basket. "Here, have one of my caramel cashew bars. I made them for Josh's birthday tomorrow but I thought maybe we could use them for bribes or something."

"For bribes."

She shrugged. "You know, to get somebody to talk who doesn't want to."

He opened his mouth for a second, his eyes astonished, then closed it with a snap. "That good, are they?" he finally said.

She managed a smile, despite her worry for Josh. "See for yourself."

After a moment's hesitation, he picked one up and bit into it. As he chewed it slowly and then swallowed, his eyes glazed with sheer ecstasy.

"Okay. You win," he said after a few more bites. "Right now, I would tell you anything you want to know."

She laughed, though a hundred questions tumbled together in her mind she would have asked him if circumstances between them had been different.

She held out the tin. "I've got a dozen more in here. You're welcome to eat them all if you want."

He gave her a half smile as he put the SUV into gear before backing out of her driveway. "Wrong thing to say to an ex-cop," he said. "We're like locusts. If there's food available, we eat it."

She had a sudden wild urge to make a hundred different home-baked treats for him. Dutch apple pie, jam thumbprint cookies, snickerdoodles.

It was a silly reaction but she couldn't help remembering all the bleak details Susan had told her about Ross's childhood. His mother didn't sound like the sort to cook up a batch of warm, gooey chocolate chip cookies for her kids after school and Julie wanted suddenly to make up for all those things Ross never had.

She sighed and pushed the impulse away. Right now they needed to concentrate on Josh, she reminded herself.

"Where to first?" she asked.

"Nobody answered at his girlfriend Lyndsey's house but I figured that's a logical place to start."

The small tract house was in a neighborhood with dozens more that looked just like it. The siding might be a little different color and a few details varied from house to house, but Julie would be hard-pressed to tell them all apart, if not for the house numbers.

No lights were on inside and only a low-wattage porch light glowed on the exterior.

"Doesn't look like anybody's home," he said.

"Her mom works nights," Julie said. "Josh told me that once in passing. I think she's a nurse or something."

"Well, it doesn't hurt to double-check since we're here."

Julie opted to stay in the SUV while Ross walked to the front door and rang the bell. Even with her vehicle window rolled up, she could hear a dog's deep-throated barks from somewhere in the backyard.

The neighborhood shouldn't have seemed ominous. It had obviously seen better days and some of the houses had peeling paint, with a few junk cars up on cinder-blocks in the driveways, but it was equally obvious that families lived here. She spotted multiple bikes, trampolines, play sets.

Still, she was immensely grateful for Ross's solid presence. She wouldn't want to be here by herself.

She watched him ring the doorbell once more, then to her surprise, he reached down and tried to jiggle the doorknob, without success.

"Would you have gone in if the door hadn't been locked?" she asked when he returned to the SUV a moment later.

He shrugged and she didn't miss the gleam of his smile in the darkness. "Don't know," he admitted. "I'm always glad when the opportunity doesn't present it-self to find out exactly how far I'm willing to push the law I've always tried to uphold. Any ideas where to try next?"

"Actually, yes. I made a list."

"Why doesn't that surprise me?" Ross asked, a rue-ful tone to his voice. "Something tells me I'm going to need another caramel cashew bar."

By midnight, they had run out of friends that either of them had ever heard Josh mention. They had hit all the usual hangouts—the quarry, the pizza place, the lover's lane that curved through a forested area south of town. They had even checked beneath the bleachers on the football field.

On a Friday night the week before graduation, they had interrupted a group of half-stoned skinny-dipping seniors, found a half-dozen cars with steamed up windows and nearly found themselves in the middle of a verbal altercation that looked to have been shaping up into one heck of a fistfight.

All the way around, it seemed an exciting night for Red Rock. But Josh was nowhere to be found.

In the parking lot of the high school—their last stop—Julie leaned against the hood of his SUV while Ross stood next to her and dialed the number to the police station.

It was a last resort, a call he didn't want to make, but he thought there might be a slim chance Josh might have tried to contact his mother.

To his surprise—and consternation—he was patched right through to the police chief and he had an instant's sinking fear that Josh might be in custody.

"Hey, Jimmy. It's Ross Fortune."

"Oh. Ross. Hello. This is a surprise. A little late for social calls, isn't it?"

"Yeah, it's late. Oddly enough, you're still there. I wouldn't have thought the Red Rock police chief would pull the graveyard shift. Is something up?"

Jimmy hesitated just long enough for Ross to figure out his guess was correct. He drew a deep breath. *Damn it, Josh. What have you done?*

"Just another wild Friday night in Red Rock. You know how it is. The high schoolers are done with finals so they're all a little nuts. We're busting 'em like crazy on underage drinking and some minor drug possessions."

Ross thought about narcing out the skinny dippers at

the quarry, then figured he'd let Jimmy's officers find the party on their own.

"We're a little busy tonight," the police chief said after a moment. "What can I do for you?"

He picked his words delicately. "I'm looking for my sister's kid, Josh. Any chance he stopped in to visit her tonight?"

The police chief was silent for a long moment that seemed to last forever and Ross held his breath, aware of Julie watching the one-sided conversation carefully.

"Not today," Jimmy finally said. "Think he came by earlier in the week. Just a minute. I can call the visitor log up on my computer to double-check for you."

Ross could hear keys clicking and then a moment later, the police chief came back on. "Nope. He was here on Tuesday but hasn't been back. Why do you ask?"

Ross debated telling him the kid had taken off but decided that information could wait. Jimmy was too damn smart and just might look at the puzzle pieces and come up with the same picture Ross was beginning to find.

"Oh, Frannie just asked for some warm socks and I wondered if Josh had had a chance to take them to her. No big deal. I'll stop by with them tomorrow."

"You sure that's all it is?"

They were both circling around each other like a couple of mangy old junkyard dogs after the same bone. "Positive. That's it. You know women and their cold feet."

"Don't I ever!" He gave a jovial laugh that sounded false to Ross's ears, but he wondered if he was imagining things. "Christy Lee just about freezes me out every night. Her feet can be like two little popsicles on the end of her legs."

"Well, thanks for the information. Guess I'll see you tomorrow when I drop off the socks."

"You be sure to do that."

After Ross hung up, he gazed out at the night, replaying the conversation in his head. Something didn't fit with his usual interactions with the police chief.

"Josh hasn't been at the police station?"

"Not that the chief was willing to tell me, anyway."

"Maybe he didn't know."

"There's not much happens at the Red Rock police station that Jimmy doesn't keep an eye on."

It made no sense for the chief to be at the station this late at night unless something big was going down. But short of busting into the police station, Ross had no way of knowing if Josh was there confessing to a murder.

And he could only hope that Josh would have the presence of mind to make a lousy phone call first before he did anything so rash.

"I think we need to check back at the house and see if he came home," Ross said. "I left a big note for him to call me on my cell but maybe he didn't see it."

She looked doubtful and he didn't add that the police station was on the way and that maybe they would just casually take a little drive through the parking lot, looking for a beat-up yellow RX-7.

He didn't see Josh's car in the parking lot of the police station, though. Nor was it in the driveway of Frannie's house.

He must have cursed aloud because Julie reached a comforting hand to touch his forearm. "I'm sure he's fine, Ross. He'll probably turn up any minute, full of apologies and explanations."

"I hope so," he muttered. He led the way inside the

house and went immediately to the answering machine. It was blinking to indicate a new message and he stabbed the button.

To his vast relief, Josh's tenor filled the kitchen.

"Hey, Uncle Ross. Sorry, I must have left my phone somewhere in the…somewhere. It was almost out of juice anyway. Anyway, I can't find it right now so I'm calling from a pay phone. Since I couldn't remember your cell number, I'm leaving a message here and hoping you get it. Don't worry about me. I've got a few things I need to take care of. I don't know when I'll be back but I'm fine, I promise. Everything's fine. Don't worry about me! Just take care of my mom and I'll be back as soon as I can. Thanks, Ross. Sorry about the fishing trip in the morning. Tell Ms. O to forget about the dinner, too. I'll make it up to you both, I promise."

Ross looked at the time stamp on the message and growled a harsh curse. "We only missed his call by half an hour."

"He said he was calling from a pay phone," Julie said. "Did the number show up on the caller ID? I don't know how these things are done but maybe you could trace it and at least narrow down where he was a half hour ago."

"Great idea." He scrolled through the numbers, then stopped on the most recent, noting the San Antonio prefix. What in blazes was the kid up to? He didn't know whether to be angry or relieved that Josh wasn't calling from the Red Rock police department.

He could do a reverse lookup to find the number but it would be faster just to call it, he decided. He dialed and waited through six rings before somebody picked up.

"Yeah?" a smoker-rough, impatient-sounding female voice answered.

"Hey, my friend called me a little while ago from this pay phone and needed a ride but he forgot to give me an intersection to pick him up," he quickly lied. "Can you tell me where you're at?"

"Hang on. This ain't my usual stroll. I don't know this neighborhood. Just a sec." She returned a second later. "My friend says we're on the corner of Floyd Curl and Breezy Hill."

"Near the hospital?"

"Yeah. That's it. Hey, man, I think your friend might have found another set of wheels. Ain't nobody else here but us. You could give me a ride, though. Me and my friend can wait right here for you."

"You two might be waiting a while, sugar. But thanks anyway."

He hung up on her protests and found Julie watching him with a curious look in her eyes.

"That was quick thinking, to say you were picking up a friend."

He shrugged. "Old cop trick. I've got a million of them."

"I'm beginning to figure that out," she said. "We're going to go check it out, aren't we? Maybe we can find Josh's car somewhere in the vicinity."

"That's exactly what I was thinking. But you don't have to do this, Julie. I can handle things on my own."

"I know you can, but I'm worried about him, too."

She paused, looking uncertain for the first time all night. "If you would rather not have me along for whatever reason, I certainly can understand but I would like the chance to help if you want me."

"It's not that. I want you."

He heard the echo of his words and wished he could yank them back, but they hovered between them.

She cleared her throat. "That's good."

"I want you along," he corrected, trying not to be too obvious about amending his statement. "It's only that it's already past midnight and I know an all-nighter trip to the city wasn't in your plans for the evening."

"I can be flexible, Ross. We can keep each other awake."

Inappropriate images popped into his head and refused to leave there. He could think of far more enticing ways for the two of them to stay awake than looking for his recalcitrant nephew, but he knew those kinds of thoughts about Julie were dangerous.

He wanted to tell her to forget it, that he was better off on his own. But she had been wonderful all evening, helping him get into teen hangouts that otherwise might have been off-limits to him.

"All right," he said. "Let's go to San Antonio. It's a good thing we've already got all your provisions, isn't it? Looks like it might be a long night."

Three hours later, they were no closer to finding his nephew and Ross was beginning to wonder if they should even be looking. The kid was now officially three hours past eighteen. He was an adult. If he wanted to take off for a night, was Ross really in a position to have any objection?

Or even to worry about him?

Maybe he should have left Julie at the house in case Josh tried to call again. He had taken the precaution of changing the message on the answering machine, leaving pointed instructions for Josh to call Ross's cell phone immediately if he happened to call home and got the message, and they had left scrawled messages all over the house saying the same thing.

As Ross drove through some of the rougher neighborhoods of San Antonio, he worried he was putting Julie through all this unnecessarily.

He glanced over at the passenger seat. She was hanging on, but just barely. For the last half hour, her lids had been drooping and her face was tight with fatigue.

"All right. I'd say we've tried long enough. We've covered a three-mile perimeter around the pay phone and come up empty. Let's get you back to Red Rock."

She scrambled up in the seat. "I'm sorry. No. I'm fine. Don't stop searching on my account."

"This is worse than looking for a needle in a haystack. We don't even know if the needle's here at all or in some other haystack altogether. You need a little rest. And to be honest, I could use some sleep myself."

She slanted him a look. "What would you do if I weren't here?"

"My apartment isn't far from here. Under other circumstances, I would probably catch a few hours of sleep there and head out again first thing."

"Let's do that, then. I can bunk on your couch. It's silly to drive all the way back to Red Rock if you're going to be here bright and early in the morning looking for Josh anyway."

Even for 3:00 a.m. logic, her words made sense. Beyond the time it would save in the morning, he wasn't sure she would make it all the way back to Red Rock.

And Josh was close. He sensed it somehow, with that cop's intuition that had never failed him yet. He had learned not to ignore it—even if that meant sharing his apartment for a few hours with Julie Osterman, the woman he had vowed to do his best to stay away from.

By the time they reached his place she was nearly asleep, but she managed to stumble out of his car and up the steps to his third-floor apartment.

He didn't know if it was the night air or the climb, but by the time they reached his door, a little color had returned to her cheeks and her eyes didn't look nearly as bleary.

As he unlocked the door and flipped on a light, he told himself the apprehension was completely his imagination.

She did a slow turn then walked to the window.

"Oh," she breathed.

"It's not much, I know."

"No, it's great! What an incredible view."

Though his apartment was only on the third floor, he overlooked the River Walk. His favorite evening activity was sitting out on the small terrace with a beer, enjoying the lights in the trees, the boats on the water and all the activity below.

He opened the sliding door and she walked out, lifting her face to the night air.

Though the lights of the city muted the stars much more than they did out in Red Rock, the heavens still offered an impressive display, a vast sea of tiny pinpricks of light against the black silk of the night sky.

Just a few hours before daylight, the River Walk was quiet now compared to how it probably had been even an hour or two ago.

"This is great. If I lived here, I would have a tough time wanting to do anything but sit here and enjoy."

She was beautiful, he thought. Lovely in that serene way that sometimes stole his breath.

And tougher than she looked, he admitted. She had stuck with him all evening, even through some of the rougher neighborhoods where he had looked for Josh. She hadn't shied away from situations that might have made her uncomfortable. Instead, she had been right there with him, keeping an eye out for his nephew.

And her provisions. He fought a smile all over again. How adorable was it that she had packed everything from his favorite cola to bandages, just in case?

"Come on," he said after a moment. "Let's get you settled. You can take the bedroom. I'll show you where everything is. I might even have an extra toothbrush."

She arched an eyebrow. Though she didn't say anything, he could read the speculation in her eyes.

"Josh comes to stay with me sometimes and he always seems to forget his so I try to pick up a few extras when I'm at the store."

He had no idea why he was compelled to defend himself but he didn't want her thinking he was in the habit of bringing strange women back to his apartment. He rarely even brought women who *weren't* strange here. The last time had been further back than he cared to remember.

He led the way down the hall to his bedroom, grateful he had taken time to pop over and clean up a bit just a few days ago, when he was in town catching up on things at the office.

"I'm sure I've got a T-shirt or something you can sleep in."

"Thanks. That would be great."

He opened a drawer and pulled out one of his less

disreputable T-shirts and tossed it at her. She caught it one-handed and clutched it to her chest.

"Thank you."

She looked so soft and rumpled, with her hair a little bit messed from dozing in the car and her eyes wide and impossibly blue. As he gazed at her, she swallowed and offered a tremulous smile and his body burned with sudden, insatiable hunger.

Her smile slid from her features though she didn't look away, and he wondered if he was imagining the sudden tension, the swirls of awareness that seemed to eddy around them.

"I'm sorry to take your bed," she murmured.

"No problem. I don't mind the couch." His voice sounded raspy and tight. He cleared his throat. "Good night, then."

"I...good night."

He watched her for a few seconds more, then swallowed a groan and stepped forward. One kiss. Surely they could both survive one little kiss. It seemed a small enough thing when he had spent all night with her and managed to keep his hands to himself, when his body was crying out for so much more.

Chapter 11

With a breathy, sexy little moan that scorched down every nerve ending, she slid into his kiss as if she had been waiting all night for his mouth to find hers.

She tasted of coffee and something sweet and cinnamony and he couldn't get enough. He pulled her closer, relishing the soft curves against his chest and the way she wrapped her arms around his neck as if she couldn't bear to let him go.

He wanted more. He wanted *everything*, all of her gasps and the inhaled breaths and those infinitely arousing little sounds she made.

Her mouth was soft and luscious and so welcoming that he lost track of time. For several delectable moments, all the stresses weighing on his shoulders lifted away and the only thing that mattered to him was this woman, this moment.

He deepened the kiss, his tongue tangling with hers,

and he felt the little tremor that shook her body as she responded, heard the little hitch in her breathing. His body was rock hard in an instant and a slow, unsteady ache spread through him.

He slid a hand to her back, under her shirt, and the sultry softness of her skin against his fingers was irresistible.

One kiss wouldn't be enough.

How could it be, when he found just the small brush of her skin against his hands so heady, so addictive?

If he didn't stop now, though, he wasn't sure he would be able to find the strength. Even now, it took all his control to wrench his mouth from hers.

"We have to stop, Julie."

"Why?" she murmured against his mouth. He groaned at the note of genuine confusion in her voice.

"We don't…it's not…"

She kissed the corner of his mouth before he could form a single coherent thought and his brain took a siesta when, with tiny, silky little darts of her tongue, she began licking her way across to the other side.

"What were you saying?" she murmured, her voice low and husky.

"No idea," he answered truthfully, and returned the kiss with all the fierce hunger raging through him.

When she had walked into his apartment earlier, Julie had been emotionally drained and physically exhausted from their futile all-night search for Josh. But his kiss was as invigorating as a straight shot of high-octane caffeine.

Her body buzzed with heat and energy, like she was

standing in a desert windstorm, being buffeted from every direction.

She had enough energy right now to run a marathon without even working up a sweat.

Or to spend what was left of the night in his arms.

She shivered as he trailed kisses down her jawline to the sensitive skin of her throat and then down to the open collar of her blouse.

Desire surged through her, wild and potent, as he pressed kisses to the curve of her breast above her bra. His mouth tasted her, exploring every inch he could reach that wasn't covered by her clothing, but it still wasn't enough.

Not nearly enough.

Her gaze held his as she shrugged out of her sweater and reached trembling fingers to unbutton her shirt.

His brown eyes blazed with desire as he watched her and she saw a little muscle jump in his cheek.

"Are you sure about this?" he asked, his voice little more than a growl. "We can still stop now, though it just might kill me."

"Absolutely sure," she replied. To prove it, she pulled her arms through the sleeves of her shirt, quickly worked the front clasps of her bra and then stepped out of her jeans.

The raw hunger in his eyes did crazy little things to her insides. She wasn't sure a man had ever looked at her like this, as if she was every fantasy he had ever conjured up.

She shivered a little at the force of that look but she didn't back away. How could she?

"Your turn," she murmured, and her hands found the buttons of his shirt, then his pants. She wasn't sure where this eager response was coming from but she liked it.

She had always enjoyed the closeness of making love with her husband in his better years, but it had been a long, long time for her. She couldn't remember this kind of urgent ache inside her, this insistent, undeniable need to be closer.

She had to touch him. All of him. He was masculine and tough and his lean strength beckoned her, seduced her. She trailed her fingers across the planes of his chest, relishing his hard muscles and the leashed strength beneath her hands.

His abdominal muscles contracted tightly when she gently dipped her thumbs into the hollow below his ribcage and he stood immobile under her exploring touch for only a little longer before he groaned under his breath and pulled her against him again.

She didn't mind. He was warm and solid against her bare skin. As he kissed her, he pulled her close enough that her breasts were pressed against that hard chest she had been exploring earlier and she couldn't breathe around the delicious friction of her skin against his.

At last he lowered her to his bed and she could see the lights of the city spread out beyond his window. He had angled his bed to take full advantage of the view through the wide windows and somehow she found the idea of him lying in his bed looking out at the night sweetly charming.

And then she forgot all about the city lights and everything else but Ross when his mouth covered hers for another long, drugging kiss at the same time his hand found her breast, his fingers clever and arousing on the peak.

She gasped, arching into him. His thumb teased her nipple, rolling it around and around until she thought she would implode from the tension and the heat inexorably building inside her.

When he slid his mouth away from hers and lowered his head to her breasts, she nearly came off the bed from the torrent of sensations pouring through her. He teased and tasted for a long time, until she was writhing beneath him, desperate and aching for so much more.

At last, those deft fingers headed lower, toward the core of her heat. She clutched him tightly, pressing her mouth to the warm column of his neck as his thumb danced across her thighs, coming close but not quite reaching the place she ached most for him to touch.

He circled around it and continued to tease until she finally growled with frustration and nipped at his shoulder.

His low laugh rang through the room. His gaze met hers and her heart seemed to swell at the lighthearted expression in his eyes, a side of Ross she rarely saw but which she was coming to adore.

"Very carnivorous of you, Ms. Osterman."

"I have my moments, when provoked," she answered, her voice husky.

"Remind me to provoke you more often, then," he murmured.

She smiled and he stared at her mouth for a long time, his expression unreadable and then he kissed her again, his mouth slow and unmistakably tender on hers.

Oh, she was in trouble here, she thought as heat began to build again, as he continued to tease her.

"Just touch me already," she all but begged.

He laughed roughly. "With pleasure. And I absolutely mean that."

His fingers finally found her and she cried out as she nearly climaxed with just one slight touch.

She thought she knew what to expect. She had been married for five years. Before her husband's illness, she had always considered their lovemaking fulfilling, an enriching, important part of their marriage.

This insatiable need for Ross was something completely out of her experience. She thought of that desert windstorm again, fierce and violent, ripping aside a lifetime of convention and restraint.

It frightened her more than a little, this lack of control, this urge to throw herself into the teeth of the maelstrom and let it carry her away.

She could feel herself begin to withdraw, to scramble back to the safety and security of that restraint, but Ross wasn't about to allow it.

"Let go," he whispered in her ear. "Let go for me, Julie."

His words were all it took to send her tumbling into the storm. He lifted her higher, higher, and then she cried out his name as she climaxed.

He quickly donned a condom from the bedside table and entered her even before the last tremor shook her body. His gaze locked with hers as his body joined hers, and she felt truly alive for the first time in forever.

She wanted to burn every sensation to memory— his scent, of cedar and sage and something citrusy she couldn't identify, the salty, masculine tang of his skin, his strength surrounding her, engulfing her. She wrapped her arms around him as tightly as she could manage.

He could hurt her.

The thought slithered into her mind out of nowhere and seemed to take hold, despite the hazy satisfaction still encompassing her.

She wasn't sure if she could treat this moment with

the same casualness she knew Ross would. This meant something to her, something rare and precious and beautiful. She only hoped she could hold on to that and remember it as such after he pushed her away once more, as she was quite certain he would when the night was over.

That wild hunger began to climb inside her, insistent and demanding, and she pushed her concerns away. She would savor every moment with him. She wasn't going to ruin the magic and wonder of this moment with regret, with needless worry about the future.

With renewed enthusiasm, she threw herself into the kiss and after a surprised moment, he responded even more intensely.

His movements became more urgent, more demanding, and she arched to meet him, welcoming each joining of their bodies.

"Julie," he gasped after a long moment, and then he arched his back one more time as he found completion.

In the sweet, languid afterglow, she lay in his arms, trying to burn the memory into her mind. She couldn't regret this, even though she could already feel the tiny cracks in her heart expanding.

He would hurt her. She only hoped she was strong enough to endure it.

It was her last thought before she surrendered to the *other* demands of her body and finally slept.

Julie was beautiful in sleep. Her hair curled around her face in a filmy, sensuous cloud and long lashes fanned high cheekbones.

She looked delicate and lush at the same time and he couldn't seem to look away.

How could he ever have guessed a few short weeks

ago that the prim and tight-lipped do-gooder he had thought her to be that night at the Spring Fling art fair would be so wildly passionate in bed?

He should have guessed it by the fierce way she defended the scruffy teenager he erroneously thought had been stealing her purse. He had been so busy snapping back at her that he hadn't allowed himself to see past her anger to the breathtakingly beautiful woman behind it.

She fell asleep as easily as a kitten in his bed and with the same liquid stretch of her limbs.

He pulled her closer and she purred and snuggled into him. It gave him the oddest feeling, this complete trust she had in him. He found it exhilarating and terrifying at the same time and wasn't quite sure how he should react.

Over her shoulder, he could see the lights in the trees outside on the River Walk. He watched them flicker and dance on the breeze, as he did many nights. This time his mind wasn't busy running through the details of a case. It was too occupied with Julie and the mass of contradictions she presented. She could be sweet one moment, fiery the next; pensive with one breath, then wildly passionate the next.

Everything about her fascinated him, from the courage she displayed after becoming a young widow under such tragic circumstances to the dedication she devoted to her job.

He thought of the huge basket of provisions she had packed earlier tonight and smiled all over again. It didn't last very long, though, when he suddenly remembered just why she had packed that basket.

Josh.

He hadn't thought of his nephew once in the last

hour. Not once. Josh was out there somewhere, possibly in trouble, and Ross had forgotten all about him, simply because he found Julie so enticing.

He let out a breath, feeling chilled even though his bedroom was a comfortable temperature.

He needed to focus. He should never have given in to the hunger to kiss her. He was being pulled in too many different directions and right now his family needed him. He couldn't regret it, though. Not right now, with Julie warm and soft in his arms and this curiously appealing tightness in his chest.

He must have drifted asleep eventually. When he awoke, pale dawn sunlight was coyly peeking through the windows where he had forgotten to draw the curtains.

He stretched a little, struck by a curious feeling of contentment inside him. He wasn't used to it. In truth, the quiet peace of it left him a little unsettled and he didn't quite know how to react.

He gazed down at Julie, still sleeping beside him. If anything, she looked even lovelier than she had a few hours earlier.

Her mouth was slightly parted in sleep and she made a tiny, breathy little sound. He wanted to kiss her, with an acute, concentrated desperation.

He couldn't do it. It wouldn't be fair, not when she needed her sleep.

He tried to shift away but even his slight, barely perceptible movement must have disturbed her.

She blinked her eyes open and gazed at him for a moment, then she smiled softly and he had the random thought that the sun breaking across the city after weeks of rain couldn't be any more lovely or more welcome.

"Good morning," she murmured, her voice throaty and low.

"Hi."

"How long did we sleep?"

He glanced over at the digital readout on his alarm clock. "Not long enough. Only a few hours. It's almost six-thirty."

She reached her arms over her head and stretched until her fingers touched the headboard. "That's funny. I feel oddly invigorated."

He had the sudden, painful awareness that she was naked beneath the sheet that barely covered her. She was inches away from him, all that soft, glorious skin and those delectable curves.

His body snapped brightly to attention.

"Invigorated. Yeah. I know what you mean," he muttered.

She smiled again, her eyes half-lidded and knowing, and he couldn't mistake the sultry invitation. He held out as long as he could manage—oh, maybe a second and a half—before he lowered his head to hers and kissed her.

She responded just as sweetly as she had a few hours earlier, her mouth warm, slick and eager against his. Those arms she had just stretched out above her slid around his neck now and she pulled him close.

He loved when she touched him. Whether it was a casual hand on his arm in the middle of a conversation or her lips brushing his or her body arching against him in the sweet throes of passion, he couldn't seem to get enough of her.

A weird feeling seemed to trickle through him as that sensuous magic surrounded them again. It welled in his chest, clogged in his throat. Something warm and tender and terrifying. He wasn't sure what it might be—and he wasn't sure he liked it.

He wanted to take care of her. To cherish her. To rub her feet at the end of a hard day and make sure her car was filled with gasoline when she needed it and cook her fish on the grill just the way she liked it.

What was happening to him? For one jittery, panicky minute, Ross wanted to jump out of bed and rush out of his apartment and not look back. He didn't want this. Any of it. He didn't need another soul to take care of in his life, especially not a woman whose heart was so huge and full of love.

Anyway, she didn't need somebody else to watch out for her. She was doing fine on her own. She especially didn't need a cynical ex-cop with more baggage than an airline lost and found.

"Something wrong?" she asked, watching him carefully out of those big blue eyes, and he realized he had wrenched his mouth away and was staring at her as if she had just sat up in the bed and started spouting pig latin.

He quickly forced his emotions under control. He'd had plenty of practice at that when he was a kid and again as a cop.

This weird feeling wasn't love. It couldn't be. He wouldn't *let* it be.

He liked her well enough and he was more grateful than he could ever say for her help with Josh. That's all it was.

"What is it?" she asked.

"Nothing. Nothing at all," he said.

He pushed away the jumpy feeling and turned his

attention to that spot on her neck that he had discovered drove her crazy. She shivered and tightened her arms around him.

He might have thought their second time making love wouldn't have been as intense, as shattering, as the first. He knew what to expect, after all. He had already had the exhilarating chance to explore all those delectable curves. He had already discovered that little mole above her hipbone and he knew she made those soft, sexy little sounds when she was close to finding release.

But if anything, the repeat performance was even more astonishing. It was slower-paced, sweeter somehow, as if they were moving through soft, warm honey. Every sensation seemed magnified a hundredfold. He had never known a woman to give herself so generously, without any reservations, and it stunned and humbled him.

Even more, she acted just as stunned by her own response, which only seemed to accentuate his own.

She cried out his name when she climaxed, then wrapped her arms tightly around him when he joined her with a groan, and Ross never wanted her to let go.

All those scary feelings crowded back as he held her afterward, her head nestled in the crook of his shoulder, but he forced himself to hold them all back.

He *wasn't* in love with her. No way, he told himself.

He was still trying to convince himself of that when his cell phone suddenly bleated from somewhere in the bedroom.

Chapter 12

He might have been tempted to ignore it, to dive back into the heat and magic they shared, if not for the sudden recollection of just why they were there in his apartment in San Antonio.

But who else would be calling him at 7:00 a.m., unless Josh had just bothered to return to the house and found all his strongly worded orders to do just that?

"Is it Josh?" Julie asked.

"It had better be," he muttered. He grabbed his phone from the bedside table.

"Where the hell are you?"

A long silence met his growled question and then a small female voice spoke. "Um, still at the jail. But my lawyer assures me that's only for another few hours. They're releasing me on my own recognizance."

"Frannie?" He scrambled up against the headboard

and pulled the comforter up to his waist, as if his sister could see through the telephone.

"What are you talking about?" he demanded. "What's going on? Why are you calling me so early?"

She let out a strangled sound that was half sob, half laugh.

"You haven't heard, I guess. Nobody has picked up the story yet this morning since the police aren't releasing any details. They're letting me go."

"Dropping the charges?"

"The next best thing to it, my attorney says. They've dropped my bail to nothing. They're not holding me any longer. I'm going to be freed, Ross. Can you believe it? They've brought someone else in for questioning. I'm going home to Josh. It's like some kind of miracle, isn't it?"

His sister started crying in earnest but Ross felt as if his heart had jerked to an abrupt stop.

He couldn't believe it. He didn't *want* to believe it. But how could it possibly be a coincidence that Josh goes missing a few hours ago "helping out a friend" at the same time somebody gets hauled in for questioning about killing Lloyd?

Josh, what the hell have you done?

But, maybe he was way off base. If Josh had confessed and was now in custody, wouldn't Frannie be hysterical instead of reacting to the news with this sort of stunned jubilation?

"Who killed him?" he asked, unable to keep the wariness from his voice but hoping she didn't notice.

"I don't know. Nobody's telling me anything," she answered. "All I know is that they've got some 'person of interest' and they're ready to let me go. Oh, I can't wait to be home. Will you come get me?"

He slid out of the bed, already reaching for his khakis. "Of course. Stay in touch and call me the minute you hear from your attorney. I'll be there as soon as I can."

"Don't wake up Josh, okay? I want to surprise him."

Ross frowned. Somebody in the family was definitely in for a surprise. He could only hope it was indeed Josh who was surprised at learning his mother had been released and not him and Frannie when they found Josh already in custody.

"I'll see you in a little while," he said, instead of responding to his sister's plea about her son.

He hung up, his mind racing in a hundred different directions as he yanked on his socks and thrust his arms through the sleeves of his shirt.

"Ross, what's going on?"

He looked toward the bed and found Julie watching him with consternation. How could he have forgotten Julie? She looked soft and tousled, her hair messed and her lips swollen from his mouth. He gazed at her, wishing with everything inside him that things could be different, that he could stay with her, right here in this warm, cozy bed.

But his family needed him. And just like always, he had no choice but to help. Still, the choice had never seemed so damned hard before.

"I've got to hurry back to Red Rock. That was Frannie."

Her features tightened with concern. "What is it?"

"They're letting her go. They've brought someone else in for killing Lloyd Fredericks."

* * *

She stared at Ross, not quite sure she had heard him correctly. "Letting her go? Are you serious?"

"Completely." He started buttoning up his cotton shirt and it was only as she watched his grim features that Julie realized why all this seemed so discordant and unreal. He wasn't reacting like a man who had just learned his sister was about to be freed from jail.

"Okay, my brain obviously isn't working correctly yet this morning," she said. "Tell me again why you're not throwing the world's biggest party? Isn't this what you've wanted? What you've been working so hard to bring about for the last two weeks? Frannie's coming home, Ross! Why on earth do you look like you're heading to a funeral, instead of celebrating?"

He was silent as he started to slip on his boots, but his features looked even more austere than normal.

"Ross, tell me. What's wrong?"

At last he lifted his gaze to hers and she nearly gasped at the haunted expression in his brown eyes. Her mind sifted through the pieces, Frannie, Lloyd, the Spring Fling and the events of that awful night.

And Josh.

Josh was the missing piece, she realized, as everything clicked into place. She thought of his determined efforts to find his nephew the night before, and the odd phone call he had made to the police station, their seemingly casual route back to the Frederickses' home that had led them right past the station house.

She gasped and stared at him. "You think it's Josh they've hauled in. You think he killed his father!"

He didn't respond for a long moment but his silence was answer enough. "I don't know what I think," he finally said. "All I know is that Josh fought bitterly with his father that night and uttered what could be taken as a direct threat. He was seen with the murder weapon, not long before his father's body was found. He knows something, something he's not saying. I told you that since the murder, he's been secretive. He takes these mysterious phone calls and I can tell he's troubled."

"He's had a rough few weeks, losing his father and his mother at once. You can't honestly think he had anything to do with killing Lloyd! That he would let his mother go to jail for his own crime!"

"Where is he then?"

She had no answer to give him, though she fervently wished she did.

"I'm sorry about this," Ross said, "but I've got to go back to Red Rock right away. I can drop you off at your house on the way."

"Okay. I only need a moment." She rose and quickly began to dress again, thinking with regret of the brief, stolen time they had shared together. Something told her those moments were as elusive and rare as a wildflower growing on a harsh, unforgiving rock face.

As she dressed, she listened to his one-sided conversation with the police station. She could have guessed the outcome, even before he hung up the phone in disgust.

"They're not saying anything until charges are officially filed, which might or might not happen any moment. I need to haul out of here."

"Of course." She threw on her blouse and sweater, doing her best to block out the dull ache of regret.

"I need to make some phone calls on the way back to Red Rock to see if I can find out what the hell is going on, just who it is who's confessed. How do you feel about taking the wheel so I'm not distracted by talking while I drive?"

"Anything I can do to help. You know I want to do whatever I can."

"Thanks."

Though gratitude flashed in his gaze, it was quickly gone, replaced by a deep anxiety. She wanted to soothe it but she knew nothing she said would help him right now. But she could do as he asked and take at least one responsibility from his wide shoulders by driving them back to Red Rock.

He must have spoken with a half-dozen people as she took the shortest route possible away from San Antonio. Listening to him probe each contact for information was fascinating. He seemed to know exactly the right buttons to push with every person he spoke with. He could be brash and abrasive when necessary, but he could also pull out unexpected wiles that completely charmed her—and whoever he was talking to.

As they neared the Red Rock town limits, she listened to him try to skillfully pry information out of a source in the police department.

"You're not holding out on me, are you, Loraine?" he asked after a short conversation where he had exhibited a delicate finesse that surprised her.

He was quiet for a moment and Julie would have given anything to know what the person on the other end of the line was saying.

"How sure are you on that?" he asked after a long moment, his features unreadable. "Ninety-nine. That's good. And the other one percent?"

Loraine said something that made him laugh. When

the worry left his features, even for a moment, he looked younger, lighter. Almost happy.

She jerked her gaze back to the road, her heart tumbling around in her chest like a bingo ball in the chute.

She was in love with him.

The knowledge burrowed into her heart, as clear as the exit sign on the freeway. She wanted to push it away, to deny and disclaim, but she couldn't. She knew exactly what this dangerous tenderness curling through her meant.

She was in love with Ross Fortune, a hard and cynical man who seemed the last one on earth she ought to fall for, a man who was an expert at protecting himself from any deeper emotions.

She loved him. His deep core of decency, the care and concern he doled out to his family, his complete commitment to doing what was right.

She loved him—and he so desperately needed someone to love him, even if he would never admit it.

Why did that someone have to be her? she wondered with grim fatalism. She didn't want to love him. She wanted to go back to the way things had been just a few short weeks ago, before he had barreled into her life.

He would hurt her.

The knowledge hovered around her like the wavy mirages on the highway. Pain, harsh and unforgiving and unavoidable, waited for her. He would hurt her and she could do absolutely nothing to hold it back.

The time for protecting her heart might have been before that fateful night when he had accused poor Marcus Gallegos of stealing. She had been heading for this moment, for this inevitable pain, since then.

She might have been able to reduce its severity if she

had walked away after that evening, if she had maintained all her careful defenses. Instead, she had let her life become entwined with his through Josh. Each time she saw Ross, she had allowed him to sneak a little further past her defenses.

Tears burned behind her eyes, blurring the road in front of her, but she blinked them away. He hadn't hurt her yet. She refused to waste this particular moment in anticipation of the future pain she knew was on the way.

He ended the call a moment later and Julie knew she wasn't mistaken that his mood seemed lighter. His eyes seemed brighter, his expression less anxious.

"That was a friend of mine who works in central booking at the jail. She said the guy they're holding is a 40-year-old male."

"So not Josh."

Her voice sounded like she'd just swallowed a handful of gravel but she hoped he didn't notice or that he would attribute it to an emotional reaction to the news of his nephew's apparent reprieve.

"I won't be completely convinced of that until I find the little bugger and figure out where he's been all night. But no, at this point it looks like somebody else in Lloyd's legion of enemies had it in for him."

"How tragic, that so many people in Red Rock could have enough motive to want a man dead."

When he said nothing for several moments, she glanced away from the road just long enough to catch the quizzical look he threw at her.

She flushed, her hands tightening on the steering wheel. "Why are you looking at me like that?"

"You didn't even know Lloyd, did you?"

She shook her head.

"You didn't know the man but as far as I can tell, you're the only one besides his own mother and his mistress who finds anything to mourn in his death."

"I just think it's terribly sad that someone could take the precious gift of life and all the opportunities given him to make the world a better place and then twist them all so hideously that most of the world is glad he's gone."

He reached across the width of the seat and picked up her hand. Before she quite realized what he intended, he lifted her fingers and pressed his mouth to the back of her hand, in a very un-Ross-like gesture.

"Do you know what your greatest gift is?" he asked.

She let out a shaky breath, wondering how on earth she was going to collect the tattered pieces of herself when this was over. "What?"

"You make everyone around you want to be better. To try harder to see the world through those same bright, optimistic eyes."

She loved the feel of his hand holding hers, the safety and warmth of him, even as she wanted to snatch her hand away, to protect herself from any more encroachment on her heart.

"You didn't get nearly enough sleep last night if you can wax philosophical this morning."

"No, I didn't."

Heat scorched through her at his words as she remembered all the ways they had kept each other awake in the night. She was almost positive she was able to keep her fingers from trembling in his.

"Do you mind if we swing by Frannie's house before I drop you off? I want to make sure Josh hasn't checked in. For all we know, he could be asleep in his own bed, not knowing that everything has suddenly changed."

"No problem," she answered, trying not to be too disappointed when he released her hand so she could use both of hers for driving.

Ross must have been listening to his cop's intuition again. The very moment she pulled into the Fredrickses' driveway, a battered yellow sports car pulled up beside them and Josh climbed out.

He looked tired, Julie thought. Tired and worried and somehow older than he had appeared the last time she saw him.

She wondered how he would react to seeing them together so early at this time of the day but he didn't so much as raise an eyebrow.

"Hi," he said when they joined him outside their respective vehicles. "You two are out and about early this morning."

Already the morning was shaping up to be a warm one. But the sun-warmed heat was nothing compared to the anger suddenly radiating from Ross.

"Well?" he snapped to his nephew. "Let's hear your explanation? I'll warn you, it better be good."

Josh looked genuinely bewildered and a bit wary. She also thought she saw a little guilt there, as well. "Explanation for what?"

"For what?" Ross's voice rose on the last word. "Let's start with where the hell you've been all night. Julie and I drove around Red Rock and San Antonio half the night looking for you!"

His eyes widened with shock. "Why? I left you a note and then I called and left a message on voice mail. Didn't you get it?"

"Sure we got your note," Ross answered tightly. "Do you think you could try to be a bit less cryptic next time? We didn't know *what* was going on. And then when you didn't answer your blasted phone all night long, what were we supposed to think?"

"I told you a friend of mine needed help." Josh suddenly seemed as taut and angry as his uncle and Julie wondered how much of his reaction was due to fatigue.

"Did it ever once occur to you that saying only 'a friend needs help' could mean anything from algebra homework to changing a flat tire to running drugs across the border? You said you were going to help this friend but you didn't say anything about it taking you the whole damn night."

"I didn't expect to take all night. It was a…routine thing. But there were…complications. But everything's okay now. She…everything's okay."

An echo of worry flickered in his eyes and Julie reached a hand to rest on his arm. "Are you sure everything's okay, Josh? You look tired."

Josh's gaze met hers and for an instant that illusion of maturity disappeared and he looked suddenly desperately young. He seemed to want to lean on someone. He opened his mouth and she held her breath, hoping he would choose to confide in her and his uncle, but then he changed his mind and closed it again.

He straightened his shoulders. "Yeah. It's been a long night. Sounds like for you guys, too. I'm really sorry you made an unnecessary trip to San Antonio, but you can't blame me for your own overreaction. I told you not to worry or wait up. And I left you a message, too. I told you not to worry about me."

"Easy for you to say!"

"I'm officially eighteen, Uncle Ross. An adult in the eyes of the law. You don't have to treat me like a baby and run off and look for me like some kind of bounty hunter."

Ross looked angry and uncomfortable at the same time. Julie cut him off before he could voice the angry words forming in his eyes and possibly say something he might come to regret after their respective tempers had cooled.

"We were worried about you," she said to Josh. "It seems uncharacteristic for you to just take off like this."

He suddenly seemed inordinately fascinated with the bluebells growing in his mother's flower garden. "It was an emergency. And that's all I can tell you right now."

Ross knew his nephew was holding out on him. The boy—no, not a boy anymore—had secrets in his eyes. Ross was an expert at extracting information from unwilling subjects and sifting through lies and subterfuge to the truth but somehow none of his techniques seemed to work on his nephew.

That was what happened when he let his emotions overrule his good sense. He ought to sit Josh in a room and make the kid tell him what was going on. But Josh was right, he was eighteen and Ross supposed he was entitled to a few secrets.

He was so relieved that Josh hadn't been involved with his father's murder that he supposed he could let the mystery of his whereabouts overnight remain just that for now—a mystery.

"If your cell phone had been working, I might have been able to call you to tell you the news," he said.

"What news?" Josh asked, his hand on the open doorframe of Ross's SUV.

He paused. "Your mom is being released from jail any minute now. I'm on my way to get her."

Josh stared at him as if he had just announced they were flying to Saturn later. "What?" he exclaimed. "Why didn't you say so?"

"You just got here. We haven't exactly had much time to chat."

"This is huge! What happened? Did the stupid district attorney finally agree to reduce her bail?"

"She's being let out on her own recognizance. According to my sources, they've got someone else they like for the murder."

He watched his nephew's reaction carefully and saw a mix of emotions chase across his features, everything from shock to disbelief and finally a deep, pure relief.

"Who did they bring in?"

"I'm still trying to get answers to that. Your mom called me a little while ago and said her attorney was working on getting the charges against her dropped but she didn't know many details. I've been able to find out a little but not a name or anything like that. I'm heading down to the police station right now to see what else I can find out."

Josh's hand tightened on the doorframe. "I'm coming with you."

His nephew had obviously been up all night, judging by the fatigue lining his eyes and the heavy sag of his shoulders. But he was young enough to survive an all-nighter. Ross had a feeling he wouldn't be able to keep Josh away.

"Get in, then. We can drop Julie off at her place on the way."

He took over behind the wheel from Julie and she slid into the passenger seat beside him. The three of them were mostly silent on the five-minute drive to her house. Ross found himself grateful for the buffer of Josh's presence, suddenly aware of the monumental shift in his relationship with Julie after the night they had shared.

He wasn't ready for things to change. He enjoyed her friendship too much to ruin things with sex but he was afraid that's exactly what he had done.

He didn't want things to get messy with her but he knew with brutal self-awareness that he sucked at relationships. He was much better at short-term flings, where women had few expectations beyond a few dates and a good time.

Julie wasn't like that. As he pulled up to her small, tidy house near the elementary school, he could see the proof of it.

He walked around and opened her door—manners instilled in him by his uncles. He walked her to the front door, past colorful terra-cotta containers full of bright flowers and a trio of birdhouses.

This was just the sort of house that made him nervous. The flower gardens spoke of settling in, of commitment and permanence, all the things that seemed so foreign to him. He couldn't remember a single plant his mother had tried to grow. They had never been in one place long enough to see a seedling sprout anyway, so why bother?

He had been in his condo for five years, though. Why hadn't he ever tried to grow anything on the patio?

He had perfect light out there and it wouldn't be a big deal to plant some tomatoes and maybe a pepper plant or two.

At her door, he paused, feeling intensely awkward, in light of all they had shared together the last few hours. She seemed to sense it, too, and fiddled with her purse and the keys she had used to unlock the door.

He struggled for something to say but everything sounded lame. *Thanks for the most incredible night of my life* sounded like it came right off the pathetic bachelor's morning-after playlist.

"Let me know what happens with Frannie, okay?" Julie finally said.

"I'll be sure to do that," he answered. His chest ached a little as the morning sun lit a halo around her. She looked as pretty and bright as her flower gardens and he knew she wasn't for him.

He was going to have to break things off with her. She was digging in too deep and he couldn't let her. Not when she scared the hell out of him.

He hated being one of Those Guys, who slept with a woman and then brushed her off, especially when he had a feeling she expected more. But he also wasn't willing to string her along, not when he already was coming to care far too much for her.

Chapter 13

Ross's heart ached in his chest. He wanted nothing but to pull her against him and hold on forever, which was more than enough reason to push her away.

"Julie, I…"

She shook her head and for just a moment, he thought he saw something like sorrow flicker there before it was quickly gone. "Ross, don't say anything. What happened earlier was…wonderful. We both wanted it to happen. But I completely understand that it was only a one-time thing."

He scratched his cheek. "Twice, technically."

She laughed roughly, though again he thought he saw regret in those soft blue eyes. "Okay, twice. My point remains that I don't expect anything more than that. You can put your mind at ease. I promise, I'm not going to be clingy or throw a scene or rush inside my house and cry for hours. Don't worry about me, okay?"

He should be relieved. Wasn't this what he wanted? So why did his chest continue to ache like he'd been punched?

"I'm not the kind of man you need, Julie. I wish I could be. You have no idea how much I wish I could be. But I'm not."

"How did you become such an expert on what I need?"

"It's my job to understand people. I have to be able to read things about people that even they don't always see. I have to be able to understand their motivations, their triggers, their personality types."

"And what's my personality type?"

She asked the question with deceptive casualness but he heard the sudden tightness in her voice, in the way she compressed her lips just a little too hard on the last consonant so it popped. He was in quicksand here, he suddenly sensed.

He glanced at the car where Josh watched them curiously, too far away, thank the Lord, to hear their conversation.

He didn't want to get into all this right now. But he had started things and he owed it to her to finish.

"You're a nurturer. A natural healer. You take people who are hurting and broken and you try to fix them. It's what you do with the kids you work with at the Fortune Foundation but I've seen you put the same effort into everyone. I saw you slip more than a few bills to anybody who looked like they had a sob story last night while we were looking for Josh."

A tiny muscle flexed in her check. "And you don't want to be healed."

He bristled. "I'm not broken."

"Aren't you?"

Her psychoanalytical put-the-question-back-on-the-poor-patient crap suddenly bugged the hell out of him.

"I'm fine," he snapped. "Absolutely fine. I've got everything I need."

She said nothing, only continued to study him out of those eyes that saw entirely too much.

"Everything was going just great in my life until two weeks ago when somebody whacked my brother-in-law. Now that they've found whoever it was who did it and Frannie's coming home, I can return to the life I had before and everything will get back to normal."

"In my business, we call that self-delusion."

"Call *what* self-delusion?"

"You're supposed to be an expert on figuring out what makes everybody else tick. Their motivations, their triggers, their personality types. Isn't that what you said? Can you really be so blind to your own?"

"What's that supposed to mean?"

"Nothing. Never mind. Goodbye, Ross."

She opened the door and though he knew Josh and Frannie waited for him, he couldn't help himself. He followed her inside.

"Tell me what you meant," he growled.

She studied him for a long moment, then she sighed. "You keep everyone away, don't you? Because of the instability of your childhood, you're so determined not to count on anybody else, to be so completely self-sufficient now that you're an adult, that you close off everybody except your family. Frannie and Josh. And even then, you feel like you have to shoulder every burden for them, not share a single worry. As a result, you're probably the most lonely man I've ever met."

He stared at her, thunderstruck by the harsh analysis. Her words sliced at him with brutal efficiency. How did she know anything about his childhood? Fast on the heels of the shock and hurt came the sharp flare of anger. She had no right to think she could sum up his world in a few neat little sentences.

"I take back everything I said," he snapped. "You're not a nurturer. You're just plain crazy. I'm absolutely not lonely. Hell, I can't get people to leave me alone long enough for me to be lonely!"

"I guess we can both be wrong about each other, then," she said, sounding so damn calm and reasonable, he wanted to punch something.

"I guess so. Better to find out now than sometime in the future after we've invested more than just a night with each other."

"I'm sure you're right," she murmured. "You'd better go, hadn't you? Your sister's waiting for you."

He gazed at her for a moment, wondering how this whole thing had taken such a wrong turn, then he nodded. "Yeah. I guess I'll see you around, then."

She only smiled that impassive smile at him and opened the door, leaving him no choice but to stalk through it and down the sidewalk.

Julie watched Ross drive away, his white SUV suddenly anything *but* unobtrusive as its tires spit gravel and careened around the corner.

Apparently he couldn't wait to get away from her.

Drat the man. She swiped at a tear trickling down the side of her nose and then another and another, grateful at least that she had the strength of will to hold them back until he was out of sight.

She wanted to rant and rave at Ross Fortune's stubborn self-protectiveness, his apparent willingness to walk away from the magic and wonder they had shared, just so that he could guard his psyche.

A good tantrum would at least be an outlet for the wild torrent of emotions damming up inside her, but the hardest thing to accept was that none of this was Ross's fault.

She walked into bed with him with her eyes open. She might not have consciously admitted she was already in love with him but deep down she must have known, just as she had to have realized somewhere inside that Ross was completely unavailable to her, at least emotionally.

She had convinced herself she was strong enough to live in the moment, to seize the chance to be with him without regrets or recriminations later.

What a fool she was. And she called *him* self-deluded! How could she have ever believed she could share that intimacy with him, let him inside her soul and not feel battered and bruised when he walked away from all she was willing to offer?

This was goodbye then.

Their respective worlds weren't likely to intersect again. With his sister on her way to freedom, Ross had no reason to stick around Red Rock. Frannie would be able to care for Josh from now on and accompany him to the Fortune Foundation for counseling sessions if he still needed them.

Ross would return to San Antonio and his private investigation practice and that lovely, impersonal apartment and his self-contained life that struck her as immeasurably sad.

She pressed her hands to her face for just a moment then dropped them to her knees. She would survive a broken heart. She had no choice. As Ross said, she was a healer, a nurturer, and she couldn't do any of that if she turned inside herself and wallowed in her own pain.

He was an ass.

Ross sat in the reception area of the police station, replaying his conversation with Julie over and over in his head.

Had he really called her crazy? He burned with chagrin just thinking about it. He had reacted like some kind of little kid, lashing out first to protect himself from being wounded by her words.

She deserved better from him than that. Julie had always been nothing but warm and kind to him. She had just spent the entire night helping him look for Josh, for hell's sake. And then when she gave him an opinion that *he* had solicited, he snapped back at her like a cornered grizzly. It was unfair and unnecessarily hurtful.

He had to make it right, somehow, but he had no idea where to start.

He still didn't buy what she was selling. He had moved past his childhood a long time ago. Yeah, he might still have scars. The insecurity of growing up with Cindy Fortune would have been rough on any kid, he wouldn't deny that. But he didn't dwell on it anymore. He hadn't for a long time.

And lonely. She said he was lonely. He didn't buy that, either. He had plenty of friends, good ones. They went to basketball games together and had barbecues and fishing trips out on his boat.

Okay, he would admit she was right that he didn't let too many people close. But that didn't mean he was some kind of freaking hermit.

He thought of the nights alone in his apartment when he would stand at the window gazing down at the River Walk, at the lights and the activity and the people walking together, content and happy in their tidy little family units.

More often than not, he would attribute the nameless ache inside him as he watched them to heartburn. It sure wasn't loneliness. Was it?

"Ross? You in there?"

He glanced up to find Josh staring at him with a quizzical look.

"Sorry. Did you say something?"

Josh rolled his eyes. "Only about a dozen times. I asked if I could borrow your cell phone to check on my friend."

The same friend whose troubles had occupied him all night? Ross wondered. He wanted to push his nephew to finally come clean and explain what was going on. But since he had screwed everything else up this morning, he decided maybe he ought to keep his mouth shut for now.

He handed over his phone and wasn't surprised when Josh walked outside to make his call. More secrets. He was getting pretty sick of them all.

Despite the fact that Frannie was to be released any moment now, Ross still didn't know much more than when she called him two hours before.

Try as he might, he couldn't manage to worm more information out of anyone in the department except what he already knew. A forty-year-old man was the new suspect in Lloyd's death.

He didn't understand why everyone was being so closemouthed about the whole thing, but he could guess. They were no doubt engaged in the age-old police game of CYA. Cover Your Ass. No doubt they realized they had rushed to judgment with Frannie without looking around for any other suspects and wanted to avoid making the same mistake again and possibly jeopardizing their case.

He didn't care who killed Lloyd, as long as it meant his sister could return home where she belonged and he could go back to San Antonio where *he* belonged.

Josh returned a few moments later and handed his phone back.

"Everything okay with Lyndsey?" Ross hazarded a guess.

"Yeah, she's doing tons bet—" *Better.* Josh cut his word off but Ross completed the word for himself, even as his nephew frowned at being tricked into revealing more information than he wanted.

"What happened to her?" Ross asked. "Has she been sick?"

For an instant, he thought Josh would confide in him. He opened his mouth and Ross sensed he wanted to tell someone whatever was bothering him. Ross sat forward with an encouraging look, but before Josh could say anything, the door leading to the jail opened.

He and Josh both turned to look and found Frannie standing in the doorway, looking frail and exhausted, with no makeup and her blond hair scraped back in a ponytail.

Despite the outward signs of fatigue, her eyes glowed with joy.

"Josh. Oh sweetheart."

Josh rose from his seat, stumbled forward and then swept his mother into his arms. Both of them were crying a little, even his tough-guy, eighteen-year-old nephew. Ross watched their reunion, aware of a niggle of envy at the love the two of them shared, a love with no conditions or caveats.

Josh had probably never spent one moment wondering at his place in his mother's heart. Frannie loved him with everything she had.

Frannie touched Josh's face as if she couldn't quite believe he was there in front of her and then after a moment she remembered Ross and turned to hug him, as well. She felt like nothing more than fragile bones.

"You're fading away, Frannie," he growled. "Have you been on some kind of hunger strike in here?"

She shook her head. "I just... I haven't been very hungry. It was too hard to drum up an appetite when I could only think about how afraid I was."

If you were so blasted afraid, why didn't you defend yourself? Who were you covering for? Ross wanted to rail at his sister but he knew this wasn't the time. "We need to get you out of here and get some good cooking into you. What do you say we stop at Red on the way home for a huge brunch? We'll break out the champagne."

"That sounds delicious." She gave him a tremulous smile just as Loraine Fitzsimmons walked through.

"Hey, Ross." She smiled.

"Hi, Loraine. Thanks for the information earlier."

She looked around to make sure no one else could overhear them.

"Just thought I'd give you a heads-up. They're questioning him again."

"Who is it?"

She cast another furtive look at the doorway. "You're not going to believe this. It's one of Mendoza boys. Says here it's Roberto. Isn't he the one who's been living in Denver?"

Ross had just half a second to wonder why the man had hated Lloyd enough to kill him and to entertain the possibility of trying to post bail for the guy, whoever he might be, when suddenly he was aware of Frannie's small sound of distress. A moment later his sister's eyes fluttered back in her head and she started to fall.

"Mom!" Josh exclaimed. He dived for her and though he wasn't in time to catch her completely, he slowed the momentum of her fall.

Josh lowered her to the carpet and both he and Ross knelt over her.

Loraine hovered over them, her eyes wide with shock. "Do you want me to call a medic?" she asked.

"Give us a minute," Ross said. Frannie had looked so weak when she came out. Was it any wonder she had succumbed to exhaustion and nerves and fainted?

"Come on, Frannie. Come on back, sis."

"Come on, Mom," Josh added his voice. "You're scaring us."

She blinked her eyes open, then a moment later she scrambled to sit and looked around, trying to regain her bearings.

"Are you all right?" Ross asked. Her pulse seemed

a little thready to him and he wondered if he ought to let Loraine go ahead and call a medic.

Frannie blinked a few more times, then her gaze met Loraine's and Ross saw full awareness come back in a rush. Frannie tried to stand but couldn't make it to her feet without his help.

"Take it easy," he said, but Frannie seemed to barely hear him.

"Who did you say they're holding?" she asked Loraine, and Ross couldn't miss the sudden urgency in her voice.

"Mendoza. Roberto Mendoza."

Frannie inhaled a ragged breath and, for a moment, Ross was afraid she would pass out again. "Do you know the guy?" he asked.

"I...no."

She was lying. No doubt about it. Frannie had always been a lousy liar. Maybe that was why she had opted instead to keep her mouth shut when she had been accused of killing her husband.

He knew most of the Mendozas on a casual basis, mostly because they were good friends with his family here in Red Rock. He tried to remember if he had ever met Roberto Mendoza and had a vague memory of bumping into the guy years ago on one of his visits to Red Rock.

What was his relationship with Frannie?

He was royally sick of all these Fortune family secrets. Though he wanted to drag his sister to one of the interview rooms in the police station until he got to the bottom of all this, he knew this wasn't the time. This should be a celebration for Frannie, a chance for her to start taking back her life.

As soon as things settled down for his sister, his

own life could get back to normal. To stakeouts and
paperwork and catching up on cases. He would be far
too busy to pay any attention to those moments standing at his window in San Antonio, watching life go on
below without him.

Chapter 14

He really disliked weddings, even when they were family obligations.

A week after Frannie's release from jail, Ross stood in the extensive gardens at the Double Crown watching his cousin Darr dance with his very pregnant bride of less than an hour, Bethany Burdett. Bethany Burdett Fortune, now, he supposed.

It was a lovely evening for a wedding. Little twinkly lights had been strung through all the trees and the garden smelled sweet, like flowers and springtime.

Darr beamed with pride and his new wife looked completely radiant. That was what they said about pregnant women and brides—and since she qualified on both counts, Ross figured *radiant* was an accurate description. She also couldn't seem to take her eyes off Darr.

The two of them seemed deliriously happy together,

he would give them that. He hoped things would work out for the two of them and for Bethany's kid, which wasn't Darr's—and nobody was making a secret about it. The baby needed a dad and Darr appeared more than willing to step up and take responsibility. Ross just hoped he didn't grow to resent raising another man's kid.

They wouldn't have an easy road—a cynical thought to have just moments after their wedding, he knew, and he was slightly ashamed of himself for even entertaining it.

How did he get to be so pessimistic about happily-ever-afters? He couldn't really say he'd never seen a good marriage at work. His uncle William had adored his wife Molly before her death and they had been married for decades. Lily and Ryan had known several happy years, too, before Ryan's surprising death.

He couldn't deny there were many couples in his extended family who, by all appearances, had good, fulfilling marriages. He didn't begrudge any of them their joy, he just figured maybe Cindy's particular branch of the Fortune family tree had picked up some sort of withering disease that blighted their prospects of happy endings.

His mother had never stayed with any man for longer than a year or so. His brothers didn't seem capable of settling down, and God knows, his sister's marriage had been a farce from the beginning.

He glanced toward Frannie, sitting at a table with their cousin Nicholas and his fiancée Charlene. She looked as if she were only half-listening to their conversation and he wondered again why she didn't seem more ecstatic about being released from jail. She still

seemed thin and withdrawn and she evaded and equivo-
cated whenever he tried to probe about why she hadn't
defended herself in Lloyd's murder and her strange reaction to finding out one of the Mendozas had confessed to it.

Something was up with her and it bugged him that
she still refused to tell him what was going on, even
after all they had been through the past month. She was
a grown woman, though. If she didn't want to tell him
what was troubling her, he couldn't force her.

He glanced at his watch, wondering if twenty minutes into the reception counted as fulfilling his familial
obligation so he could go. When he looked up, his heart
seemed to catch his throat when he saw Julie Osterman
walk into the garden, wearing a soft yellow dress that
made her look as if she had brought all the sunshine
along with her.

In the week since he had left her at her house with
such heated words, he had forgotten how breathtaking
she was, with that soft brown hair shot through with
blond and those incredible blue eyes and delicate features. He suddenly realized with some vexation that
if he had the chance, he would be quite content just to
stand there and gawk at her all night.

As if she felt him watching her, she shifted her attention from her conversation with his cousin Susan
and looked up. For a long moment, the two of them
just stared at each other, their gazes locked. Emotions
swelled up inside him, thick and heavy and terrifying.
He saw something in her eyes, something that made
them look huge and liquid and sad, and then she deliberately turned back to answer something Susan said to

her, though he knew she was still aware of him, of this strange bond tugging between them.

He wanted fiercely to go to her. His chest ached and he actually lifted a hand to rub at it then caught himself and shoved it into the pocket of his dress slacks instead. It still throbbed though, an actual physical ache that made him feel slightly ridiculous.

He had missed her. More than he had ever dreamed possible. In the week since he had seen her—since those stunning few hours they had shared at his apartment in San Antonio—she hadn't been out of his mind for long. Everything seemed to remind him of her, from shooting hoops with Josh to the starlit view from his bedroom window at night to—of all silly things—the scent of the particular brand of fabric softener he used, just because that day in the grocery store he had talked to her while they were standing in the laundry aisle.

It had to stop. He was miserable and he hated it. Surely this ache in his chest would eventually go away. He had to start sleeping again, instead of tossing and turning all night, reaching for someone who wasn't there.

Any day now, things would get back to normal. Or at least that's what he kept telling himself.

Lucky for him, he wasn't in love with her, he thought. Then he *really* would be miserable.

He told himself he wasn't staring at her but he couldn't help but notice when Ricky Farraday asked her to dance a few moments later. Ricky was slightly shorter than she was and only fourteen but she took the arm he held out for her with a shake of her head and a laugh he would swear he could hear clear on the other side of the plank dance floor set up in an open area of the garden.

"You're watching those dancers like you'd like to join them."

He jerked his gaze away to realize Frannie had joined him. "No. Not at all. You know I'm not much of a dancer."

"Neither am I. Why don't we trip all over the floor together?"

"I don't think so."

"Come on, Ross. Don't be a big chicken. We haven't danced together since I was twelve years old on my way to my first junior high school dance and you and Cooper and Flint put on some of Cindy's records and took turns trying to teach me a few steps."

He laughed at the memory of him and his brothers almost coming to blows about who could waltz better. Even though they had bickered their way through it, they had all had a great time that Saturday night. He'd forgotten the whole thing. It was so easy to focus only on the bad times that he often forgot how much fun they could all have together.

"Come on. I'd like to dance," Frannie pressed, showing more enthusiasm about this than she had toward much of anything since her release. How could he say no?

He shrugged. "Don't blame me if I ruin your fancy shoes with my clunky feet."

"I can buy more shoes," she said, and led him out to the dance floor. As he expected, he was rusty and awkward at first but Cindy had passed on at least some small degree of her natural ability and they quickly fell into something resembling dance steps.

The entire time, he was aware of Julie across the dance floor. She laughed at something Ricky said and his heart started to ache all over again.

"Okay, what's wrong?" Frannie asked. "Are you completely miserable to be out here dancing or is something else bothering you?"

He raised an eyebrow, finding her question the height of irony since he'd been hounding her to confide in him about one thing or another since the night her husband was killed.

"Nothing." He could equivocate with the best of them. "I'm just not a huge fan of weddings."

"I love them," she said promptly. "Bethany and Darr look so happy together, don't they?"

He stared at her. "How can you? Love weddings, I mean?"

She gave him an arch look. "Do you think I can't be a romantic, just because my own marriage wasn't the greatest?"

That was just about the biggest understatement of the decade, but he decided to let it slide. "I was thinking more about how tough it would be to love weddings when you grew up with a front-row seat to Cindy's messed-up version of relationships. That's enough to sour anybody on the idea of hearts and flowers and happily-ever-after, don't you think?"

"Oh, Ross." Sorrow flickered in her eyes and her fingers tightened around his. "Don't look to Cindy for an example of anything. Or at me, either."

"You don't think we've inherited her lousy relationship gene?"

"Oh, I hope not. I would hate to think you and Cooper

and Flint could never find the same kind of happiness that Darr and Bethany share today."

Against his will, his gaze flickered to Julie, then he looked quickly back at Frannie, hoping she had missed that quick, instinctive look.

"Maybe Cooper and Flint might eventually settle down and you're still a young, beautiful woman," he said. "There's no reason you couldn't find someone someday, someone who will finally treat you like you deserve. But I think at this point, it's safe to say it's not in the cards for me."

She was silent for a long time and he hoped she would let this awkward conversation die. Instead, when her gaze met his, Frannie's eyes were filled with sadness and regret.

"We have all treated you so poorly, haven't we?"

"What do you mean? Of course you haven't!"

"We all counted on you for too much, made you believe you were responsible for everything in our lives. Even Cindy. Maybe especially Cindy."

She squeezed his fingers. "You're not, you know. Not responsible for any of us. You're not responsible for Cindy's failed relationships or her lousy mothering or for my own mistakes or for anything but your own life, Ross, and what you make of it."

So far, he hadn't made much of it. Oh, he had a decent career that he enjoyed and had found success at. But what else did he have to show for forty years on the planet?

"Do you remember teaching me how to ride a two-wheeler without training wheels?" Frannie asked.

He blinked at what seemed an abrupt change of topic. "Not really."

"I do. I can remember it like it was yesterday. I remember exactly what you said to me. I was seven years old, far too old to still be riding a little-kid bike, which means you would have been about eleven. You worked with me for days trying to get me not to wobble. You were so patient, even though I'm sure there were a million other things you would rather have been doing than helping your stupid, clumsy baby sister. Finally one day, you just gave me a big push, let go of the bike frame and told me to forget my fears and just enjoy the ride."

He remembered they had been living in an apartment in Dallas and had gone to the park near their place every afternoon for two weeks. No matter what he tried, Frannie couldn't seem to get the hang of balancing on two wheels. Only after he gave her no other choice except to fall over on the sidewalk did she manage to figure it out. After that, there was no stopping her.

"Can I give the same advice back to you?" Frannie asked, her voice solemn.

"I know how to ride a bike," he muttered, trying to figure out where she was going with this.

"Yes. But do you know how to *live*, Ross?"

He bristled. "What's that supposed to mean?"

"Take it from somebody who feels like she's been one of those ice sculptures over at the bar for the last eighteen years—if a chance for happiness comes along, you have to take it. You can't be afraid because of our messed-up childhood, because of what Cindy did to all of us. Don't give her that much power, Ross. You deserve so much more."

Her words seemed to sear through him, resonating through his entire body. He was doing exactly that. He was still letting Cindy control his life, with her whims and her capriciousness and her instability. He was so convinced he was just like her, that he would mess up everything good and decent that ever came his way, that he was deathly afraid to let go of those fears and take a chance.

Frannie was exactly right. Just as Julie had been right a week before in everything she said to him.

He was afraid to count on anyone else, afraid to open his life to even the possibility of someone else touching his heart.

"I didn't mean to leave you speechless," Frannie said.

He blinked and realized the song had ended—a good thing, since he had stopped stock-still on the edge of the dance floor.

"Think about it, Ross. I just want you to be happy." Frannie kissed his cheek, then slipped away.

The music started up again and somehow Ross managed to make his way off the dance floor before somebody collided with him. He needed a drink, he decided, even if it meant he had to stick around a little longer to give the alcohol time to wear off before he drove home.

Before he could reach the open bar and those ice sculptures Frannie had been talking about, Julie twirled by on the arm of his nephew, who must have asked her to dance the moment Ricky led her off the floor. Her gaze met his over Josh's shoulder and this time he was certain he saw something like sorrow there.

His chest ached again and he had no choice but to rub it as the truth seemed to soak through him.

He couldn't lie to himself anymore. He was in love with Julie Osterman. With her smile and her gentleness and her compassion for everyone around her. He loved the way she touched his arm to make a point and her enthusiasm and dedication to the rough-edged kids she helped and the way she always had everyone else's interests at heart.

He let out a shaky breath, feeling as if a dozen ice sculptures had just collapsed on his head. He *couldn't* be in love with her. He didn't know the first damn thing about being in love.

His instinct was to run, to climb into his SUV and head back to San Antonio, where he was safe. But he had supposedly been safe all week from Julie and these terrifying emotions she churned up in him and he had been miserable.

Just let go and enjoy the ride.

Frannie's words echoed in his mind. Did he have the courage? Could he let go of the past and seize this incredible chance for happiness that had been handed to him?

He watched Julie twirl around the dance floor with Josh and knew he had to try.

Ross was staring at her.

Julie tried to keep her attention on the dance steps, on not tripping all over her partner and making a complete fool of herself, but she was painfully aware of Ross's hard gaze scorching her all over. But why did he bother looking?

He had made it abundantly plain he wasn't interested in anything more than the one night they had together. She had spent all week trying to get over him, to convince herself her heart wasn't broken, and then he had to show up at her friend Bethany's wedding looking rough and masculine and gorgeous in a Western-cut dark suit and tie.

If he didn't want her, why was he looking at her like she was a big plate of caramel cashew bars he couldn't wait to gobble up?

She drew in a shaky breath and tried to answer something Josh said, though she wasn't sure if she made any sense. She barely heard what he said in reply, but his next words suddenly penetrated through the haze around her brain.

"What happened between you and Ross?" Josh asked.

She stumbled and nearly stepped on his foot but quickly tried to recover. "What do you mean? Why do you ask?"

His shoulder moved beneath her hand as he shrugged. "I just thought you two were getting along so well. I'm not blind. I could see the vibe between the two of you the night we had dinner. And suddenly it's like you're nowhere to be found and Uncle Ross is acting like a grizzly bear who needs a root canal. What happened between you two?"

She knew it was petty of her to find some satisfaction that Ross was acting cranky but she couldn't seem to help it. "Nothing happened," she lied. Other than they shared one incredible night together and then he broke her heart. "We're just friends."

"Are you sure? He really seemed to like you, more than anyone else I've ever seen him with."

She let out a breath and pasted on something she hoped would pass for a smile. "I'm positive. Just friends."

"Too bad. I think you would have been good for Uncle Ross. He needs somebody like you."

Though she knew Josh didn't realize it, his words poured like acid on her already raw wounds. She was still reeling when the music ended. One of Josh's extended cousins called to him and he excused himself with a smile.

She stood for a moment, aware of Ross across the dance floor talking to his cousin J.R. and J.R.'s lovely fiancée, Isabella Mendoza, who was Roberto's cousin. His gaze met hers one more time, his dark eyes unreadable, and she let out a shaky breath.

Julie couldn't take anymore. She had done her duty by her friend Bethany and had told her how thrilled she was for her and for Darr. There was no reason to stick around for more of this torture.

Quickly, she made her way toward the grassy field that was serving as a parking lot for the wedding, pausing only long enough to say a hasty goodbye to a few friends. Just as she reached the outskirts of the crowd, she heard Ross calling her name.

She briefly entertained the idea of pretending she didn't hear him, but that would be the coward's way out. Besides, as quickly as he moved, he would catch up to her before she could reach her car anyway.

As he approached, she turned slowly, cursing him all over again for making her heart flip in her chest. His features wore an odd, unreadable expression and his eyes were gazing at her with an intensity that made her suddenly breathless.

"Hi, Ross," she managed.

"I thought I saw you leave. I'm glad I caught you. I…needed to talk to you."

"Oh?" She did her best to hide the tremble of her hands by folding them tightly in front of her.

For a long moment, he didn't seem inclined to say anything, he just continued to watch her out of those deep brown eyes. She wasn't used to seeing him at a loss for words and she didn't quite know how to respond.

Finally he let out a long breath. "Do you…would you like to take a walk with me?"

She ought to tell him no. She wasn't at all in the mood to dredge everything up again and she wasn't sure her fragile emotions could handle another encounter with him. But she was curious enough about what he wanted to talk about that she finally nodded. They walked side by side on the gravel pathway around the house in the gathering twilight, through more gardens, their shoulders barely brushing.

The silence between them was jagged, awkward. As a trained therapist, she certainly knew the value of a good silence to allow for thoughts to be gathered, but she couldn't endure this one.

"What did you want to talk to me about?"

He sighed. "I said I *needed* to talk to you. Not that I *wanted* to."

His words stabbed at her already-tender nerves and she stopped abruptly, then turned on her heel and headed back the direction she had come. "Fine," she said over her shoulder. "Let's forget the whole thing. I can find my own way back to my car, thanks all the same."

He grabbed her arm to stop her departure but quickly released her again when she turned back around. "Ah, hell. That didn't come out right. I do want to talk to you."

He was silent for a long moment. When he spoke, his voice was low and rough. "The truth is, I want to do more than talk to you. You're all I've been able to think about for a week."

Her stomach shivered at his words and she folded her

arms tightly across it, as if he could see her tremble. "What am I supposed to say to that?"

He looked so uncomfortable that her heart tumbled around all over again in her chest. "I don't know. That maybe you missed me, too."

Only every moment, with every single breath. She swallowed and looked away. "What did you want to talk to me about, Ross? I was just on my way home."

He didn't answer, only started walking again and curiosity gave her no choice but to follow him. He finally stopped near a small, burbling creek that cut through a small copse of trees near one of the outbuildings.

They found a bench there, a weathered iron and wood creation that looked as if it had been there as long as the hills around the ranch. He must have known it was here, she realized, since he had led her directly to this spot. She sat, her emotions in turmoil. After a moment, he sat beside her.

"I love this place," he finally said, his voice low. "It was always my favorite spot whenever we came to the ranch when I was a kid. We didn't do it very often. Come here, I mean. Maybe only two or three times I can remember, but I loved it. I cherished those times because I always felt…*safe* here."

She held her breath, more touched than she knew she ought to be that he had shared this secret place with her, though she still didn't understand why.

He gazed out at the creek, without meeting her gaze. "I didn't feel safe in very many places," he said after another long silence. "You were absolutely right, Julie. Everything you said to me the other morning at your house was right on the money. I keep everyone away because it's easier than letting myself count on people who let me down."

He finally looked at her. "I spent my entire childhood with nothing solid to hold on to but a few fragmented memories of this place."

She couldn't help herself—she reached out to touch his forearm. He looked down at her hand on his sleeve, his eyes deep with emotions she couldn't begin to name, then he covered her hand with his tightly to keep her fingers in place on his arm, to keep the two of them connected.

She could feel the heat of him through the fabric of his suit jacket, feel the muscle tensing beneath her hand. If he found some comfort from her touch, she wasn't about to move.

"My mother should never have had kids," he said hoarsely. "I don't think she wanted any of us and she didn't know what to do with us when we arrived. I was the oldest and it was left to me to take care of everybody else."

"And you did."

"I didn't have a choice. There was no one else. What you said, about keeping everybody out, counting only on myself. You were exactly right. I had to at the time for survival, and it just became a habit, I guess. I denied what you said at first because I didn't want to believe I could be giving my childhood, my *mother,* that much power to control my life. I'm forty years old. It shouldn't still be so much a part of me."

"We can never completely lose our childhoods," she said softly. "It's part of what shapes us. We just have to learn as adults to accept that we don't have the power to change it. All we can do is try to move forward and make the rest of our lives the best we can."

"You also called me the loneliest man you ever met."

Her eyes stung with tears at the bleakness in his voice. "I'm so sorry, Ross. I should never have said that."

"No. Don't apologize."

He was quiet. In the distance she could hear the music from the wedding, muted and slow. "You were right about that, too," he finally said. "I have been. I never wanted to admit it before. I think I was afraid to face that. I told myself I was perfectly happy, that I liked being on my own, making my own decisions, not having to be responsible for anyone else. But it was only an illusion."

"Oh, Ross."

He let out a shaky breath. "I don't want to be lonely anymore."

Hope fluttered inside her chest like fragile butterfly wings but she was afraid to acknowledge it, afraid to even look at it for fear of crushing it.

He shifted and before she quite realized what he intended, he grabbed both of her hands in his. Her heart began to pound and she couldn't seem to catch her breath.

"This scares the hell out of me," he said, "but I had some good advice thrown back in my face tonight and I'm going to take it. It's time for me to let go of my fears and enjoy the ride."

"I don't know what you're talking about," she murmured. "I'm sorry."

He laughed a little, but his features quickly grew solemn. "I'm in love with you, Julie. That's what I'm talking about."

"What?" Her fingers clenched in his and she would have jerked them away but he held on tightly.

"It's true. I think I've been in love with you probably since you just about whacked me over the head with that silly flowered purse I thought had been stolen."

"You can't be!" The delicate little butterfly of hope inside her became a fierce, joyful dragon, flapping furiously to take flight.

"That's exactly what I've been telling myself for the last week. I've never been in love before. I thought I would get over it, get over you. But seeing you tonight just made me realize this is too big, too deep, for me to just forget about. I can't pretend anymore."

"Ross, I..." her voice faltered and she couldn't seem to string two coherent words together.

"You told me first love was wonderful and terrible at the same time. Do you remember that?"

She nodded, vaguely remembering their conversation about Josh and Lyndsey.

"I've had the terrible part this week, without you. I'm ready for the wonderful part to kick in any time now."

She gazed at him there in the gathering dusk, looking so big and gorgeous and dear. She gave a sound that was half laugh, half sob and crossed the brief distance to throw herself into his waiting arms and press her trembling mouth to his.

He gave an exultant laugh and gripped her tightly, returning her kiss with all the passion and heat and wonder she had dreamed about for the past week.

"I love you, Ross," she murmured against his mouth. "I love you so much. I've been completely miserable this week."

"I probably shouldn't be happy about that, should I? You know what they say about misery loving company."

She laughed. "You could show a little compassion for my suffering."

"That's something you'll have to help me work on. That whole compassion thing you do so well."

"I'll do my best," she promised.

His features grew serious and he drew away a little. "I'm not the greatest bargain out there, Julie. I can't lie about that. I've still got some things to work through that might take some time. You and I both know you could probably do a whole lot better."

"No, I couldn't. There is no one better." She pressed her mouth to his again and poured every ounce of the love flowing through her into the kiss.

When she drew away, they were both breathing hard. "You are a wonderful man, Ross Fortune. The best man I know. I think I fell in love with you that first night, too, when I saw how concerned you were for everyone else around you but yourself. For Frannie, for Josh. You were even worried about me, and you didn't even know me then. You're good and decent and honorable, Ross. The kind of man a woman knows in her heart will watch out for her and protect her and do everything he can to make her happy."

"You make me want to be all those things and more."

He lifted her until she was sitting on his lap, her arms still wrapped tightly around the strong column of his neck.

"And just so you know," he said, his voice just a whisper against her skin, "you're it for me, Julie. This might be my first time falling in love but it's also my *only* time."

She fought back the sting of tears again and kissed him softly in the pale, lavender light, wondering how she had been blessed enough to love and be loved by two such completely different men.

A tiny part of her heart would always mourn Chris and all the possibilities that had been extinguished too soon. But she was more than ready to move forward, to take this incredible chance she had been given for happiness.

She had a sudden vision of a future with Ross, one that was bright and beautiful and shining with promise. She saw them taking on challenges and causes, opening their lives and their hearts to wounded children, filling their world with joy and laughter. A place where both of them would always feel safe and cherished and loved.

The image was as clear and as real as the huge, round moon beginning to gleam over the treetops. Only this was better.

Worlds better.

As beautiful as it might be, that moon was always just beyond their grasp. But Julie suddenly knew without a doubt that together, she and Ross would grab hold of their future and make it perfect.

* * * * *

THE FIVE-DAY REUNION

Mona Shroff

To Shakuntalaben and Vasantbhai Shroff,
whose love made sure I never had in-laws
but instead blessed me with a second set of parents.

Acknowledgments

This is my first Harlequin Special Edition book but actually the fourth book that I have written. And like the other three, it's never a solitary effort.

First, I'd like to thank editor Susan Litman for reaching out and offering me this incredible opportunity. Anytime someone comes to you and says they enjoy your writing enough to ask you to do more is fabulous. As always, my incredible agent, Rachel Brooks, has been encouraging and supportive and protective and wonderful, and I truly appreciate her for all of that and more!

Ishara Deen and Shaila Patel helped me flesh out Nikhil's and Anita's characters and their growth, which is always such a wonderful thing. You both are incredible! Thanks also to Angelina M. Lopez, who gave me the quickest turnaround ever on a first draft with helpful notes and thoughts. Christi Barth is a fabulous mentor and brainstormer and answered my cry of "What comes next?" in addition to giving me invaluable advice as I started writing my first series. These are all amazing writers and their support is priceless.

Thanks to my daughter and son for dealing with Deadline Mom even while they were visiting! My extended family and friends have not yet tired of me saying, "I can't, I'm on deadline!" and for that I love them!

And last but never least, love and thanks to my personal romantic hero, Deven, for patiently waiting for me to turn in my manuscripts and being equally excited every single time.

DAY ONE:

MEHNDI PATTERNS
Things that are hidden...

Chapter 1

Nikhil Joshi slipped the cream silk jabho top over his head. The soft material floated over his body. He fastened two of three buttons, leaving the topmost one on the collar undone, then ran a hand through his thick hair and proclaimed himself ready. His younger sister, Tina, was getting married, and today was the first of the five days of festivities. The rhythmic beating of the tabla and the fabulous aroma of contemporary Indian street food wafted up to his room from the kitchen downstairs.

The sounds of laughter and wedding music filled him with a mixture of anticipation and dread. His entire family had congregated in DC from India and various states for Tina's big week. He had to at least appear to be over Anita. Three years was long enough. He inhaled deeply and exhaled slowly.

His phone dinged, alerting him to a text from his agent.

His third book was to be released next week and his agent and publicist were plotting to fill every free moment he had to promote it. He needed to be available; there was no resting on the laurels of bestseller lists. Sure, that reputation helped, but each book was unique. Each book had the power to make or break him.

He would not be broken.

His agent, Chantelle Ellis, had just scheduled a livestream interview for him for tomorrow afternoon. She was sorry that it was so last-minute, yada yada, but he should do it. Could he sneak away from the festivities for an hour, hour and a half, max?

Nikhil hadn't even thought twice about taking the meeting. Work was work. If he was going to be successful, sacrifices needed to be made. How many times had he heard that from his mother over the years?

He glanced at the small picture of him and his father that he kept here on the nightstand. His dad would have loved all this. House full, people partying. At least Nikhil thought so, but it was getting harder and harder to remember him sometimes.

He tossed his phone on the bed and focused on getting ready to face the family and all their questions about his divorce.

The toughest interrogation would be from his recently widowed, elderly grandfather. Nikhil hadn't seen the patriarch of their family since his own wedding close to five years ago. Somehow, every time he'd tried to go to India to visit him, something else had always come up, and he'd been unable to make the trip. There was no way around that conversation. Just through.

He checked his phone again and sure enough there was an email from his publicist, confirming next week's tour schedule, which started on Monday, with a launch party at a local bookstore. This was what he'd been waiting for his whole life. He was finally reaching the level of success he needed to prove to his family that he wasn't a complete screwup. That he was worthy of the Joshi name.

And he'd done it on his own.

Without Joshi Family Law.

Nikhil slipped his phone into his pocket and left his childhood bedroom suite. It was time to allow the festive spirit to fill him as he joined the mass of people in the Joshi house. His sister's wedding was a time for elation and looking to new beginnings. No more reliving his past.

His mother's house was wall-to-wall people enjoying sumptuous food, with musicians playing the tabla and harmonium, a fabulous soundtrack for the event. Maybe it wouldn't be so bad.

Suddenly, he was smothered in hugs by his cousins Hiral and Sangeeta, who had just arrived from Delhi that afternoon. "Nikhil! Where have you been? We've been hanging out for over an hour!"

"I had a couple emails I needed to answer." He returned their hugs. It had been too long since he'd seen them.

Hiral clapped him on the back. "That's what it takes to get a bestseller, huh? We haven't seen you since your wedding, I think."

Nikhil froze. Why would they so casually mention his wedding? "What?"

"Like five years—"

"Well, Tina finally found someone who would put up with her, so…" Nikhil tried a smile.

His cousins looked behind him and around the crowded room. "We thought we just saw Anita-bhabhi, but she looked busy. We'll catch up with her later."

Nikhil furrowed his brow. How was that possible? There was no way they could have seen their former sister-in-law. Why were they even looking for her? He and Anita were divorced. Before he could question them about it, more cousins approached and Nikhil was lost in a sea of greetings and hugs and someone pushed a shot of tequila into his hands. They took turns toasting Tina and her fiancé, Jake, and tossed back the shots.

After another round, Nikhil broke free. "I want to see my sister while I can still walk."

Nikhil made his way through the large house, grabbing a spinach pakora from a tuxedoed waitress and popping it into his mouth. If appetizers were still being served, at least he hadn't missed dinner.

Tina was wearing a simple cotton blue chaniya choli as she had her mehndi done. She was seated in a chair in their largest living room, the mehndi artist beside her. The artist's hand was almost a blur as she applied the mehndi paste in an intricate pattern, using Tina's hands and feet as a canvas for her intricate art.

His sister's besties were seated on the ground around her as if she was a queen holding court, as opposed to a bride having her wedding mehndi applied. Maybe it was the same thing.

Joy filled and lightened him. His baby sister was a force to be reckoned with, and she'd found her equal in Jake. She quite literally glowed with happiness. He grabbed a tray of prosecco from a waiter and approached the circle of women, most of whom he'd known all their lives. They all laughed and accepted the drinks.

His mother was not among the women in the circle. Hmm. That was odd.

Nikhil made his way through to his sister.

She looked up at him, panic in her gray eyes. The mehndi certainly looked beautiful, but didn't seem to be relieving his sister's stress as it was purported to do. He grinned. "Hey, Teen." He put down the near-empty tray and squeezed her shoulder. "What do you look so worried about? Everything'll be fine."

She shook her head. "I'm sorry. I had no idea. I thought you'd be here earlier and I wanted to talk to you."

"I had to finish emails. And I know why you wanted to talk to me."

"You do?" Her already big gray eyes bugged out.

He nodded. "It's just now hitting you what a production a wedding can be." He shrugged. "I told you to try going to city hall like I did." He laughed and held a glass of prosecco out for her to sip. Not that his had lasted.

She looked at it longingly and then down at her mehndi-covered hands. "That's not it."

Nikhil chuckled. "Such a princess." But he held the glass to her mouth so she could take a sip.

She gulped at it like it was water and she was in a desert.

"Easy there, Butthead. You have five days to go."

Tears filled her eyes. "You have to believe me, Nikhil. I didn't know they were going to do this."

Small pricks of panic went through his body. "Who? Do what?"

She bent her head down. He knelt down close to her. "What are you talking about? And why are you crying?"

"*She's* here."

Nikhil had no idea what she was talking about. But the look on her face, the alarm in her eyes unsettled him. "Who is—"

"There you are, beta!" Seema Joshi's voice cut through the din. She was the mother of the bride, and her outfit reflected that to perfection. Her peach-colored sari was exquisitely wrapped, her hair was up and her delicate jewelry sparkled. Nikhil looked away from his sister to see his mother grinning too widely, her eyes too sparkly.

His stomach roiled. Something was clearly up. This was not good.

"Come and say hello to your grandfather. He just got here," his mother called.

Nikhil glanced at Tina. Her eyes were wide, and she bit her bottom lip. His entire being went into high alert as he approached his mother. As he reached her, his heart nearly fell into his stomach.

Standing behind his mother, looking drop-dead gorgeous in a simple peacock blue sari, her black hair in a high, sleek ponytail, amber eyes wide, was none other than Anita Virani.

His ex-wife.

From the look on Nikhil's face, it was clear that he had not expected to see her here. Anita widened her eyes at her former mother-in-law, shocked that she hadn't told her son about the ruse. She hadn't intended to bombard Nikhil with her presence.

She met Nikhil's eyes, trying to communicate intuitively that she hadn't intended to surprise him in this way, at the same time willing him to play along as she smiled as big as she could. "Sweetheart! I've been looking all over for you. Dada—" she paused for emphasis, hoping Nikhil would see the light "—has just arrived from the airport and has been asking to see us, and I didn't want to go without you."

There was nothing of the kindness she had come to love in his face. Instead, she was met with hard, cold eyes, lips pressed together in muted anger and a clenched jaw. Much the same expression she'd seen on his face frequently in their last days and months as a married couple.

Her hands shook and heat flushed her face as she reached for his arm. He flinched at her touch, inexplicably sinking her heart into her belly. She should not care about his reaction. After all, she had been the one who left.

No matter. She gently threaded her arm through his, continuing her silent, eye-based communication that did not really seem to be working.

"Dada wants to see us," she repeated, squeezing his bicep to steady her hand. Which was worse? Nikhil knowing she was shaking, or squeezing an arm that was so familiar yet foreign it broke her heart? Didn't matter. She'd made her choice three years ago and she made her choice now. *"Together."* She tilted her head toward his mother and tightened her lips. Help would be great right now, since she clearly had avoided this conversation as well.

Seema-auntie used one of her powerful move-it-mom looks, which worked no matter the age of the child. Anita hoped it worked on her children like that someday. Should she ever have any. She and Nikhil had talked about children, but that seemed very far away now.

Nikhil looked down at Anita, his eyes narrowed. He smelled exactly like she remembered. Same cologne, same underlying masculine scent that had given her comfort so many times. She nudged him forward, hand still squeezing his bicep. Was it bigger than she remembered? Well, no matter now. Actual explanations would have to wait.

Right now, they were on. The happily married couple.

As they followed his mother through the small mansion, the party continued around them. Aromas of Indian street food made her stomach growl. Loud voices and laughter competed with the tabla and harmonium. Nikhil grabbed a cocktail from a passing waiter.

Anita eyed his drink with envy. Alcohol would be fabulous right about now. There had been a time when he would have grabbed a drink for her as well, but clearly, that time was behind them. The flash of sadness that swept through her was fleeting, but familiar. It happened whenever she thought about Nikhil, which was more often than she should.

Anita remembered Dada from her own wedding. He had been a strong force, full of vibrant energy and opinions. He had stood a solid six feet, had always maintained fitness in his body as well as in his mind. His laugh had been infectious, wrinkling his dark brown skin, and rumbling from deep within. He'd had a full head of white hair which had strongly resembled Nikhil's in its unruliness.

As they approached him, the toll of his sickness and grief became apparent. Dada had lost some weight, making him appear frail and weak just as her former mother-in-law had told her. Anita sighed with relief when the old man's dark eyes lit up with amusement upon seeing them. When she had really been married to Nikhil, she and Dada had bonded almost immediately, giving her the comfort of family that she craved.

It was the first time she was really glad she'd agreed to do this.

Even if it was a lie.

She and Nikhil bowed down to touch his feet. Dada placed his hand on their heads in blessing and motioned for them to sit. Nikhil sat in the chair next to his grandfather without so much as glancing at Anita. It was the only chair. Dada steeled Nikhil with a sharp look.

"Beta, let Anita sit. Don't be rude."

Nikhil pressed his lips together and forced a smile as he stood. "Of course."

Anita was unprepared for the pain and sadness that accompanied his anger as he made eye contact with her. He had once looked at her as if she were his entire world. Now he looked at her as if she'd ruined it. Well, maybe she had.

She tore her gaze from Nikhil and smiled at his grandfather as she sat down.

"Ah. That's wonderful." Dada-ji beamed. "Tell me. What are you both doing with your lives these days?"

She leaned toward him, squeezing his hand. "I'm so sorry about Dadi, and I'm sorry I haven't called you. I really have no good excuse."

Dada squeezed her hand back. "Thank you, beti. Your mother-in-law passed on your sympathies."

"You must miss her," Anita said softly.

"That, I do." His voice was rough with grief, and his eyes turned down briefly before he squeezed her hand again and made eye contact. "If she were here, she would want to know why you two haven't given us great-grandchildren."

And there it was. The first of the million times she bet she would hear that question over the next five days.

Nikhil's handsome face darkened. "Come now, Dada. You know better than to bring up such things." He glanced at Anita, his expression unreadable. "Anita and I aren't even—"

"Ready just yet," Anita cut in. "We're busy with our careers." She sharpened her gaze at Nikhil. *Play. Along.*

He narrowed his eyes at her, but nodded to his grandfather.

"Dada," Anita continued brightly, "you know Nikhil published a second book and is getting ready to go on tour for his third." So maybe she'd followed his career. It didn't mean anything. She paused, looking him in the eye.

"Seema told me that you are finishing your second year of law school. And you are working at the local legal aid center. A fantastic way to get started." Whether Dada had noted her glare at her "husband" or not, he dropped the baby subject and beamed at her. "I did something similar when I was a young barrister in India."

Anita saw clear as day the disappointment that flashed across Nikhil's face as Dada made no mention whatsoever of his accomplishments. He covered it quickly, and most people probably didn't notice.

But she did.

Seema-auntie arrived with a plate of food for her father. Anita stood. "Here, let me take that." Nikhil's mother gave her a tight smile and handed her the plate.

"Mom, come with me, I have to show you something in the kitchen." Nikhil glared at his mother.

Anita stood between them, the tension building like waves around them.

"I'm busy just now." She fussed over her father.

"It's really important," Nikhil spoke through gritted teeth and stared his mother down.

"I can sit with Dada—" Anita made eye contact with Nikhil's mother and forced out the next word "—Mom." She hadn't used it in years. She smiled at the older man. "I want to hear his stories."

"Actually, *dear*—" Nikhil narrowed his eyes at her "—it's wedding stuff. I need you both."

Dada, apparently oblivious to the tension, focused on his food. "I'm old. I'm not an invalid. I can eat on my own. Besides, the whole family is here." He gestured with his hand. "Go. Take care of your business."

Anita walked beside Nikhil, the backs of their hands brushing together, electrifying her. He still had that effect on her. She took this opportunity to really look at him. To try to glean from his face and body what he had been up to for the past three years. He towered head and shoulders over her. His cream silk jabho complemented his dark skin, and conformed to his muscles quite nicely. He was bigger than she'd remembered. But they had still been practically children back then. He was clean-shaven, as always, which allowed her to see exactly how hard he was clenching his jaw. He'd need emergency dental work if he kept that up.

Nikhil stopped at the door of his mother's study, opening it to allow them to enter. Anita had always loved this room. She inhaled deeply and the scent of the books lining two of the walls calmed her nerves, if only just a bit. She remembered all of the books she'd read from this library and then discussed later with Nikhil. It had been one of their favorite things to do.

Anita was just about to shut the door when Nikhil's older brother, Rocky, slipped in. He raised his eyebrows at her in surprise, then smiled at her. She smiled back— finally a friendly face. She shut the door and found Nikhil glaring at the two of them. He turned to the room and boomed, "What the hell is going on here?"

Chapter 2

"Language, beta." Nikhil's mother was the picture of calm. Her accent was slight, but still present. She straightened her sari, patted her hair.

Rocky was standing next to Anita, grinning, and Nikhil had an overwhelming urge to punch him for doing so.

"Ma!"

His mother sighed magnificently. "Fine. I would think it was obvious. My father doesn't know you're divorced. So, I asked Anita to come to the wedding and behave as though she was still married to you." She spoke as if Anita wasn't standing right there.

He caught Rocky shaking his head in the periphery. What the hell was he doing here?

He stared at his mother, incredulity seeping into him. He allowed himself a moment to pass his gaze over his ex-wife as if to confirm she was actually there. It quickly returned to his mother as if gazing at Anita had scorched him. Which it had.

"What do you mean they don't know we're divorced?"

His mother shifted uncomfortably. "I couldn't tell them at the time."

From the corner of his eye, Nikhil saw Anita fidget with her wedding rings. The magnitude of his mother's words hit him as the diamonds glinted in the dimly lit room. "Wait, *what*?"

"I knew they would be disappointed, so I kept putting it off. It was humiliating to admit to a divorce in the family. It reflects badly—and could have made it difficult for Tina to get married."

Nikhil clenched his jaw harder. Of course it would be all about how his failed marriage reflected on them.

"Before I knew it, a couple years had passed. Then Dadi passed and Dada had his heart attack." She paused and swallowed. "I just didn't think he could handle it. Now Tina is getting married—and since she's marrying a non-Indian, it's a good thing my father did not know about the divorce."

That didn't sound right. Dada would not have a problem with a non-Indian. But the divorce? Maybe.

She turned away and threw up her arms as she sat down in the large leather seat. "At least Jake is a lawyer. It was the one saving grace."

"Well, that seems to fix everything, doesn't it?" He shot an accusatory look in Anita's direction even as he flushed.

"It'll never work." Rocky wore a cocky smirk.

"Dad would never agree to this," Nikhil shot back.

"Well, he's not here, is he?" His mother's voice softened. "What was I supposed to do, Rakesh? Tell my father that Nikhil was divorced?" His mother spoke to her older son as if Nikhil wasn't even the room.

"What does it matter? Dada doesn't expect Nicky to fall into line. He always does whatever he wants anyway." Rocky knew Nikhil hated the use of that nickname, but he used it anyway—most likely on purpose.

"Your grandfather would be humiliated, knowing there was a divorce in the family," their mother insisted.

"Not if it was Nicky," Rocky said.

They were literally talking about him like he wasn't even in the room. It was choosing colleges all over again. Back then, Nikhil had gone against everything Rocky and his mom had suggested. He had stayed local and attended University of Maryland as an English major.

Nikhil felt himself flush. None of this was anything he hadn't heard before. He was the one who didn't fall in line, or follow the rules, or become a lawyer. Or stay married. He stared straight ahead, as though he could feel Anita's eyes on him.

"And with Tina getting married before him…" She shrugged and finally turned toward Nikhil. "It's just five days."

"What about your friends?" Nikhil asked.

"I only told my closest circle. They know to just go along. Most people think you are still married. Just too busy to attend the parties, et cetera." She glanced at Anita and a small smile came over her face. "It is good to see you, beti."

"She's not your beti anymore," Nikhil snapped.

"Nikhil!"

"It was her choice, Ma." He stared straight ahead at his mother, but he might as well have reached out and pointed a finger at her. Without turning his head, he knew Anita had lifted her chin in defiance.

His mother waved a dismissive hand. "I honestly did not think Dada's health would allow for him to make it to the wedding, until he called a few days ago to say he could make it after all."

Rocky opened his mouth again. "No way Nicky's going to be able to pull off an act like that. He doesn't have the savvy for it."

Nikhil fired up at his brother. "I have the savvy for it just fine. It's just that it's ridiculous." He turned to his mother. "You're lying to your dad. And you want me to do the same." He leaned toward her. "I'm not doing this. Either you tell him, or I will."

His mother was unfazed. "Nikhil! This is not about me. He's my father and he is close to being on oxygen, for god's sake. A divorce in the family would…*crush* him. He would never get over the humiliation. He would never be able to get over the fact that people were talking ill about you."

"But doesn't the rest of the family know?" This wasn't happening. This kind of thing happened in soap operas, not real life. Besides, the family had been talking about him since he was a child. The middle kid, never quite as good at things as his older brother, the golden child, never quite as accomplished as even his younger sister.

Nikhil had had little interest in grades, preferring to play with his friends, or read books or get in trouble. As he got older, it became apparent that he had no interest in the family business, and that was the last straw.

Rocky lived for the law, and Joshi Family Law would be his someday. He had also found an amazing woman to marry him. Easha was a brilliant lawyer, abundantly kind, and an all-around lovely person. Nikhil couldn't believe Rocky was lucky enough to meet someone like her.

Out of the corner of his eye—because that's all he could give her—he saw Anita take a step back.

"Well, beta…" His mother continued her confession.

Nikhil froze and scanned the room as if looking for answers. Clarity dawned. Hiral and Sangeeta. And all their other cousins. This wasn't a soap opera; it was a sitcom. Except it wasn't that funny. "You never told *anyone* I was divorced, did you? When you say closest circle, who is that even?" He racked his brain for a moment, recalling their meeting with Dada and coming here to this room. Realization hit him hard. "*No one* was surprised to see her here."

He finally turned to Anita to face her head-on. "You knew about this?" The question burned through him. Looking at her head-on had him slightly off-kilter. Maybe because he hadn't seen her in a while, but even in his mounting anger, she was more beautiful than he remembered.

Anita shook her head, amber eyes ablaze. "Seriously? How could I possibly know what your mother told people?"

He paced the office for a moment to gather himself, before turning back to his family. "No." He shook his head. "I'm going to go tell Dada the truth, that she and I are no longer together." It was too hard to even say her name. "I'll make an announcement. Tell everyone at the same time." *Damn.* It was like getting divorced all over again.

"Subtle," his brother mumbled.

His mother paled. "Please think about what you're proposing to do. You will make a scene."

"What did you think he was going to do, Mom? Nicky always does whatever he damn well pleases." Rocky pursed his lips at him.

Nikhil tried to ignore his brother.

"Think about your sister," his mother implored.

He threw his hand out in a dismissive fashion. "Don't use her against me." She was the only one he would reconsider for, and his mother knew it. "Besides, they'll find out anyway. Our friends know."

"That's like maybe ten people out of the hundreds that will be attending," Anita finally spoke up. "If we get to them first, then it shouldn't be a problem."

Why the hell was she so invested in this? "How did they get you to do this?" He turned to face her again, this time braced for the impact of seeing her. He hadn't seen her in over three years. Maryland law required them to live apart for a year before they filed for divorce. They never tried to see each other during that first year. Things were said, they were who they were and they couldn't be together. She had walked out, and that was the last he'd seen of her.

And sure enough, a year to the day that she had moved out, he was served with papers. Anger had made him sign them and send them off. Any second thoughts he might have had were crumpled up and stored in the back of his mind.

She looked him in the eye, calm and confident. "I could tell you that it was to protect Dada, but that would only be part of the reason." She glanced at his mother, and lifted her chin before turning back to him. "Your mother is helping me with my law school tuition."

Nikhil felt like he'd been punched in the gut; acid and bile churned. Of course. She was one of them. Seeing her in person for the first time in years, that sari hugging her curves just so, her voice with that unnamable soothing quality that he'd always found irresistible, he'd forgotten for a moment who she had turned out to be.

He remembered now.

She had tried to return the engagement and wedding rings to him when she had collected her things, but he didn't want them back. They were hers. And always would be.

"If we get to them first? Are you listening to yourself?"

"What? A group text and it's done. 'Dada doesn't know about the divorce. Pretend Neets and I are still married.' Simple." She froze as she used his nickname for her. Clearly it had not been intended.

He shook his head. "This is crazy. I'm telling him." He stormed out of the study with every intention of finding his grandfather and telling him the truth. Lies never worked. He'd find out eventually. This was real life. Not a sitcom.

His mother's sari rustled softly behind him as she followed as closely as she could without running. Without creating a scene.

He knew Anita was with her because he could smell her perfume. Its familiarity was like drifting into the past. He fought it.

Nikhil found the tabla player and whispered something. The bearded young man handed over his mic.

He caught sight of his mother at the front of the crowd, gripping his ex-wife's arm. His. *Ex.* Wife. Rocky was on her other side, his mouth smashed together, su-

periority oozing from every cell in his body. Rocky
glanced down at Anita, shaking his head, secure in the
knowledge that Nikhil would once again screw things
up.

"Hey, everybody! If you'll excuse the interruption,
I need a moment of your attention."

A hush fell over the assembled crowd of friends and
relatives as everyone gave him their attention. Tina sat
stiff and helpless as her brother took center stage.

"I'm Nikhil, one of Tina's brothers, and I just have
an announcement to make."

Anita's gaze met his and she gave a slight shake of
her head, glancing toward the corner with her eyes. He
looked over to see his grandfather sitting next to his
cousin Sangeeta. The man was still distinguished at
eighty-eight, still a force to be reckoned with. But what
Nikhil saw here was a much older, almost delicate version of that powerhouse. He saw an old man—frailer
than he remembered—surrounded by his family, beaming with pride as he looked around and chatted with his
grandchildren, and even one great-grand. The fruits of
his lifetime.

Nikhil caught Anita's eye and something inside him
jumped.

Nikhil did not speak for a minute. If he did, the truth
would be revealed. Dada really did look frail enough
to have another heart attack. And the reality was that
his mother was right. Dada would be humiliated that
there had been a divorce in the family. Whatever his
parents and brother said about him, Nikhil had a special
place in his heart for his grandfather, and his grandfather for him. Not to mention, that bond had extended

to Anita, and if nothing else, Nikhil knew Anita adored his grandfather.

Damn it.

"The truth…is I didn't think any guy would ever be able to put up with my sister." He turned to Tina and winked as laughter erupted. "And any guy who would want her, wouldn't have been good enough for her anyway." Laughter rang through the house. "But Jake is an incredible person. And you know that's true because I'm saying it and he isn't even here." More laughter. "The important thing is that he loves my sister." He smiled at Tina, his gaze passing over Anita briefly. He turned and whispered to the musicians, who began playing an old Hindi song about brothers and sisters. Nikhil stepped closer to the mic, his eyes on his sister, and began to sing.

Anita fell in love with Nikhil's written words first. Then his chai—hands down, he made the best chai she'd ever had. He had never revealed his secret, but after trying it just once, Anita only drank Nikhil's chai.

But it was his voice that sealed the deal.

His voice was as angsty and rich as she remembered, and a flush hit her cheeks as she recalled the love songs he used to sing to her.

Their first date had come after weeks of getting to know each other, and she remembered that exhilaration, the excitement of finally being able to go out with him. They had gone to dinner, then back to his place. She woke in the morning to the sound of Nikhil singing as he had prepared her breakfast.

He had been singing an old Hindi love song, his voice soft and unassuming, almost as if he didn't even realize he was singing. Anita couldn't imagine a better sound to wake up to. He had flushed slightly when he found her watching him.

"You sing."

He shrugged. "I don't even notice I'm doing it half the time."

"Your voice is…heart melting." Her heart had raced at showing her vulnerability.

But he had simply handed her a mug of that incredible chai, kissed her and returned to breakfast prep and his singing.

All of that came rushing back to her as she took in his beautiful voice, as he sang a classic Bollywood song about the enduring bond of brothers and sisters.

As he continued singing to his sister, she remembered how she had seen his affection for Tina when they'd first started dating. She'd thought that any guy who loved his sister like that was worth being with. For a moment, she allowed herself to remember how it felt to love and be loved by him.

Once the song was over, his gaze landed on hers and for a brief second, she could have sworn some love shone through, but before she could fully grasp it, his dark eyes hardened, and she clearly remembered why she had left.

She'd had no other choice.

Chapter 3

Tina separated herself from her circle of besties and made her way to her brother, encircling her arms around him, trying not to smush the still-drying mehndi on her hands, now covered in plastic.

She stood on tiptoe and he bent down to her.

"I'm sorry, Nikhil. I had no idea until this morning…"

"It's fine." He pulled back and smiled at her. They were only a year and a bit apart, but he always thought of her as his little sister. "Really. It'll be okay. It's for Dada, right?"

His sister, his rock, nodded. "Dada is the best. And I have always loved that song."

He glanced behind her at Anita.

Tina followed his gaze. "You going to be okay hanging out with her all weekend?"

He shrugged. "It's just five days."

Tina nodded, but concern furrowed her brow. When he and Anita split, Tina had been the one who checked on him every day. Made sure he ate. He'd tried to hide his misery, but Tina had always seen right through him.

"Well," he said, grinning at her, "lucky for me, this is not a dry wedding." He grabbed a drink from a passing waiter and stepped back from his sister. "Don't worry about me. You have bride things to do—whatever they might be." He shooed her back to her friends, and glanced to where Anita stood chatting with Jake's mother and sister.

He grabbed a second drink and walked over to her. Might as well get the show on the road. "Hey…" *Sweetheart. Honey. Neets.* The endearments wouldn't come. He held out the second drink for her. "I got you a drink." He smiled at her, hoping he was convincing. "I see you've met Jake's mother and his sister." Nikhil leaned over and hugged Christi Collins. "Really good to see you, Mrs. Collins."

"You too, Nikhil." She smiled warmly at Anita. "You'll meet the rest of the family at the rehearsal dinner tomorrow."

"I look forward to it." Anita smiled at Mrs. Collins as someone else approached her.

She grinned at Nikhil and took the drink. He thought he saw gratitude flit across her features. But it was gone before he could confirm it. "Thanks…" She sipped. "Just what I needed."

"You two are the cutest." His cousin Sangeeta came bounding up to them, drink in hand. She was easily twenty-six years old, but she bubbled over with energy. Sangeeta's mom, Neepa, and Nikhil's mom were sisters. "Ohh! You two should renew your vows on your fifth anniversary—you know, since you never had a whole big wedding thing! That would be such fun."

"Oh no. That's not necessary. Mom had a fabulous reception—" Anita started to say, darting a glance at him.

"But half of us couldn't make it," Sangeeta insisted. "Since you married at city hall and then Seema-masi had a last-minute party." She nearly pouted. "But no worries. I'll plan it with my mom and Seema-masi. We'll even get Deepa-masi to help." She hurried off, leaving Nikhil and Anita alone.

Their fifth anniversary would have been next month. They looked at each other and sipped their drinks, the silence between them thick with unsaid words. Better that way.

Thankfully, his phone buzzed. He grabbed it like a drowning man grabs a life preserver. His publicist, confirming that he was good to go for his launch next week. "I have to take this."

"Sure." Anita shrugged. "Whatever." She stepped away to give him space and was immediately approached by some of his mother's friends.

Nikhil downed his drink and stared after her for a moment, then turned away and opened the text.

Anita sipped her drink and made small talk with the extended family and friends. She remembered most of them and found it surprisingly easy to fill in the gap of the past three years with general answers. The most popular question was about children. Those questions might have been annoying had she been married— seriously, who was she kidding? She wanted children eventually, but even so, the questions about her reproductive state were irritating.

Her former in-laws had excellent taste, and demanded the best in everything, including the liquor they selected, so her Manhattan was incredible. As were her surroundings. She'd always loved this house despite its large size, because she'd imagined it filled with people for parties and gatherings, just like this.

Her parents had enjoyed entertaining, and they had been the type to cook everything at home—no catering in the Virani household. It's how she and her brother learned how to cook. The four of them would plan the menu based on the guest list and then map a plan of execution for the big day.

She missed planning those parties. Her brother, Amar, still cooked—it was his job after all. But being in the family kitchen was never the same for her, after... everything. She cooked to feed herself, but ate anywhere but in the kitchen. Her brother basically lived in the kitchen. She gave herself a little shake to bring herself back to the moment, plastering a smile on her face. *Focus, Anita.*

The house she grew up in was hardly at this level, however.

Not only were she and Nikhil staying here, but so were Rocky and Easha, their cousin Hiral and his fiancée, Meeta, Sangeeta, and Seema-auntie's sisters and, of course, Dada.

Nikhil had never particularly enjoyed being here, but they'd had dinner here every Sunday evening as per his mother. It was the one day a week that the whole family sat down together. Nikhil had told her they had been doing it since his father was alive, and his mother didn't see any reason for it to stop just because her children were grown. It was the only time that all devices were nowhere near them, and they talked to each other. It was the one time that JFL was not a priority, if only for an hour or two.

Anita had reveled in the feeling of family, but Nikhil had always been tense and gruff at these dinners, itching to fulfil his duty and leave.

The bourbon warmed her body and relaxed her muscles as it soothed down her throat. She hadn't realized how tense she'd been. It had seemed harmless enough when Auntie had asked her to do this, but now, in Nikhil's presence, and everyone expecting them to be this happily married couple, it became quite real.

Nikhil returned after answering his text, a fresh drink in his hand. He stood next to her, with enough of a gap between them that only the air around them touched. But Anita felt that air solidly.

"Here comes Neepa-masi." She nodded as one of his mother's older sisters approached. She slipped her hand into his and tightened her grip against his instinct to pull back. She put on her best oh-my-god-I'm-happy-to-see-you smile. "Hi, Neepa-masi! It has been too long. You must be so excited about Hiral and Meeta's wedding."

"We are very excited." Neepa-masi's answers were always measured. It had always seemed to Anita that Neepa-masi was not a fan of enthusiasm. "Seema has managed to arrange things beautifully." She drew her gaze around the room. "Even though she claims to be so busy with the business."

Anita nodded and forced a smile. "Well, Mom has always planned beautiful events, even with running JFL." She shouldn't care about the slight. After all,

Seema Joshi was no longer her mother-in-law. But she did care. She was simply playing the part, she told herself. "I would expect every attention to every detail, Neepa-masi. You know how particular Mom can be."

Neepa-masi nodded and glanced at Nikhil, her eyes scanning their clasped hands. She seemed to nod with satisfaction. "So good to see you both here. Law school is so demanding, Anita, but it's good to take a break and spend time with family."

"Of course, Neepa-masi," Anita answered.

"You will be coming to Virginia for Hiral and Meeta's wedding, of course." It was a statement, an order. Anita was struck by the differences in the two sisters. And the similarities.

"Of course, Masi. We wouldn't miss it for anything." Anita couldn't stop herself.

Nikhil squeezed her hand. She was making promises she knew she wouldn't keep. But she couldn't give Neepa-masi the satisfaction of knowing she wouldn't be at Hiral's wedding. Neepa-masi would not miss the opportunity to lord it over her younger sister.

"Well, maybe by then you two will have some good news for us." She gave Anita a meaningful look. "I'm sure my little sister would love to be a dadi."

They both froze for an instant, with no response. Neepa-masi grinned and walked away.

No sooner had Seema turned her back on them than Anita let go of Nikhil's hand. No need to touch him any longer than was necessary. A waiter passed and Nikhil exchanged his empty glass for another. He raised an eyebrow at her.

"Oh hell yes. Please." She placed her empty on the

waiter's tray and Nikhil grabbed her another drink. He took a huge gulp of his.

"Easy there. It's five days." Anita glanced at his bourbon.

"Whatever."

Anita shrugged. "It's your hangover."

That was their first direct interaction with each other.

They walked around together, saying hello to guests as they would have if they had been a real couple. It was actually a relief to be forced to socialize, since Anita had no idea what she would say to Nikhil if they were alone.

Anita was quite surprised Nikhil was going along with the ruse, given how angry he'd been a few hours ago. After an hour or so, they found themselves alone on the patio, everyone having gone in to eat.

Nikhil's phone buzzed and he pulled it out and started typing.

"Wow. Working at your sister's wedding," Anita deadpanned.

Nikhil arched an eyebrow and glanced at her from beneath his shock of black hair. It would have been sexy if it hadn't been accompanied by a grimace. "Work is work. You know that. It's basically the Joshi family motto. Or did you forget?" He went back to his text.

"I didn't forget. I'm just surprised *you* adapted to that particular family motto."

Nikhil stopped typing and turned his full attention on her. "I *am* a member of this family."

Disappointment flooded Anita. "So you are."

Nikhil put his phone away and shrugged. "However, the truth is if you're not a lawyer around here, you have no value."

Anita had noticed that the guests' conversations were primarily directed at her and law school. "At least they aren't bombarding you with the best times to have a baby."

He raised his eyebrows at her. "Says you."

"Shut up, people are telling you when to have a baby?"

He shrugged. "Not exactly. They're wondering how we will make it work when you're in school and so busy as a lawyer." He turned away and mumbled. "As if I didn't exist. As if I couldn't take care of my own child while my wife worked."

"You know we're not really married or considering having a baby, right?"

He side-eyed her.

"So what does it matter what they say?"

He looked at her, his eyes narrowed. "Are you saying it's not getting to you?"

Anita sipped her drink and looked away. It did bother her, but maybe not for the same reasons it annoyed Nikhil. She did want a family one day, and every time people asked, she was reminded of exactly how far from having that family she was. Further now that she had walked out on her marriage.

"Right." He nodded and downed his drink. "That's what I thought."

"Come on, you two. Dinner." Hiral called them in. "Your honeymoon's been over for years. Give it a rest."

Nikhil jutted his chin at his cousin with what Anita clearly read as a forced smile, and motioned Anita into the house by placing his hand at the small of her back. She tensed from the sudden intimacy, and, at her flinch, he pulled his hand away and simply followed Anita through the door.

The enticing aromas of Indian street food circulated in the air, a backdrop for the laughter, chatter and music of the celebration. A buffet of chaat, frankies and pav bhaji tempted the guests. Hiral introduced Meeta to Anita and handed them each a plate.

Anita grabbed a frankie and scoop of chaat, while chatting with Meeta. The guys filled their plates, and the four of them found a place to sit. Hiral grabbed a bottle of bourbon and some glasses from the bar and brought it to them.

They drank and ate and laughed, and Anita almost felt like she'd never left, except for the fact that Nikhil kept avoiding her gaze, where at one time, making eye contact across a crowded room was their most intimate form of foreplay.

"You know, I have heard so much about you from Hiral and Sangeeta, I feel like I know you. I can't wait for you to come to Virginia for our wedding. I love that you and Tina are so close. We're all going to be like sisters—I just know it!" Meeta pronounced.

Anita smiled and nodded, unable to bring the lie out. She and Tina had been close, but Anita lost her in the divorce. Meeta was amazing, and Anita knew if she had the chance she could be close to her—but she wasn't really part of the family, was she? She had given up her place.

"Well, that would be interesting, wouldn't it?" Tina appeared behind Meeta, passing a hard gaze over Anita.

Meeta grinned, oblivious to the tension. "Yes! It's going to be great!"

Nikhil stood. "Have a seat, Princess Bride. I'll get you some food."

Tina took Nikhil's vacated seat on the sofa, turning her body slightly away from Anita, while she chatted wedding plans with her cousins. She stiffly held out her mehndi-covered hands so as not to ruin the artist's hard work while the paste dried.

"Let's not forget Nikhil and Anita-bhabhi's five-year anniversary party next month." Sangeeta joined them with her plate towering with food. "I mentioned it to Mom, and she thinks it's a great idea. Kind of extending your wedding celebration, Tina."

Tina raised an eyebrow at Anita. "You agreed to this?"

"Why wouldn't she?" Sangeeta asked.

"Bhabs is not really the party type," Tina explained stiffly.

"She doesn't have to be," Sangeeta continued. "She just has to keep loving Nikhil-bhai. I'll do the rest."

Anita shrugged. There was no reining Sangeeta in.

Nikhil arrived with a plateful of food. Anita scooted over to make room for him next to Tina. He sat and held out a frankie sandwich for Tina. She bit into it and groaned.

"Oh my god. Soo good."

Nikhil smiled. "Here—try this." He held out a spoonful of the chaat.

Tina's eyes widened. "Amazing!"

Nikhil continued to feed his sister, all the while calling her a princess, although his love for her was apparent even in his teasing.

"I don't remember this caterer," Tina said.

"Yes, you do." Nikhil rolled his eyes. "We tasted the food."

"Yeah, but this is way better than what we sampled at the tasting." Tina closed her eyes and continued to chew. "No way this is Taj's usual spread."

Anita froze. "Who?"

"Taj. You know—" Nikhil started to say.

"Oh, I know." She widened her eyes at him, and as if the universe hadn't messed with her enough, a familiar and slightly unwelcome voice called to her.

"Anita? Is that you?"

Anita closed her eyes and inhaled before popping up from her seat and going to greet Sonny Pandya before he could come to her. He had on a navy chef's jacket with "Taj" embroidered on the breast and was carrying a small tray of samosas. She had gone on one date with Sonny a month or so ago, and while he was a lovely person, there hadn't been any sparks. Anita simply wasn't interested in him that way. And he wasn't getting the hint.

"Hey, Sonny. What are you doing here?" She walked away from the group.

"Your brother and I are helping Taj with this wedding." He looked over her shoulder. "Isn't that your ex-husband?"

"Yes, well. It's complicated."

"You never answered my texts after our date. I was hoping—"

"Hi, honey." Nikhil came over and dropped his hand on her shoulder and kissed her cheek. She flushed and froze.

"Hi."

"Oh, hi. I'm Nikhil, her husband." Nikhil extended his hand to Sonny.

"You're still married?" Sonny's eyebrows shot up and in the next instant they furrowed. "I'm confused. Amar said you were divorced. And you went out with me…" He looked from Anita to Nikhil and back.

Anita felt Nikhil's body tense next to her. She lowered her voice. "Well, we are divorced. I did not lie to you, Sonny. It's just—"

"We're back together," Nikhil laughed. "And I'm jumping the gun by hoping we'll get—" he cleared his throat "—well, remarried." He squeezed Anita, drawing her closer to him. "Right, honey?" He looked at her. They had never once called each other *honey*. And now he'd said it twice in as many minutes.

"Yep. That's right. Jumping the gun." She nodded at Sonny. "But yes, we are giving it another chance."

"Oh. That's why you didn't respond to my texts."

"Right. And I probably should have just come clean, but you know how it is when you're not sure where something is going…" Anita nodded at him.

"Sure." Sonny nodded, looking slightly sad. "Well, okay then. I should get back to work."

"Um, so, Sonny…" Anita threw a furtive glance at Nikhil. "We don't have to mention this to my brother—"

"Anita?"

She tensed and closed her eyes again, Nikhil withdrew his arm. This voice belonged to her brother.

"What are you doing here?"

"Hey, Amar!" She brightened up as if this was just a funny coincidence. "Imagine seeing you here! Though Sonny here was just telling us how you both were helping Taj with this wedding."

Amar looked from Sonny to Anita, his gaze landing on Nikhil and their proximity to one another.

"Amar, I wish you'd told me they were getting back together," Sonny said.

"What?" Amar's already big brown eyes nearly bugged out.

Anita widened her eyes to her brother to not blow it. But she was having less and less faith in her eyes' ability to communicate accurately. The universe must have had pity on her in that moment because a tuxedoed waiter approached them.

"Sonny. Boss needs you in the kitchen."

Sonny nodded and turned to Anita. "Good luck to you." He left.

"You two are getting back together?" Amar whispered loudly.

"Well, no. Not exactly," Anita began.

"Not exactly?" Amar's eyes were still bugged out, and a vein at his temple was starting to throb.

She pulled him aside, gesturing for Nikhil to follow. "We're faking being married, but then Nikhil told Sonny we were getting back together, which is actually helpful because he won't stop texting me. So now at least, that's taken care of." Anita spilled out the words quickly and smiled at her brother as if it all made complete sense. *Fake it till you make it.*

He stared at her. "Do I have to ask why you are faking being married?"

"Well, it seems my mother never told anyone we were divorced," Nikhil finally offered, but all the fun had left his voice.

"She *what*?" Amar raised his voice, then immediately lowered it again. "What do you mean?"

"I mean she didn't tell anyone, especially my grandfather. He recently had a heart attack, and she's afraid he's too frail to handle the truth," Nikhil said, his tone flat.

"That's ridiculous! And why is that Anita's problem?"

"Hey. This wasn't my idea. It was all my mom. Trust me, spending five days with my ex-wife isn't really what I'd call fun."

Anita fired up. "It's not a joy for me either."

"Then why are you here?" insisted Amar.

"Because…" She paused, glanced around. "It's like Nikhil said. Dada's health is bad."

"Anita." Amar frowned at her. "Still not your problem. It was hard enough—"

"Don't worry. She'll be fine." Nikhil's voice was bitter. "She's only here for tuition money. It's strictly business."

Amar's eyes bugged out. "Tuition? Anita, what the—"

"Hey, Virani. Boss needs you. Now." A waiter had come to get him.

Amar looked back at the waiter who had called him, then turned back to Anita. "This is not over, little sis."

"Whatever." Anita rolled her eyes. "Just don't tell Sonny."

Amar waved a dismissive hand at her as he walked away.

"Well, that went well, don't you think?" Nikhil said.

Anita threw him a withering look. "Let's just get through the next four days, huh? We don't have to actually like each other or anything—we simply have to act like we do."

"I can do that."

"Fine. Me too." Anita just needed to ignore how good it felt to have his arm around her and have him kiss her cheek.

It was going to be a long five days.

Chapter 4

Nikhil knew Anita's brother had never really been his biggest fan, even when they were married. Amar had always felt that Anita had married him too quickly. Her brother was a fan of taking things slow and steady.

Maybe he was onto something. Maybe if Nikhil and Anita had taken their time, they'd still be married. Or maybe they never would've gotten married to begin with.

He had no idea what had possessed him to tell that guy that he and Anita were back together. He'd had no idea that Anita was dating; maybe that's all it was. It couldn't have been because he was jealous. He'd been on a few dates. No second dates, just a few first dates, during which he either found himself bored or finding fault with the young woman. It was no surprise that he was the one with the problem, so he stopped subjecting perfectly wonderful young women to his unwarranted scrutiny.

He really was dreading the next few days here, pretending to be married to his ex-wife while his sister got married. Especially since it had felt nice to hold Anita for those few minutes. They still fit together, just so. Not to mention she smelled like citrus and flowers. And her skin was soft.

Stop. It was five days and then everyone would go their separate ways.

Frustrated, Nikhil signaled a passing server. He grabbed two cocktails from the woman's tray and handed one to Anita. "You're dating?" What could he say? He was a glutton for punishment.

Anita shrugged, still clearly thinking about her brother. "Not really. Sonny and Amar went to culinary school together. I guess Sonny was interested and asked Amar if I would be. I thought it couldn't hurt. You and I have been—divorced—for almost three years. So I went."

"And?" He couldn't help it—the curiosity was stabbing at him. He quickly gulped his drink.

"And nothing." She looked him in the eye, trying not to smile. "There was absolutely no chemistry." The smile broke through and she chuckled. "We have nothing in common except food—" She shook her head, tossing her ponytail a bit. "He's a very nice guy, but I just couldn't."

Nikhil chuckled along with her, an inexplicable feeling of relief coming over him.

"What about you?" She lifted one sari-draped shoulder. "Date much? Seeing anyone?" She sipped her drink.

He shrugged, looking into her amber eyes. He was

going to lie. He knew it even as the words came out. They didn't play games, but they were playing the ultimate game right now, so why not max it out? Why not make it appear as though he had moved on from her? "I do date," he heard himself saying. "Regularly."

Did her face fall? If it did, she masked it pretty quickly. He took a gulp of his very excellent Manhattan.

"Oh. Well, that's great. I'm happy for you." She took a sip of her drink. "Anybody…special?" Anita fidgeted with her rings as she widened her eyes, trying to appear nonchalant. It was her tell. She was nervous asking the question.

Warmth flooded through him, as he held her eyes, and this time he opted for honesty. "No. Not even close."

He thought relief flashed across her face, but his cousin was calling out to them.

"Hey, guys. Outside, impromptu dance party." Hiral came over to get them.

Nikhil chugged his Manhattan. It burned on the way down, tingling his limbs. "Let's do it." He followed Hiral toward the sound of the tabla outside and assumed that Anita followed him.

The live band had been enticed into singing a garba to great applause. Concentric circles were spontaneously formed as each circle did a different step. Garba was basically a line dance done in a circle. The outer circles did easier steps, while Nikhil and Anita always danced in the centermost circle, which featured the most challenging steps. The beat started slow, but steadily increased. The alcohol was starting to hit Nikhil, but he managed.

Then a blur of blue nearly hit his face as Anita's sari

flew while she danced next to him. He missed a step, bumping something, and the blue fell into him, falling.

Nikhil caught Anita midfall with one arm around her waist, before she hit the ground. He pulled her up toward him, her skin soft and cool beneath his hand.

Damn, but she felt great as he wrapped his other arm around her to steady her. Her breath came hard as he held her close, her smart and sexy mouth open as she tried to catch her breath.

She leaned into him, so their bodies touched, her beautiful eyes focused on his mouth.

The rhythm of the tabla faded into the background, and the laughter of the dancers blurred into the night.

There was only Anita in his arms. Things were spinning, and he forced himself to focus.

"Neets?" he whispered. He must have had too much to drink, because the next thing he knew, his lips were on hers and he was kissing her deeply, as if they were still married.

He thought he must really be drunk, because kissing Anita felt like the most natural thing to be doing. Not to mention, she was kissing him back.

And despite the wrongs and mistakes of the past three years, it felt so very, very right.

Nikhil's mouth on hers felt like coming home. Like the thing she'd wanted more than anything, but she didn't even know she'd missed it.

His hands at her waist were strong and warm and she gave in to the feeling of security she'd always had with him.

She kissed him as if the past three years hadn't happened, melting into his arms.

Then all at once, the beat of the tabla and the sounds of celebration rushed back to her, and she pulled away from Nikhil's embrace. Her heart raced as she stared at him, the taste of him still on her lips. What the...?

By the time guests had cleared out, Nikhil was swaying as he stood. Tina had removed the plastic and scraped off the paste, so her hands were free. She helped Anita get Nikhil up to their room.

"You know something?" Nikhil slurred.

"What's that, Bhaiya?" Tina laughed as they made it to the top of the steps.

"I am invisible." He looked at Anita.

Tina laughed. "Jeez, Bhaiya, how much did you drink? I can see you just fine."

"But I am. To everyone but you and Dad."

Anita snapped her head to Tina and Nikhil at the mention of their father.

Tina's expression had softened. "You're right. Dad saw everybody."

They reached their room and Tina helped Anita lay Nikhil down in the bed. She removed his shoes. "Thanks, Tina. No way I could've gotten him up here myself."

All the mirth was gone from the young bride. "He's my brother. I wouldn't leave him lying around downstairs, drunk. And just so you know, that kiss outside was fake, for show."

"Of course it was. Did you think I wasn't playing along?" Anita retorted. But it hadn't felt fake, on his part or on hers. It had felt strangely good, right. She had broken off the kiss when she had come to her senses, but the way Nikhil had been looking at her...it didn't matter. Clearly he was intoxicated, and Tina was right. She should remember it was all for show.

Tina stood there for a moment, not quite glaring, not quite kind. "Look, I don't know how Mom got you to come and do this marriage act. Just don't make him fall for you again. He was a mess the last time. I don't think he could stand it again."

Anita's heart fell into her stomach with the reminder of how she had hurt him when she left. She nodded, numbly. "No danger of that. He clearly doesn't want me here. It's all for show. For the family. For Dada."

Nikhil groaned in the bed. Tina glanced at her brother as she left. "Grah shanti at 8:30 a.m."

Another groan.

Anita turned to the form of her ex-husband splayed across the bed. Tousled dark hair, brown skin with a slight five-o'clock shadow on a purposeful square jaw… At six feet tall, he took up almost the whole bed lying diagonally like he was. Say what you wanted about Nikhil Joshi, but there was no denying those classic movie-star good looks.

Anita sighed. *Definitely hot.*

Nikhil groaned again. "Hey." He sat up and looked at her, his voice barely even a drunken whisper. "You look like my wife." He waved a hand. "My ex-wife. Her name was Neets." His words were slurred. "I lost her because she couldn't see me. Because I'm invisible."

"Uh-huh." Anita tried to move him so he wouldn't roll over and have his head hanging over the side. She was barely registering his words.

"You know why she couldn't see me?"

Anita grabbed the empty trash bin and put it next to the bed. Just in case. "Why couldn't she see you?" This was going to be good. She placed electrolyte water on the end table.

"Because I wasn't successful. Because I was never going to be a lawyer, like the rest of my family. Like her. Wonder if she can see me now?"

Anita stared at him, her heart thumping inside her chest. "That's not true." Sadness gripped her as she started arguing with a drunk man. "I never cared about—"

Before she could finish, he fell back onto the bed and passed out.

PERSUASION

~POWERFUL WOMEN~

Chapter 5

Five Days Ago

Anita slipped her laptop and lesson planner into her bag. Her students rarely ever hung out after class. They all had families and jobs to get to, so by 8:05 p.m., her classroom was usually empty. She'd rather do her paperwork at home, plus she still had some homework to do for her own classes, so she packed her stuff quickly. She grabbed her water thermos and took one last glance to be sure she hadn't forgotten anything before heading for the door.

She must have been going at quite the clip because she nearly bumped into a woman who was coming in.

"Oh, I'm so sorry. I—" Anita froze as she found herself staring into the face of a slightly older woman. The woman still wore the same mild floral perfume, and

Anita recognized the scent almost before she recognized the woman.

Seema Joshi. Her former mother-in-law. For some reason, tears burned behind her eyes, and she swallowed hard as she stepped back.

"Auntie?" The word sounded foreign to her as she addressed the woman she'd once referred to as *Mom.* Anita had lost her own parents in a car accident, so when her mother-in-law had embraced her as a daughter, Anita had been more than willing to accept her.

"Beti." The word trembled coming off of Seema-auntie's lips.

Anita searched the woman's face for a reason for her sudden appearance. "Auntie—did something happen? Is…he…all right?" It was a reflex. *He* might be her ex, but certainly she wished him no harm.

"Nikhil is just fine," Seema-auntie answered, her mouth going tight and the soft, loving tone she'd just used to address Anita became clipped.

So some things never change. Mother and son had always bashed heads. Probably, because they were so alike. Though neither one could ever see that.

Seema-auntie's eyes widened, and she reached out a comforting hand on Anita's shoulder. Seema Joshi must have been in her late fifties, but good genes and skin care had her looking no older than forty. Truthfully, she could easily pass for thirty-five. She was smartly dressed in white jeans and a floral top with a light sweater. She still carried herself almost regally. Seema Joshi was one of the founders of Joshi Family Law, her late husband being the other. When Vikash Joshi had passed at the age of forty, Seema had taken it over. JFL now the preeminent law firm in the area.

"Do you have a minute?" Seema-auntie's voice was tentative, cautious. Unusual. While Seema Joshi was kind, she was never timid or unsure of herself. She commanded every room she was in. But not this one, today.

"Of course." Anita backed up into the fluorescent-lit classroom and sat down at one of the desks, all of her belongings basically clattering to the floor. She motioned for her former mother-in-law to sit beside her.

"Teaching English as a Second Language, I see." Her smile was achingly similar to her younger son's. "How wonderful."

"I really do enjoy it."

"And being at night, you are free to work for the Herreras' firm," she added, a bit of pride in her voice.

Anita nodded. "Well, I'm only there occasionally now."

"Of course—law school."

At Anita's look of surprise, Seema-auntie quickly added, "I have lunch with Priscilla Herrera on occasion, and she always has wonderful things to say about you and your work."

There was a point to this conversation; Anita was sure of it. She just didn't know what it was, or when it would show itself.

"Let me get to the point, beti."

Anita nodded.

Seema-auntie fidgeted with her bangles (real gold) and rings (real gemstones) for a moment before she finally sighed heavily and looked Anita in the eye. "I need a favor. A huge one, and I hesitated to ask, but I'm worried about Dada's health…"

"What's wrong with Dada?" Anita perked up. Nikhil's grandparents had always been so warm and welcoming to her. Nikhil and Anita had visited them in India after they were married, and whenever Dada and Dadi were stateside, they always made a point to see them. She'd lost touch with Dada after the divorce, but that was to be expected.

"He had a heart attack six months ago." Seema-auntie's lip quivered. "And Dadi passed a year ago."

A heaviness filled Anita's heart to hear of Dadi's passing. She quickly pushed it aside. Those feelings were misplaced. She no longer had a connection to this family. They weren't her family anymore, were they? "Oh, I'm so sorry," she somehow managed to say.

Seema-auntie nodded, tears filling her eyes. Anita took the older woman's hands in her own. She knew how it felt to lose a mother.

"What do you need?" Though Anita could not imagine what she could possibly offer.

Seema-auntie swallowed hard, and cleared her throat, squeezing Anita's hands. "Tina is getting married."

Anita steeled her face to show nothing but happiness. Tina had become one of her closest friends when she'd met Nikhil, almost a sister. Anita lost her in the divorce. She was happy for her former sister-in-law, but there had been a time when Anita would have been among the first to know. Not anymore. "That's fantastic!"

"Thank you. We're very excited." Seema-auntie paused and looked Anita in the eye.

"His name is Jake Collins, and she met him at JFL." A genuine smile came across her auntie's face as she spoke about her future son-in-law. "Not on Tina's team, but he's in line to run the real estate division, while Tina's just doing amazing work in the administrative and regulatory branch of the practice."

Anita nodded, her face still frozen in fake happiness. Still all in the family. Everyone in the immediate family was in the practice. Everyone except for Nikhil, that is.

"The thing is…see…" Seema-auntie continued. "I was never able to… What I mean is… I never told any of our family or friends that you and Nikhil divorced." Her last words came out in a rush.

The fake smile dropped into real astonishment. "What?"

"I just couldn't. My mother died and my father had a heart attack—there was no good time. Plus a divorce in the family would be very humiliating for Papa. I never even told my friends, because I was afraid it would get back to him."

"What do they think? I mean, when Nikhil and I don't come to functions?" She stared straight ahead at her auntie. "What did your sisters and Dada say when we didn't call them when Dadi passed?"

She shrugged. "We called as a family. Dada asked about you—I said you were busy. Our friends understand busy children. So I just say you're both busy. Working. Studying."

Anita's mouth gaped open for a second before she responded, her words firm and commanding. She wasn't this woman's daughter-in-law anymore and this was beyond anything Anita could have imagined. "You have to tell them, Auntie." She couldn't believe this. How was it possible that people—lots of people—thought she was still married to Nikhil? "You have to tell Dada. He'll want to know why I'm not there at Tina's wedding." Her heart pounded in her chest.

Seema Joshi sat straight in her chair and leveled her gaze on Anita.

"Not if you're there." Her former mother-in-law fixed her in her gaze. This was why she was here.

"What does that mean, if I'm there? You can't possibly want me to come to the wedding? How is that even—"

"You'll have to behave as if you and Nikhil are still married." The older woman spit the words out fast.

Anita shook her head while she tried to calm her breathing. "That's not… I mean, that will never work."

"Why not?"

"Because it's a lie." And how could she spend five days with a man she once loved but no longer had? "Besides, Nikhil will never agree." Of this, Anita was certain.

Seema-auntie continued as if she hadn't spoken. "Beti. Listen. It's just five days. I know you're in law school and that you applied for a loan." She stared Anita down. "You put us down as cosigners."

"I needed to be sure I'd get the loan. I'd never ask you to pay—"

"Of course. I understand. I also know your scholarship only covers two-thirds." She paused as only a lawyer can, before speaking with methodical preciseness, as if she was a surgeon wielding a scalpel as opposed to a lawyer wielding her words. "Do this. Spend five days as a part of our family, and I will take care of that remaining third. Imagine, your education will be paid for—you will have no added debt. No other strings attached. That is all. Then I promise not to bother you again."

No one knew about the scholarship except for Anita and the school. And her best friend, Divya. Because Anita hadn't mentioned it. She had been a shoo-in for a full ride, but at the last minute, she got a letter telling her she only got two-thirds. She and her brother, Amar, had the remaining third in their savings, but it was his dream to open his own catering business, and she had already told him to use that money as start-up funding. She had been that sure of the full ride.

"That is crazy." She frowned and shook her head. She'd have to pretend to be married. To her ex-husband. For five whole days. She hadn't even set eyes on him since she'd walked out three years ago. How could she possibly be in the same room as him after all this time?

After the way she had left?

What would her parents have said? She shook her head. That was irrelevant, because chances were she might not have married Nikhil so quickly if her parents had been alive.

It didn't matter. No way. She would just have to take out the loan and pay off the debt after she graduated. Lots of people did it. "No, Auntie. I'm sorry." She started gathering her things. "It's just such a crazy idea—"

"I know, beti. But you have to understand, that's how desperate I am." Her auntie watched her grab her computer bag and purse, with increasing panic on her face. "Please listen. I went to India after my father's heart attack. He was so weak and frail back then. And according to Neepa-masi, he hasn't shown much improvement." She leaned in toward Anita. "You know how crucial the first year after losing a spouse can be. And you know the stigma of divorce in our community."

Anita pressed her lips together. "I am *fully* aware of the stigma of divorce in our community, Auntie." People stared at her at the mandhir, and she heard whisperings from her parents' friends. Divya tried to downplay the whole thing, but even Divya's parents had told Anita that it would be very difficult for her to remarry within the community.

Which was actually fine by Anita, since she had no intention of starting a new relationship right now anyway. She was focused on finishing law school and getting a job. She and Amar were struggling to make the mortgage payments, but it was easier than selling their family home and getting an apartment. Besides, Amar would never leave the house.

Although…not having any school debt might solve her problems. Not having any debt would certainly make her feel more grounded. It was five days out of her whole life. She and Nikhil simply had to put on a show. The computer bag fell from her shoulder.

"Of course you are." Seema-auntie stood. "You're right. This is crazy. I don't know what I was thinking." She walked to the door. "Sorry to have wasted your time. I'll just tell them you have a big case in another city."

"But won't Nikhil tell them?"

"Don't worry about Nikhil." She dismissed him with a wave of her hand and left.

Anita sat back down, stunned, though her mind was whirring away. Seema-auntie had left her card with her cell number on it. Of course she did. Thirty grand for five days. How hard could it be? What was she afraid of, anyway? Nikhil was probably well over her by now. She had no intention of getting back together with him. It might be uncomfortable, but that little bit of discomfort would pay off nicely in the end.

She dug her phone out of her bag and dialed. Auntie picked up on the first ring. "Yes?"

"I don't have clothes for this kind of thing," Anita said.

Seema-auntie appeared in the doorway, relief oozing from her. "I will provide all of your outfits. The mehndi is in five days."

"I haven't said yes yet."

She smiled. "Why else would you call?"

DAY TWO:

MORNING OF OBSTACLE REMOVAL
Making way for new things

Chapter 6

Anita woke to a stabbing pain in her hip and a crick in her neck as her payback for being chivalrous and sleeping on the sofa. Not that she'd had a choice, given the way Nikhil had drunkenly sprawled across the bed. Truth was she wouldn't have slept with him on the bed anyway.

Their "room" was a small suite, with an area for the king-size bed and a separate sitting room, and their own private bath. There was also an overlarge walk-in closet that allowed Anita to have "her" side and Nikhil to have "his" side. Anita's side had been empty when she had first arrived, so she had unpacked her small suitcase in there. Part of her deal with her former mother-in-law was that she would provide her wedding attire, as Anita had no time—or money—to purchase the nine outfits required in less than five days. At some point yesterday, her closet had been filled with saris, chaniya choli and lehnga, as well as a bridesmaid's gown. Shoes and jewelry were also tucked in there. Seema-auntie had seen to every detail.

On the few occasions that Nikhil and Anita had spent the night when they were married, they had stayed here, in his old room. It smelled of sandalwood and his cologne, and was comfy and familiar and brought back memories long forgotten.

Memories she had spent the last three years trying to squelch.

Her phone dinged. Amar. Her stomach quivered seeing his name. He had been pretty pissed last night when he saw her here.

Tuition money? Seriously, A. It's not worth it. We'll figure it out...

She muted the conversation and turned away from her phone.

No sooner did she shake off the guilt that had washed over her than her phone dinged again. Divya.

How's it going with the butthead?

She had ceased being a fan of Nikhil's after the divorce. No matter that she had thought he was amazing when Anita was married to him. Divya's loyalty was pure.

He's still sleeping off the shock of being fake married to me.

Drunk?

Yep. Get this. Taj is the caterer. So Amar is here. *shocked face emoji*

shocked face emoji Good luck. I'm in grocery store hell.

Divya was an incredible pastry chef but her skills were currently being wasted at a grocery store bakery. It paid the bills but was far from what she wanted to do with her life.

She sat up and peeked over at the bed. There was no movement from Nikhil, save the regular rise and fall of his fabulous chest.

Anita grabbed her laptop and checked her email. She glanced at the date and a pang hit her heart. She tamped it down and turned her focus to her work. A couple emails from the local law clinic where she volunteered. There was nothing pressing, but one of the emails hinted at a client of hers possibly facing eviction. She pulled up some paperwork and emailed it over. Hopefully this would buy them until Monday, when she could physically go down and talk to someone.

The puja was still a couple hours away, so she got to work on her homework. Anita started her third year of law school in a couple months, but they had already been assigned readings. She washed up, then settled in to complete an assignment. This wedding would put her behind on her schedule, but not having any debt would more than make up for it.

Once she finished the assignment, she showered and put on her sari.

Well, she did the best she could. She always needed help with a couple safety pins. Nikhil used to help her.

She was struggling with pinning pleats behind her left shoulder when Nikhil groaned. She watched him through the mirror as he slowly attempted to sit up in bed. He ended up lying back down, holding his head.

"Electrolytes next to you," she said, finally securing the pin. The sari sagged a bit, but whatever. She'd managed it in the end.

She tried not to look at him. He was ridiculously handsome first thing in the morning. Tousled dark hair and scruff on his chin. The soft, bewildered look in his dark eyes, matched with a slight pout of full lips.

She had always loved waking up next to him. He was sexy and handsome—some mornings, she couldn't believe her good fortune. That *she* was the one who got to wake up next to him every day. That she was the one he loved above all else.

Or so she had thought.

"Electrolytes." She raised her voice a bit. "On the nightstand."

He started at her voice, which only made him moan again. "Neets?"

He really needed to stop calling her that. "Anita," she corrected him as she donned large dangly earrings and a necklace and reached for her matching bangles, desperately trying to ignore how sensual her name sounded in even his dry-throat voice.

"What the hell are you doing in my room?" he croaked at her.

"Right now, it's our room. We're supposed to be married, remember?" Her bangles jingled as she slid them on, the sound reminding her of wedded bliss.

"I'm trying to forget."

Did he remember kissing her? Didn't matter. "You

certainly tried to forget last night." She looked at her phone. "You have forty-five minutes to get up and be presentable. The grah shanti starts at eight thirty."

He grunted. She walked over and shook him. He reeked of alcohol.

"What are you doing?" he grumbled, clutching his head in obvious pain.

"Tina's first puja is in forty-five minutes, downstairs, and you need to be there." She handed him the glass of electrolytes. "Though I get paid regardless of whether or not you show. I told your mother I would not be responsible for your attendance."

He sat up and took the glass, looking at it like it might bite him. "I'm sure she drew up the appropriate documents."

"No. I did." She smirked at him.

He scowled at her as he sipped the electrolytes.

"Pithi today too."

The grah shanti would start with a Ganesh puja, to remove all obstacles—spiritual and otherwise—from the upcoming wedding ceremonies and would end with everyone taking turns applying a turmeric and chickpea flour paste, pithi, to all parts of Tina's skin. This part of the ceremony tended to disintegrate into everyone spreading the pithi on everyone else. Almost as if everyone wanted to be cleansed and purified for the wedding. Well, not really. Everyone just wanted to rub paste all over each other because it was fun.

Anita and Nikhil had never done this as they had opted to get married at city hall and forgo all of the traditional celebrations. A big wedding seemed odd, since her parents wouldn't be there, and Amar and Anita couldn't have afforded a big multiday wedding with all the trappings, anyway. The city hall idea had appealed to Nikhil's rebellious nature. Only his mother, his siblings and Amar and Divya had been at their small ceremony.

Of course, Seema-auntie had still insisted on throwing them a huge wedding reception, which Nikhil had been opposed to.

"She just wants to showcase us. It's not because she really cares," Nikhil had argued.

"So what? It's a party to celebrate our marriage. What's wrong with that? Besides, she seems really excited about it," Anita had countered.

The party had been a mix of both. Yes, Seema-auntie had wanted to show them off, but she was genuinely happy for them.

"Yeah. I got it."

Nikhil's sullen voice jarred Anita back to the present.

Silence floated between them and Anita was visited by the thought that they were both thinking about what they had missed out on by not having a wedding.

Anita found everyone gathered in the large great room, which encompassed the family room and eat-in kitchen with a large central island that could seat twelve.

"Jay Shree Krishna, beti." Seema-auntie greeted her with warmth and praise to god, which felt truly genuine, and not just for show.

"Jay Shree Krishna." Anita returned the greeting. The comforting scents of chai and coffee mixed with warm laughter and fond calls of "Hey, Bhabhi," "Anita-ben" and "beti" filled her heart momentarily with the joy of family. Until she remembered that they really weren't her family at all, which was accompanied by a pang of grief for her parents. It had been close to nine years since they'd been taken from her, but grief reared its spiky head when she least expected it.

The priest was already there (a good sign for a timely start) and the family was enjoying hot chai and coffee along with breakfast. Anita was catching up with cousins when Nikhil ventured down.

He was wearing a blue cotton tunic with the sleeves rolled up, over the traditional slim-fit bottoms. His hair was still damp, the curls starting to dry. Simple, but he looked amazing. And not even a little bit hungover. How the hell did he do that? He was all smiles and jokes with his cousins, working so hard to not look in her direction, to not acknowledge her, that she knew that he was more than aware of her presence in the room.

Anita had plastered a smile on her face but something of her true feelings of awkwardness and sadness must have shown through because when Dada finally entered, the first thing he did was bark at Nikhil.

"Nikhil! What is your wife doing so far from you? Sit with her. You never know how many days you have left."

The loss of his wife must have hit him hard. Dada furrowed his brow at Nikhil, though he looked well rested and stronger than he had yesterday. The flight must have been rough on him.

Ever the obedient grandson, Nikhil made his way to Anita and stopped at the coffee service. She watched as he put in the exact amount of cream and sugar that she liked, before continuing toward her. So sweet of him to bring her coffee. She reached out her hand for the cup, at the same time he took a sip himself.

"Way to make me look like an ass," he mumbled from the mug as he glanced at her outstretched hand.

"You don't need my help for that." She rolled her eyes. "How the hell was I supposed to know the coffee wasn't for me?" she mumbled, a smile on her face for the crowd. "You used to bring me coffee all the time."

"We aren't married anymore." He spoke through gritted teeth. "And I used to make you chai all the time." He dropped an ice-cold glare on her. "How soon we forget."

She hadn't forgotten. Though she had insisted on coffee in the morning, it was his chai that got her through the afternoons. She had gone back to mainlining coffee when they divorced.

She grinned for the people watching them. "We're supposed to be married. Just hand it over."

A smack upside his head caused him to spill coffee down his front. He jumped and turned.

"Dada!" Nikhil was dripping hot coffee. "What was that for?"

Anita tried not to smile. She failed.

The old man had moved to the coffee service to make a cup of coffee.

"It's okay, Dada. You don't have to get me another cup," Nikhil said.

"I'm not," the old man grumbled. "This is for your wife."

Anita flushed, mortified that an elder was getting her coffee. She popped up from her chair, meeting Dada halfway. "Oh no. That's okay, Dada. I can get my own coffee."

He handed her the mug and a huge smile. "I know, beti. But how much better it is when given with love." He glared at Nikhil. "Treasure the people you love. There is never enough time."

Nikhil simply stood there, mopping his shirt. His mother passed by, slightly frazzled, a tray of sweets in her arms. She took one look at Nikhil, Anita and her father and barked at Nikhil, "Nikhil, quickly, go change. You and Anita are sitting in the puja."

Nikhil ran up to his room, taking off the wet jabho as he walked. He ran the stain under cold water, then tossed it toward the hamper. It landed next to the hamper. Close enough. His head still pounded; the acetaminophen had yet to take effect.

It was just his damn luck that his sister-in-law didn't feel well enough to sit the puja, so Dada had volunteered him and Anita. They weren't even really a couple! Of course, his grandfather didn't know that.

Last night was something of a blur. He remembered lots of alcohol and joining the dancing outside, but then things got very swimmy. There was the fleeting memory of cool lips on his.

Wait. Did he kiss Anita last night? Did she kiss him back? No. That was the alcohol talking.

He'd have to sit next to Anita for the next few hours as they performed the rites the priest asked of them that would serve to remove obstacles from the wedding of his sister. Didn't bode well. Not that he couldn't sit next to Anita. Of course he could. Her body next to his didn't mean anything anymore, right? It didn't help that his head was pounding.

Did he really kiss her?

His phone rang. What? A glance at the screen revealed that Chantelle was calling again. It must be something huge for her to call two days in a row, because she never called. She preferred email. He glanced at the door. He needed to get downstairs. This wouldn't take long. Nikhil answered.

"Chantelle?"

"Hey, Nikhil—great news! That publisher we are wild about? The one who can take N. V. Joshi to the next level? They have an editor in your town. This weekend. She's attending a wedding, but she's willing to meet with you on Saturday!"

"What?" Nikhil couldn't believe what he was hearing. This was what he had been waiting for. He didn't even think about it. "Yes. Yes. Schedule it. Uh…"

Saturday was the fourth day of all the festivities. The Indian ceremony would be that day. Which meant he had a small gap in the afternoon for this meeting. Couldn't take more than thirty minutes, right? "Say Saturday afternoon? I'm kind of at a family thing this weekend myself, but I can make myself available for a while."

"I'll let them know and I'll be in touch."

She hung up and Nikhil stood there, trying to take it all in. This was it; this was his time. If he got this publisher to offer him a contract, his family would finally be able to see him as a success. They would finally have to acknowledge that he wasn't a screwup just because he didn't want to be a lawyer.

A pang hit him as he thought about how proud his father would have been of him. Lawyer or not, his dad had always had his back.

Nikhil used to spend hours reading in the den while his father worked. From time to time, Vikash Joshi would look up from his papers and smile proudly at his younger son. "Keep reading, Nikhil. Success is in those books."

Maybe he took it a bit too literally, but those words were always with Nikhil.

Even Anita would have to acknowledge that he was a success. Something he had never been sure she'd believed when they were married.

Laughter from downstairs brought him back to the festivities. He rifled through his closet and found a red silk jabho. That would work for sitting in the puja. He donned the tunic and hurried back downstairs, praying the meds would kick in soon.

The familiar sound of Anita's hearty laugh had him turning toward the priest. There she stood, her mouth open, body relaxed, black hair catching the morning sun, her sari wilting off her shoulder.

Nikhil strode over and he knew the instant she saw him, because the light in her eyes was replaced by apprehension.

"Jay Shree Krishna." He greeted the priest with his hands together. "I need to steal…my wife for a moment." The words came out easier today than yesterday.

The priest nodded his approval and went back to his preparations.

"What's up?" Anita looked up at him, a forced smile on her face. Her eyes betrayed her apprehension around him. For just a moment, he found himself longing to see the relaxed smile and taunting eyes she used to save just for him.

"I, uh." He pointed to her shoulder as he asked permission to touch this woman. This woman whose body there was hardly an inch he hadn't touched at some point. "Your sari is falling… Do you have pins?"

"Oh, yes. I do." She reached into the little purse attached to her sari. "But it's okay. I can just get your mom to—"

"She's busy."

"Well, then Easha-bhabhi…"

"She's throwing up."

Anita grinned, an inquiring yet knowing eyebrow cocked. "Is she?"

"Yes, she's pregnant. She's not past the first trimester, so we're not telling anyone just yet. Rocky wants to keep it quiet." Nikhil looked around. "We'll use Mom's study." He extended his arm for her to lead the way.

He walked behind her to the study, and her floral perfume wafted back to him, conjuring memories of their life together. What was it about certain scents that could make you believe the past was present? That maybe the divorce never happened, and they were still happily married? They were stopped at least four times on the way to greet cousins and friends, some of whom they hadn't seen since their marriage party.

Nikhil placed his hand on Anita's lower back to guide her back to the study. This time, she didn't flinch, but seemed to relax into his touch. It shouldn't please him so much…but it did.

Once in, Nikhil closed the door, shutting out the exuberance of the house and locking in the thick silence between them. Anita handed him the extra safety pins and took out the one on her shoulder. Nikhil watched as she gracefully brought the fabric back and forth, making perfectly even pleats. The sari was half-off, revealing the short blouse beneath, as well as the smooth bronze skin of her toned torso.

Nikhil forced himself to look away.

When she was done, she flipped the pleats around her body and over her shoulder, coming down back to front, toward her torso, and waited for him expectantly. He was trying so hard not to look at her, he didn't move right away.

She cleared her throat. "Nikhil. Safety pin."

"Of course." He leaned over her shoulder to fasten the pleats. His fingers grazed the skin of her back. Goose bumps appeared on her skin. Well, at least he wasn't the only one affected.

She pulled the bottommost pleat free, pulling it across and covering her breasts and torso. Another safety pin was required near her lower back to secure this piece.

"Nikhil." Her voice was soft. She turned her head toward him, their faces were inches from one another. "Back here."

For a moment he forgot they weren't married.

"Hmm." He forced his focus onto the safety pin. She tossed her hair, the soft tresses landing on his hand, obscuring his view.

"Oh sorry," she said.

"No problem." He gently picked up her hair and moved it aside so he could fasten the safety pin. He fastened the pin and turned his head. Mistake. Now their mouths were mere centimeters from each other. A foggy flashback came to him.

"You kissed me last night." It was almost an accusation.

"You kissed me first." She turned and stepped away from him, the moment gone.

So it had *happened.*

"That's not how I remember it." He shrugged.

"Well, I'm surprised you remember anything. Let's just chalk it up to alcohol and forget about it." She checked the rest of her sari and nodded at him.

Kissing her had always been one of his favorite things. In fact they'd made out in this room more than once during their short but intense dating days.

A phone chirp interrupted his wayward thoughts.

Anita reached for her phone from the small purse hooked to her sari. Nikhil saw the name before he could help himself.

Amar. Her brother. Who obviously knew they were actually divorced.

Anita made a face and put her phone away.

"You're not going to answer him?"

"He's still irritated that I'm here." She rolled her eyes. "You know how he gets."

She sighed. Amar had missed the call when the police had phoned to tell them their parents were in the hospital. The officers had called Anita next. Amar had never forgiven himself for missing that call, and he would get worried if Anita didn't respond, automatically assuming the worst. "Fine. I'll send him a text." She quickly texted him and put her phone away.

He patted the area he had secured her safety pin. It wasn't an excuse to touch her again—it wasn't. "Well, at least Mom can't glare at you for not being properly put together. You look amazing."

Anita flushed under his open admiration. "She never glared at me for that—she made eyes at you. Because *you* couldn't bother to be 'properly attired.' Who shows up for family portraits in a T-shirt?" There was laughter in her words, and Nikhil knew she was remembering the admonishment he'd endured from his mother for doing just that. His mother had had no sympathy for his antics, even back then.

Nikhil warmed to the first real smile on her face he'd seen since she arrived. He quickly reminded himself of how she had given up on him all those years ago. How she had hurt him. And how she had left him.

Chapter 7

Anita kept her back stiff and straight during the small ceremony and focused on the pandit. The goal was to avoid touching Nikhil as much as possible as they performed the various rites. From the caution that Nikhil was showing with his hand movements, he clearly had a similar goal.

He never looked at her or reacted to her. It was almost as if she wasn't sitting next to him.

They were both sitting cross-legged on the floor, heads bowed. It was his turn to offer flowers in the ceremony. Nikhil sat, hands clasped together, eyes closed, the epitome of serene. He didn't move. She nudged his elbow with hers. He remained still. The pandit cleared his throat and continued chanting. She nudged him again. His eyes popped open and he looked at her from the corner of his eye. She motioned in front of them with her eyes.

He smiled sheepishly at the pandit. "Oh, sorry," he murmured as he completed the action.

Finally, her eye-based communication was working.

She carefully met Nikhil's eyes and caught him biting his bottom lip, trying to hold in a chuckle. She pressed her lips together to stifle her own laugh. The pandit instructed them to hold a spoon of water. They both reached for the spoon together, fingers grazing each other. Neither of them pulled back.

Shortly after they had married, they held the traditional housewarming ceremony for blessings in their new apartment and invited their friends and relatives. The puja was set for 8:00 a.m. on a Saturday morning. Nikhil and Anita had attended the engagement party of a close friend the night before. Anita may have had more to drink than she should have, because when she woke at 6:00 a.m. the next morning, she was still a bit tipsy. They sat in the puja, and every time they closed their eyes, Anita fell asleep. Nikhil had had to continuously nudge her elbow to get her to pay attention.

She shook her head at him as that memory filled her simultaneously with happiness and melancholy.

The puja finished within the allotted time, and it was time to apply the pithi on Tina. Nikhil's mother was first to apply the yellow paste on her daughter. As the bride's older sister-in-law, Rocky's wife, Easha, was next. Then Anita. Anita dipped the two betel leaves into the paste and approached Tina. Tina avoided looking at her, so Anita simply dabbed Tina's hands and feet with the paste and moved on, an incredible sadness weighing her down.

She found herself sitting next to Dada as the rest of the family and friends took their turn. It was only a matter of time before all the guests were covered in turmeric paste.

"Come, beti. Let's walk." He stood and grabbed his cane. Anita allowed him to lead her outside, noting that he wasn't really using the cane. They walked side by side on the sidewalk. Dada was tall and not even slightly hunched. He might have been thinner than she remembered, but he certainly looked better than last night.

"You're looking more yourself today, Dada," Anita said.

"The flight always makes me nauseous. I feel much better today." He was silent for a time, seemingly lost in thought, though he walked at a good pace. Finally, he spoke. "You and Nikhil. You remind me of me and your dadi." He smiled at her. "She was so like you. Smart. Witty. Beautiful." He shrugged. "Active in the community. Not much of a cook."

He looked at her. "Do you cook?"

She grinned. "Yes, I do. In fact, Nikhil and I used to cook together." Wait, where did that come from? She had almost forgotten. It had been something they looked forward to when their schedules lined up. They even used to cook at the house with Amar, from time to time, helping him with new recipes or spice combinations.

"You don't anymore?"

Uh-oh. "Well, we're so much busier these days, you know. He's busy writing. I'm busy with law school."

The older man grinned with pride. "The family must be thrilled. Another attorney in the family business."

Anita stared at the older man. He had no idea that he had just fallen onto the major reason she and Nikhil were divorced. Nikhil had hated the fact that she wanted to be a lawyer. Better not to say anything.

He patted her hands. "You have been through quite a bit at such a young age. Losing your parents so young. How fortunate that you and Nikhil have each other to lean on."

She had leaned on him. Her parents had been gone a couple years when she'd met Nikhil. She'd been out of college a year or so, was still floundering, trying to find her way. She found work teaching as a substitute teacher during the day. In the evenings she was the assistant to an English professor who taught creative writing. It was how she met Nikhil.

She had still been grieving and lost from the loss of her parents. He had been there for her. Until he wasn't.

"You know, beti. What I have learned these past years is that we are always stronger than we think and that it is never too late for anything."

Anita stared at the old man. If she didn't know better, she would have thought he was trying to get her back with Nikhil.

They had returned to the house, and Anita heard her name being called as they entered.

"There she is! Anita-bhabhi!" The Joshi cousins were nothing if not loud and affectionate.

Nikhil waved her over and bits of dried paste fell from his hands. He had turmeric paste on his cheeks and clothes and hands. Anita covered her mouth with her hands as she walked over and took in Tina. Every inch of the girl's exposed skin was completely covered in turmeric paste. Anita was sure the girl's girlfriends had probably gone under the sari a bit as well. Her hair was caked yellow. She glanced at Nikhil.

He had the audacity to grin with pride. "I did the hair."

"How am I going to get to the shower?" Tina widened her eyes. The thing about turmeric was that it was multifunctional. It was used to cure a sore throat, mend a cut and beautify skin. It also permanently stained just about anything, except skin and metal cooking utensils. But most certainly, it would stain the cream-colored carpet that ran all through the Joshi household.

Anita grabbed a nearby towel, likely set out for just such a purpose, and laid it in front of her. "Walk." When Tina had walked the length of the towel, another friend or cousin would bring one forward and lay it down before her. Pieces of dried turmeric paste fell onto the towels as she walked.

Anita shook her head. "Total princess."

Tina simply humphed and slowly continued her journey to the upstairs bathroom. Anita continued to direct the path from towel to towel, ignoring Tina's curious glances at her. They finally reached the door of Tina's bedroom and Anita opened it. Tina entered, not meeting her eyes.

One of Tina's best friends came up behind Anita. "Hey, Anita! So good to see you!" She pulled Anita into a warm hug.

"Anu!" Anita fell into the young woman's embrace.

"It's been a while." Anu pulled back, beaming.

Anita shrugged. "Well, you know…"

"I know. I heard about the divorce." Anu nodded, glancing quickly at Tina. "But hey, I'm super excited to hear that you and Nikhil are getting back together."

"What?" Both she and Tina chorused their surprise.

"Sonny Pandya? Sonny is like my cousin's cousin on the other side of their family. Anyway, he's here with the caterer and he told me that you told him that you and Nikhil are getting back together."

"That is one hundred percent—" Tina started to say.

"True," Anita interrupted, giving Tina a *look* to just go with it.

Tina's eyes widened and she opened her mouth, but Anita spoke over her. "Nikhil and I are giving each other another chance, and Tina's wedding came up while we were figuring all that out. But hey, do me a favor and don't say anything about any of this. We're trying to put it behind us and move on."

"Um, yes. Sure. Of course. Makes sense," Anu agreed, looking slightly confused. "I already told the girls—we were so excited you were here. Is that okay?"

"Sure. Just let's keep it between us." Anita smiled sweetly at Tina and silently begged her to keep quiet.

Having accepted what Anita said, Anu was talking. "Well, I missed you! We used to have so much fun together."

They had had a lot of fun together. Anita had gotten to know Tina's closest friends while she was married to Nikhil. They had all been on more than one girls' night together.

But when Anita left, she left them all. She really missed that sisterhood.

"I missed you all, too."

"Ooh," Anu squeaked. "Maybe we could all hang out again, you know, since you and Nikhil are a thing again."

Tina cleared her throat. The two women turned to her. She was covered in drying turmeric paste, standing in the middle of the room glaring at Anita. Anu shook her head and started laughing. Anita joined her.

At first, Tina remained stoic, but within minutes she, too, was laughing hysterically. She bent over.

"Oh no! Stop!" Anita called out, still giggling. "It'll fall off." She turned to Anu. "You got her?"

"Well," Anu answered, eyeing Tina, "I could use a hand for getting that sari off."

"It's fine, Anu. The two of us can handle it," Tina spoke up, all her mirth gone as she flicked her gaze to Anita.

Anita shrugged as if she didn't care that Tina was angry with her. That was fine. Getting Tina ready was not part of the contract. "No worries, I'll see what they need downstairs." She threw what she hoped was a nonchalant look at the girls and headed for the door.

"Are you kidding?" Anu screeched. "Wait, Anita. With both of us, there'll be less to clean up."

Anita stopped and looked at Tina. Tina pressed her lips together. "Fine."

"Great." Anu grinned. "Let's get her in the bathroom."

Anita and Anu started to unwrap Tina's turmeric-caked sari in the bathtub. Once the sari was off, Tina was able to take over. Anu and Anita left Tina to shower.

Her job done, Anita headed for the door when Anu's phone dinged. "Ugh! I have to go talk to the tabla guy."

"Right now?"

"I'm in charge of the music this weekend, and the tabla guy is having some crisis."

"Well, I'm sure I can take care of that for you, since you're also getting the bride ready." Anita grinned.

"Well, actually, no, you can't." Anu waved her hands at Anita. "I'll go. Besides, you do such a great sari." She was nearly pouting.

"Um, I don't think that's a good idea." She shifted

her gaze to the bathroom. She didn't really need to be alone with Tina.

Anu's phone dinged again. She glanced at it as she rushed out the door. "You'll be fine."

"Anu—" It was no use; she was gone. The emergency was probably concocted so she could flirt with him, but either way, Anita was left alone to help with Tina's sari.

Great.

Anita walked around Tina's room while she waited, grateful for a moment where she didn't feel like she was pretending. There was a picture of Anita, Nikhil and Tina from a beach weekend. They looked happy. They *were* happy.

A knock at the door tore her from her reverie and Nikhil's voice called from the other side. "Can I come in?"

"Sure. She's still in the shower," Anita called. She cleared her throat and started to smooth her hair but stopped herself.

Nikhil slowly opened the door, avoiding her eyes. "Just wanted to see how long she'd be." His hair was still damp from his shower and curled a bit at his neck. He had on a fresh, rust-colored kurta shirt and nice jeans, and was paste free.

"Pithi can be hard to take off…"

His gaze bounced around the room. "Thanks for… the puja." He waved an elbow.

Anita shrugged. "Returning the favor. Besides, can't have you falling asleep at a puja. Your family would never let you live that down."

"Especially Rocky," Nikhil agreed.

Silence lay thick with memories between them. Nikhil pointed at the picture Anita was still holding.

"I remember when that was taken." He walked over with his hand out. Anita handed him the photo. "It was just after our first anniversary. Tina had tagged along on our beach vacation." He didn't step back, simply gazed at it, the smile on his face fading into a tight-lipped frown.

This close to him, Anita caught the scent of his shower. Clean, fresh, him.

"We were so happy." He met Anita's eyes. "Is Amar still pissed at you?"

"Probably. But he's busy. He's getting overtime to work this wedding, which is fabulous, since he needs to start his own business."

"That's still the goal?" Nikhil smiled.

Anita nodded. "He just has to jump in and do it. Not sure what's holding him back."

Nikhil nodded, not saying anything. Maybe he was thinking about when they used to cook together at her parents' house.

"Oh, and the bridesmaids think we're, uh, well… getting back together." Anita flushed.

"What?"

Anita shook her head. "It's a whole cousin thing, Anu knows Sonny. He told her."

"Yeah. So why are you perpetuating that lie?" Tina emerged turmeric-paste free, makeup done and dressed in her sari blouse and floor-length petticoat.

"So that Anita can let down an admirer softly and not have to tell him she's not interested." Nikhil's jaw was set as he placed the photo back and addressed his sister. "Mom wants to know how long."

Tina glanced at Anita. "Give me thirty minutes and I'll have my hair done, too."

"I'll tell her." Nikhil left without even looking at Anita again.

Anita was left in thick silence with her former sister-in-law. Tina looked around. "Let me guess. Emergency with the tabla guy?"

"You called it. She assumed I would stay and help you with your sari."

"Let's do it then." Tina sighed.

Anita motioned for Tina to turn and sit in front of the large vanity-style mirror. She started rolling sections of Tina's hair in hot rollers.

Bride or no, waves of irritation were flowing off Tina right now, so Anita did not feel the need to fill the silence as she normally might. There had been a time when they had talked about everything, late into the night, grudgingly succumbing to sleep when one (or both) of them fell asleep on the sofa in the apartment Anita had shared with Nikhil.

Understandable, since Anita was her brother's ex-wife, but come on, they had been friends. "Stand up and I'll get the sari."

"She's paying you or something," Tina stated as if they had been having this conversation. Maybe they had.

Anita pressed her lips together. That was between her and Seema-auntie. Tina did not need to know everything. She handed Tina the sari so she could get it started.

"It's ridiculous." Tina shook her head. "Not to mention dangerous." She turned and tucked and then handed the rest to Anita.

"How is it dangerous?"

Tina met Anita's eye in the mirror. Her gaze was hard. "For my brother."

"I'm not going to do anything to him." Anita made the pleats and pinned them. She then wound the sari around Tina, tossing the pleats back and over her left shoulder.

"You were kissing him last night!" Her voice was hard, accusatory.

"He kissed *me*." It was her defense, and she was sticking with it.

"Your being here is enough. And Mom has you in the same bedroom. I tried to get her to at least give you separate bedrooms—it's a recipe for disaster."

"There's no need for you to be concerned. I'm over him. Or I wouldn't have agreed to come." Anita was really getting good at this whole lying thing. "Besides, I slept on the sofa."

Tina narrowed her eyes as Anita turned her away from the mirror to face her and make final adjustments before securing everything with safety pins. "Well, good for you, but Nikhil hasn't been the same since."

Anita paused in her primping. "What do you mean?"

"My brother was a mess after you left him. All he did was sit in that apartment and write all the time. Mom didn't even know if he was eating." Tina spit the words at her.

Anita looked away, heartbreak and shame overcoming her. "I—I had no idea."

"How could you? You never looked back, did you? You just walked away."

Anita forced herself to raise her chin at Tina, even as sorrow filled her with the idea that Tina (or Nikhil) thought she could just walk away. "Not that it's any of your business, but I didn't just walk away. We weren't happy." She swallowed to hide the fact that her voice had cracked. "What was the point of staying together?" Walking away from Nikhil had been one of the hardest things she'd ever had to do. But he hadn't supported her, he hadn't been there for her, so she'd had to go.

A fleeting glimpse of pain in Tina's eyes was quickly replaced by anger. "He told me that you were the one who filed the papers."

Filing those papers had taken every bit of strength she'd had. "That's true." She secured the last safety pin in the sari. Tina looked beautiful, even with the anger in her eyes.

"You be careful around him. Just remember that this whole weekend is pretend. Just because we're acting civil around you doesn't mean that we've forgotten the pain you caused us."

"Us?" Anita asked.

Tina blinked as if she had revealed too much. "The family."

Anita had had no idea that Nikhil had been so distraught, nor did she have an inkling that this weekend would be difficult for Nikhil in any way. He had made it clear at the time how he felt about the law, more specifically, how he felt about Anita going into law. He'd shown very little concern for the fact that being a lawyer was a way for Anita to have that sense of security she had lost when her parents were suddenly taken from her.

Anita became very interested in fussing with the sari, even though it was perfectly put on at this point. She had given up the family when she divorced Nikhil because, well, they were his family, and she was no longer a part of it.

"You're getting married this weekend. Let's focus on that. Nothing is going to happen between me and

Nikhil. We had our chance. We blew it. End of story." Anita sounded more matter-of-fact than she felt, but it was the truth. "Turn."

Tina was gorgeous. Her sari was a light silk of a solid deep pink color with a silver-threaded border and draped beautifully over her curves. Elegant enough for a bride, yet casual enough for the in-between time right now where they would be simply mingling with whoever stopped by.

"Sit." Tina sat back down in front of the mirror as Anita unrolled the hot rollers and finger-combed her hair. "All set. With five minutes to spare."

"Thank you." Tina's gratitude was softer than Anita had expected. "You still are the best at putting on a sari."

"It's easier on someone else." Anita shrugged. "I—I always need help with the pins."

She had learned from her mother. Anita had spent hours over the years watching her mother don a sari to go out or just dress up. She had started learning as soon as her hands were large enough to make pleats. To this day, Anita could still hear her mother's words of guidance on how to tuck the ends just so, or make the pleats in perfect alignment. She could almost smell her mother's perfume in the air and feel her gentle touch in the silk. When she was married, Anita helped all the women and girls in the family put on their saris. She had thoroughly enjoyed it. Right now, she swallowed the tears that burned at her eyes.

"You should go down. Everyone's waiting for you," Anita said. "I'm just going back to my room to change."

"Remember what I said." Tina arched a perfect eyebrow before leaving the room.

Anita nodded as Tina shut the door. Tina was only

protecting her brother. Anita didn't blame her for that. She would do the same. But she missed that closeness, and Tina's anger only added to the emotional weight on her shoulders.

Anita went to her room and quickly changed into a beaded emerald green salwar kameez she found hanging in the closet. The matching jewelry was on the bureau. Her former mother-in-law had thought of everything.

Tears built hot and insistent behind her eyes as she fastened the dangling earrings. She closed her eyes to fight them, but she failed. Turns out she had missed the family more than she had thought. Especially Tina.

DAY TWO:

REHEARSALS AND PRACTICE
When the past meets your present.

Chapter 8

Nikhil opened the door to the private room in the back of the restaurant to the sounds of laughter and a live band playing background music. Jake's parents were hosting a rehearsal dinner, and everyone was already here after the dress rehearsal.

He searched the crowd. His mother caught his eye and walked to him.

"Nikhil! You missed the rehearsal! The Collinses were asking for you." His mother's admonishment hardly landed.

"My interview ran long. I couldn't very well leave in the middle of it." He inhaled. "It's work. I'll make nice with Jake's parents. I promise." He scanned the room as he spoke.

His mother pressed her lips together, following his gaze. "What is so important you can't focus on what I'm telling you?"

"Nothing." He turned to face his mother. He certainly wasn't looking for his ex-wife.

The restaurant decor was simple and understated, and Jake's father, Michael, had proclaimed the food to be phenomenal. The band was actually quite good, and Nikhil found himself humming the tune to himself.

Anita was in the center of the room, surrounded by his mother's friends, when she caught his gaze. She looked like prey being hunted. She widened her eyes at him and bit her bottom lip. It had always been their unofficial sign for 'get me out of here!' He found himself smiling at her and motioning to the bar. When she nodded, he headed for the bar to grab them drinks. He was waiting for their Manhattans when a familiar voice reached him.

"Nikhil Joshi." The voice was smooth and confident, and it made the hairs on the back of his neck stand up.

Jalissa Sheth. What in the hell was she doing here? And why did his family feel the need to surprise him with every woman he'd had a relationship with? He turned to face her. She was laser focused on him and sauntered closer until she was leaning against the bar next to him. She was wearing a low-cut green cocktail dress, her dark hair cascading around her shoulders.

He narrowed his eyes. "What are you doing here, Jalissa? It's family only."

She shrugged. "I must be family."

"Whatever." Thankfully the bartender put two Manhattans in front of him. Nikhil picked them up and started to walk away from Jalissa.

"It seems talk about your divorce is exaggerated." She nodded in Anita's direction.

Nikhil clenched his jaw. "What do you want, Jalissa?"

"Well, I had hoped to make amends." She stepped closer to him, resting a hand on his chest. "We ended things—poorly."

Nikhil laughed. "Are you serious right now? You dropped me like a hot potato as soon as my family hired you."

"That's an extremely simplistic way of putting it, Nicky."

"No. It's an exact way of putting it." Nikhil stepped back so her hand would drop. "It's Nikhil. And it's over." He turned away from the nightmare that was Jalissa and scanned the room for Anita.

When he finally caught sight of Anita, it was like finding oxygen after talking to Jalissa. She was easily the most beautiful woman in the room, gorgeous in a simple black cocktail dress that skimmed her curves, leaving one shoulder open. Her hair was curly and swept over to one side, revealing her neck and bare shoulder. Nikhil walked over to join her.

She was being given the third degree by some of his mother's friends about why they didn't have children. Neepa-masi was very interested in the topic in particular. "You have been married nearly five years." She smiled as she directed her conversation at Anita. "It is time. You aren't getting any younger."

Before either of them could respond, a squeal at the door grabbed everyone's attention. Nikhil recognized it immediately. Deepa-masi, his mother's middle sister.

Neepa-masi made a beeline for her sister, embracing her and taking her in. "So great you made it!"

"Of course! I wouldn't miss it!"

"You missed the mehndi and grah shanti." Nikhil's mother had approached. "And the rehearsal."

"Good to see you, too, Seema." Deepa-masi rolled her eyes. "I couldn't get a flight any earlier and traveling from the West Coast takes all day."

Neepa-masi put her arm around her younger sister. "It doesn't matter. You're here now. Come. Papa has been asking about you."

"Of course. Why would it matter to miss the beginning of my daughter's wedding?" his mother mumbled.

The two women swept past Nikhil's mother like she wasn't even there. Dada greeted Deepa with open arms and hugs. That's how it was. Deepa-masi was the middle child; she could do no wrong. Total opposite of his family.

"Some things never change." Jalissa was standing on his other side, her hand on his bicep. Nikhil had been watching his mother and hadn't noticed her coming up to him.

Anita glanced at her, her face darkened as she swept her gaze over Jalissa's hand on him.

"Hi. I'm Anita Joshi." Anita extended her hand to Jalissa.

Nikhil stared at Anita. Even when they were married, she went by Anita Virani. Was she staking a claim right now? Why would she even care?

"Jalissa Sheth." Jalissa let go of his bicep to shake Anita's hand. "I had heard it wasn't Joshi anymore." She smiled in what to anyone else would appear to be a sweet manner. Nikhil saw it for it was. Challenge.

Anita smiled back equally sweetly. "Clearly you heard wrong."

Jalissa took her hand back and glanced at Nikhil. "Clearly. Good seeing you, Nicky." She dragged her fingers over his arm as she walked away.

Anita raised an eyebrow at him. "Nicky?"

He shook his head and grumbled. "Not now."

"Nicky." Rocky came striding over, clearly agitated.

"Nikhil," Anita corrected.

Nikhil did a double-take at her, before facing his brother to see what he had done wrong now. "Rock."

"You totally missed the rehearsal." Rocky was flabbergasted. "How could you do that? You have to know where to stand, and when to walk—"

"How hard is that?" Nikhil dismissed his brother's concerns. "Anyway, I had a work thing that ran long. So, I'm sorry. But that was important. I'd think that you and Mom of all people would understand work being a priority."

"Nicky—"

"Nikhil," Anita stated as she sipped her Manhattan.

"This is family—it's more important than work." Rocky narrowed his eyes as if he were speaking to an idiot.

"Since when?" Nikhil stared at his brother, speechless for a moment. His whole life, he'd heard that work was the most important thing. Anything having to do with JFL always took precedence. "Or maybe because my work isn't associated with JFL it's not as important?"

"No. Mom and I aren't working these few days either."

"You took off for Tina's wedding?" Nikhil couldn't believe what he was hearing.

"Yes. And before you think about it too hard, we all took off when you got married, too," Rocky stated.

"You went in late," Nikhil corrected.

"We were there," Rocky insisted.

"Damn, Rocky, who *are* you?" Nikhil shook his head.

"Me? Who are *you*, Nicky?" Rocky shot back.

"Nikhil." Anita turned to face Rocky. "His name is Nikhil. How hard is that to remember? He's your brother, for god's sake!" Anita spit out.

Rocky looked like he'd been slapped. Nikhil took the opportunity to take Anita's hand and walk away. "That was awesome. Did you see his face?" Nikhil laughed and squeezed her hand. He snapped his gaze to her when she squeezed it back.

"He's right, though," she whispered when they had made it back to the bar. "It's your sister's wedding. Maybe don't schedule work things."

"I only have one more thing. Saturday afternoon. But it's huge. My agent actually called to tell me about it. This publisher we have been after has finally agreed to meet with me to talk about my potential future with them. This publisher can offer everything I've ever wanted. So it's a big deal."

Anita sipped her drink. "I'm happy for you—honestly—but it's your sister's wedding."

"I thought you'd be all for it. Finally seeing me work." Nikhil smirked at her, all of his gratitude at her for standing up to Rocky gone. "I believe the word *lazy* was used more than once at the end of our marriage."

Anita just stared at him. She shook her head at him, her lips twisted in disgust. "Is that what you got out of it? That's what you remember about the end of our marriage? That I used the word *lazy*?" She inhaled deeply. "You know what? That bitch in the green dress can have you."

"What the hell does that mean? You're leaving this farce?" What was she so mad about? She was the one who left. His next words belied the surge of panic that rushed through him at the thought that she might actually leave. But he bit them out anyway. "Feel free."

He remembered much more than the words she'd used. What haunted him in those moments that he thought about the divorce were the words he never used. Words like *I'm here for you. Go for it. Do what makes you happy.*

Her eyes hardened. "No. I'm not leaving. Not until this wedding is over."

"Don't you mean not until you get your tuition money?" Until he said it, he didn't realize how much that hurt him. That she was only here for a payoff.

Familiar sadness and pain flickered in her eyes before she hardened them again.

It didn't matter if he spoke or not. He was always hurting her.

Anita turned away from Nikhil. Blood pounded in her ears, her heart raced and she was sure her jaw was clenched so tight it might never open again. Many things were said at the end of their marriage. But that hadn't been the point. Nikhil had been clueless then, and he was clueless now.

She couldn't even look at him right now. Green Dress was watching them from across the room. If Anita stomped off right now, they risked their little ruse being exposed. Or it would just look like a husband and wife having an argument. Though the look on Green Dress Bitch's face said she was on to them anyway. Anita stayed put, not looking at her ass of an ex-husband.

He was right. She had said he was lazy. He had quit a nicely paying job at a local bar so he could concentrate on his writing, while Anita worked two jobs. Which she really did not have a problem with. She knew he would be successful one day. The problem was when she had decided that she wanted to go to law school and he flipped out.

"Why would you want to be a lawyer?" Nikhil had looked up from his computer to ask this question.

She had gone to him, excitement bubbling out from her. "You should have seen it. This family lost their daughter to DUI. Priscilla Herrera found the driver and prosecuted. The family got closure. I want to do that."

Nikhil had not said much at the time, but over the next few weeks, Anita would come home with information on classes she needed to take, scheduling of the LSAT, which schools were best, and each time she brought it up, he became more and more distant. Until one night she had called him on it.

"What's going on here, Nikhil? I feel like you're not on board with the law school route."

"I'm not. I've seen this my whole life. My mom, my brother, my sister, everything revolves around JFL. They miss everything and anything, if JFL needs something. I can see you going down that road, and it scares me."

"That won't happen. I probably won't even work for JFL—"

"Ha! Like you'll have a choice. The family will get their hooks in you. They already have." Nikhil had dismissed her.

His dismissal of their discussion and her dreams had infuriated her. He was supposed to love her, shouldn't he have been supporting her? "Well, at least I won't be sitting around all day staring at my computer, doing nothing," she had retorted, biting the words out in anger.

"Are you calling me lazy?"

"If the shoe fits."

Not her finest moment.

Not really his either.

Anita watched Jalissa walk around. She was drop-dead gorgeous in a low-cut, curve-hugging cocktail dress. Anita swore the woman was swaying her hips with the knowledge that Nikhil was watching her. A quick glance at Nikhil confirmed that he was.

Well, she couldn't really blame him. The woman was clearly interested in him, and she was beautiful. What Anita could not understand was her urge to gouge the woman's eyes out. Nor did she have an explanation for why she introduced herself as a Joshi. It was like she was marking her territory. Except that he really wasn't her territory at all. And if she had been married to Nikhil for real, she never would have staked her territory anyway. It wasn't her style.

In any case, Nikhil was clearly irritated and didn't want to talk about it, so she dropped it. She sipped her Manhattan.

"I was insensitive." Nikhil faced the bar, next to her. His suit jacket brushed against her bare arm. "I didn't want you to work for JFL." His soft tone surprised her after the words they had just spit at each other.

"I got that. But here you are, doing exactly what you hated your family for doing."

"It's not the same thing." He swirled his drink.

"What do you mean?"

"I mean—"

"Hey, you two! Give Deepa-masi some hugs!"

Deepa-masi was the most fun of the sisters. She was married with a couple children who were still in college. Her husband traveled quite a bit for work, frequently leaving Deepa-masi on her own, which she did not seem to mind.

"Deepa-masi." Nikhil turned to greet her with a hug. "Good to see you."

Deepa-masi glanced at their joined hands. "Here you are! Look at you two. Still honeymooning." She hugged them both. "You haven't made it out west yet. I'm waiting."

"Soon, Masi. I promise," Anita said. There she went again, making promises she knew she wouldn't be keeping.

"Well, I was hoping to come out here for a baby shower." She grinned at Anita.

"Oh, we're not ready for that quite yet," Anita responded.

"She's in law school," Nikhil added. "She wants to focus on that."

"That's nice." Neepa-masi was back. "But keep in mind your priorities."

"Their priorities are just fine," Seema-auntie interjected, coming up behind her sister.

Anita stared at all three sisters. She couldn't remember seeing them all together like this. They must have been for the wedding reception the Joshis had had for them, but Anita met so many people that day, it was hard to remember.

In any case, it was clear to Anita that Neepa-masi and Deepa-masi, the oldest and the middle, were quite close, while Seema seemed to simply tolerate them. Or maybe it was the other way around.

"Come," Seema-auntie spoke to her sisters, "let's get a drink."

Anita simply stared as the sisters walked away. "What the hell was that?" she said, turning to Nikhil, their earlier tensions having subsided with the appearance of the masis. Nikhil had his lips pressed together, trying not to laugh.

"Is this funny for you?" Anita exclaimed. She tried to sound indignant, but a smile fell across her face as a chuckle escaped Nikhil.

"I mean, come on. Yes." He shook his head. "You're in law school, doing very well, I'm sure. And all they can focus on is when you're planning on having a family. And then they use that as a reason to one-up each other. The best is that now, you're the one getting bent out of shape." He leaned in close to her ear. "And we're not even married."

"Well, they don't know that." She shouldn't, but she leaned into him, his breath sending goose bumps up and down her spine.

They shared a chuckle, before looking at each other again. "Do you think we would have had children by now?" he asked.

Anita twisted her rings. She had thought she might be a mother by now. She shrugged. "Maybe." She looked up at him.

He grinned. "Two boys."

"And a girl." She smiled back. "Maybe two." That had been their plan. She had loved the idea of a big family, an always-full house. They had lain awake some nights, naked and spent, thinking about the children they would have, what they would name them.

Nikhil held her gaze.

"Nikhil." Michael Collins, Jake's father, walked over and offered Nikhil his hand. Nikhil shook it. "Good to see you. Books are doing well." He beamed at him, just as his wife came up to them as well.

"Mr. Collins, so sorry to have missed the rehearsal. I was on an interview that ran long and—"

"Nikhil Joshi, do not worry one bit about it. You can make it up to me with an early copy of your next book." Christi Collins squeezed his hands. "I absolutely love your books. I can't wait for the next one. Bestsellers, all of them!"

Nikhil grinned. "Done! And thank you."

She fixed him in her gaze. "And we would not say no to a song."

"Mrs. Collins—" Nikhil started to protest. But Anita knew it wouldn't take much to convince him to sing. He loved it.

"Christi. And I won't take no for an answer."

"He'd be happy to sing tonight," Anita interjected. "He should. He missed the rehearsal."

"It's all set then." Mrs. Collins cut her eyes to Anita. "Good to see you again, Anita. I've heard so much about you."

"Have you?" Anita asked, glancing at Nikhil. Surely Jake's parents know about the divorce.

Christi pulled Anita into a hug. "I have." She whispered, "Tina always talks so fondly about how close you two were." Christi pulled back, a smile on her face. "You are good to come and do this for Seema. She was quite distraught."

Unexpectedly, tears burned Anita's eyes. "Well, they're a good family. Though I will say, Tina is quite—"

"Don't get me started on Tina," Michael interrupted. "I couldn't ask for a better daughter-in-law."

Christi smiled at her husband and rolled her eyes a bit. "They like to test wits, my husband and Tina, and it literally makes his day."

"Good luck with that, Mr. Collins." Nikhil grinned. "I never win. In fact, no one in my family has."

"Well, they should all know better than to take me on." Tina smiled at the group as she and Jake joined them.

Michael shook his head, grinning. "She's a tough one, Jake."

"Ms. Virani?" A young woman's voice called to her from behind Tina.

Anita shifted her position to see who had called her name. A young woman in a waiter's outfit approached her, an empty tray in hand.

"Yes." Anita could not place the petite woman.

"You may not remember me, but you helped my dad get disability when he was injured on the job. From the law clinic, downtown?"

Anita smiled. "Yes, of course. Megan, isn't it? How's your dad doing now?"

"Much better, thanks. He should be back to work in a week or two." The young woman sighed relief. "Your help with that made all the difference."

"I'm so glad to hear that. Please give him my best." Anita squeezed Megan's hand before she left.

"You work at the law clinic?" Nikhil asked.

Anita nodded. "Well, I'm an unpaid intern. I love

the work, and it's great experience. I'm hoping they'll hire me when I graduate."

"Well, if they don't, I'm sure JFL will," Jake said. "We've been trying to get a community division going forever."

"That's generous, but Jake, the firm is not affordable." Anita shrugged, and sipped her drink.

"No, that's the point. We'd all be taking a couple cases basically pro bono to give back to the community, but we need someone to run that. You'd be great," Jake insisted.

Anita beamed. "Really? So I could do all that work for the community and you all would help, and we wouldn't charge?"

"Yep."

"Is that even possible?" Anita was interested, but it had to be real, not just a thought.

"If you're interested, we'll make it possible." Jake beamed.

She glanced at Nikhil. "I'd love that. But I'd have to think about it. I still have a year left and then there's the bar."

Nikhil pressed his lips together. "I'll get us another round."

"Everyone," Christi said, nodding at the group, "we're seating for dinner now."

"Seriously, Rocky?" Nikhil was pissed but trying not to draw attention. "What the hell is Jalissa doing here?" They were at the bar waiting for drinks, while dinner was being served.

"It wasn't my idea." Rocky pressed his lips together.

"Why would I believe you? You're the one who hired her," Nikhil said.

"How was I supposed to know she'd dump you after she got the job?" Rocky sipped his drink and cast his gaze around the room.

"Well, you didn't fire her." And now they were offering Anita a job. Good thing they weren't together anymore.

"You know we couldn't do that. It opens us up to retaliation." Rocky shook his head.

What Nikhil knew was that a woman he thought he loved had used him to get a job in his family's company, then dumped him within six months. Granted they had started dating while she was in law school. The family took her on as an intern and hired her upon graduation, pending passing the bar. She passed the bar, secured her position, and then dumped him. And his family kept her on. He met Anita a few months after that breakup.

He couldn't stop himself from watching Jalissa throughout the night. Something about her presence made him uncomfortable because he couldn't place why she would even want to be here. So it was best to know what the enemy might be up to.

Christi Collins took the mic. "We have a treat tonight. As your dinners are being served, our daughter-in-law-to-be's brother is going to treat us to a song." She smiled in Nikhil's direction, and he raised a glass to her.

Great. What had he agreed to? Actually Anita had volunteered him.

"In any case," Rocky whispered in his ear, "you're supposed to be married, so stop watching her." Rocky looked him in the eye.

Nikhil shook his head at his brother. "I have to sing now." He widened his eyes in mock innocence and went to take the mic from Mrs. Collins. Turning to the crowd, he thought for a moment before speaking.

"This is a song you all know, but it is my wish for my sister and her new husband in their new life together, that they have a love and life that is all these things." He nodded at the band and began.

He sang about new beginnings and reasons for living. Anita stood in the back, next to one of the bridesmaids, watching him with her whole body. She seemed oblivious to whatever was happening around her.

Without realizing it, he was singing to her again. Telling her his hopes and wishes and there was nothing but the two of them.

No divorce. No fake marriage.

No regrets.

Nikhil and Anita said their goodbyes to the Collins family and headed on home, carpooling with Rocky and Easha. Easha was still barely keeping food down, but she was being a trooper, attending whatever events she could.

"You could just stay back and rest," Rocky was saying as he drove.

"Why? I'm going to be sick whether I'm alone or out here celebrating," Easha insisted.

Rocky took her hand and kept the other on the wheel. "If you're sure."

"I'm sure." She smiled at him.

"Okay then." He lifted their joined hands and kissed her hand.

Nikhil and Anita exchanged looks in the back seat. Rocky? Showing PDA? What was going on in the universe?

When they finally got back to their room, they went about getting ready for bed.

"Do you want the bathroom first?" Nikhil asked.

"Um, no, you go ahead." She pulled out her laptop.

Nikhil went into the bathroom and took off his shirt. He popped his head out. "Are you going to work for my family?" Nikhil blurted out.

"What? I don't know." Anita looked up from her computer. "It still matters to you whether I work for them or not? We aren't even together anymore. And you're more of a workaholic than us all."

"Whatever." Nikhil hoped he sounded nonchalant and went back into the bathroom.

"Okay." Anita appeared at the door. "Why? Why is it such a big deal if I work for JFL? They *are* the biggest practice around here. Their reputation is incredible."

"I don't care." He looked at her in the mirror and began brushing his teeth.

Anita folded her arms across her chest, watching him in the mirror. "It sounds like you might."

"Nope."

The way she stared at him in the mirror, there was no way she believed him. "You never could be happy for me, could you? If there was anything to do with your family, you just couldn't stand it." Anita was fired up.

Nikhil finished brushing his teeth, and wiped his mouth, suddenly very aware of the fact that he was shirtless. "That's not true." But it kind of was. Just not how she was saying it.

"Isn't it, though?"

"Do you honestly believe I was unable to be happy for you?" He watched her in the mirror.

"Yes." Her eyes widened and she threw back her

shoulders while raising her chin to him. "I wanted to go to law school, actually follow my passion, and you freaked out. Your family was happy for me, and you couldn't be bothered." She was nearly shouting. "Why do you think I left? And now, you're all bent out of shape because I might work for JFL. They're huge, and you don't work there."

"You left because you thought I wasn't happy for you?" He didn't shout back out of confusion. He had not once said he wasn't happy for her.

"You weren't. You didn't want to talk about law school, or me working at the firm, or anything."

He turned to face her. "I heard you." The memory that was never far from the surface came front and center.

"What are you talking about?" Anita's voice was raised in irritation.

"Back then? I heard you talking to my brother. So *grateful*—" Nikhil made air quotes here "—that he understood you, and that he was helping you with the LSAT. I heard you tell him there was no way that I could understand. As if I wasn't even capable of being happy for you and your success. You had already decided." The bathroom wasn't small, but Nikhil had stepped closer to her to make his point.

"You had told me you didn't like that I wanted to go to law school. Every time I came to you excited about something, you clammed up, which was completely unfair. I was looking for stability—for family—and every time I got close to it, you pulled me back. They're your family. You would think that—"

"That what? That I would be happy for you? I was."

"Did you think there was something going on between me and Rocky?"

"Of course not." Nikhil shook his head. "But it was clear to me that you were getting closer to them. That you shared something with them that you did not share with me." He knew where that led. It started out as small conversations, then led to meals, then the meals ran into the meetings until it was all one meeting, one conversation all day long. He'd seen it happen with his siblings to the point where Nikhil was completely invisible. Or it led to her being offered a job and then ditching him anyway.

"So what was wrong with that?" Anita challenged him.

He stared at her, knowing that if she had joined JFL when they were married, he would have lost his connection to her. He froze, unable to voice his fears that he might not be enough for her, unable to form the words that would confirm that he in fact could never be enough for her.

Because the connection to JFL was stronger than any other connection there was. That was the lesson he'd learned less than one year after his father's death.

Young Nikhil's nose had pulsed with pain from the punch he'd taken from one of the guys. He had been sure it was bleeding, if not broken. The ominous sound of his mother's heels clunking toward him from the hallway filled his stomach with more apprehension than actually facing down the boys he had fought.

The principal looked up from her desk.

"Mrs. Joshi. I'd like to say it's good to see you, but under the circumstances..." She glanced at Nikhil.

His mother turned to look at him and clenched her

jaw. She turned back to the principal. "What happened?"

"He was in a fight with at least three other boys."

"He's suspended?"

The principal nodded. "It's the third time this month."

His mother nodded at the principal and had turned to him at that moment. "Get up." She had handed him a handkerchief, which he had mildly registered as being his dad's. She was silent until they got in the car. She pulled out of the lot before she spoke.

"I'm at my wit's end with you, Nikhil. I am fed up with all the fighting. What has gotten into you?"

He opened his mouth.

"I do not want to hear it. I don't even care at this point. Just stop. Just stop fighting. I do not have time to keep leaving the office to come down here and take care of your mishaps. You're suspended for three days this time. You're coming to the office to do scut work. Your dad never believed in it, but I do. And since he's not here anymore to handle you, you'll do things my way!"

Nikhil had actually been excited at the prospect of going to the office with his mother. Maybe he'd catch her in a good mood and be able to explain his side of the fight.

But when he had gone to the office with her the next day, she had assigned him to an intern and he didn't see her again until it was time to go home.

He said nothing now, nothing to explain himself, his feelings or fears. Though why he cared if Anita worked for JFL now, he had no idea.

Anita fumed, her eyes registering a sudden realization over coming her. "You have got to be kidding me!

You let me go because your family *actually liked me*? That is completely ridiculous." She shook her head in disgust. "I can't believe I married you in the first place."

She turned away from him and marched out of the room.

The door slammed and Nikhil was left shirtless and alone, once again.

Chapter 9

Anita marched down to the kitchen and was greeted by the scent of lemon cleaning products, as the staff put finishing touches on the cleanup and prep for tomorrow. She headed for the bar and poured herself a bourbon—the good stuff, neat, screw the ice. She took the drink and collapsed into one of the oversize leather chairs in the family room.

Floor-to-ceiling windows in this room overlooked a small brook. The night sky was clear midnight blue, leaving the backyard to be lit by the crescent moon. The small brook babbled along happily, as if she hadn't just found out that she was divorced because her husband was jealous of his family. She closed her eyes and inhaled. Though that didn't really make any sense to her. He had his issues with his family, sure, but he loved them just the same.

His almost hypnotic singing voice echoed in her ears. She had been completely mesmerized by him earlier that evening. Every time he sang, she felt as though he sang only to her. There really wasn't anything sexier than a man who could sing like that. She shook her head as if to dislodge his voice and her thoughts. More thoughts came in instead. Memories of him singing to her on their first date. She squeezed her eyes shut against those thoughts.

Three more days. That's all she had to endure. Three more days. Maybe some old feelings for Nikhil would pop up. Hell, maybe they'd never left. But she was done for now.

She sipped her bourbon, staring out at the brook, and that last argument came back to her. Anita had needed law school like she needed breath.

Her world had been turned upside down when her parents were killed. Up until that point, she'd led a charmed life. She had a life plan, a loose one, but a plan nonetheless. She would go to college, start her career, fall in love, get married and have children.

Dilip and Varsha Virani were all about their children's dreams. Amar had always had his—he was almost born a chef. Her parents had encouraged her to find her passion, and that was what she had been searching for when they died.

The fact that she would never be able to share her passion with her parents always left her feeling slightly hollow.

The call from the police at the scene of the auto accident had come to her cell phone. Everything had slowed down and sped up all at the same time. Her first call had been to Amar. She remembered meeting him at the hospital and she hadn't even cried yet. It was as if she had shut down a part of herself so she could function. When the doctors confirmed their parents' deaths, Amar had broken down, but she had felt nothing. Maybe she'd been too numb to comprehend what was happening.

There was the house to take care of, bills and so much more. Amar had been so overcome with grief that he had been barely able to function for a day or two, so she had made all the arrangements. After the funeral, Amar seemed better, and they shared the responsibilities. It made sense for them both to live in the house and finish school while they worked. They had sublet their respective apartments and moved back into their childhood home. That was where Anita lived now, with her brother.

It was almost two months after her parents died that the well-wishers had stopped coming by. It was as if they had done their part, and now the rest of the way was up to her and Amar. It was true, in a way. No one could grieve for them. But it left them feeling...not abandoned, exactly. Just...empty.

Not long after, Anita had gone grocery shopping to get some basics, and something she and Amar could use to cook dinner together. It had felt almost normal to be buying fruit, veggies, milk and cereal. She had even gone to the Indian grocery store to replenish spices. She was unloading the groceries and putting them away when it happened. She started talking to her mother, like she used to when she was a teenager helping to put away groceries. She just went on about this new recipe she'd found online and how they should test it before telling Amar about it.

What do you think, Mom? We could add that tan-

door masala instead of what everyone else uses. Amar
would love it. What do you think? Mom?

She had turned away from the fridge where she was
going to put away the milk to see why her mom hadn't
answered. Then she remembered. Her mother was gone,
and she'd never be able to talk to her like that again.

Just like that, the ground beneath her gave way. She
slid down the fridge to the ceramic tile floor, hard and
cold. The room spun and her stomach roiled. Her foundation, her rock, was gone.

She was shaking when her brother found her, still
clutching the milk, unable to get off the kitchen floor.
Everything around her seemed to move in slow motion, only to suddenly speed up to a pace she couldn't
match. That's when the tears finally came. She had
wrenched out sobs in her brother's arms right there on
the kitchen floor. How long they sat there, she had no
idea. But when she was finally drained, she and Amar
had stayed up talking, not finding sleep until the wee
hours of the morning.

They each found a therapist who guided them through
those first months and stages of loss, but Anita could
not shake the feeling that she was floating through life
with no one or nothing to ground her.

When she'd met Nikhil a couple years later, he seemed
so stable, and his family was so wonderful—she'd missed
the closeness of gathering, the intimacy of family, and
they welcomed her with open arms. They'd even looked
into her parents' case, since the driver of the vehicle had
never been found. She had felt like she had a foundation again.

Shortly after they married, she'd gone to work as a
secretary in a small law firm that was owned by a friend

of the Joshi family. Her mother-in-law had gone to law school with Priscilla Herrera. The money was good and the Herreras were wonderful to her. She helped with research, and one case involved a hit-and-run. Though it hit close to home, the actual work made her feel grounded again, and she knew that this was what she was meant to do. When she had excitedly told Nikhil about it, he had seemed excited, but there had been a reticence about him.

Soft footsteps sounded over the kitchen tile and she turned, expectant. "Nikhil?"

"No. Rocky." Rocky was the same height as Nikhil, but with a slighter build, and the same Bollywood movie-star good looks. Right now, he was in shorts and a T-shirt and carried a glass of bourbon.

"Hey." Disappointment filled her. Huh.

"No need to sound so excited," he joked, sitting down on the sofa beside the chair. He took a gulp of his bourbon and nodded at hers. "What's your excuse?"

Anita glanced around to see if anyone else was wandering around. No one was there. Even the staff had finished up. "I'm sharing a room with my pain-in-the-ass ex-husband. What about you?"

Rocky laughed. "You win. I needed to relax before going to bed. I worry about Easha." He took another gulp. "Let me guess. He doesn't want you to work for the firm."

"How'd you know?"

"I know my little brother. He's had a chip on his shoulder his whole life." Rocky was dismissive. "Not to mention Jalissa."

"Let's not mention Jalissa," Anita nearly snapped. The mere mention of that woman had Anita seeing green.

Rocky raised his eyebrows at her. She shrugged. "Or maybe the chip is because you are a very hard act to follow."

"That is bullshit. Our parents loved us all the same. Nicky—"

"Damn it, Rocky, he's not a kid anymore. You know he hates when you call him Nicky, and you do it all the time."

Rocky held his hands up in surrender. "When he acts grown-up, I'll reconsider. *Nikhil*—" he rolled his eyes at her "—is actually lucky he didn't have to be the first-born. There was never even a question as to whether I would go into law. It was always assumed I would."

"It wasn't the same for Nikhil?" She drank some of the amber liquid, relishing the warmth as it went down.

"I don't know. But what I do know is that Nikhil made it be known, early on, that he had no interest in going to law school. That he was going to follow his heart. It's a luxury in this family, being able to follow your heart." Rocky looked into his drink. "And damn if he didn't do it. Three books in. Already a bestseller." Rocky shrugged and Anita caught some brotherly pride there.

"How's Easha holding up?"

Rocky grinned. "Best she can. She's still nauseous and throwing up. Don't say anything, huh? To anyone outside the immediate family. About the baby."

"Of course." She didn't bother to correct the fact that she wasn't really family at all. Maybe it was pretend, but she could at least enjoy being a pretend part of the family for a few days.

She was pathetic.

He glanced at his watch. "I should get back to her."

He threw back the last of his bourbon. "Listen. Thanks. For doing this for Mom. I know Nicky isn't easy."

"Actually, *Nikhil* is fine." Not sure why she felt the need to defend him, but there it was. "Mom—Seema-auntie," Anita corrected herself, "didn't tell Neepa-masi and Deepa-masi about the divorce?"

"Hell no. They would be the last ones to know." Rocky shook his head.

"Why?"

"It's like she feels like she has to prove to them that she can be good at things." He shrugged. "Like they underestimate her all the time. I think it got worse when Dad died and they couldn't understand why Mom wouldn't just sell JFL and take a salary."

"But she wanted to maintain JFL. I mean, she loved it—she loved the law. She had lost her husband. She didn't want to lose her dreams, too. If anything, she wanted her dreams even more." Anita could completely understand.

"I remember phone arguments over the years with the masis asking her to come to India, and Mom being unable to go for more than a week at a time, because she had to take care of things here. Although, I suspect on some level, she didn't want to have to deal with her sisters." Rocky sighed, sadness coming over his eyes. "When Dadi fell ill, a year ago, she left things to me and went to India for a few weeks. Dadi passed a week after Mom returned home. She'd been with her mother for weeks and still wasn't at her side when she passed, and her sisters were unsympathetic.

"Mom went back to India when Dada had his heart attack six months ago. She stayed for a month to care for him and then returned. Granted, Neepa-masi took the brunt of caregiving, but Mom offered to bring Dada back with her. Neepa-masi wouldn't allow it. She babies Dada. Mom can't stand that."

He stood. "Anyway, that's the abridged version. She won't want them to know about the divorce because it'll make her look like she can't handle her own children. They'll say she allowed shame to come to the family." He shook his head. "She's already hounded me to be able to tell them about the baby. So she can brag about being a dadi. But I can't, not yet."

"Rakesh Joshi, what aren't you telling me?" She looked up at her former brother-in-law, her chin up, jaw set. She was getting an answer.

He sighed. "Easha had a miscarriage a few months ago, and it really tore her up." He paused, and Anita caught tears in his eyes.

"It tore you both up," Anita said softly.

He nodded. "Yes. Well." He cleared his throat and looked at her, his eyes still wet. "We just want to be *sure*, just pass the first trimester before we say anything, you know."

"Sure, Rocky." She stood and hugged him. "It'll be fine. I heard that morning sickness is a good sign."

"Really?"

She shrugged. "I have no idea. But it sounds good." She grinned.

Rocky smiled and hugged her again. "It's great having you around." He glanced once more at the time. "I really have to go. Good luck with Nicky." Rocky wished her good-night and left.

"Nikhil," she corrected him as he ran off. Anita returned to staring out the window and sipping her drink.

"Hey."

This time, she recognized his voice, and it sent a warmth through her. She turned to Nikhil and found him holding two glasses of bourbon. He had changed into shorts and a T-shirt, and his hair was pleasantly tousled. Her insides turned to goo, as held out a glass to her, his voice as smooth as the alcohol he offered. "Peace offering."

She raised her still half-full glass to him, and he shrugged and poured half of the extra drink into her glass, and the other half into his and leaned back against the bar. She swiveled the chair around to face him.

He was calmer, as was she.

Silence floated between them. "I just heard about the miscarriage."

Nikhil nodded and sipped his drink. "Anita... I owe you an explanation. I wasn't jealous of you and the family. It's just—my whole life, everything was about JFL. It was more important than anything."

"What happened with Jalissa?" Anita asked.

He sighed and stared into his glass before looking at her with his response. "We dated while she was in law school, before I met you. Then my family offered her a job at the firm. She took it. Six months later, she dumped me."

Anita knew there was a reason she hadn't liked her on sight. "They couldn't fire her."

He set his jaw. "Well, that's what they said."

"You really loved her?"

"Not like I loved you," he mumbled into his drink and flushed.

"You were afraid I'd leave if I worked for your family." She stood, looked him closely in the eye.

Nikhil shrugged, unable to meet her eyes. "You left anyway, so the joke's on me." He gulped his drink.

"I never actually had any regret over marrying you." She sipped her bourbon. "Remember our city hall ceremony?"

He nodded, this time looking at her.

"Happiest day of my life," she blurted out without thinking.

His eyes never left her. "Mine, too."

"We just—didn't work." She closed her eyes. The pain in his face, just now, was real.

The sliver of moon provided enough light that she could just see him. She stepped closer to him. The bourbon relaxed and warmed her. She was close enough to feel the heat from his body. He was leaning, his back slouched against the bar.

"You really thought you would lose me if I went to law school?"

He nodded, his gaze still fixed on her.

"We had some good times, though, didn't we?" she asked.

His perfect lips curved into a smile. "We did."

"Remember how we used to cook together?" she asked.

He stared at her, his eyes darkening, and she knew he was thinking about the times they would spend the weekend making love, dressing only to make themselves some food, before discarding their clothes and returning to their bed. Or wherever.

She cleared her throat. "I mean when we used to tweak old recipes from our moms and grandmothers."

He nodded, amusement falling across his face. "They didn't technically have recipes…"

"True." She grinned. "But we figured it out, adding things, whatever."

"That was your talent. You were good at figuring out all of that. Must be in the genes—your brother always loved what we came up with." He was smiling full-on right now. Anita loved that smile.

She shook her head. "Nah—I remember you being pretty good yourself."

"We said we would write a cookbook. Like an homage to our moms and grandmoms." He smiled with the memory, and Anita hadn't seen him this relaxed since she had shown up.

She couldn't look away. Maybe it was the moonlight. Maybe it was the apology. She was drawn to him as ever before. Kissing him yesterday had been…an accident. Kissing him now, on purpose, would be a mistake. It would be a really, really good mistake. But a mistake nonetheless. Her heart raced as he pushed away from the bar and moved closer to her. Could she kiss him and still walk away? She tilted her head up to him. She was about to find out.

The lights flicked on in the kitchen. Anita stepped back from Nikhil, squinting to see who had saved her from herself.

Tina.

The bride-to-be stood there in loose shorts and a T-shirt, her hair in a messy bun, her arms folded tightly across her chest, shoulders slumped. "I need you guys to come with me and tell Mom the wedding's off." Then she burst into tears.

Chapter 10

Nikhil wasn't happy to hear his sister sobbing, but she saved him from kissing his ex-wife.

Again.

He and Anita looked at each other and went into action. Nikhil poured his sister a bourbon while Anita tried to get her to sit down.

"I'm not sitting down." She glared at her brother.

"Well, we're not coming with you until we hear what happened." He held out the bourbon to her.

She looked from him to Anita and back. "You two always were a united front." She sighed and sat down as she took the bourbon. "I don't know what happened behind closed doors, but you were a force when you were on the same side."

Nikhil flicked his gaze quickly at Anita, but she was determinedly looking at Tina.

They waited until Tina had a sip. Then Anita spoke first. "What happened?"

Tina's deep inhale spoke of all the drama of a bride unable to come to terms with her groom. "He doesn't want me to change my name."

Nikhil and Anita stared at Tina for a minute in silence and blinked. "But I thought you wanted to keep Joshi as your last name." Anita spoke slowly as if her normal cadence might spook the young bride.

"I do." Tina looked at them like they were the idiots for not understanding.

"Help me out here. I'm just a guy," Nikhil said.

She sighed deeply again and took a sip of her drink. "We were talking about last names. And I said, 'What about hyphenating?'" She looked at Anita, for support it seemed, because Anita nodded and Tina continued, "Like Joshi-Collins."

"Okay." Nikhil had no idea where this was going.

"And he said, 'Why do you want to do that? Just keep Joshi,' and I said, 'Why? Don't you want me to be a Collins?' And he said, 'Why do you want to be a Collins? I thought you were just keeping Joshi.'"

At this point, Nikhil had no idea what was happening, but Anita nodded with deep understanding. "Somebody enlighten me."

Anita pressed her lips together and looked at him like he was a child. "She's upset because she wants him to *want* her to change to Collins, even though he knows that she's keeping Joshi."

Tina frowned and nodded. "So you see? We can't get married."

"I don't see," Nikhil said. "You're getting what you want. He's supporting whatever decision you make. It's your name, and he's in favor of what you want." Maybe he needed another drink.

"God, Bhaiya. You really don't understand anything, do you?" Tina rolled her eyes.

"See, Tina?" Anita grinned. "Sometimes, guys don't get it. Even when you spell it out for them. Nikhil is the perfect example of not getting it."

Hey. Wait a minute. He opened his mouth to protest, but Anita shot him a look that told him to shut it and shut it fast. "It doesn't mean he doesn't love you. Maybe you just need to talk. Weddings are stressful—"

"Tina." Jake's voice came from the front door. "Tina?"

Tina's eyes widened and she turned to face him as he entered the kitchen.

Anita leaned over to Nikhil. "Uh, how did he get in here?" she whispered.

He smiled, whispering back, "You kidding? He's practically been family for ages now. He's had a key and the codes to the house for months." Nikhil rolled his eyes. "He's here more than me."

"Tina. You didn't talk to your mom yet, did you?" Jake was in athletic shorts and a T-shirt and flip-flops and he was slightly out of breath. His hair was tousled and his green eyes held panic. He'd clearly rushed over here as fast as he could.

"Not yet." But Tina's voice was soft and had lost all the angst and determination of five minutes ago.

Jake sighed relief. "Oh thank god. Listen. I would *love* for you to be a Collins, if that is what you want." He walked toward her until he could touch his hand to her face. "It would be an honor to share my name with someone as amazing as you. But it's your name. You do what feels right for you. Either way, you're part of my family, the same way I'm part of yours. My parents will love you, the same way your mom loves me. Regardless of what your last name is. I love you either way. We're family. That's how it is."

"You came all the way out here to tell me that?"

"Well, yes. I want us to be married." He frowned, clearly upset. "Were you—are you—going to call it off?"

Tina fell into his arms.

Nikhil whispered to Anita, "Isn't that what I said?" She shushed him.

Nikhil cleared his throat. "So, everyone, still getting married?"

Tina wrapped an arm around her fiancé, and turned to them, grinning broadly. "Yes." She turned a look of complete adoration on Jake, before turning back to Nikhil and Anita.

"I just wanted it to be like—like the way our family loved her." Tina focused on Nikhil as if Anita suddenly wasn't even there. "Mom loved her like she was one of us."

It was true. Seema Joshi had always treated Anita like she was one of her children, not an in-law. Anita had always felt loved and accepted by the family. She had missed them dearly when she divorced their son.

"They absolutely liked you better than they liked me." Nikhil turned to Anita. "That's for sure, regardless. They still like you better." Nikhil shook his head, a small smile on his face.

"It's true." Tina nodded, finally looking at Anita.

"Well, I have no doubt that the same is true for the Collinses as Jake has said," Anita said. "Though be careful using us as a bar to measure by." Anita elbowed

Nikhil and laughed. "Because in the end, it didn't really work out."

Nikhil's eyes widened. Tina's head snapped up and flicked her gaze between them both. Nikhil seemed horrified, but then broke out into a half smile. "I mean…" He shrugged. "She's not wrong."

Jake joined Anita's laughter. "I'm never letting this one go." He squeezed his fiancée tight.

Tina's eyes widened. She didn't seem to think this was funny. "You two are unbelievable."

Nikhil just stared at Jake. He had let Anita go. Why had he done that? What had been more important than having her in his life? He absolutely couldn't remember.

"Nikhil. Nikhil." Tina was waving a hand in front of his face. "Good night."

He snapped out of it and nodded. "Good night. See you at wedding number one." He forced a smile, still lost in his own thoughts.

Tina and Jake left the kitchen, arm in arm.

"Well, crisis averted," said Anita softly. The two of them were alone, in the now brightly lit kitchen. While Nikhil rinsed out the glasses, he thought about how close they'd come to a near disaster. Maybe it was the moonlight, maybe it was the bourbon or maybe it was the reminiscing, but here in the stark light of the kitchen in the middle of the night, he knew he should not be kissing Anita Virani.

He never should have let her go, so now he certainly did not deserve to have her back. If he kissed her, he wouldn't want to stop.

While Nikhil changed for bed in his ample walk-in closet, Anita was checking email on her phone. When he came out in just his shorts, he found Anita sitting on the bed, staring at her phone, a melancholy look on her face.

"What's up?"

"Nothing." She looked up, her eyes glassy. He glanced at her phone. She had been looking at a picture of her parents. Dilip and Varsha Virani had been a handsome couple. The photo she had pulled up was from her high school graduation. Proud parents on either side of their young grad and big brother towering over them behind her.

"They were already gone for over a year when I graduated from college. Amar was there, and Divya. We weren't even going to take pictures, but Divya insisted." Anita shook her head. "She's good like that."

He donned a T-shirt as he sat down next to her. "Doesn't get easier, does it?" He recalled holding her as she had marked Mother's Day and Father's Day and birthdays and anniversaries without her parents. Just as he had marked many of those days without his own father.

She looked back at the photo. He put his arm around her shoulders and squeezed her to him as he mentally reviewed the date. He chided himself for not remembering sooner. "Your mom's birthday. Jeez, Anita. I'm sorry I didn't remember."

She shook her head, wiping her eyes. "No. It's okay. I couldn't face it today. I just—" She let out a sob. "What kind of daughter does that? I didn't even call my brother today. He called and I ignored it because I didn't want to talk to him about why I'm here."

"Call him now." Nikhil nodded at the phone.

"It's almost midnight."

"So what?"

She stared at her phone for a moment.

"He's your brother. If anyone knows what you're going through, it's him." Nikhil kissed the top of her head without thinking.

She nodded at him and calmed her breathing before tapping his number on her phone. "Hey, Amar."

Nikhil removed his arm from her shoulders to give her privacy. She grabbed his hand before he could stand and motioned for him to stay next to her.

"Sorry I missed your call earlier. I...forgot what day it was. Well, I didn't really forget. I just couldn't..."

She nodded and her eyes filled with tears. Nikhil scribbled something on a sticky note: "Dance while she cooked?" She smiled.

"Remember that time we caught her dancing in the kitchen?" She laugh-sobbed. "Celery!"

She nodded at whatever he was saying, a smile coming through her tears. "No. It was 'I Will Survive,' remember?" She laughed at something he said. "Mom had moves!" She wiped her eyes dry and leaned on Nikhil's shoulder.

"Church and reception tomorrow." She nodded at whatever he was saying. "So a different caterer tomorrow?...Okay...You're working the Indian ceremony and the sangeet-garba reception on Saturday?...So, I'll see you then...Miss you...Will do." She tapped the phone off and looked at him. "Thanks for that. And for sitting with me."

"No problem."

She fidgeted with her phone for a moment before looking at him. "You don't really have to, you know, since we really aren't anything to each other."

Nikhil had no answer for that, so he said nothing about it. "What was the *Will do*?"

She rolled her eyes and shook her head as she sniffled. "He wants me to say hi to Divya if I talk to her."

Nikhil widened his eyes. "Divya, huh?"

Anita turned and sat cross-legged on the bed facing him. "He's got it bad. Though he'll never admit it."

"Did you tell Divya?"

Anita dropped her mouth open in horror. "Sibling code. No way. Besides, he's never actually even admitted it to me."

She glanced at the sticky note in her hand. "Mom was so full of life." She looked at Nikhil. "Too bad you never met her. Or my dad."

"You and Amar used to talk about them so much, I felt like I knew them. Besides, I could never imagine my mother singing and dancing while she cooked, using celery as a mic. She's too stoic."

"Reserved."

"Also—I think the last time she cooked was the night she met you."

"She's a really good cook." Anita turned on the bed to face him. "That can't be the last time she cooked."

Nikhil nodded his head. "And I was surprised even then."

"That was a fun night." Anita grinned.

"Was it, though? Meeting my whole family, all the law talk. And Tina and Rocky arguing. I was surprised you didn't break up with me right then."

"I loved all the law talk. But what I really loved was the loudness and even the arguing. I had missed that sense of family." She paused. "It was nice having it

again. Even if it was only for a while." She looked away
from him, sadness covering her face again.

"Rocky was pretty pissed when we broke up. Not as
angry as Tina, but still." Rocky had bugged his eyes in
anger, shaking his head at Nikhil as if he was a complete idiot. *She's the best thing that ever happened to
you, schmuck. How could you let her walk? How could
you not do everything in your power to keep her?*

His mother had shared the same sentiment. That he
was the one at fault for the breakup. It never mattered to
them that Anita had been the one who filed for divorce.
He had dismissed Rocky's admonition at that time as
simply typical Rocky. But he had wondered many times
since then if his older brother wasn't right.

Tina had been the only one who seemed to be on his
side. The only one who had been angry with Anita. And
actually, the only one who still was. His mother and
Rocky seemed actually happy that Anita was here, at
the wedding. Nikhil had long since passed anger when
it came to Anita. He was firmly at longing.

"I think you'd be surprised at what Rocky really
thinks of you." She caught his eye.

"I doubt that. He has always made it clear." Nikhil
leaned back on to the bed, resting his head on one elbow
as he faced Anita.

Anita shrugged. "Has he made it clear that he's proud
of you? That he respects you for not falling in line with
your parents' expectations?"

Nikhil shook his head in disbelief. "He said that?"

"Maybe you should talk to him yourself." She un-
crossed her legs and hopped off the bed. "We should
get some sleep. Tomorrow is a long day." She stretched
before heading for the bathroom.

He made up the sofa and closed his eyes when he lay down. He heard the water running and imagined her doing her nighttime routine.

He shifted and inhaled deeply, willing sleep to come. It would not. He'd gotten so close to kissing her, but that wasn't all that was keeping him awake. He'd enjoyed their camaraderie in helping Tina, in warding off nosy aunties, in actually making their fake marriage work.

And yes, that almost kiss was definitely keeping him awake.

In a bit, he heard her come out and head toward the sofa. She stopped when she found him there, "asleep." She quietly turned away and he heard her climb into the bed. She always applied lotion before bed, and the clean scent always reminded him of her. It floated to him now, taking him back to when she was his.

DAY THREE:

I DOS AND CHAMPAGNE TOASTS
Make it to the Church on time…

Chapter 11

By the time Anita woke, the sofa was tidy, and Nikhil was not in the room.

Probably on another call. She did not remember him being such a workaholic when they were married. In fact, one of the things she had really loved was his ability to prioritize and know when to work and when to take time off. He seemed to have lost that ability. It was not attractive.

She freshened up and pulled out her laptop and was contemplating coffee when Nikhil entered the room, the aroma of hot chai coming in with him. He had on athletic shorts and a fitted T-shirt, but his hair was still attractively mussed from sleep. He carried two large mugs from which emanated the most luscious aroma. She closed her eyes and inhaled. "That better be your chai, because—"

"You'll only drink my chai in the morning." He grinned at her. "I'm not new."

She nearly grabbed the mug from him and wrapped her hands around it, inhaling and savoring the luxurious aroma of cinnamon, cardamom and clove before she finally indulged in the first life-giving sip. Nikhil really did make the best chai.

She had made chai a few times after the divorce, had even had her brother make it, too. It really wasn't that complicated, but even as a culinary student with a developed sense of taste, he couldn't quite replicate the flavor she remembered. It remained lost to her.

Like so much else she remembered about him…

"Are you ever going to tell me the secret to this chai?" She nearly moaned, closing her eyes.

She opened her eyes to find Nikhil staring at her, his eyes dark. "Nikhil?"

He startled and refocused, a sly grin on his face. "I make my own spice."

Anita widened her eyes. "You mean, you actually grind out the spices and make it yourself?"

"Yes."

"If you had told me that when we were married, I might not have left." She pursed her lips and cocked an eyebrow at him.

He rolled his eyes. "And before you ask, no, I am not going to tell you how I make it, or what I put in it."

"Fine." She took her chai to the desk and sat down in front of her laptop. "I have some work to do before we leave for the church."

"Me too." He pulled out his laptop and made himself comfortable on the sofa.

"We almost kissed last night." Anita tried to keep her tone focused, even businesslike. "Again."

"I know." He looked at her over the top of his laptop.

"That can't happen." Anita was firm.

"Agreed."

"Probably too much alcohol."

"Exactly," Nikhil agreed. "Plus reminiscing…" He waved his hand.

"And we used to be really good together."

Nikhil paused, a slight grin coming over his face. "That is true. We were really good together…" His voice drifted off.

Anita cleared her throat. "Well, it's probably best we don't dwell on that. Nothing good could possibly come of it. Right?"

"Right."

They stared at each other a moment, during which she recalled exactly the good that used to come out of them being together, and she flushed.

She snapped her attention back to her computer. "I need to get this done."

"Okay." He grinned.

They were working in quiet companionship for a while, when her phone buzzed with a text from the clinic. She called in.

"Hey, Marisa."

"Anita, I know you're busy this weekend, but I have Charlotte Montgomery here. She's freaking out about the hardship-stay hearing today. She said the landlord keeps threatening to throw them out on the street."

"Okay. Put her on."

"Hey, Ms. Virani." The young woman's voice was shaky.

"Charlotte, please call me Anita."

"Okay, Ms. Virani."

Anita rolled her eyes. "What's going on?"

"The landlord keeps threatening to throw us out. I told him we're going to court today—but he won't listen. I'm scared and I don't know what to say…and I can't mess this up. My kids and my mom need me." Charlotte's voice cracked, and Anita's heart broke for her. The poor girl probably hadn't even slept in days.

"Okay. I'll be there. Look at the paper—there should be a time on it. Read me the time."

When Charlotte read her the summons, Anita's nerves hummed. She would be cutting it close to the wedding. Still, there was no way she was going to leave her client alone to face an eviction hearing. She'd figure out the timing. "Okay. No problem."

"I'll have to bring the kids," Charlotte said. "There's no one to watch them."

"Even better." Anita grinned. "We'll take them with us."

"Everything okay?" Nikhil asked after she hung up and went straight into her bag for papers.

"Yep. Nothing an email can't handle," she lied. She pressed her lips together, her mind whirring. She had all the paperwork and necessary signatures. She was supposed to be meeting with the landlord on Monday, but he was just being a dick. Finding Charlotte a better place to live was the ultimate goal, but right now, Anita needed to make sure that Charlotte wouldn't be homeless by tomorrow. She could email all the documents, but it really sounded like Charlotte just needed someone by her side to make sure things went smoothly. It was a no-brainer. Anita would simply go down there and attend the hearing with her. And be back in time for the wedding and hope no one noticed.

If she made her hair appointment earlier, and left the dress in the car, she could deliver the papers and be back in time to meet the limo before it left for the church.

She called the hairdresser and changed her time slot. She had been added on to the end at the last minute, so she simply asked to be shifted as early as they could push her. She quickly did her makeup and gathered all her things.

"You're taking the dress to the hair thing?" Nikhil asked.

"Well, sometimes they run late and we want to make sure everyone is ready for pictures. You know." She shrugged, knowing it was a lame excuse.

He studied her closely for a moment, and Anita thought he might be on to her, but he shrugged. "Okay… you better go before you lose your spot in the hair line or whatever is happening over there. The limo is coming here half an hour before the wedding."

"I'll see you then." She grinned and grabbed her bag, which had all her papers and computer in it.

"You're taking that with you?"

She hesitated. She should probably tell him. But didn't she just lecture him on working during the wedding? "It takes time to get hair done. I can get a bit of work done while I sit." She walked out the door, ignoring the pit that was developing in her stomach from her simple lie of omission. Though why it mattered that she was lying to him when they were both being untruthful to a few hundred people this weekend was beyond her. She pushed those thoughts from her mind as she drove to the salon and parked in front.

Only Easha was in the salon with Laila, the hair-dresser, when Anita got there. Tina and the other brides-maids were scheduled for a bit later. Perfect. Anita could get her hair done and sneak out without running into anyone.

Easha had thick dark hair that Laila was teasing and twisting into the same updo they would all have. She hadn't yet put on her makeup, but her brown skin was flawless, except that Easha looked a bit green.

"Can I get you something?" asked Anita. "Ginger tea?"

Easha pointed at the table. "I have some, thanks."

Anita greeted Laila and took a seat. "I'm very excited for you and Rocky. You must be very happy."

Easha nodded. "It's been a long time coming. Just weird timing. The wedding and all that."

"Rocky told me everything," Anita blurted out. "I'm so sorry for your loss."

"Thank you. We're…well, we're excited about this one." She nodded, tears in her eyes. "I'm sorry. I cry all the time. Hormones, I guess." She chuckled through her tears. They sat in awkward silence for a moment. "You know, Nikhil didn't come to Sunday dinner for months after you left."

Easha and Rocky had gotten married a year before Anita and Nikhil. At the time, Anita and Easha were quite friendly, but Easha had been new to JFL and was working all the time. They basically met at Sunday dinners. Anita didn't know what to say with the informa-tion Easha was offering her.

"It was Tina who finally dragged him over, and even then, he wouldn't say much and he would leave as soon as possible."

"He used to do that when I was around, too."

Easha shook her head. "No. He was getting better about staying after you two were married for a bit."

"And now?"

Easha shrugged. "Since he's found success in something he loves, he's better. But there's always a loneliness about him." She fixed Anita in her gaze. "I think he misses you."

"But he works all the time now. I mean, I understand working hard, but it's almost like he's scheduling interviews and meetings during the wedding to prove how successful he is."

"Maybe he is. He's always acted like he had something to prove—" Easha met her eyes "—to the people around him. Rocky. You. His mother."

Anita shook her head. "I don't know." That couldn't really be true, could it? "Rocky seems different." Anita changed the subject.

Easha beamed as she nodded. "I think the prospect of becoming parents has changed us both. Like we love our work, but we want to be there for our kids. So we're taking on more associates so we can have some family time."

Anita shook her head. "Who would have thought of Rocky Joshi as a family man? The Rocky I remember was a tough, take-no-bull litigator. It took a while to find his soft side."

"You're telling me." Easha rolled her eyes.

"Even you, Easha-bhabhi. I think you were tougher than him." Anita smiled. How easily Anita called her sister-in-law.

Easha laughed. "I still am tough at work. I've just

shifted my priorities." She looked Anita in the eye. "People change."

Anita simply nodded, not taking the bait. Maybe.

Laila finished Easha's hair and motioned Anita to her chair.

Easha gathered her things. "I'm going to carefully lay down and get some rest before the craziness starts." She started for the door and turned back. "You know, neither one of you has ever said that you don't love the other anymore."

Easha's parting words hung in the air while Anita watched her leave. She pulled out her laptop while Laila did her hair and focused on work. She needed to make sure everything was in order for the court hearing today. Laila tugged and twisted Anita's hair into the same updo she'd given Easha.

Hair done, documents gathered, Anita was just leaving when the other bridesmaids all showed up at the same time.

They squealed with delight as they walked in, and literally slammed into her with hugs.

"Oh my god! It's so good to see you," Miki squealed. "Why did you never answer our texts?"

Anita hugged them back. She hadn't seen these ladies since the divorce. "How's the tabla guy?" she teased Anu.

"He's a fantastic kisser. Thank you for asking." Anu grinned, not even trying hide that she'd deceived Anita earlier.

"You didn't have to leave us just because Nikhil was acting like a dick." This was Julie. "Oh, but how cool that you two are getting back together!"

"Yes." Anita nodded. She had forgotten that these

ladies thought she and Nikhil were together now but
knew that they had been divorced. Hard to keep track
of the lies. "And he wasn't acting like a dick. He was…"
So many things that Anita had not known about. Trying to prove himself. Trying to protect himself. It was
too much to think about.

"Well, you'd say that now, anyway. Maybe we'll get
to come your wedding soon!" gushed Anu.

Oh god. How was she going to keep all this straight?
"Where's Tina?"

"She's on her way."

"Has anyone talked to her today?"

"Why? What's happening?" asked Anu.

"Nothing. I'm fine." Tina's voice from behind them
was commanding and joyous, perfectly befitting a bride.

The bridesmaids all squealed like teenagers again as
they welcomed the woman of the day. Anita held back,
gathering her things. She needed to leave soon if she
was going to make it back in time.

"Anita." Tina's voice was soft and without anger.

Anita looked at her. "Congrats. I'm sure all will go
well today."

"Thank you for last night." She gave a small smile.

"Of course."

Silence filled the room. "I should go." Anita walked
to the door. "I'll see you all at the limo."

Anita parked in front of the courthouse and scanned
the area for Charlotte and her children. She got out of
the car and saw the young woman, who at twenty-two
years old still looked like a teenager, with one toddler
on her hip and one by her side. The most adorable, well-
behaved twins Anita had ever seen.

Charlotte was a single mom and the only caretaker for her ailing mother. She'd missed a few shifts at her job, because she'd had to accompany her mother to the doctor, so she'd lost several paychecks and as a result was behind on rent. Charlotte's boss was threatening to fire her for not showing up, but Anita would deal with *him* on Monday.

"Hi, Charlotte." Anita grinned and presented her with a coffee and a bagful of bagels that she'd picked up on her way out there. She squinted in the sun, despite her sunglasses, as the humidity threatened her updo.

"Hey, Ms. Virani." Charlotte's face immediately relaxed and she broke out into a huge smile. "Thank you so much for coming."

"Of course." She greeted the children, and they shyly waved to her.

"This is Elizabeth—" she indicated the little girl on her hip "—and Evan," Charlotte said, introducing her children. "Your hair looks nice. You look like you're going to a wedding," commented Charlotte.

"Well, thank you, and I am in fact going to a wedding today. So let's go meet with this judge and secure your apartment. On Monday, we'll talk to your boss."

Charlotte beamed. "Thank you so much." She looked at her kids. "Hear that? Ms. Virani is going to make things all better."

Anita took in the young mother and her two children and butterflies filled her stomach. If this didn't go well, this family would be on the street. She would return to the Joshi mansion and attend her fake sister-in-law's wedding.

What was she thinking? She should have called her boss, let her handle this. But her boss wouldn't have been able to come out like this. She had so many other families just like this who needed her. Anita was Charlotte's only chance.

Anita inhaled deeply and drew up her shoulders, a smile plastered on her face. There simply was no room for a bad outcome here. This family was staying in their apartment while they looked for a more suitable place to live.

"That's right," Anita told the children. "We're not taking no for answer." *Behave like the person you want to be, even if you're not quite there yet, because eventually that's who you will become.* Her father used to say that to her and Amar all the time. Basically, his version of "Fake it till you make it." She certainly did not feel that confident, but there was no alternative.

She took Evan's hand and led the way into the building and found the assigned courtroom. She walked with purpose, as if she did this all the time, when in fact, she had only been here a couple times before. Her dad's voice echoed in her ears. *If you don't believe it, no one else will. So move with purpose and the force of your convictions.* He used to say this to her whenever she was nervous. "No kidding, Dad." She smiled to herself. It was almost as if he was right there with her.

They arrived in the small courtroom just as their case was being called. Charlotte tensed as she pointed out the landlord, a middle-aged man who looked rather unassuming, but who, Charlotte guaranteed Anita, was anything but. Anita reassured her that all would be well and seated the little family next to her.

Anita stepped forward with confidence she hardly felt and raised her chin. She swallowed and cleared her throat and then calmly addressed the court. She barely even noticed that people were watching her. It was nothing like her dance days, because right now, Anita's performance was about Charlotte and her family.

"We request a hardship stay, to give Ms. Charlotte Montgomery extra time to find a place that can accommodate her children and her mother. Ms. Montgomery is hardworking and up until her mother fell ill, she never missed a day of work. As of right now and the foreseeable future, there is no one else to care for Ms. Montgomery's mother. We have a meeting with Ms. Montgomery's employer on Monday, to secure her position as well as come up with a schedule that will allow Ms. Montgomery to care for her mother and provide for her family. I have provided the court with medical records detailing the mother's illness with relevant dates." She passed the paperwork to the bailiff and took her seat.

The judge was a middle-aged black woman whose expression revealed nothing. She eyed Anita and Charlotte and the two children before nodding at the young man who was representing the landlord.

The landlord's attorney stood. "Your Honor, rent has to be paid. You cannot live somewhere for free. Ms. Montgomery is not alone in having hardship. Everyone else manages to pay rent."

Anita stood. She was out of turn, but there was no taking no for an answer. "Ma'am. Charlotte Montgomery is an extremely hardworking young woman. She was unable to finish college when her mother fell ill, as her mother was her primary source of childcare. Her mother's condition worsened, requiring Ms. Montgomery to become the primary caregiver for her mother. She is one year shy of a bachelor's degree. Putting her on the street because of missed rent would be a great disservice to her family and her children, as well as to Ms. Montgomery herself. Not to mention the greater society as well."

"Ms. Virani." The judge turned a frown on Anita. "I am well aware of Ms. Montgomery's situation, as you have provided extremely detailed documentation of the facts."

"Yes, Ma'am. I just wanted—"

"Sit down, Ms. Virani," the judge told her.

Crap. Her heart fell. She shouldn't have opened her mouth. She should apologize to the judge. Anita started to stand.

The judge looked at her and shook her head. "Do not stand. I have made my decision."

Anita sat back down, her back completely straight, and took Charlotte's hand. It seemed an eternity before the judge spoke again.

"Very well, four months' hardship extension ought to do it." She shuffled some papers and called out. "Next."

Anita stood. "Thank you, ma'am. Your Honor. Ma'am."

The judge passed a glare over Anita. "Next!"

Anita nodded and led Charlotte and the children out of the courtroom. Charlotte hugged Anita tight, and beamed. "Thank you so much, Ms. Virani!"

"My pleasure. I will meet you on Monday, and we'll take care of your job, okay?"

"My boss is going to be tougher. It's really hard for me to get in for shift work. I have a neighbor who can sometimes watch the kids, but not always. Mom is too weak to keep two toddlers, and there just isn't enough money for childcare."

Anita looked at Charlotte as an idea dawned on her. "Can you type?"

"Of course."

"Okay. Listen, I have an idea. I'm not sure if it will work or not, so check in with the clinic from time to time this weekend, okay?"

"What—"

"I don't want to say anything until I work out the details. Listen, I have to get to the wedding. Do you need a ride somewhere?" Technically, she wasn't supposed to do that, but she didn't want to leave Charlotte just standing there.

"No. It's just a couple blocks and the kids need to run off some energy before we get to my mom."

"Okay. I'll be in touch."

"Thank you so much, Ms. Virani. Now you better get going if you're going to make that wedding."

Anita ran to the car, elated. *This* was why she wanted to be a lawyer. Charlotte had a place to live until she found something better. It wasn't perfect, but she wasn't on the street. She sent a small thank-you to her parents, started the car and raced to the church.

Chapter 12

Nikhil stood by the limos in front of the house and glanced at the time on his phone again. He was starting to sweat in his tux in the summer sun. He pulled open his bow tie. He'd retie it in the limo. Anita should have been here fifteen minutes ago. The limo would leave in ten minutes, with or without her. Where was she?

He called her. Voicemail again. He left a message.

"She'll be here," Rocky whispered in his ear.

"No doubt," retorted Nikhil. If Anita agreed to something, she was in a hundred percent.

He turned to his sister, the bridesmaids, his mother and Neepa-masi. "Go ahead and get in. I'll find her."

Tina pressed her lips together. His mother squeezed his sister's hand. "Don't worry. She'll show."

"Meeta has been here for half an hour." Neepa-masi pursed her mouth with pride.

Nikhil's mother closed her eyes and inhaled. "Yes, we know that your daughter-in-law-to-be is wonderful, Neepa. Easha is also here. I'm sure Anita will show any minute now."

Neepa-masi shrugged. It was clear she found it doubtful. She smiled her approval at Meeta. Meeta, for her part, smiled back, but made eye contact with Easha. The two young women rolled their eyes at each other and smiled.

Meeta and Easha were both in floor-length blue gowns, as they were part of the bridal party. The masis were also in floor-length gowns similar to what Nikhil's mother wore, but all three in different colors.

"It's not me that cares, Mom," Tina said. "I told you this was a bad idea. You just should have told Dada—"

"Told Dada what?" Neepa-masi asked.

"Don't worry about that, Neepa," his mother snapped at her sister. "Just get in. Where is Deepa?" She looked around for her other sister.

"I'm here." Deepa-masi came running up. As long as he could remember, Deepa-masi was always running late.

"Where's Papa?" his mother asked her.

"He's coming." Deepa-masi waved her hand behind her.

"Jeez, Deepa. You couldn't wait for him?" Neepa-masi called from the limo.

"He can walk, Neepa," said his mom, with exaggerated patience.

"He's had a heart attack." Neepa-masi glared at her.

"Six months ago, Neepa." Deepa-masi rolled her eyes. "He's a lot stronger than you think."

"Thank you, Deepa." His mother seemed shocked that Deepa-masi had actually taken her side.

"Neepa treats him like an invalid," Deepa-masi said. "Even the doctor says he's fine."

"He still has that cane," Neepa-masi insisted.

"Which I don't think he really needs," said Seema. "Stop babying him."

"Seema, you really don't know anything about it. You're never there," Neepa-masi snapped.

"I have a business to run, and children—"

"The children are grown." Neepa-masi rolled her eyes. "All you ever think about is your business. All these years, all we ever hear about is your business this, your business that. Your father needs you. It's *your* business—why can't you take time off?"

"I did take time off for him, and I am going to take time off when I become a grandmother in six months!" Seema snapped. She immediately pressed her lips together and glanced at Easha, realizing she'd said too much.

"Mom." Easha shook her head, as both masis' eyes popped open. "What are you saying?"

"Seriously?" Rocky raised his voice from next to Nikhil, where he and the other guys were trying to stay away from the sister squabble. "Unbelievable. We specifically asked you *not* to say anything, but no. When it comes to the masis…" He threw his hands up and shook his head.

Neepa-masi and Deepa-masi grinned. "Well, you blew that secret."

"I'm sorry, Easha. It just came out," his mother tried to explain as Easha made her way past her mother-in-law and into the air conditioning of the limo, still shaking her head.

"Why do you let them get to you?" Easha whispered softly to her mother-in-law before she sat down. Rocky was still glaring at his mother.

She looked away from her older son and turned to her younger son. "Do you know where she is?" His mother looked at him, desperate for an answer.

"Don't worry. Anita would never let you down," Dada said as he finally joined them, looking quite dapper in a tuxedo as well.

Nikhil and his mother turned to the older man. He did not have his cane and he was smiling.

"What do you mean?" Nikhil's mother asked.

"I mean Anita is a good daughter-in-law, and she will be here." Dada smiled at his daughter. "If she is late, there is a good reason. Right, Nikhil?"

"Absolutely true," Nikhil said. She was acting odd when she'd left for her hair appointment. She had made a call...something must have come up at the clinic. She wouldn't risk everything for nothing. "You need to go. Come on, Deepa-masi, Meeta. Get in with Tina and Mom and get to the church. We're right behind you."

Seema Joshi inhaled and closed her eyes as she entered the limo. Nikhil knew she was dreading sitting in there with her sisters.

Nikhil helped his grandfather get into the limousine that was taking the men. Rocky was still fuming and already seated along with Hiral.

"Come on, Nikhil," Rocky called. "Don't make us late."

Nikhil looked around before getting in, hoping to

catch sight of Anita's car. The street was still. He checked his watch one more time and climbed in behind Dada.

Anita parked her car in the church parking lot, grabbed her strappy sandals and dress and made a bee-line for the bathroom. She had been too late to make the limo, so she came straight to the church. Even so, she saw the limos pulling up as she entered the church. She quickly put on the bridesmaid's dress in the bathroom, a beautiful and elegant strapless baby blue gown that just grazed her curves and trailed an inch on the floor. She freshened up her makeup and checked her hair before finally going out to meet the family. She nearly floated, still excited from the hearing.

She found Nikhil in heavy discussion with his mother and sister.

"I'm telling you, she will be here," Nikhil was saying.

"But where would she go?" Tina asked.

"I think she went to help someone at the law clinic downtown. She said something yesterday about a client being evicted." He shrugged. "But she'll be here. I know it. She won't let you down."

"So, work?" Tina pursed her lips.

"No. Helping someone—I'm sure of it." He was standing up for her. Confident in the fact that Anita would be there as promised. Nikhil had faith in her.

"Hey, everyone!" Anita stepped up as if she'd just gotten there. She squeezed Tina's hand. "You look like a fantasy." She met Seema-auntie's eyes. "Sorry I missed the limo."

"No problem, dear. We're just happy you're here." She looked at Nikhil. "Go. Both of you, take your spots."

"Bridesmaids line up over there." The wedding planner pointed to the door to the chapel. "Groomsmen across from them."

Nikhil took Anita's hand and led her to the lineup. He was very handsome in his perfectly fitted tuxedo, though Nikhil had always cleaned up nicely. He squeezed her hand and she looked at him. He looked at her with a mixture of intimacy and pride that was completely new to her. The old Nikhil had never looked at her this way. Come to think of it, the old Nikhil would have assumed she wasn't coming when she was late.

Not this guy. This version was calm and confident that if she made a commitment, she would stand by it. It was the truth, but his faith in her and the way he was looking at her rendered her almost speechless.

Almost.

She grinned at him, still high from what she'd done that morning. "Wait until you hear where I was." The next instant, the chapel doors were open. She placed her hand in the crook of Nikhil's arm as she had been instructed and they followed Rocky and Easha down the aisle. They separated at the end and turned to watch Tina arrive.

Jake was focused on the door Tina would come through, his excitement almost palatable. His cousin Matthew stood next to him as his best man. A memory popped into Anita's head. She and Tina had been talking about weddings, and Tina had proclaimed that if she should ever get married, Anita would be her maid of honor. Today, Anu stood in the maid of honor position.

Jake's green eyes were bright and the smile on his face was a gateway to his feelings. All of his love for Tina was right there for everyone to see.

She caught Nikhil's eye and caught him watching her. Her stomach actually fluttered in excitement. What had gone wrong between them? Were they just too young at that time? Too selfish? Too immature? She honestly could not remember in this moment.

She hadn't even told him where she was going to be this morning, and yet, he had calmly defended her, knowing she would not abandon either of her responsibilities. He trusted her. This was not the Nikhil she had been married to.

Nor was she the Anita he had been married to.

After the ceremony, the bridal party was whisked off for formal pictures before the reception. Tina had chosen to go to Lake Kittamaqundi in town. The lake sported an outdoor amphitheater and was itself picturesque.

The photographer was quick and efficient, lining them all up in the predetermined poses. Being a "married" couple, she and Nikhil were put together often. A few times, Anita tried to duck out—they certainly did not need Nikhil's ~~fake wife~~ ex-wife in the wedding pictures—but someone would always call her back. Not that she was in any way opposed to having Nikhil's muscular chest pressed against her back—or her front— depending on the pose. And this photographer was a fan of having Nikhil's hand at her waist at almost all times. By the time they were done, Anita didn't know if she was sweating because of the hot Maryland summer sun, or because of the constant touch of her ex-husband.

The smiles on the bride's and groom's faces never dimmed. There was laughter, there were a few emotional tears, but the couple's happiness infected everyone around them. They could not take their eyes off each other.

"Your sister looks really happy," she whispered during one pose when they were facing each other, Anita's chest against his.

Nikhil smiled and his face lit up, taking Anita's breath away for just a second. "Jake's a good guy. They are well matched."

"They really are." She couldn't stop looking at him. "People probably think we're well matched as well."

Nikhil raised an eyebrow at her.

"By the way, thanks for having my back earlier," she whispered as the photographer posed the others.

"Of course. I didn't think you'd bail or even risk being late for no reason." Nikhil's voice was calm and sincere.

"I had to keep a client from being evicted."

Nikhil's eyes popped wide, but the photographer returned before he could say anything.

"Hey, middle brother and the wife. Not your day to make googly eyes at each other. Look at the camera," the photographer admonished.

Nikhil's hand at her waist tightened as he pulled her closer and they shared a quiet laugh as they turned to face the camera.

The group made it to the cocktail hour in time to grab drinks and be seated for the start of the reception. Tina was radiant in her dress, and Jake couldn't keep his eyes off of her.

Nikhil and Anita were seated with Rocky and Easha, as well as Hiral and his fiancée, Meeta, and Miki and her fiancé, Nitin, and of course, Sangeeta. Rocky had put aside his anger with his mother for the time being and doted on Easha, getting her ginger tea and crackers to nibble on. Hiral and Meeta were hilarious, entertain-

ing the group with stories of the over-the-top engagement party Hiral's parents had thrown for them in India.

Miki and Nitin were the youngest of the group and
had just gotten engaged a month ago. They could barely
keep their hands off of each other.

"So, how did you propose, Nitin?" Anita asked as
the salad was being served. She sipped her wine, a crisp
summer white that just hit the spot.

"Well, actually, Miki proposed." Nitin kissed her
cheek. "Thank god." He grinned. "I wanted to, and I
was hashing a plan, but she beat me to it."

"Wow, Miki. Awesome. How did you do it?"

"Nothing outlandish. We were walking one evening
after having a lovely meal with our families, and it felt
right. Our parents had introduced us, so I knew they
were on board. So I just asked him to marry me." She
flushed as she looked at him. "And he said yes. And the
next day, we bought a ring." She waggled her ring finger, upon which was a beautiful diamond ring.

"That's such a great story," Easha gushed and took
Rocky's hand. "Rocky actually picked out my ring—it
was perfect. Then he got down on one knee and everything right in our favorite restaurant. I could barely see
the ring through my tears." She laughed and tilted her
head toward him. Rocky looked at her with such fond-
ness. Anita had never seen that before. It was touching.

"What about you, Hiral? How did you propose?"
Rocky asked.

Hiral and Meeta looked at each other, glanced at
Sangeeta and flushed. "We'd rather not say," Meeta
mumbled, clearing her throat.

"What, you can't say it because I'm here?" asked
Sangeeta.

"Yes. My little sister doesn't need to hear…" He drifted off as Meeta burned red.

Sangeeta rolled her eyes. "You might want to come up with some G-rated version because everyone will ask at your wedding."

The other three couples exchanged raised eyebrows and grins. Meeta finally turned to Anita. "How about you two?"

Tension rent the air for a moment while Anita gathered herself. After all, only Meeta, Hiral and Sangeeta didn't know about the divorce. Besides, she hadn't thought about this in a long time. She then glanced at Nikhil, who also looked lost in the past. He cleared his throat. "Well. We hadn't really known each other long."

"But we were very much in love," Anita added, for Hiral's and Meeta's benefit.

"Of course." Hiral winked at them. "We can still see it."

"Most certainly." Dada's voice reached them as he walked up behind them. He held up a hand as they all turned to look at him. "Continue with the story. I've never heard it. And back in our day, our parents did all of this, so we didn't get to be so romantic until after we got married." He nodded at Anita.

"Well." She turned back to the table. "Nikhil was very romantic. He took me to the beach. The only light that night was a sliver of the moon." She glanced at Nikhil quickly, then back at the group. "He sang to me." Anita smiled at the memory. It really had been wonderfully romantic. The barely crescent moon, the stars in the clear night sky, the empty beach. Most people would think that a full moon would be more romantic, but that crescent sliver suspended in the clear night sky was as mesmerizing as any full moon. The salty scent of the ocean had lingered in the air, the crashing of waves was their playlist and it had felt like they were the only two people on the planet. There was no way to say no. And she hadn't wanted to. Being with Nikhil had steadied her for the first time since her parents had died. And she had wanted that. She had wanted the stability that came from being with someone you loved. That she had thought marriage would offer. She had been mistaken.

Sangeeta had tears in her eyes. "That's so romantic!"

"What was the song?" asked Meeta.

Everything seemed to stop and focus on them. Anita remembered the song but she couldn't look at Nikhil or say the name of the song. "Oh, that's not—"

"'Janam Janam' from *Diwale*," Nikhil answered, his voice soft and low, as if he were sharing an intimate secret. Which he was.

"Perfect." Hiral smiled in admiration.

"Oh! We'll use it for your anniversary party!" Sangeeta made a note in her phone.

"Absolutely," agreed Dada. "*Mera Hoke hamesha hi rehna, Kabhi na kehna alvida.* Beautiful." *Always be mine, Never say goodbye.*

Anita glanced at Nikhil. His jaw was tight and his gaze was focused in front of him. Of course, she had said goodbye. "I toasted you, as well." Nikhil's voice had turned heavy, tight.

She had not forgotten. She nodded, unable to tear her gaze away from him. "With chai."

"What?" Easha exclaimed.

"Um, Nikhil makes the best chai." Anita turned back to the table, forcing a smile on her face. She glanced at him, but his jaw was still tight. "I never could resist his chai."

"I needed a guarantee," Nikhil finally spoke. "The chai was the best way."

"So how did you two meet? Did Seema-masi arrange it?"

Nikhil looked away. Anita took over the answer. "I was assistant teaching a nighttime graduate-level creative writing class that Nikhil was taking at the time." She paused. "I did most of the grading because the professor had been already overtaxed when they assigned her this class. Anyway, Nikhil did not like the grade I gave him on a paper." She smiled at the memory and glanced at Nikhil. He remained silent. "He stayed after class one night to discuss it with me. After that he stayed after every class to discuss something about the lesson. And he always brought a thermos—seriously, a thermos—filled with chai."

"I had to." Nikhil perked up. "I really didn't care about the grade." He looked at her, dark eyes soft, a small smile peeking through on his lips. "I just wanted to spend time with her, but she wouldn't date me because she was kind of my teacher. So I brought chai and we would have chai in Styrofoam cups after class and talk about—" he looked directly at her "—everything."

Anita grinned at the memory. He had been quite persistent when she had refused to go out with him. She needed the money and couldn't afford to lose that job because of a guy. No matter how handsome and charming she had found him.

On the last day of the semester, after grades had already been turned in, Nikhil had waited for her after class as he had been doing. This time without his thermos.

"Where's the chai?" she had asked, quite disappointed that they weren't going to hang out together.

He shrugged. "Last day of class."

She tried to hide her disappointment and nodded. "So, nothing to discuss, I suppose."

"Did you turn the grades in?" he asked.

"I did. But no, I will not tell you your grade." She jutted her chin at him.

He smiled and placed his hand over his heart, moving closer to her. "I expect nothing less."

He was now close enough that she felt his breath on her ear when he bent down and whispered to her, "If grades are in, you're not my teacher anymore."

Goose bumps had covered her body from his proximity. She still remembered the musky scent of the last of his cologne and how she had simply wanted to melt into it. "No," she had whispered back, "I'm not."

"Then today is the best day of my life," he continued in that whisper as he moved yet closer to her.

"Why is that?" She tilted her head up.

"Because today is the first day of you and me." His eyes darkened, and his voice grew gruff. Her body outright tingled in anticipation. "And I'm finally going to get to kiss you." With that, he lowered his mouth to hers, finally closing the distance between them, and kissed her.

He was gentle at first, but she captured his mouth with hers and they kissed each other senseless.

When they stopped to breathe, Nikhil turned his beautiful smile on her again. "I didn't bring the thermos, because I was hoping we might have chai later," his eyes had glinted with mischief, "like first thing in the morning."

As Anita found out, morning chai was even better.

She met Nikhil's gaze and flushed as he met hers. He clearly remembered that night, too.

"So what happened on the last day of class?" Meeta asked.

Nikhil cleared his throat. "I, uh, I asked her out to dinner. And that was our first official date." That was the G-rated version.

"Fantastic," Dada proclaimed. "Worthy of Bollywood." He chuckled. "I must insist the two of you treat us to a performance tomorrow evening at the sangeet-garba reception after the Indian ceremony."

"I'm sure Nikhil is already singing. Aren't you?" Anita asked, panic rising in her.

"Yes, Dada, I am."

"No, beti—a dance. I am sure Anita can dance. Nikhil can sing, Anita can dance," Dada insisted. "I'm an old man. Humor me."

Anita shook her head. "Oh no, Dada. I don't really dance like that—in front of people. Nikhil can sing." She had no problem throwing him under the bus. "That will be great."

"No," Dada insisted. "You two are the picture of love. Maybe Easha and Rocky would like to join you?"

Both Rocky and Easha shook their heads emphatically.

"Very well, just you two then. Just something simple."

"But, Dada…" called Anita, but Dada was already in conversation with someone else.

She turned to Nikhil, who still watched her.

"I can't do this." Anita was panicked. "You know how I have stage fright. I'll just freeze."

Nikhil shrugged. "No way out of it. Got to keep Dada happy."

She placed her hand on her belly. Her stomach churned at just the thought of dancing in front of people. She shook her head again.

"I'll be right there with you. I'll be singing, so I can cue you." Nikhil looked her in the eye. "I promise." He smiled and while her belly did not relax, she melted a little under his gaze.

Chapter 13

The table resumed normal chatter after Dada's little visit, so Nikhil relaxed a bit. He should have expected these questions, but he hadn't been prepared for that little trip down memory lane.

Nikhil had taken Anita out to dinner that night, and it was their first official date. He had already fallen for her over the course of their after-class meetings during the semester. His writing had also drastically improved, but he chalked that up to the fact that he wanted to impress her in every way possible.

He wasn't sure exactly when it had happened, but he had fallen for her as they sat and drank chai after class in the classroom. At first they discussed his writing and how to improve it. But that quickly morphed into conversations about anything and everything. She had told him about her parents and how she and Amar were surviving, leaning on each other. Nikhil had been in awe of her strength and positivity.

Nikhil and his siblings had certainly leaned on each other when they lost their father, but they had been much younger. Nikhil and Tina had been there for each other as their mother channeled her grief into JFL, and Rocky pulled back from them, becoming more serious and focused in school.

Where Anita had remained focused and positive, Nikhil had frequently found himself in detention. His method of problem-solving had usually involved fists, which led to more than one suspension.

Before she even went back to his place that night, he knew she was the one. But when she confirmed that she felt the same way, Nikhil felt that his life was turning around. This was the woman he wanted to spend the rest of his life with. He had known it in his soul.

Dinner was served, and Nikhil picked at his food and simply watched Anita. She teased Meeta and kept an eye on Easha. She patted Rocky's hand from time to time, and laughed heartily at Hiral's antics, all the while trying to include Nitin in the craziness. In that instant he was struck with a solid fact. Anita Virani was his family, more than anyone else at this table, more than anyone else in this room. She was his home, and he was the idiot that had let her walk out of his life.

He was still in love with her. Which basically meant he was screwed, because she had been the one to leave, and he had no idea how to get her back.

He had been so caught up in what he might lose, and how he might lose it, he hadn't ever seen what he really had. And what he'd had was this woman's love. Was it still there?

He continued to watch her, and every so often, she turned her head toward him and gave him a smile that weakened him. It was that secret special smile that was just for him, because it said *I'm thinking about you right now.*

Maybe. Maybe it was still there. Though he hardly deserved her.

His phone rang. It was his agent. He tapped Anita's shoulder to indicate he was stepping out to take the call.

It was Chantelle. "Nikhil. Good news. The publisher's representative is excited to meet with you."

"Great. You'd said she was here for a wedding. Do you know where it is?"

She named the hotel, and he couldn't believe his luck. It was the same location as his sister's wedding. For a second, he considered telling her that no, he could not take a meeting *during* his sister's wedding. But then he thought about all the times his mother and brother and father had scheduled meetings during vacations, or even dinners out. And this was one of the most important meetings of his career. No, he was as hard a worker as they were.

He pulled up the wedding schedule. He could fit in a quick drink between the post-wedding ceremony lunch and the reception. Thanks to Dada volunteering them, he really needed that time to practice for his performance with Anita.

Well, how long could a drink take? He'd make it work. "Perfect. Text me the time."

He returned to the table to loud voices, the dominant one of which was Anita's easy tone. Except that she was riled up.

"Who said Nikhil wasn't successful?" Anita demanded, not bothering to lower her voice, despite the guests around them.

His mother stood next to Anita, both of them half-turned away from him. "No one, beti." She sounded surprised. "Of course, Nikhil is successful, in his own way." Her smile was oversweet for the benefit of the others at the table.

Anita pulled herself to her full height and took a step closer to his mother. "Nikhil is successful in *any* way, Mom." This time, she measured her voice, but did not back down. Nikhil's heart leaped.

"He writes books. Fiction." Nikhil's mother shook her head as if writing books was an easy way to gain success. "*You* at least are helping people."

"He has written three books, in the past three years. Two are published and on the market, the third releases in ten days and he is currently working on a fourth." There was pride in her voice. He had never allowed himself to consider that anyone in his family was following his career, least of all Anita. Happiness—and hope—bloomed inside him as she spoke, rattling off titles and the outlets that had reviewed them. "He's on bestseller lists, has had rave reviews and people are talking about his books."

At this, his mother turned all the way to her, giving Anita her full attention. "He makes up stories." She shrugged, that one action making Nikhil's accomplishments completely inconsequential.

"Have you even read his books?" Anita lifted her chin. From where he stood, Nikhil could hear the challenge in her words. "Because I have."

She read his books? After all this time, that little bit

of knowledge had the power to undo even the insult of his mother minimizing his work.

His mother continued to appraise Anita. "Were you impressed?"

"You read them and see if you are impressed," Anita said.

Rocky interrupted, "I've read them."

What?

Anita turned his way and Nikhil could see her profile. She was not surprised.

His mother looked taken aback.

"They're really good, Mom," Rocky confirmed. "Well written and insightful."

"Rocky, you read my books?" Nikhil said as he stepped up to the table. He couldn't stop himself.

Rocky flushed and shrugged. "Well, yes. You are my brother." He flicked his gaze toward their mother. "And you were brave enough to forge your own path."

Nikhil was speechless. Rocky had never given any indication he wanted something other than to dedicate his career to the law.

"Besides, I had to make sure you were good before I acknowledged that N. V. Joshi was my brother." Rocky laughed as he surveyed the group, but landed a serious gaze on Nikhil.

"Hey, how about we toast our little sister and wedded bliss?" Nikhil called out into the silence. "I'll go grab some champagne."

"I'll go with you." Rocky nodded at him.

"Okay."

"Listen, Nikhil." Nikhil turned to his brother. It was the first time he hadn't called him Nicky. "I really am proud of you. I know I don't say it or even act that way.

But you went off and made a name for yourself without relying on the family name. You're braver than I am for sure."

"Are you saying that you don't want to be a lawyer?"

Rocky shook his head. "No. I'm saying I never even considered another possibility. Probably neither did Tina. But you did."

"Only because Mom gave up on me years ago."

"She didn't."

"It doesn't matter." Nikhil shrugged. It mattered. To him.

"Listen, not for nothing, but Anita is *here*. Right now. Making nice with the family. And it can't just be for whatever Mom promised her. Maybe it started that way but that's not what's happening now."

"What are you saying?" His heart lifted. Did Rocky think there was a chance for him and Anita?

"I'm saying she was the best thing that ever happened to you and you're being granted a second chance, so don't screw that up."

"I don't know about that."

"You don't want her back?"

"It's complicated."

The bartender handed over a bottle of champagne and went to get glasses, when someone tapped him on the shoulder. Expecting Anita, he turned around with a huge smile. "Hey, you."

But instead of Anita's beautiful amber eyes, he was met with Jalissa's green contact lenses.

"Jalissa." Nikhil pressed his lips together and nodded to Rocky. "All set?"

Rocky pointed to the champagne bottle and grinned. "Just waiting for glasses."

Nikhil stepped back from her, but she rested her hand on his bicep.

"Nikhil." Her voice was soft. "Have a drink with me."

"Um, not only no, but hell no." He grabbed the bottle, thinking he'd just make Rocky wait for the glasses, but she held on to his arm. "Jalissa, I'm not having a drink with you."

"Nikhil. One drink. I just want to talk. We ended things so badly..."

"We?" His eyebrows shot up. This woman could not be for real.

"Nikhil, come on. For old times' sake. One drink. What's the harm?" She pouted overlipsticked lips at him and Nikhil was struck with the thought that he couldn't for the world imagine why he'd ever had any feelings for this person.

Nikhil sighed. He shouldn't. Jalissa was nothing but trouble. She did nothing without an agenda. She also did not take no for an answer.

"One drink," Nikhil relented.

The glasses arrived and Rocky grabbed them and the champagne. He gave Nikhil a warning look before leaving.

Jalissa grinned and motioned to the bartender for two beers. She grabbed their drinks and sat down at a table close by. Nikhil sat in silence while he waited for her to speak.

"So how are you?" She kept her voice low and soft.

"I'm just fine, Jalissa."

"No, really. You seem happily married." She grinned. Nikhil stared her down without speaking.

"Or are you?"

"What actual business is it of yours?"

"Just...well...if you're happily married, I'll walk. But if not, then maybe I have a chance."

"A chance at what?"

"At you."

Nikhil could not help the laughter that escaped him. "There's no chance for us." He started to stand.

"You haven't even touched your beer." Jalissa nodded.

"Whatever, Jalissa."

"I know you're divorced and that you're faking for your grandfather." Jalissa sneered at him as she stood, all the softness gone from her voice.

"Get to the point, Jalissa."

She leaned into him, her hand on his. "Another chance. I get it—you're putting on some kind of show with her for this wedding. It's all over in a couple days. Call me next week, and we can pick up where we left off." She placed her hand on his chest and drew her fingers down.

It had been her go-to move when they were together.

But now? Nothing. Nikhil felt absolutely nothing for her, from her.

He placed his hand over hers as she quite literally grabbed his belt. "No, thank you."

She leaned closer so her mouth was inches from his. "I'll call you."

"The hell you will." Anita's voice came from behind him.

Nikhil turned to find Anita staring down Jalissa. Those amber eyes he loved so much were twin lights of heat. If she'd had the power, Anita could have set Jalissa on fire with that look. "What part of *he's married* do you not understand?"

"He's not married—I know you two are divorced." Jalissa had the nerve to sneer.

"Are we, though?" Anita stepped into her face and Jalissa backed off. "Would we do this if we were faking?" She grabbed Nikhil and kissed him full on, on the mouth. He responded to her instantly. He trailed his tongue over her lips, enticing her—no, daring her—to open her mouth. Once she did, there was no returning.

He had no idea how long they kissed each other; he just never wanted to stop. When they broke, he was a bit dizzy and shocked. "What the hell was that?" He stepped away from her, instantly regretting his action.

Her eyes widened as she seemed to realize what she had just done. "I—I..."

Jalissa's smile was victorious. "I knew it." She pursed her lips at Nikhil. "Like I said, call me when you're done with the farce." She walked away.

Chapter 14

Someone had taken over her body. That was really the only explanation she had for kissing Nikhil like that. She had come to find out if he was okay, after he'd overheard Seema-auntie's comments, and saw Jalissa with her hands all over Nikhil. A green haze had come over her.

Who did that woman think she was, touching her husband like that? The fact that Nikhil was not in fact her husband seemed irrelevant and Anita had gone and staked her claim like some alpha dog. She wasn't even thinking; she simply acted.

She was frozen to her spot as Nikhil stared at her in disbelief after kissing her completely senseless and pulling away. Jalissa finally left, but Anita had the feeling that the woman was on to them and their marriage act.

Neither she nor Nikhil moved for what seemed an eternity. Everything appeared to be moving in slow motion. Until all at once, Anita was brought back to her reality.

Damn it! She had kissed Nikhil and he had pushed her away, in front of his ex-girlfriend.

Her hand flew to her mouth where she could still taste him. She was such an idiot. What the hell had possessed her?

"Oh no. I'm sorry." Heat crawled up her neck and into her face. She was sick to her stomach. "I don't know why I did that. I had no idea you were trying to… Never mind. Clearly it was a mistake. I'm sorry. Let's pretend that never happened, okay?"

Nikhil nodded, a glazed look still lingering in his eyes. "Yes. Of course—a mistake. Just probably got carried away with the role."

"Yes." Anita clung to that idea like a lifesaver. "Yes. Of course. We used to be married and we're pretending now, so I just got carried away. Sorry if I messed things up for you."

"What? Oh no. Actually I'm grateful. She was coming on very strong. Doesn't like to take no for an answer." Was he as flustered as she was, or was that just wishful thinking?

"Wait…so you're not trying to get back with her?"

"Oh hell no. I told you. She used me to get a job at JFL. That'll never happen."

"Right." Nikhil would never be with someone who worked for his family. It was actually Jalissa they had to thank for that, damn her.

Stop. Nikhil was not really hers anymore. She needed to remember that.

"Gather around, everyone. Time for Tina and Jake's first dance as a couple," the DJ announced.

Everyone turned to see Jake lead Tina out to the dance floor. They were a beautiful couple. All eyes followed them as they moved in unison.

"I know it may seem cheesy, but now that I see Jake and Tina together, I kind of miss that we never had the big wedding." Nikhil was smiling at her.

Anita had been thinking the same thing. "Well, I suppose it's just as well. Considering how things turned out."

Nikhil nodded, and she thought she caught some sadness flit over that smile. The DJ called for the family couples to join the newlyweds. Nikhil turned to her, his hand extended. "Might as well continue the farce."

She nodded and took his hand, almost eager to be in his arms again, fake or not. It was definitely dangerous for her to dance with him, but if he could do it, so could she.

See? She was fine.

Nikhil led her to the dance floor, where he wrapped one arm around her waist, the other still holding her hand. He held her close, their bodies just touching. The song the couple had chosen was about a man trying to understand his good fortune at being with the woman. He was simply thrilled that this amazing woman loved him.

"You were right to leave me," he said softly as they swayed back and forth.

"Why would you say that?"

"Because it's true. I was too young. Too self-absorbed. Not there for you." He was looking directly at her, not behind her or around the room. She could see the vulnerability on his face, in his eyes.

Anita digested that a moment. "I was also too young,

too vulnerable. Too ready to cling to anyone who could stabilize me after my parents' death." She shrugged. "Wrong time for us both, I guess."

She looked up at him. He met her gaze with a small smile and she could swear he was thinking about kissing her again. He shifted his gaze to something behind her, so she took the opportunity to study him. Clean-shaven, but with a just a hint of evening scruff on his brown skin, strong jaw, fabulous mouth. That kiss was still imprinted on her lips. She thought she had been making progress in steeling herself against him. But that kiss had now set her back. Not to mention what dancing in his arms was doing to her. She was enjoying being wrapped up in him just a little too much. She inched closer so now their bodies were pressed against each other.

He looked down at her and smiled. She had forgotten what a heart-melting smile Nikhil had. At least when he had looked at her. She could watch him smile at her forever.

"You know, I never really understood why you were with me in the first place," he said without looking away. "I fell for you after maybe that second time we stayed after class."

"Is that why you kept coming back?"

"I had to. I couldn't be away from you. I wanted to debate with you, listen to you laugh, take the sadness from your eyes." He paused. "You didn't know anything about the family business or wealth—you seemed to like me for me."

"Of course, I did." She shrugged. "I saw your potential as a writer. Your use of words was poetic and seemed to flow so naturally from you. You were tough, but kind and strong." She grinned. "I loved you when you were just a wannabe writer. Now look at you."

"No. Now look at *you*."

Why had he been such an idiot as to let her go? True, that kiss had taken him by surprise. But then she back-tracked so fast, he wasn't sure what to make of it. Had she just pressed against him on purpose?

He led her in a small waltz, even twirling her around. They were in complete sync without so much as a word being spoken between them.

Too soon, the song was over and a faster song started. Anita stepped back and started dancing with him, show-ing no interest in leaving the floor. When they were married, they couldn't always afford to go out, so they would move the furniture and turn on music and dance in their little apartment.

Nikhil still lived in that apartment, much to the an-noyance of his mother. She never could understand why he hadn't let her help them get a bigger place, and after the divorce, she had assumed he would move back into the family house.

His mother had been insistent. "Why are you stay-ing in that tiny little apartment? I understand you and Anita wanted to play house, but now she is gone. Just let it go and move back home."

"We were not playing house. That apartment was our home," Nikhil had stated for the millionth time. He hadn't bothered to explain why he wanted that apart-ment. It was what he could afford. He didn't want to use her money.

And besides, he felt closer to Anita there.

Miki and Nitin joined them on the dance floor, along with Meeta and Hiral. Anita laughed and the sound filled his heart with a happiness he hadn't felt since they had first been married.

No, he never should have let her go. He took her hand and spun her on the dance floor, bringing her into him when she stopped the spin. She smiled up at him.

"Remember when we used to move the furniture?" She laughed.

"I was just thinking about that. Those were the best times. You would dance in my arms."

"You would sing to me." Her voice was breathless and everything around them fell away. All that existed was her.

"Lovebirds!" Hiral's voice cut through their moment. "Come over here! We're doing shots at the bar!"

Nikhil nodded without looking away from Anita. "We're coming."

Anita broke out in a smile and grabbed his hand. "Come on!"

He trailed after her. Hiral was handing out shots of god-knows-what to everyone. He held his up. "To Tina and Jake!" They clinked glasses and downed the shots.

It burned on the way down. Anita crinkled up her face. "Damn, Hiral. What the hell? At least spring for something that goes down easier." Turning to the bar, she ordered another round for the group. "Try this," she challenged, passing glasses around, then holding hers up in a toast. "To Tina and Jake and their happily-ever-after." They all drank the alcohol.

"Much smoother, Anita-bhabhi. You're right," Hiral conceded.

Hearing Anita called "bhabhi" was like a balm to Nikhil's heart. "We have wedding number two tomorrow," Nikhil reminded them. "Because of course, Tina has to get married twice. So let's do this again tomorrow. But Hiral does not get to pick the shot."

"Anita-bhabhi!" the cousins all chorused.

She flushed as they cheered her, basking in the love. She deserved this. She deserved the love and family and all that.

But he just wasn't sure he was the one to give it to her.

At the end of the night, they crammed into an Uber with Rocky and Easha and Hiral and Meeta.

The laughter was free flowing as was the comfortable conversation.

"Rocky does that all the time! Like, how hard is it to pick up your socks?" Easha was laughing.

"Hiral gets his socks—for him it's the wet towel! I'm like, hang it up so it'll dry." Meeta shook her head at her fiancé.

"Nikhil couldn't get clothes into the hamper. Remember the coffee spill on him yesterday? I get back to the room and it's *next to the hamper*! They play basketball, and can get that ball into a stupid hoop, but they can't get a shirt into the hamper!" Anita laughed and the girls all high fived each other.

Nikhil shook his head along with the guys. "Listen to these women complaining about their husbands." He looked at Anita. "We have no complaints whatsoever about our wives."

"Duh. We're amazing!" Meeta laughed.

Anita met his eyes.

Once home, Nikhil loosened his tie and Anita tugged off her strappy heels and held them in her hand. "Good night, you guys! More wedding tomorrow." He took

Anita's hand and they walked to their room together, still hand in hand.

Like a real married couple. And no one was even watching.

Chapter 15

Anita took Nikhil's hand and spun in toward him, landing with her back against his very solid, very muscular chest. He had removed the bow tie, unbuttoned the top of his dress shirt and draped the jacket on the sofa. She was still in her bridesmaid's gown and bare feet. Her hair was slowly falling out of the careful updo Laila had managed this morning. They'd been practicing for their dance tomorrow night for the past couple of hours.

She tilted her head up to him and he met her eyes with his before spinning her out again. The beat carried them the rest of the way through. They ended in each other's arms and the music finished.

"Perfect." Nikhil grinned at her. "I forgot what a natural you are at this. I don't know why you get so nervous."

Anita grimaced. "You know I hate being the center of attention."

"But you did all that bharat natyam dancing when you were growing up. Amar showed me the pictures."

She had done years of classical dance training, but that hadn't cured her of stage fright. "You know, between you and me, I never really enjoyed that kind of dancing."

"But it's such hard work—hours of practice."

She nodded. "It was. But the more I think about it, I was doing it to please my mom. Not that she forced me. I just knew it would make her happy if I did it, so I did."

They were in the sitting room area of their bedroom suite, and Nikhil had insisted on showing her the video of the dance they would be doing the next day.

"Are you sure you want to be a lawyer?" he joked as he sat down on the sofa. "I mean, you'll have to stand up and argue your case in a courtroom."

"It's different." She shrugged. "I did it today. When I was in front of all those people, including a judge, I was focused on being an advocate for my client. So, I wasn't self-conscious. It wasn't about me, so I was able to power through. You know, part of becoming a lawyer was the fact that it was what I really wanted to do with my life. I wasn't doing it to make someone else happy, or fulfil an obligation. It was for me. Still is. Being a lawyer is who I am." Anita stood and stretched.

"I always knew you'd be great."

Anita froze. "You always thought I'd be a great lawyer?"

"Of course." His tone was matter-of-fact.

"You never said that before."

Nikhil frowned. "Didn't I?"

Anita shook her head. "No. You were pretty much against the whole lawyer thing."

Nikhil rubbed his forehead. "I was too young and stupid at the time to realize that it wasn't always about me."

Anita nodded. "Well, we were both *young*." She caught his eye and smiled.

"Ha ha." Nikhil grinned at her and her belly did a small flip.

Silence wafted between them.

"Thanks for standing up for me tonight," Nikhil said.

Anita shrugged. "Of course. You should stand up for yourself. Your mother is not going to know what you do if you do not include her."

"You know, Rocky said he was actually proud of me."

"Well, he should be." Anita widened her eyes. "Though you should be proud, regardless."

Nikhil nodded. "Tina is the only one who ever came to my book launches."

"Did you ever ask your mom or Rocky to come?"

"I stopped asking my mom to come to things a long time ago." He shrugged.

"Maybe they don't come because you don't ask," Anita suggested as she gathered her things and went into the bathroom. "Try them again. People change."

Anita undressed and hopped into the shower, trying not to think about how naked she was with Nikhil mere feet away. She had thought he would be angry with her for cutting it so close this morning, but instead, he had been supportive and understanding.

Huh.

She shook her head. If she was having warm and fuzzy thoughts about Nikhil, it was only because they had taken that trip down memory lane. Which is probably why she kissed him. Not because she was jealous. Or she was trying to stake some claim on him so Jalissa would back down.

After the first couple after-class chai meetings, Anita had gone from being irritated with them to looking forward to them. Nikhil was funny, charming and forging his own path.

By the time she had finally been able to kiss him and he had invited her to stay for morning-after chai, she was already in love with him. She hadn't even known about JFL or his family's wealth until the day he brought her home to meet his family, because their relationship had had such tunnel vision.

Nikhil had been so sure of his path, and his family had been so welcoming, it was no wonder that Anita fell for him and for them.

She toweled off and came out of the bathroom to find Nikhil shirtless and doing push-ups on the bedroom floor.

Damn, but the man was beautiful. His bronzed skin was touchably smooth as she watched the muscles of his back contract and relax as he moved down, then up. Down, then up. A small, tiny part of her brain tried to tell her to stop watching, but the rest of her brain and her body insisted she continue. Majority rules.

"Bathroom's open."

He grunted.

"You're doing push-ups." She bit her bottom lip.

He stopped his push-ups and stood. His skin shone with just a shimmer of sweat from his activity. "Just waiting for you to get out of the shower." He raked his gaze over her from the towel on top of her head to her feet and back up again until he caught her eyes with an intensity she hadn't expected. He might as well have touched her.

Her breath caught. "You didn't have to wait." This was not wise. Yet she couldn't stop the words.

His eyes darkened and he shook his head. But he did not move.

Anita stepped toward him, close enough that the only thing between his hard muscles and her skin was the towel.

"This is not a good idea." His voice was husky, and he hadn't torn his eyes from her or moved.

"It's not," she agreed.

"I was a mess when you left." He leaned into her. Heat from his body emanated through the towel.

"So was I," she whispered, barely able to get the words out.

The way he was looking at her, though. Hooded eyes, full, parted lips.

"Terrible idea." He brought a finger to her shoulder and ran it across and up her neck, goose bumps in its wake. He rested his hand gently on her face.

She couldn't make a coherent thought right now if you paid her. Nikhil leaned down and gently touched his lips to her shoulder. It was just the whisper of a kiss, and yet her whole body responded instantly.

The towel was in her way.

She brought his face to hers and pressed her lips against his, properly kissing him, demanding that he open his mouth to her. Demanding that he kiss her back. He obliged, taking over just as he had earlier, deepening their kiss. This time, Anita pressed closer, drawing her fingers lightly over those muscles on his back, reveling in his moan of pleasure.

He continued to kiss her and brought his other hand gently across her shoulder and down her collarbone, gripping the towel in front of her chest. She might have moaned or maybe he did, but he tugged on the towel and finally she was free of it. The towel slipped to the floor and, exposed, Anita sighed as his skin touched hers.

This was not the plan. There were maybe a hundred reasons not to do this, but she couldn't think of any of them right now. She couldn't think right now, and she didn't want to. She just wanted to feel.

Anita groaned into his mouth, wrapping her arms around his shoulders to pull him yet closer to her.

They eventually broke for air. "Anita?" Nikhil's voice was husky and soft.

She just looked at him, unable to speak. She loved him. Damn it. She had never stopped. She had simply squished all those feelings down into a small, locked box in her heart, and they had just burst open. Being with Nikhil tonight was going to set her back, but right now, she could not think of one good reason not to be with him.

Just this one last time.

Nikhil searched her face. He was looking for her doubt.

He wouldn't find it.

"Yes?"

"Want to take another shower?" Nikhil's grin was delightfully devilish.

She stepped back from him and grabbed his hand, leading him back to the bathroom.

DAY FOUR:

DROPPING THE WHITE CLOTH
AND DANCES
Two souls becoming one...

Chapter 16

Nikhil's eyes fluttered open in the darkness to find Anita curled up into him, their legs entwined. A quick glance through the skylight showed him the moon high in the sky, so there was plenty of night still left. He shifted slightly, trying not to wake her.

"Nikhil?" Her voice was groggy with sleep.

"Hey. Sorry. I didn't mean to wake you," he whispered.

"It's okay." She shifted closer to him.

He wrapped his arm around her and pulled her closer and wished this night could last forever.

"Nikhil?" Her voice was soft in the darkness, but no longer laced with sleep.

"Hmm."

"How did you finally start writing?"

Of all the questions… He half smiled to himself. She wanted to know how he finally got moving.

He had had the hardest time getting started on his dream when they were married. He had taken some writing classes, and then had quit his one paying job as a bartender to pursue his writing. Which basically consisted of him staring at his computer for hours on end. While Anita worked.

He really had been a complete ass. He wondered again why she had ever married him to begin with. Though why she had left was becoming increasingly more clear.

"Why did you ever even marry me?" Nikhil countered.

"I asked first."

"I know."

Silence. The sound of Anita's deep, resigned sigh reached him through the darkness. "I was in love with you. You were sweet and charming, and you could have followed in your family's expected path, but you wanted to find your own way. I thought that was admirable. Especially since I was—lost."

"Lost? You were so busy when we met. Substitute teaching during the day, assisting professors at night and helping Amar with recipes in between. You had almost no downtime."

"That's how I wanted it. I didn't want to think about my parents being gone—I couldn't handle that sense of floating I felt when I thought about them being gone. I was looking for solid ground." She paused. "I clung to you. That was completely unfair."

"Well, I was truly a selfish bastard. I was too caught up in myself to even see what you were going through. I'd let my mother's expectations—or lack thereof—

control my decisions for so long, I was truly blind to the good relationships in my life. Like you. Rocky."

"You didn't answer my question. How did you finally start writing?"

He drew his fingers gently down her spine. She wiggled closer to him. "Are you trying to distract me?"

"Is it working?" He grinned into the dark and pulled her gently on top of him.

Her hair tumbled forward, grazing his chest. "It is."

Nikhil never wanted to leave this room. He was conscious of this before his eyes opened to the early-morning light pouring in from the skylight. He patted the space next to him and felt a jolt of disappointment when he found the bed empty. The shower was running and he smiled to himself as he left the bed to join his wife in the shower—again.

His ex-wife.

What the *hell* was he doing?

He stared at the bathroom door. It was ajar. She left it open for him. The water turned off and he listened to her hum while she toweled off. Just as he decided he was doing what he wanted, and what he wanted to do right now was her, she walked out, a towel wrapped around her, hair damp.

"Isn't this how we started all this?" he asked as he went to her.

She shrugged and dropped her towel just as their bedroom door opened.

"Bhaiya— Ah! What is happening?" Tina shrieked, squeezing her eyes shut and turning away.

"Oh s—!" Anita muttered a curse, quickly reached

down and grabbed her towel before fleeing into the bathroom.

Nikhil quickly grabbed at his shorts, which happened to be on the floor. "Knock much, Tina?"

"Well, how was I supposed to know—you two are divorced!" Tina screeched.

"Still," Nikhil growled. He found a T-shirt and put it on. "What do you want?"

Tina slowly turned around, opening only one eye at first, checking if it was safe.

Anita slammed the door to the bathroom shut and leaned against it, her heart racing. She looked down at herself and quickly wrapped the towel around her tighter as if Tina could still see her.

What the hell was happening? And she didn't mean just Tina barging in. Last night had been incredible with Nikhil. But— Loud voices from outside the bathroom interrupted her thoughts.

"What is the matter with you, Bhaiya?" Tina was whisper-shouting. "Don't you remember how you were when she left the last time? She broke your heart. Just because she's here doing something nice, it doesn't mean that she's going to stay." Tina softened. "Unless she is?"

Anita may have imagined it, but there seemed to be a flicker of hope in Tina's softened voice.

"Maybe." Nikhil's voice was heavy. "No. I don't know."

Anita's heart fell. She couldn't explain why. She was a grown woman. She knew that one night of sex did not equal a relationship. No matter what her feelings for him were. If he didn't know if he wanted her, then that was that.

"All I'm saying is, be careful with your heart. She's only bound to us for a few more days."

"Us?"

"You. I meant you."

"No, you meant us." Nikhil's voice gentled.

Anita couldn't believe what she was hearing. When she divorced Nikhil, she left the whole family. Even Tina. She had thought about reaching out a few times via text, but at the last minute, she never did.

"Well, I couldn't very well go on seeing her when the mere mention of her name had you either in a rage or moping," Tina countered.

"Well, all that is past now. You can, and should, do whatever you want."

Anita wanted to rush out and hug her. Tina had been like a sister to her, and she had missed her terribly. But Tina was right: Anita was leaving in two days. There was no point in renewing bonds that were bound to be broken again.

Maybe she should have thought about that last night instead of giving in to her feelings.

"This isn't about me, Nikhil. It's about you. And her."

"Aren't you getting married again today?" Nikhil had forced humor in his voice. He was done talking to his sister.

"Nikhil…"

"Tina…" Nikhil sighed. "I'm a grown man. I can take care of myself."

"Mmm-hmm."

"Why are you even here?" Nikhil asked, feigning irritation.

"I just…wanted to see you before I got married." Anita heard muffled sounds and smiled to herself, realizing Nikhil was hugging his little sister.

"Good luck today. You're a lucky girl. Jake's amazing."

"Wait. Aren't you supposed to tell me how lucky Jake is, to get someone as amazing as me?"

"Why would I say that?" The amusement in his voice made Anita shake her head. "Jake made his choice. He's stuck with you. You were born into this family—I had no choice."

"You're the worst," she admonished, but the laughter in her voice was just as clear. "I'm sure Rocky will be nicer than you."

"Little Sis, if you're waiting for Rakesh Joshi to be nicer than me, you have a long wait."

"Ha ha."

"Go. Go make yourself into a beautiful bride."

Anita heard the door open. "Love you," Nikhil called.

"Love you, too, Bhaiya."

Anita heard the door shut. She stared at the bathroom doorknob, waiting to see if Nikhil would try it, to pick up where they had left off or not. She wasn't sure what she would do if he tried the knob. Would she throw caution—and her heart—to the wind and open it?

She stared at the knob for a few minutes.

"Anita?" he called from the other side of the door.

She opened the door.

"You heard?"

She nodded. "Probably best if we didn't—" It seemed the safest thing to do.

He nodded. "Yeah, probably right."

"Last night was—" she started to say.

"Amazing."

The way he was looking at her, she was going to melt into him again, her heart be damned. Time to back it up. She used her best nonchalant tone. "I was going to say *expected.* I mean we were married. We always enjoyed each other. We're grown, consenting adults, we were bound to sleep together since we were in close proximity."

"Grown, consenting adults." Nikhil stared at her a moment, then shook his head, stepping back from her. "Of course."

Silence hung in the air, during which Anita tried to convince herself that her words were true.

"I'm going to get dressed. Be out in a minute."

"We need to practice." He spoke after a moment.

"Can we just forget about the dance?" Anita pleaded.

"Um, no. We promised Dada."

"Well, I have hair and makeup in an hour, so we can practice until then." She smiled gamely. "We certainly wouldn't want to disappoint your grandfather."

Anita was stiff in his arms as they practiced, not anywhere near as relaxed as she had been last night. But who was he kidding? He was keeping his physical distance as well. Tina was right. He couldn't afford to forget that he and Anita had had their chance and it hadn't worked out.

Besides, what had Anita said? *Grown, consenting adults.* It was just sex. She didn't have any real feelings for him. Though as much as he had been trying to deny his feelings for Anita, they were there, and had probably never left. He had simply gotten used to dealing with them.

Or maybe he had hoped that one day, he would be able to get her back.

"I'm definitely going to need your cues to get through this," Anita said as they finished up.

"Of course." Cues. That's what he was good for. He reminded himself that Anita was here for a reason. To put on a show and get her tuition paid.

"I'm just going to put on my sari and get going for hair and makeup."

"Sure."

The distance between them seemed larger today for some reason. They were extra polite.

She went into the bathroom to change into the sari blouse and the slip. Nikhil sighed—just as well. Not six hours ago, they had been naked together.

She came out and stood in front of the long mirror in her heels, floor-length sari slip and short sari blouse. She turned on a YouTube video on her phone and put it in front of her as she started to put on the sari. Curious that the sari master was going to the internet for help, Nikhil peeked over her shoulder.

"Um." He reached out to touch the sari. "Can I?" he asked the woman he had been married to. Who he'd just had his hands—and mouth—all over.

"Oh. Yeah. We're supposed to wear it mermaid style, which is cute, but—"

"Here. You just need someone to hold this." He held the sari in place while she wrapped and made pleats. Once she had everything secure, she handed him a safety pin and he pinned the sari in place.

He looked at her in the mirror. The sari was the same color blue as the bridesmaid's dress she had worn yesterday. Tina had picked a simple chiffon sari with a thick silver beaded border, which was perfect for the way Anita had wrapped it. The border drew a long line across her body from shoulder to calf, the rest of the sari hugging her curves tight. Hence the term *mermaid*.

But Anita didn't need the sari to make her beautiful. Nikhil studied her in the mirror as she made final adjustments. She was beautiful in a way he had never noticed before. "You look different."

"Do I?" She turned her face to him.

"What were you just thinking about?"

"Oh," she said, then hesitated, still looking at him. "I was thinking about my case yesterday and how I still have to take care of things, but I think I have a solution."

"Yeah? What is it? Tell me." He took her hand and sat down on the bed.

She bit her bottom lip. "I don't want to jinx it before I've gotten it, you know?"

"Of course." But he desperately wanted her to share her thoughts. It was not lost on him that had he listened to her while they were married, they might still be married.

She took back her hand and he felt slightly empty. He sat as she gathered her things and made to leave.

And just like that, Anita was out the door.

Chapter 17

Anita needed to get away from Nikhil and all the warm, fuzzy feelings she was having for him. Having him help her put on her sari, just like old times, had all those feelings buzzing inside her again. Not to mention that incredible night, the hours they'd spent in each other's arms.

She had been thinking about *him* when he asked. So, of course she lied and told him that she was thinking about work. If not, who knew what she might say—or god forbid—do? They'd had their chance and it was over. Only a fool would go down the same road twice. And she was done being a fool.

She might no longer be the person she was back then, and he might be different, too. But that didn't mean they should be together. No matter how good the sex was.

She made a detour at the house before leaving for the

hotel, so she could talk to Seema-auntie. She knocked on Seema-auntie's study door, knowing there was no way she was still in bed. She was likely answering emails, or setting up a brief before things got going here today. But no answer. She cracked the door and found the room empty. Hmph.

"Can I help you with something, beti?" Seema-auntie's voice came from behind her.

Anita spun around, startled. "I was actually looking for you. I assumed you had work to do." She indicated the study.

Seema-auntie chuckled. "My daughter is getting married. I am not working at all this weekend. I have the associates to handle any emergencies that come up."

Anita was stunned.

Seema-auntie continued to grin at her. "People change, beti."

Apparently.

"What can I help you with?"

"Let's talk in the study."

Seema-auntie nodded and led the way in. She shut the door and turned to Anita.

"I was wondering if we could change the terms of our agreement." Anita got right to it.

"Oh?"

"I'll keep my end, of course. I'm not trying to leave." Although, it might be easier to move on from Nikhil if she left now. "But I was wondering if instead of tuition money for me, you would be willing to hire a young woman who is a client of mine. She's hardworking and a quick learner. The caveat is she needs childcare, as well."

Seema-auntie stared at her. "You want to forfeit your tuition to get this young woman a job?"

Anita continued as if Seema-auntie hadn't spoken. "I know you have childcare on the premises. She could earn a decent living and her children would be taken care of. Every so often, she might need to work from home, as she has an ailing mother. But I looked it up, you *are* looking for secretarial help, and she'd be perfect. Maybe a bit of training, but I know she'd be an asset to JFL."

Seema-auntie eyed her carefully. "Why are you helping this girl?"

"She's a client. Her mother is ill and needs care. She wants to move her mother in with her, but she's currently working shift work for an hourly rate and can't afford a bigger place. She's barely making rent on her current place. She also has two small children."

"You're trying to ground her, give her something solid she can believe in."

"I suppose I am. But I also know she has potential. She won't be a secretary forever." Anita smiled.

"I thought you wanted to be debt free."

"I'll manage. I'll be fine. Just give this young woman the job and we'll be even. Anything beyond that is up to her." Anita found she wasn't even exaggerating. She was fine taking a loan. Debt wasn't the end of the world. It was one year's tuition. She'd been through worse. She would find a way to handle it. But Charlotte was stuck, and this was a way to help her.

"What if she's not as good as you say?"

Anita shrugged. "Fire her. By then, the wedding will be over—you'll have gotten your end. I'm only asking you give her a chance."

Seema-auntie studied her a moment, then held out her hand. "Done. I'll make the changes."

Anita shook her hand, but then went in to hug her. "Thank you so much! You won't be sorry."

"I'm not worried."

"I better go." Anita smiled. "Hair and makeup."

Her heart was light as she drove to the hotel where the wedding would be. Charlotte would be taken care of at JFL as long as she worked hard.

Anita arrived in the bridal suite expecting to see all the girls, but instead found only Tina, her hair and makeup done. She tried not to think about how Tina had caught her naked with Nikhil that morning.

Too late, she felt the flush rise up her face. "Oh." She looked around as if maybe the other girls were hiding. "I thought we were all meeting here today."

"We are. The others are running late." Tina shrugged as if she'd expected it and didn't make eye contact. "I think they're hungover. Anu went to get chai. She'll be back in a minute." Tina motioned for Anita to sit.

"Sure." Anita looked at Tina. Her hair had been done in a beautiful updo that left some strands free. Flowers sat in almost a crown around the updo. Her makeup was natural, her jewelry, simple gold. All in all, she was a beautiful bride. "Need help with the sari?"

Tina nodded. Anita stood and retrieved the sari from the closet. "This is a beautiful panetar," gushed Anita. It was the traditional white sari with a thick red border. It had simple bead work and sparse design, but the material was exquisite. They stood in front of the full-length mirror and Anita started wrapping the red-and-white bridal sari.

"Yours looks good," Tina said, making eye contact in the mirror.

Anita cleared her throat. "Nikhil helped me."

Tina pressed her lips together, her body stiff. "You're messing with my brother's heart. I warned—"

Anita tensed and looked Tina in the eye through the mirror. "I most certainly am not."

Tina pursed her lips. "That's not what I saw this morning."

"What you saw is really none of your business," Anita snapped, despite the flush she felt rise to her face. "Knock next time."

"Lock the door," Tina retorted.

"I would have if I had thought— It wasn't *planned...*" Anita slowed down and inhaled deeply. "Not the point. The point is whatever happens or doesn't happen between Nikhil and me is between us."

"Until I have to pick up the pieces. Again," Tina spit back.

"There will be no pieces." Nikhil would have to have real feelings for her for him to break into pieces. But he had agreed that they were simply consenting adults with a past, who were good together in bed. So...no pieces. "Nikhil and I are adults. We know what we're doing." Ha. *Good one, Anita!*

"Whatever." Tina rolled her eyes. "It's not just him, you know. You left us all."

"You mean you." Anita softened her voice.

"Yes. I mean me. You were the closest thing to a sister that I had. We confided in each other, and just like that you're gone." She snapped her fingers.

"What was I supposed to do—have coffee and lunch with my ex-husband's sister?" Anita defended herself.

"No, you were supposed to be my friend."

"Well, I couldn't." Anita tried to concentrate on making pleats.

"Why not?" Tina was nothing if not challenging.

"Because it would have been awkward and weird. And I thought he might need you. He's closer to you than anyone else in the family." It was true. That was a part of it.

"Sure, it might have been in the beginning. But it wasn't like he was coming with us. I reached out to you. And you ignored me."

Anita let silence flow in the air. Tina was getting married today; they didn't need to get into all that now.

"So you're not going to say anything?" Tina insisted.

"It's your wedding day." Anita tried to remain calm, focused. She restarted the pleats. They weren't working today.

"So what?" Tina snapped.

"What do you want me to say?" Anita dropped the pleats again but didn't bother to pick them up. The sari pooled in a mound of red, white and gold at their feet. "That I ignored your texts because it was too hard to see you? Because seeing you would remind me of him? And I missed him so damn much, some days it was all I could do to not call him or, worse, show up at the apartment and beg him to give our marriage a second chance?" Anita was shouting into the mirror now, close to tears. That was the truth of it. She *had* ignored Tina's texts because she knew Nikhil needed his sister. But the whole truth was that Anita could not have anything to do with anyone who was part of Nikhil. It was too hard.

"You're angry because I hurt your brother and stopped talking to you. I'm sorry I hurt you. But I lost *all* of you when I left." And after losing her parents a few years before, the loss of the Joshi family… It was too much. It had been easier to simply cut everyone off at the time.

Tina gazed at her in the mirror. "You still love Nikhil."

Anita shook her head as she fought back the tears that burned at her eyes. "No. Don't be ridiculous."

Tina turned away from the mirror and looked at Anita head-on. "I'm not." A sad smile came across her face. "I don't know why I didn't see it before. You *are* still in love with him. And he's still in love with you."

Anita's traitorous heart fluttered at the thought that Nikhil might still be in love with her. After last night, she'd hoped for just a second, but she didn't really think they had a chance. She was in law school. She might actually work for JFL one day, if what Jake had said actually panned out. Maybe Jalissa had screwed him, but Anita wasn't about to spend her whole life convincing Nikhil that she wasn't Jalissa. It didn't really matter how they felt. She ignored it. Tina didn't know what she was talking about.

She shook her head. "Not true. Any of it. Me. Nikhil." Apparently she could no longer make sentences either.

"I know you. I know my brother. And you're not here just to help my mom or Dada or for tuition money. You're in love with him. And you're afraid of what that means."

No. That wasn't true.

Except that it was.

Chapter 18

Nikhil was just donning his blue sherwani for the wedding when Rocky texted him.

Meet in Mom's study ASAP. It's Jalissa.

Nikhil didn't bother with the buttons on his sherwani, instead racing down to his mother's study with his jacket half open. He barged into the study, to find Rocky and Jalissa waiting for him. Rocky was fuming. Jalissa looked cool as a cucumber, already dressed for the wedding, a vicious smirk on her face. "What the hell is going on?"

Rocky answered. "Jalissa here wants the community division we're starting up."

"That's Anita's," Nikhil blurted out as if it were a fact. It was, as far as he was concerned. From the look on his brother's face, Rocky thought so, too. "Absolutely not."

Jalissa grinned her answer. "If I don't get the community division, I'll tell your grandfather about your divorce."

"You're bluffing," Nikhil said.

"Am I?"

"Yes. If you tell Dada about my divorce, you'll be fired. There's no way you would risk your job." He glanced at Rocky, an eyebrow raised. Rocky nodded his agreement. Felt nice to be on the same page as his brother for once.

Jalissa shrugged. "I'm not risking it. You all have been falling over yourselves to save face in front of him. Not to mention, that as the associate bringing in the highest amount of revenue, I seriously doubt you'll fire me."

"Don't flatter yourself, Jalissa." Rocky's mouth was twisted in disgust. "It doesn't matter how much you bring in if you're screwing with the family."

Panic flashed across her contact-lens-green eyes, but Jalissa quickly rallied and gave a one-shouldered shrug. She hadn't counted on money not being the most important thing at JFL. "I'm not concerned."

"She clearly has something else already lined up, Rock," Nikhil said as he walked over to his brother. "I say we fire her."

Rocky pursed his lips to hide a smile as he nodded. "I concur. You forgot that the practice is called Joshi *Family* Law," Rocky said as he turned to Jalissa. "Not only do you not get the community division, you are also fired from JFL as of right now. I'm changing your access to all files. Go take the other position, Jalissa, if indeed you have one. JFL doesn't bow to blackmail, and we stand by family. Also, leave this wedding. You never should have been here to begin with."

"You don't even have that authority. Only your mom can fire me." Jalissa's words were firm, but Nikhil caught her eye flick. She didn't know anything.

"Try me." Rocky stared her down for a minute.

"You're making a huge mistake," Jalissa nearly hissed on her way out.

"No. The mistake was letting you stay on after you treated my brother badly. We're a family firm. And he's my family," Rocky barked at her.

Jalissa left in a huff. Nikhil watched her huff away, a pang of unease settling into his stomach. This wasn't over yet.

"Thanks, Rocky," Nikhil said, still staring at the door. "We should just end this farce ourselves and tell Dada the truth."

"Let's just get through today. Let Tina have her day." Rocky was already on his phone. "Don't thank me yet. It takes a minute to lock her out of the files." He barked orders into his phone.

"Hey!" The door to the bridal suite opened. "I have chai for the bride!" Anu's singsong voice reached them along with the aroma of spiced chai. The girl was perceptive, however, and sensed something was up right away. "What happened?"

"Bhabs is in love with Nikhil." Tina sounded happy. Anita's heart ached at the sound of the shortened version of *bhabhi* that Tina had always used for her. "Which is great, because I know Nikhil still loves her."

Anu's eyes widened. "Well, duh. They're getting back together, or at least trying it out, right?"

Anita shook her head. "Yes. No. I don't know." She picked up the sari and handed it to Anu. "You can finish putting on her sari. I need to go." She stepped around a shocked Anu. "And don't call me Bhabs," she called without turning around. "I'm not your sister-in-law."

She thought maybe Tina had called out to her, but it didn't matter. This whole thing had been a mistake. How had she thought this was going to work? Did she really think that she could be in Nikhil's presence and protect her heart? Ridiculous. She needed to just leave. If she stayed, she'd only fall harder. It would be so easy to believe Tina and give in to her feelings. But the reality was that people didn't really change. Nikhil would never believe she loved him for him. And she wouldn't spend her life proving that to him.

Tears blurred her eyes as she left the bridal suite and made her way down the spiral stairs and toward the front where she had parked her car. She was moving toward the back entrance as fast as her pointy heels would carry her, wiping her eyes, when she remembered the new deal she had made with Auntie just that morning.

Charlotte's job in exchange for her presence.

She had to stay. She had no choice. It wasn't just about her anymore. Her heart heavy, she turned back and bumped into something very solid.

She stepped back, catching her balance. "Oh sorry."

"I'm sorry!"

As they apologized in unison, Anita realized that male voice was very familiar.

"Amar?"

"Anita?" He stepped back from her. He was wearing chef's whites with "Taj" embroidered over the left breast. "Have you been crying? What did Nikhil do?" His face filled with anger with a velocity Anita had not known was possible.

"Nothing, Amar. It's fine."

"It's fine, is it? You pretending to be married to your ex-husband for tuition money?"

"Well, not when you say it like that." He made it sound slightly sordid.

"And what's this about you getting back together with him? That better not be true."

She shook her head. "It's not. I was just trying to let Sonny down gently."

"Talk to me, Anita. What's happening?" Amar's voice was gentle.

She shook her head. "Not now. I just need to get through this day."

"I actually texted you a few times. I need help," Amar said.

"I must have silenced my phone during the reception last night. Sorry. What's up?"

"The pastry chef is sick."

"What does that mean? No cake?"

"No. The cake is started, and her team can finish that, but I need someone to do the desserts. Mini gulab jamun, rose truffles..."

Anita already had her phone out and was texting.

"Who are you texting?"

"Divya." Duh.

Amar's eyes widened in panic. "Divya? No, don't text *her*. I don't want her to come. I was thinking one of her pastry school friends. What was that one woman's name, who used to come over with her? Who made that whimsical cake? Emily?"

Anita rolled her eyes. "Divya is the one who taught Emily how to make that cake. And they did not go to pastry school together. Emily is a nurse." Anita looked at her brother like he was crazy. Of course he had no real idea who Emily was because when Divya was around, she was the only person he noticed. "Divya's great, she works fast and you're desperate."

"She has no experience."

"Not true. She has a ton of experience. And once again, you're desperate."

Amar threw his gaze all over the foyer for a couple minutes, as if a pastry chef would emerge from the walls. Finally, he looked back at Anita, his mouth in a line. "Fine. Text her. But she better be good."

"She is." Anita hit Send. And Divya responded almost immediately.

Will I get paid?

"She gets paid, right?"

"Of course."

Anita sent off another text, then grinned when the reply popped up. "Then she'll be here in thirty minutes."

"Thank you." Amar's gratitude was genuine, but she could see he was preoccupied by the fact that he would be working side by side with Divya.

Another catering employee walked by. "Hey, something's up in the kitchen. Boss needs you."

Amar shook his head. "I have to go." He started to walk away, and turned back. "Can you tell her to come to the back entrance?"

Anita texted him Divya's number. "Tell her yourself."

Amar threw her an irritated look. Whatever. She couldn't be his go-between right now. He was a grown man. He'd figure it out.

Anita nodded. She didn't want to go back to the girls.

So she found a bathroom to freshen up in. Her phone rang. Divya.

"Hey, Divya, aren't you supposed to be on your way here?"

"I am. I'm driving. You're on speaker." Divya paused. "Did Amar ask for me, specifically?"

"No. He thought your friend Emily was a pastry chef." Anita laughed.

"Oh."

Was it her imagination, or did her friend sound slightly disappointed?

Then Divya laughed. "Ha. Whatever. How's it going with Nikhil?"

Sudden tears choked her throat so she couldn't talk.

"Anita? Are you crying?"

"No." She sniffled.

"Aw. You just realized you were still in love with Nikhil."

"What? No. How did you know?"

"Um, duh. I'm your best friend. I know things."

"Then why didn't you stop me from agreeing to this whole arrangement?"

"Like that was even possible. And besides, when is the last time you didn't just do what you wanted?" Divya said.

There wasn't one.

"You actually never stopped loving him, in case you didn't know. You didn't leave because you stopped loving him—you left because he didn't support you." Divya was very wise.

"But it's been years—"

"Do you love him? Isn't that why you're crying?"

"Maybe."

"Did you sleep with him?"

"Maybe?"

"Oh jeez. Then what happened?"

"Tina caught us."

Divya laughed. "I wish I could have seen your face!"

"Do you, though?"

"Okay, maybe not." She quieted her laughter. "Did you talk to him?"

"About what?"

"Anita, come on. Did you tell him how you feel?"

"No."

"You need to talk to him."

"I can't tell him I'm in love with him when I'm the one who left. It's not fair." She finished touching up her makeup and walked out of the bathroom while Divya spoke.

"It's not about being fair. It's about you and him. People change, Anita. You've grown and changed. In fact, you started when you left the marriage. That was you learning to stand on your own two feet. That was you learning to live without your parents or anyone else to save you. You saved yourself. And look at you now."

Before she could completely digest what Divya had said, a familiar voice called out to her.

"Anita," Rocky asked her, "you got a minute? The shit has hit the fan."

The look on Rocky's face made her heart drop into her belly. "Divya. Amar says go to the back entrance when you get here. I've got to go." She tapped her phone off and turned to Rocky. "What happened?"

Rocky filled her in on Jalissa's threat. "Just a heads-up in case you come across her. She should be gone, but you never know. Also let's keep this from Tina for now, let her enjoy her day."

"Yeah, sure. Shouldn't we just come clean to Dada, though?"

"That's exactly what Nikhil wants to do." Rocky studied her a moment, amusement flitting across his features. "But we're going to wait until after today." Rocky became all business again. "Let's get through the celebration and then we can face the music."

"Sure." Anita nodded her agreement with the plan. "It's a risk. But it makes sense." She'd find a way to make it through the day.

After that run-in with Jalissa, Nikhil drove to the wedding hotel, checked into his hotel room and went upstairs to write for a while. It was a five-star hotel, and he and Anita were in a suite that had a small office area. He wrote words then deleted them. Wrote more and deleted. The words weren't coming, and they hadn't been for almost a month. He had a deadline and for the first time in several years, he didn't think he was going to make it.

All he could think about was Anita. And if he was honest, he had been thinking about her long before she showed up here three days ago. He had never really stopped thinking about her. She was always there, in the scent of her perfume on a passing stranger, when he made a recipe she had tweaked or watched a Bollywood film he knew she would enjoy.

His family had been in wedding-planning mode for the past three months, since Tina and Jake's timeline required they move fast. Tina had been working the administrative, regulatory and business counseling division and had recently been promoted, as her expertise in this area had expedited a business opening for a big client of theirs. She wanted to get married before things got super busy at the office.

They had hired a planner, but of course, weddings made Nikhil think of divorce. Specifically his. But Tina was his little sister, so he sucked it up and helped wherever he had been needed. So, by the time he had found Anita standing next to his mother three days ago, Nikhil had already had a brain full of thoughts about her.

He had been trying to figure where they had gone wrong, wondering if there was any way to fix it, when she'd shown up. Almost like he'd conjured her from his heart and brought her to him. The ultimate Accio spell.

Even though he was not making any real progress, he lost track of the time. Nikhil arrived downstairs at the wedding hall later than he had intended. He had wanted to dance with the jaan, the groom's procession, but he seemed to have missed it. Hopefully no one noticed.

Nikhil followed the sounds of the pandit's chanting to find the wedding hall. Had they actually started on time?

His brother greeted him at the door to the wedding hall. "You're late. I've been texting you."

"Phone's on silent." Nikhil looked at his watch. "I was working, got carried away with an idea."

"You're an hour late. You missed the jaan, so you weren't here to greet the groom. Everyone is inside. Go take your seat. Tina's procession will start in a few minutes." His brother was thoroughly annoyed with him. "Mom was asking where you were."

"How was I supposed to know you'd start on time?" He was completely bummed he missed the jaan. Not to mention, he completely sounded like a child. "I'm sorry. The time just got away from me."

"It's our sister's wedding," Rocky insisted. "Why are you working?"

"Where's my real brother and what did you do with him?" Nikhil deadpanned.

"Shut up." Rocky shook his head, softening. "I'm going to be a dad soon. And I want to make sure I'm there for my kid. I don't want to miss things, like Mom and Dad did. I mean they were building a business—I get it. But I want to watch my kids play sports or dance or whatever."

"Wow. That's a change."

"It really isn't. We just don't talk like that in our family. Whether you see it or not, you have that Joshi family crazy work ethic."

"No, I do not. I would go to my kid's things," Nikhil insisted.

"It's not just kid things, Nikhil. It's everything. It's life. Yes, work hard. But don't miss out on life because you were working the whole time. You just spent two hours in your room trying to work. You could have been hanging out with the cousins, meeting friends or even just being with Anita. Not to mention you missed the rehearsal the other day. And we had fun, which you missed out on. I bet you have something scheduled this afternoon."

Nikhil opened his mouth to protest, but nothing came out.

"Uh-huh. That's what I thought." Rocky shook his head. "What are you trying to prove?"

He wasn't trying to prove anything, was he? Nikhil was aghast but followed his brother to the mandap, where his mother was performing a ceremony with Jake before Tina arrived. Jake's parents sat on either side of their son, watching.

Maybe he was working too much. He'd reconsider his priorities after the big meeting this afternoon.

The pandit finished the welcoming-the-groom puja and excused Nikhil's mother. Michael and Christi had their seats moved back behind Jake in preparation for Tina's arrival.

Two of Jake's friends held up the antarpat. This decorated white cloth was held between the bride and groom until the bride arrived in the mandap, at which time the antarpat would be dropped. This hearkened back to olden times when the bride and groom would see each other for the very first time when the antarpat was dropped. The separation was symbolic of their individual lives, so dropping the antarpat symbolized the two souls becoming one.

The DJ started the music and everyone stood to watch the bride enter. Deepa-masi and Neepa-masi and her family were Tina's escorts today. But before them came Tina's bridal party. Anita was part of this procession.

Nikhil never even saw his sister enter with their masis because he could not take his eyes off Anita. He'd just seen her a few hours ago, but it wasn't the hair and makeup that made her so irresistible. There was something else about her. She glowed. That was all there was to it.

Tina floated into the mandap and stood, staring at the white cloth. Jake stared at the cloth from his side. He inhaled deeply and nodded to his friends. They dropped the cloth, allowing bride and groom to finally see each other. Tina and Jake each radiated the other's love. The pandit invited Tina to sit, and the ceremony began.

Nikhil watched Anita as she took her seat behind his sister. He thought his heart might burst in that moment with longing and love for Anita. It was exactly then that he realized that he was desperately in love with her. The antarpat was down, and he was looking at the woman he loved. And that changed everything.

Chapter 19

The ceremony finished to cheering and the throwing of flower petals. His sister was finally married to the love of her life, and she had never looked more radiant. Family pictures followed, during which he noticed Anita went missing. Some of the bridesmaids went to find her, but to no avail.

She was avoiding being in the pictures, because she knew she would be leaving the family tomorrow, and the charade would be over. Smart girl. Though it put a pang in his heart.

Just as well—Nikhil didn't think he could stand being so close to her like yesterday's pictures. Not knowing for sure that she would be gone.

Nikhil went to the bar at the allotted time to meet with the representative from his publishing house. Within minutes a woman in a black dress suit and slick high ponytail approached.

"Hi, I'm Mehgna Sura with ADS Publishing." She held out her hand.

Nikhil shook it and sneaked a peek at his watch. How long was this going to take? "Nikhil Joshi."

"Of course. Thank you so much for taking the time to meet with me, during a wedding."

"Aren't you here for a wedding as well?" On second glance Mehgna wasn't wearing a dress suit as much as she had donned a blazer over a cocktail dress. "Wait, are we here for the same one? There's only one here today."

"I am. I'm on the groom's side. That's so funny."

He hesitated. "I'm with the bride."

"Oh, nice. My husband went to college with Jake. How do you know the bride?"

"She's my sister."

Mehgna did a double-take at him. "Your sister? And you let them schedule this meeting?"

"I was told it was important. And that you were here."

"Well, it is. I'm just surprised to have found someone as crazy as me willing to work during a family wedding." She pulled out her laptop.

Nikhil stared at the laptop. "I thought we were just having a drink, getting to know each other."

"We are. But I want to map out your next few projects as well." She stared him down. "Is that a problem?"

"No." He shook his head. Work was work, right? Though Rocky's voice echoed in his head. "Let's get to it."

Mehgna was in no hurry and took her time to discuss his future with their publishing house. He should have been thrilled; it was everything he'd been working for. Mehgna's plan would take him from a bestselling author to a blockbuster author, with his books becoming movies or even television shows.

His focus was not as strong as usual. All he could do was keep glancing at the time on her computer. Thirty minutes became forty-five became sixty. The reception had started. He missed practice time with Anita, but he needed to go if he was to make it in time for the performance. He still needed to be miked so he could sing.

He was just considering apologizing to Mehgna and leaving, when Sangeeta came running up. "Nikhil-bhai! Come on, your dance. What are you doing here?"

His cousin literally grabbed him by the arm and started to drag him toward the reception hall. "I'm sorry, Mehgna. I need to go. Let's pick this up on Monday? I'll come to you."

Mehgna did not look thrilled, but Nikhil allowed Sangeeta to drag him to the reception hall.

"What the hell were you doing?" Sangeeta admonished. "Anita is waiting for you."

She was probably pissed. He had missed practice and now he was late for the actual performance. After all the promises he'd made. But work was work.

Or was it?

He grimaced. "Well then, let's not keep her waiting."

The music was just starting when he entered the hall and Sangeeta shouted, "I have Nikhil."

Nikhil jogged to the dance floor in the dimmed reception hall and waited while his brother miked him. "Where the hell have you been?" Rocky mumbled. "I was about to dance for you."

"I had a meeting."

Rocky's glare could have cut diamonds, and he was a bit more aggressive with the portable microphone than was absolutely necessary. However irritated Rocky was, it was nothing compared to the pained fury in Anita's eyes.

She might have forgiven him for missing their practice, if he had actually shown up on time for the performance. Anita had tried to start without Nikhil, with his brother gamely filling in for the guy's part, but the crowd was cheering and she froze, as she usually did, without the cues they'd worked out the night before.

As soon as Nikhil got there and was miked, he began singing, cueing her as he had in practice, but she was angry and already flustered, so she was a step off the beat.

Anita finally started dancing, but she knew her moves were stiff. All of her discomfort about dancing in front of crowds came rushing back to her. She reached for Nikhil as they had practiced, but instead of taking her hand, he barely grasped her fingers, and she forgot the next step. She tried to catch up with him, but instead, bumped into him. Nikhil raised an eyebrow at her and extended his hand out to her. Seriously? He was going to question *her* with that eyebrow? She bypassed his hand and they both missed the next step, bumping into each other. She glared at him. He glared right back.

They were a disaster. People were chuckling, a few people even outright laughing! They probably thought it was a comedy bit.

Anita glanced at Tina and Jake, who were seated front and center. Jake was chuckling, and Tina had plastered a smile to her face, but the horror shone through in her eyes. The music continued, never seeming to end, but not before Anita tripped, nearly falling. She was saved by Nikhil's firm grasp, though it had been his foot she tripped over.

She stood up in his arms, ready to push him away, when a hush fell over the room. Anita looked out into the audience and found everyone looking at their phones, and then looking up at them. What was going on? She glanced at Nikhil just as she heard her brother's voice booming through the speakers.

"It's fine, is it? You pretending to be married to your ex-husband for tuition money?"

"Well, not when you say it like that." She sounded pathetic.

"And what's this about you getting back together with him? That better not be true."

She shook her head. *"It's not. I was just trying to let Sonny down gently."*

She pulled herself free of Nikhil's grasp and looked behind him at the big screen that was going to be used for the photo slideshow of the newlyweds. But instead of the slideshow, there was a video clip playing of her and Amar in the hallway that morning. Amar in his catering uniform, and her in tears. It kept replaying those few lines, and an image of Tina and Jake's wedding app was stamped in the corner of the screen. She pulled out her phone from the small pouch hooked to her sari and opened the app to confirm what she already feared. She didn't even need to scroll through the pictures. Confirmation hit her like a punch to the belly. A picture of her and Nikhil's signatures on their divorce papers.

She put her phone back in the pouch and stomped to the computer that was showing the slideshow. She typed a few things and the video stopped, silence resonating throughout the hall.

She marched out of the hall, oblivious to the stares and murmurs that followed her. All she registered was that Nikhil was at her heels. She continued walking up and down the hallway.

She saw Sonny from the corner of her eye. He looked terrible, stricken. She couldn't blame him. She would apologize to him, but first—

"What are you doing?" Nikhil asked from behind her.

"Looking for *her*," she spit out from between her teeth.

"Anita—"

And then there she was. Anita knew she would stick around to gloat. There was no point to doing all of that if she couldn't watch. And that was her mistake. Every villain made one, and this was Jalissa's.

Anita ripped off the rings from all her fingers and thrust them at Nikhil. "Hold these."

The bitch didn't even move as Anita approached her, sari hiked up so she could take long strides.

Anita didn't even speak. She didn't even stop moving. She marched right up to Jalissa and punched her. Jalissa's hand went to her face, where the punch had landed, her mouth opened in a horrified O. She looked for a moment as if she wanted to retaliate, but whether it was the look on Anita's face or the fact that Nikhil was fuming next to her or that Dada called out at just that moment, Jalissa took off without even looking back.

Anita turned at the sound of Dada's voice and marched back, Nikhil still at her heels. She'd never raised a hand to anyone in her whole life. She'd never really wanted to. Her hand was really going to hurt in the morning.

Rocky was guiding Dada into a small meeting room off the hallway, Seema-auntie and her sisters close behind. And with a stab of guilt, she realized they'd seen everything.

"Nikhil Vikash Joshi."

"Yes, Dada." Nikhil tugged at the mic that was clipped to him, disconnecting it.

"Start talking." His grandfather's tone was stiffer than he'd ever heard.

"Well, Dada. Anita and I are divorced."

"That is apparent." He nodded at Rocky's phone. "Why?"

Nikhil deflated. "Because Dada, she walked out. And I let her go." He did not look at Anita; he simply focused on Dada.

"So," Dada stated, sounding for all the world as if he were addressing a courtroom, "my youngest grandson is an idiot." Dada arched a white eyebrow.

"Yes, sir."

"Disappointing." His arched eyebrow spoke volumes. Disappointment was only the beginning. Nikhil saw anger and frustration, and when he looked into his grandfather's eyes, he saw sadness as well.

Nikhil's heart broke.

"And why are you pretending to be married?" Dada's laser focus never waned, and despite his grand discomfort, and his elder's obvious disappointment, Nikhil noted that Dada was looking and sounding quite like his old self. Certainly not frail or weak.

Nikhil squirmed under that scrutiny and flicked his

gaze to his mother. "Well, we didn't want to disappoint you, and then your health—"

His mother stepped forward. "That was my doing, Papa."

Dada's eyebrow again. "Why am I not surprised?"

Nikhil's masis made noises of agreement from behind her.

His mother turned to face them. "Oh shut up, you two! I don't know why I spend so much time trying to fit in with you two. You're both basically suck-ups to Papa."

Their looks of complete indignation were a sight to behold.

Seema-auntie swallowed. "They ended their marriage after two years. I didn't want you to suffer the humiliation of a divorce in the family, so I put off telling you. Then Ma passed and you had your heart attack. You were weak and I was afraid news like this might give you another heart attack. So when Tina's wedding came up, I asked Anita to come and pretend to be married to Nikhil for the duration. She agreed."

"You are paying her." Dada's voice dripped with sadness.

"In a sense." She could barely look her father in the eye. Nikhil noticed the masis were wide-eyed and gaping. No sign of sneering or that air of superiority they carried around his mother.

"What do you mean, in a sense?" Nikhil fired up. "You can't go back on your deal. She's counting on the money."

Seema-auntie turned to her younger son. "We amended the details this morning. I will give a job to one of her clients instead."

Nikhil snapped around to Anita. But she avoided his gaze.

Dada turned to Anita, then Nikhil. "You two…" His voice cracked.

"How could you do this to Papa?" demanded Neepa-masi. "Keeping secrets, lying. You never change, Seema."

"You didn't even tell us. We're your sisters, for god's sake!" Deepa-masi added.

"Sisters? Ha!" Seema-auntie stood and faced them. "You have never once treated me like your sister. You always have your little secrets and you have never even supported my career. When Vikash passed, I ran JFL while I raised three children. The fact that you didn't help was one thing, but then you would get upset when I couldn't drop everything and come running for whatever was happening. I am a lawyer. And a damn good one, too. And if I had told you about the divorce you would have gone running to Papa and Ma and told them how I screwed up again. And I refuse to let Papa suffer more humiliation."

"Was it really Dada who would have been humiliated by Nikhil's divorce?" Rocky spoke up. "Or was it you, Mom?"

"I was not humiliated… Nikhil is my son. I felt bad that things didn't work out for him."

"Then how come *no one* knows, even here, in town?" Rocky continued. "Face it. It was easier to tell the lie that they were still together, because you could save face. You have always underestimated Nikhil, and you continue to do so, by not telling the truth."

"No. That's not true." Seema-auntie worried the end of her sari in defiance.

"Isn't it, Mom?" Nikhil finally spoke, a sadness in his voice.

"Nikhil… I…"

"Never mind, Mom. It's fine." He shrugged.

She shook her head at Nikhil and turned to Rocky. "Rakesh Joshi, you should have come to me with Jalissa's demands."

"Why? You would have given in."

"Damn right I would have." His mother shrugged. "It would have saved us this drama at your sister's wedding."

"What would have saved the drama, Mom, was not inviting Jalissa to begin with, or even better, being honest about Nikhil's divorce. I fired Jalissa rather than let her blackmail our family."

"On whose authority—"

"On *mine*, Mom. I run the day-to-day. And you have no room to talk right now, the way you told everyone about the baby when Easha and I specifically—"

"So what if they know? You worry too much."

"Not your call, Mom. You can't just go around controlling everyone, rewriting the narrative when you don't like it. Like this whole thing with Nikhil and Anita. You didn't even warn Nikhil that Anita was coming! No more, Mom. You have issues with your family. That's on you. Nikhil, Tina and I aren't playing anymore."

His mother stood there, speechless. No one had ever spoken to her like this, least of all her golden child, Rocky.

She deflated. "You know, my whole life I have raced to keep up with my sisters. They always did everything so perfect. And I was just…overlooked. I suppose I simply wanted to be seen and seen as successful and competent and—"

"Perfect?" said Nikhil.

She nodded, tears in her eyes.

"Welcome to the club," Nikhil spoke softly.

"I always focused on how you three reflected upon me. I was a single mother, and I wanted—no, needed—to prove that I was capable of doing it all myself. Any mess up of yours indicated that I was a failure. And you, Nikhil, being on your own, unknown path since the minute you were born, were a source of stress for me always. I should have embraced your spirit, but instead, I tried to push it into a mold of my making. And look what happened. You're working at your sister's wedding. Missing once-in-a-lifetime events to prove you are successful, worthy. I blame myself."

Nikhil couldn't believe what he was hearing. And a quick glance at Rocky told him his brother did not either. Their mother had always been a formidable force in their lives, more intimidating and demanding after their father had died. He couldn't reconcile that with the vulnerable woman who was confessing her fears to them right now. "Well, I didn't exactly make it easy."

She grinned. "No, you did not." She shook her head. "I have always seen so much of me in you. Your sense of independence, not wanting to follow the crowd." She cut her eyes to her sisters. "But I never once suspected that you felt that need to prove yourself, like I did." Her face fell. "I suppose I should have, seeing as how that's how I spent my life, but... I didn't." She stood. "I am proud of you, and I always have been. Even before you became a bestselling author. I was proud of your spirit and the man I watched you become. That is success."

She smiled at her father, who nodded at her. "And don't let anyone tell you otherwise. Even me."

She went to her father and lifted her chin and looked him in the eye. "Nikhil and Anita are divorced. I asked Anita to come and pretend to be married to Nikhil so I didn't have to tell you. News of your failing health was much exaggerated—" she cut her eyes to her older sister "—but even when I saw that you were fine, I continued with the charade because Nikhil being divorced meant that *I* had failed *him* somehow. And I did not want to face that I had actually failed one of my children, even though I knew it was true."

Dada looked at her, his face expressionless for a moment. "As parents, we all fail our children, somehow, even with the best of intentions." He grinned at her. "Me included." He wrapped his arms around her. "Beti. You did the best you could, as we all did. The rest is up to them. And stop competing with your sisters. It's tiresome after fifty years, and no one will ever win. I have three strong, independent, highly opinionated daughters. Each of you has unique strengths and weaknesses and I love you all equally." Nikhil's mother pulled back, and he saw tears in her eyes.

Dada, however, had a twinkle in his eye. "My grandchildren will always beat you three out." He chuckled. "Anita?" He turned toward her. "Did you just punch Jalissa?"

"Yes, Dada. I did," Anita answered tight-lipped, but with her chin in defiance.

Dada grinned from ear to ear. "She's my favorite."

Chapter 20

"Where were you?" Anita fired at him as they stood in the hall. They'd left Nikhil's mother with her father and sisters and Rocky to figure how to best handle the uproar Jalissa's bombshell had caused.

"I'm sorry. I had a meeting with a publisher and it ran long—"

"I *knew* it. You were working."

"If you knew it, why are you so mad?" He said it as if it were a completely normal thing to do.

"So you weren't there for me, when I specifically asked you to cue me, because you were working?" Her voice went up an octave.

"It was just a dance. The meeting was with that big publisher I've been telling you about. It was important." The words sounded hollow, however, even to him.

"Just a dance? In front of like four hundred people. At your sister's wedding! The person you say is your most favorite person in the world and you were *work-ing*!" They ended up alone in front of the elevators. People were coming and going; the elevator ding was constant. Anita stopped walking in a corner where the activity was minimal.

"What do you care? You're leaving tomorrow anyway. You won't see any of these people ever again," Nikhil argued.

She opened her mouth to retort, but changed her mind. "You know what? You're right. But why wait until tomorrow? This farce is over." She shook her head at him. "You have changed. I always knew you wanted to be a successful writer, but working and chasing success is what has become most important to you. Maybe your mom is right, and you're doing that to prove something. Although what that something is, I have no idea. You never were like this when we were married. What happened to you?"

"Nothing happened to me. I'm just trying to be a success. Like the rest of my family. Like I have been told my whole life. My whole family has always worked and put work ahead of anything else. I'm just doing what I'm supposed to be doing." Nikhil paused.

He was serious. Anita shook her head at him. "I married you when you had nothing. I left because you did not support my dreams and goals, even though I fully supported yours. I was looking for purpose like I needed air, and when I found it, *you*, the person who claimed to love me most, did not stand by me. I had no choice but to leave. I had to take care of myself, because you taught me that no one else would," Anita said.

Silence permeated the space in between them. Anita got onto an elevator and pushed the button for their floor. In minutes, they were on the floor and walking into their room.

"Listen to us. Listen to me." Anita leaned against the door when it shut. "Pissed off at you for not cueing me—in a dance. I'm not five." She shook her head. "To be honest, I barely even bothered to learn the steps." She shrugged. "I just figured I'd lean on you." Her voice softened.

"Anita, I'm sorry."

"It's not you. Sure, you should have shown up—but it's not all on you. I'm responsible for my part in this whole fiasco." She sighed. "I married you because I fell in love with your creativity and spirit. But I was also looking for stable ground. When my parents died, my whole life turned upside down. I was privileged and taken care of. But in an instant, I was forced to take care of myself. Like really take care of myself. No parental money or support. It was just me and Amar." She looked at him. "I thought marrying you would ground me. That it would somehow take away that lost feeling I had after losing my parents."

"Did it?"

She shrugged. "For a time, maybe. But it was wrong of me to put that burden on you—and you didn't even know."

"Did you…did you even love me?" His voice shook like her answer could change the world.

The hesitation in his voice was heartbreaking. But she had no trouble answering with the truth. "That is the one thing I know for sure. I did love you when I married you." It was all she could say.

She couldn't ask if he'd loved her. She was afraid of the answer. Either way.

She started taking off her jewelry and putting it in the small boxes that had already been laid out for her. It was time for her to leave. This marriage act they'd put on was done. She'd just run to the house while everyone was still here and pick up the rest of her few things.

Her overnight bag had magically arrived from the house, with a change of clothes. Perfect. She started to remove her sari as Nikhil watched her.

"I never answered your question," he said, watching her. "From the other night."

"It's okay. It doesn't matter." She folded the sari and started to pull pins from her hair.

"You had asked what started me finally writing. The short answer is, you left."

Anita stopped moving for a moment to turn and look at him. He was telling the truth. "I don't understand."

"Well, you left. And I found myself flailing. I had failed at marriage. I had failed you. So, I locked myself in my apartment and sat myself in front of my computer. And I forced the words out. At first just five hundred words. Then a thousand. Then a chapter."

"So? You started writing when I was no longer in your life." She harumphed. "Proof we should not be together."

"I started writing *because* you were no longer in my life. I thought that if I was successful, like the rest of my family, you might want to come back. I didn't realize how incredibly wrong I was until now." He sat in the armchair, with his elbows on his knees, and rubbed his face, before looking at her again. "You didn't leave because I was not successful. You left because you needed me and I wasn't there for you. Because you wanted to follow your passion, and instead of supporting you, I let all my insecurities rule me and I shut you down. Just like tonight. We'd rehearsed for this, I promised I'd cue you, but again, I allowed myself to get caught up in impressing you and my family with how busy and successful I am, when in fact, all I did was piss off my brother and sister and worst of all, let you down— again." He stood. "That is unforgivable. No matter how much I love you."

Anita let his words sink in to every part of her. He loved her. *He loved her.* A lightness started to move through her. She halted it.

"You have been successful for a while now." Her voice was heavy as realization set in. "You didn't reach out to me."

"That's the problem, isn't it? A little part of me always knew...that I...would never be enough, no matter how successful, because the reality is that I know that I don't deserve you."

Sadness weighed down his words and Nikhil Joshi unceremoniously turned and left her life.

Chapter 21

"What are you doing home?" Amar asked as he rolled in after midnight.

Anita was on the sofa in leggings and a T-shirt, blanket covering her, watching old home movies and eating ice cream from the carton. She was a cliché. Whatever, just add it to the pile. She shrugged. "Like you didn't hear."

"Everyone heard." He glanced at the TV and sat down. They watched a clip of one of their birthday parties. Their parents looked so young.

"How much trouble are you in at work?" Anita finally asked.

"Enough. Apparently, yelling at your sister, while not a good big-brother thing to do, is not a fireable offense in the catering industry."

"Good to know."

"Changing the recipe for three of the side dishes is."

"You did what?" Anita sat up and looked at him.

"I improved those dishes. They were bland and boring. I didn't do an overhaul—I just made a small adjustment when no one was looking."

"Small, like...?"

"Like I added some of Mom's special masala to them!"

"Wait—you know how to make the special masala?" Anita sat up straight.

"Well, it's not perfect, but I'm close." Amar grinned.

"And you used it tonight?"

"Yes, but then Ranjit, the head chef, tasted it and figured out what happened."

"How did he know?"

Amar was suddenly interested in his fingernails. "It might not have been the first time I did that."

"You're fired?"

"Looks that way." He looked sheepish.

Anita nodded. "You know I forfeited the money?"

"Yes. But who is Charlotte?"

Anita told him the whole story. "So, you have no job, and I have to take out a loan for my last year of school. We're quite the pair, you and I."

"You did the right thing, Anita." He took the spoon from her and pointed it at her. "Don't worry." He scooped up some ice cream and tasted it. "What's this? It's amazing. Cardamom, vanilla, a hint of orange."

"A Divya concoction. Seriously, that girl is going to have me the size of a house at the rate she's trying new things. How was she tonight?"

Her brother's face lit up for a moment, Anita noticed, before he realized it and masked his face. "She was good."

"That's it? She was good?"

"She was great. What do you want? She did the job."
Anita rolled her eyes.

Amar took another spoonful.

"Hey, get your own ice cream. My life just—"

"Just what?"

"Imploded."

Her big brother turned and looked at her. "You're in love with him again."

"Wrong." She snatched back the spoon.

"Oh, I don't think I'm—"

Anita put a huge spoonful of ice cream in her mouth and spoke around it. "I never really stopped loving him."

"Does he love you?"

"Yes." She couldn't deny it. When she thought about all that happened over the four days, she knew it in her heart that he was in love with her. Which made the truth sting even more. "He just doesn't think he deserves me. And it's not my job to convince him."

It was well past midnight by the time Nikhil finally made it back to his hotel room. His cousins had questions, his uncles, their parents' friends—not to mention that this had been Tina's wedding reception.

He and Rocky had taken over the reception, seen to it that there was still a celebration for their sister and new husband and that all the guests were fed. If they learned nothing from their mother, it was that no one came to an Indian wedding and left without being properly fed. They took to the dance floor in celebration, but the talk was all about Nikhil and Anita. Every time he heard her name, his heart broke just a little bit more. He simply smiled and moved on.

"So, I guess no fifth-anniversary party, huh?" asked Sangeeta.

"Seeing as how we are divorced…"

"You could have called us anytime, bhai." Hiral had slapped him on the shoulder and given him a hug. "But I have to say, she really didn't seem like she was faking while she was here."

"Thanks." Nikhil refused to allow himself the hope that she might actually be in love with him.

His mother remained reserved, quietly thanking the guests, and not commenting on much more. Dada was just as quiet, as were his masis.

The night finally ended and Nikhil was forced to make his way up to his very empty hotel room. He checked his email. There was one from Chantelle, telling him that the publisher's representative was appalled that he left in the middle of a meeting. Not to mention, she was there for all the family drama. The publisher felt that he should not have scheduled a meeting during a time when he had other priorities. They were questioning his professionalism, and strongly reconsidering whether they wanted to work with him. Chantelle was trying to smooth things over.

He was numb. That publisher had been everything he'd wanted from his writing career. Being with them would have put him on a trajectory he'd only dreamed of.

He hadn't committed to his family. He hadn't committed to his job. The only thing he really cared about was Anita. And he would never have her.

He was just getting out of the shower when there was a knock at the door. His heart leaped for a minute thinking it might be Anita. But he squelched that thought by the time he answered it.

"Hey." Rocky was still in his suit, tie draped around his neck, two cold beers in his hand.

"Hey." Nikhil left the door open and walked back in. "Don't you have a pregnant wife to dote upon?"

"She's sleeping." Rocky came in and shut the door behind him, handing Nikhil a beer. He held his out, and Nikhil tapped it. "Nicely done today, little brother. Who needs a wedding planner?"

"She took off fast, didn't she?"

"Apparently even we do not pay her enough for all that drama." Rocky took a swig of his beer. "Tina was happy in the end. That's all that mattered."

"True that." Nikhil smiled. "They're good together, her and Jake."

"She's pregnant."

"What the hell?" Nikhil sat up straight in his arm-chair, his heart racing, spilling some beer. "Does Mom know?"

Rocky started laughing. "Gotcha!"

Nikhil threw a pillow at his brother. "Jackass." He settled back into the chair. "Give me a goddamn heart attack. Forget about Dada, you're going to put *me* in the hospital."

Rocky had a few chuckles left inside him. "Your face, though."

"Why are you here, Rock?" Nikhil sipped his beer. He had no idea how much he'd wanted it until the bitter, cool, fizzy liquid hit his tongue.

"What happened?"

Nikhil knew what he meant. They were brothers, after all.

"She left. Packed her bags. Probably stopped by at the house, grabbed her stuff and left." He picked at the label on the bottle before taking a healthy swallow.

"And what? You let her walk?"

"Yes."

"You're going after her tomorrow? Just giving her time to cool off?"

"She was cool when she left."

"Then what's the plan?"

"There's no plan, Rock. We're done. We were done three years ago." He rubbed his brow. "After the way I treated her back then? Of course we're staying divorced."

"What?"

"That's pretty much why she left. She was trying to stand on her own two feet, and I couldn't be bothered to see that. I was so caught up in the idea that she would leave me—either figuratively or literally—once she went to work for JFL, that I didn't see what she wanted."

"Which was?"

"Just for me to support her, like married couples do."

"So tell her." Rocky sat up in the chair.

"I did." Nikhil sunk further into his.

"Did you ask her to come back?"

"No."

"Why not?"

"Because."

"Because *what*? You're clearly in love with her. After you got over the initial shock of her being here, I haven't seen you that happy since you guys were married."

"Just let it go, Rocky."

"Why?"

"Look, I appreciate you doing the whole big-brother

thing, but you've done your part, you can feel good about coming here and talking to me, but I'm done."

"I didn't come here to play a part. I *am* your big brother, damn it. Take a minute and remember that. We used to be close. Remember?"

Nikhil did remember. Their parents had left the three of them with a nanny more than once as children, but it was always Rocky that Nikhil and Tina had looked to. Though Rocky had become more intense after their father died, and less the fun big brother. He'd had more rules, which had not gone over well with young Nikhil.

Nikhil looked at his brother. "I guess you didn't really feel like a kid after Dad died."

Rocky shrugged. "Tell me why you can't go after the one woman you've always loved."

Nikhil shrugged. "I just can't."

"What's stopping you?"

Nikhil shook his head.

"Nikhil!" Rocky raised his voice. "What is the matter with you?"

"I don't deserve her!" Nikhil shouted back.

"What?"

"You heard me. I do not deserve her." He slumped his shoulders in admission. It cost him to reveal his fears to Rocky. "She was everything to me. She gave me her heart. And I did not hesitate to break it because I was selfish, caught up in my own fears. I'm a cliché, Rock. Didn't know what I had until she was gone." He shook his head. "She's better off without me."

"You really believe that?" Rocky asked.

"I do." Nikhil's heart sat heavy in his chest.

"Okay. Maybe you're right. She's smart, fun, gorgeous—she'll find someone new in no time."

"Sure." Nikhil nodded, his stomach churning.

"You'll find someone soon, too," Rocky said, relaxing back into the armchair. "Oh!" He sat up. "Easha told me Mom got a few offers tonight after your divorce was revealed. You'll be fine." His brother's sarcasm was not lost on him.

Nikhil shrugged. The idea of someone new for him was not appealing. Though the idea of someone new for Anita was even worse.

They drank their beers in silence for a moment.

"Answer me this." Rocky pointed his bottle at Nikhil. "Are you the same man you were when you were married to her?"

"What is this BS?"

"Just answer the question," insisted Rocky.

"No. Of course not. I was young, insecure, had a chip on my shoulder the size of your ego." Nikhil frowned and sipped his beer.

"And now?"

Nikhil stayed silent instead of throwing out the retort he had ready to go. To his credit, Rocky remained silent while Nikhil mulled. "Now… I guess now I don't have that chip on my shoulder."

"Why?"

"Because I found my own way, on my own terms."

"Exactly. You're a different man than you were back then. A better man, even. You let the Jalissa thing eat at you, when that woman simply used you from the get go. She never had any real feelings for you at all."

"What kind of idiot falls for that?" Nikhil was still a bit disgusted with himself.

"The good kind." Rocky's voice softened. "That's the part of yourself you need to come to terms with. That good, kind soul. You always rooted for the underdog. You always stood up for people, regardless of what would happen to you. But you didn't care about *winning*—you cared about people, about what was right." Rocky paused, quieted his voice. "I know you fought those jerks in high school because they were bullying that boy with the turban."

"How do you know that?"

"I heard Mom talking to his parents. They had called to thank her for what you did. The boy was too scared to come forward, so you were suspended. Why do you think Mom never punished you?"

"I thought she was too busy and couldn't be bothered." Nikhil shrugged.

Rocky was silent for a moment. "In all seriousness, do you for one second believe that Anita would screw you over the way Jalissa did?"

He didn't. He knew there had been a time when he did fear that. But that was based on his fears, as opposed to anything real that Anita had ever done. "No. Not anymore."

"Then that's your answer. You made a mistake. People make mistakes. You grow and change. Anita loves you. You deserve that. You deserve to at least try."

"You think she still loves me?"

"I know she does." Rocky finished his beer and tapped the bottle down. "Why do you think she punched Jalissa? Anita is willing to fight for you." He tipped his head at Nikhil. "Pretty hot."

Nikhil could not stop his grin. It was pretty damn hot.

DAY FIVE:

EGGS, ROTLI, AND THE NEWSPAPER
Brunch off site…

Chapter 22

Nikhil woke with a pit in his stomach and a defined feeling of loss.

Anita.

Interesting because the last time she left, he only felt anger and defiance. He closed his eyes and tried to fall back asleep. He might have dreamed about her, and he'd rather go back to that than face today's postwedding brunch with the whole family.

Sleep would not come.

He sat up in bed and inhaled. Maybe he would get used to not having her around as time went on.

Except that he didn't want to. He wanted to blow off the brunch and go find her. His conversation with Rocky was still fresh in his head as he finished showering when there was a banging at his door.

Again, his entire body lightened in the hope that it was Anita. "I'm coming."

He opened the door to find Dada standing there, dressed and ready for the day. "Dada?"

So not Anita.

"Get dressed. I need you to take me somewhere."

"Where?"

"Don't ask questions. Just hurry up before your masis wake up."

Nikhil held the door open. "Okay, sit down. I just need five minutes."

Ten minutes later they were in Nikhil's car, having sneaked out the back way to avoid running into any family members. Nikhil had no idea what his grandfather was up to, and the older man wasn't giving any clues.

"Okay, drive," Dada commanded as he fastened his seat belt.

"Where am I going?"

"Pull out of this massive driveway and I will tell you," Dada ordered. "And quickly before my daughters see us. They never let me do what I want."

Nikhil pulled the car down the long driveway and then Dada pulled out a piece of paper and directed him.

"Can I see the paper?"

"No. Just drive."

After a few turns they got on the highway for two exits, and then a couple more turns into an older upper-middle-class residential neighborhood. It was too familiar to Nikhil.

He looked at his grandfather as realization set in. "Seriously, Dada?"

"What? I want brunch." Now all of a sudden, the old man was innocent and pleasant.

Nikhil rolled his eyes. "Mom has brunch at home."

Dada actually winked at him. "True. But she does not have Anita."

* * *

Anita and Amar had stayed up too late talking and planning, but Anita was awake early anyway. Amar had helped her wrap her hand after icing it for a bit. She flexed her fingers. Stiff with bruising.

She couldn't sleep. Every time she closed her eyes, images of Nikhil bombarded her. She was debating going for a run to clear her head when the doorbell rang. She bolted for the door before it could ring again, so that her brother could sleep in.

She opened the door and her heart lifted before she could control it. Nikhil stood next to his grandfather, looking sheepish and ridiculously handsome.

"I'm sorry to bother you like this." He looked at his grandfather. "He just told me to drive, I had no idea—"

"Stop apologizing, boy. She is happy to see you," Dada interrupted.

"Come in, please. It's fine, really." She focused on Dada. It was too much to look at Nikhil. She stepped aside to allow them in. "Amar is still sleeping."

"No problem. We do not need him right now," Dada announced as he looked around her house.

"What can I do for you?" Anita asked.

"Brunch," Dada stated simply as if it was obvious.

Anita furrowed her brow and finally made eye contact with Nikhil, who shook his head, put his hands out and shrugged.

"Isn't there a wedding brunch at your place?" Anita spoke slowly.

"I have not lost my mind, children. I know that there is a meal at my daughter's house. But I want brunch *here*. And I want you two to make it." He was firm, and with that, he walked into Anita's house and sat himself at the large island in her kitchen.

Anita stared at Nikhil, her eyes wide.

"Stop staring at each other and get to work. I know that both of you were raised properly, so I know that when an elder asks for something—especially food—you comply. Honestly, it is the very minimum you could do for an old man after lying to him for four days."

With huge sighs of compliance as well as some chagrin, both Nikhil and Anita made their way to the kitchen.

"Okay." Nikhil sighed, glancing at Anita for confirmation.

Anita nodded her agreement, but she couldn't really look at him.

"Well, don't just stand there. Anita has told me that you are both excellent cooks. So? Let's see what you can do," Dada commanded.

"You told him we could cook?" Nikhil said, slightly irritated, as he grabbed two aprons from a drawer and handed her one.

Anita took the apron. *He remembered which drawer.* They'd cooked here a few times with Amar. But that was ages ago. In spite of herself, she was impressed.

"Well, we used to cook together. *I* can still cook well. Not sure about you," Anita shot back.

"Oh, I can cook just fine, *Neets*."

Anita froze in the middle of tying her apron, then looked at him. Amusement danced in his eyes; he had said her nickname on purpose. "Bring it then, *Nicky*." That was why Nikhil hated when Rocky called him Nicky, because it was what she used to call him when it was just the two of them.

They both turned to Dada and spoke at the same

time. "Dada, what would you like for brunch?" They glanced at each other.

"What kind of question is that? Just make brunch. But add an Indian kick." Dada had found Anita's newspaper and was rifling through it. He had made himself completely at home. As if he was at his grandchild's home. Anita smiled.

"Okay, then." She went to the fridge and bumped into Nikhil, who was doing the same thing. She shot him a look and he stepped back as she opened the door. She reached in to grab the eggs, just as Nikhil did the same.

"I got the eggs," Anita called out.

"Fine." Nikhil reached for the milk, just as Anita did with her empty hand. She backed away and Nikhil picked up the milk.

Anita put the eggs on the island and went back to get vegetables from the fridge.

"I got the vegetables." Nikhil put bell peppers, zucchini and jalapenos on the island.

"Fine." She grabbed the butter.

"Just get the—"

She put the butter on the island.

"—butter."

Anita raised an eyebrow at him. "I know we need butter."

He held his hands up in surrender.

"Why don't you get—"

But Nikhil already had his hands on the stainless steel container that held leftover rotli. "The rotli?" he asked, both eyebrows raised at her.

Anita made a face. "And the athanu." She headed back to the fridge for cilantro and tomatoes. She noticed that Nikhil went to the pantry and came out with onions, garlic and the jar of spicy mango pickle she'd asked for. They assembled their ingredients and considered them.

"How about some chai?" Dada asked from the other end of the island. He seemed quite content, if not extremely amused.

Anita gave a one-armed shrug with a small smile and glanced at Nikhil. "Well, that's his area of expertise." She turned to him. "But of course I don't have your secret masala here."

Nikhil shrugged. "Worth a try, anyway."

"Or you could just make the masala here." Anita pursed her lips. "I promise not to look."

Nikhil chuckled. "Nice try. But I'll make do with whatever you have."

"I have the one Divya makes for us." She reached into a cupboard and handed him a jar.

"Not a problem." Nikhil grabbed the saucepan and Anita placed the milk next to the stove, along with fresh ginger root and some leaves of fresh mint she plucked from the plant in the windowsill.

Meanwhile, Nikhil gathered the loose tea and filled the pot with water, setting it on the stove to boil.

Anita pulled out two cutting boards and two knives and set about chopping onions on hers. Nikhil peeled a few cloves of garlic and set them next to her cutting board. He set about chopping up the jalapenos and bell pepper.

"What happened with that publisher meeting?" Anita asked as she started chopping garlic.

"They were pissed. They questioned my priorities for scheduling a work meeting when I clearly had other obligations." He side-eyed her, but Anita did not hide her grimace of satisfaction. "They were ready to pull the offer. Chantelle smoothed things over and they offered to reschedule."

"I guess that's good for you." Anita kept chopping.

"I told them no."

Anita stopped chopping and looked up at him. "You did what?"

Nikhil sliced the bell pepper thinly, the long way. He did not look up from his task. "I told her no."

"But I thought that's what you wanted. That publisher was going to give you everything you dreamed of."

He flicked his gaze up at her for a brief second before returning to his task. "Not everything."

Anita watched him work for a moment. "Oh." She returned to her chopping. "So now what?"

Nikhil moved the sliced bell pepper to a bowl and started on the jalapeno. "So now we check out the other offers."

"There are other offers?"

"There will be."

"Okay. Well, that's good then."

"What about you? Will you take out a loan?"

"Most likely. Amar got fired last night."

Nikhil's turn to be surprised. "So a fabulous night for all."

"He literally got fired for improving a dish." Anita shook her head. "He used our mom's masala."

Nikhil stopped chopping and looked at her. "Seriously? He can make that?"

"Just about. Maybe now, he'll consider starting the catering business he's always talked about."

"Good for him." Nikhil moved to the stove to tend to the chai. Anita started chopping the cilantro on the other side of the stove, while she sautéed the onions and peppers.

Nikhil poured three mugs of chai and they stopped for a few moments to enjoy it with Dada. Anita inhaled the aroma of happiness before she took a sip. "This is always amazing, Nicky. Even without your special masala today."

"She is correct. Excellent chai." Dada sipped his and placed it back on the island. "You know what I heard? I heard that Nikhil had Rocky fire Jalissa that day."

Nikhil threw a furtive glance at Dada, then Anita. "Where did you hear that?"

"I'm an old man. People underestimate my ability to hear things." Dada held out his hands and shrugged.

"Is that true, Nikhil? You're the one who pissed her off?" Anita gently put down her mug and turned to him.

"Well, she was trying to blackmail JFL." Nikhil squirmed. "And while I may not be an employee of JFL, I certainly won't stand for blackmail."

"What did she want?" Anita furrowed her brow. She knew what Jalissa wanted. Nikhil. But if she was blackmailing them, she wanted more.

Nikhil pressed his lips together like he didn't want to tell her.

"What's the big deal? Just tell me," Anita insisted.

"She wanted the community division that Jake had mentioned."

Anita just looked at him.

"What? That's yours."

"I haven't even graduated yet."

"One year. And you'll easily pass the bar. You would be perfect for starting that up, and you know it. There's no way Jalissa was getting that."

"You had to know she'd retaliate. I mean, I only met her two days ago and even I could see that about her."

Nikhil shrugged. "I didn't care. And Rocky agreed with me. We don't cave in to blackmail. She should have been gone a long time ago." He smirked at her. "Anyway, *I* wasn't the one who punched her." He nodded at her wrapped hand.

Anita pressed her lips together. "Well, she deserved that, too."

"That she did," Dada agreed. Nikhil laughed and Anita joined him.

"I wasn't planning on taking it," Anita finally said as they got back to cooking.

"What do you mean?" Nikhil beat an egg and poured it over some of the bell-pepper-and-onion mixture in the pan. "The job? But why?"

"Well, we're not really together, are we?" Anita answered as she shredded some cheese.

"What does that have to do with working for JFL?"

"It would be too hard—awkward. They're your family…"

"You could do it. It might be awkward at first—but I shouldn't be getting in the way of things that are good for you."

Anita had to stop and stare at him. Who was this Nikhil? They continued to work in silence. She placed a rotli on top of the flat egg mixture and flipped it over. She added the shredded cheese and rolled it up.

"Nice." Nikhil grinned at her.

"I saw it on Instagram."

"You're amazing," Nikhil whispered.

Anita flushed. "I know." They made a few more roll-ups, potatoes and pancakes, all the while chatting as if they'd been doing this forever. By the time they got out plates, Dada was no longer at the island.

"He's asleep," Anita called from the living room. "On the sofa." She shook her head. "Let him sleep. We'll wake him after we eat."

Nikhil filled plates for them while Anita made mimosas. "What's brunch without a mimosa?"

They sat next to each other and started to eat, the conversation never stopping.

"I'm sorry, Anita." Nikhil's voice went quiet and serious.

"For what?" She took a bite of her eggs. Funny, she'd had no appetite an hour ago.

"For everything. For the way I treated you when we were married, and everything you were put through this week. You deserve better than that." He looked around and motioned with his hands. "You deserve *this*. Good chai, good food, people who love you."

Anita's heart raced. Was he saying what she thought he was? "Dada does love me."

"Yes. He does." Nikhil was looking at her with such intensity. He moved closer.

"You know what else I deserve? Someone who loves me enough to bring me fresh chai when I'm working. Someone who knows I would never cut out without a good reason. Someone who wants what is best for me, even if it isn't what's best for them." Anita moved closer to him. "Know anyone like that?"

"Hey! What smells so good?" Amar bounded into the kitchen. "Nikhil? What are you doing here? And did you two make all this?" He ran his gaze over the food. "Looks amazing."

"Nikhil!" Dada called from the living room. "Time to go."

"You didn't even eat, Dada," Anita chided him.

"Eat?" Dada furrowed his brow. "Ah well. Maybe next time, eh, beti? We need to go before my daughters send the police looking for me."

Anita exchanged a glance with Nikhil, both of them smiling. Dada's motives for brunch were clear. "Sure, Dada. Next time."

Chapter 23

Nikhil stood in the doorway of her classroom. He watched Anita pack up her bags like he had so many times before. Computer bag, purse, coffee mug, bag with snacks. He'd learned what every bag was for when he would hang out with her after class.

He hadn't seen her for a few days. He told himself it was because he had his launch, and he was hanging out with a few cousins who had stayed a few extra days. But the truth was, he had been building up his courage.

His mother had informed him that Charlotte Montgomery was a lovely young woman with a lot on her plate, and that she was happy to give her a job.

"I also offered to pay that last year of tuition, but Anita said a deal was a deal, and that she would be fine," his mother had told him as she cooked dinner for the family.

Nikhil shook his head and smiled. Of course she did.

"Maybe she'll listen to you. Talk to her. She won't have to take the loan." She was chopping cilantro, and the fresh woodsy aroma filled the kitchen.

Nikhil laughed. "It's like you don't even know her, Mom. Or me."

She waved a hand and sighed. "I knew you wouldn't ask her. But I had to try."

"It's not even Sunday, Mom, and you're cooking."

His mother shrugged. "It's time I cut back a bit from JFL. Rocky can handle things. I want to spend time with my family. Especially once the baby comes."

Nikhil watched his mother bustle around in the kitchen. The air between them felt lighter, warmer since the wedding.

"Don't just stand there. Chop onions." She pointed her knife at the onions in front of him. He suppressed a smile and started chopping.

They worked in silence for a moment. "I guess we're more alike than I thought," Nikhil offered.

His mother grinned up at him as she pulled out ginger from the fridge. "I guess we are."

"Why don't you come to the launch tomorrow night?"

"I was thinking to come to your launch tomorrow."

They spoke in unison. Then smiled at each other.

"Sounds good," they both said together.

"Maybe go see Anita," his mother suggested.

"Mom."

She held up her hands in surrender. "It's a suggestion."

Nikhil had enjoyed a delicious meal with his mother and Rocky and Easha. They had opened a bottle of wine and FaceTimed with Tina and Jake.

The only thing missing was Anita.

Nikhil leaned against the doorframe and watched her. Her hair was down, silky and straight. She tucked a piece behind her ear as she balanced the bags on her shoulders and reached for her coffee mug. It wasn't just that he found her to be the most beautiful woman he knew. It wasn't the fact that every cell in his body was propelling him forward to her. It wasn't the fact that his heart raced like he was a teenager in love when he looked at her.

It was simply that he wanted to be the one she shared her life with. He wanted to be at her side while she changed the world.

"I do know someone like that," he said as he entered the classroom.

She jumped at the sound of his voice, nearly dropping all her things.

Nikhil stood just inside the doorway of her classroom, like he had so many times before.

She hadn't seen him since brunch, but then she wasn't sure that she would. She hadn't gone to his launch because, well, frankly, it was too painful. She might have to reconsider going to work for JFL when she graduated.

He was in jeans and a plain navy blue T-shirt that fit him and all his muscles perfectly. The exact clothes she always imagined him in, when she imagined him, which was all the time. He was clean-shaven; his wavy hair was tamed back. But what put her heart and body on alert was the way he was looking at her. He carried himself with an air of confidence she'd never seen before. And he was looking at her like she was the only thing before him. Like there was nothing he'd rather do than just stand there and drink her in.

She had just gathered her many bags and coffee mug

and was ready to leave for the evening. Seeing him, hearing his voice, she stopped, and everything clattered to the ground.

"Someone like what?" She knew exactly what he was talking about, but she needed to hear him say it. Her heart pounded in her chest.

"Someone who would bring you chai when you're working. Someone who knows that you would never cut out without a good reason." He was taking small, slow steps toward her, the look in his dark eyes devastating in its intensity. Nikhil's mouth when he smiled at her was a glorious thing. "Someone who wants what is best for you even if it's not best for him."

"Oh yeah?" Anita tried to put some sass in her voice, but the words came out breathy and soft.

"You also deserve someone who will stand by your side no matter what. Someone who understands your silent eye communication." He raised an eyebrow, standing in front of her now, looking at her with no amusement at all. "Someone who will hold you when you're sad. Someone who wants to kiss you senseless all the time." His eyes darkened. "Someone who knows you love them, no matter what. Someone who won't break your heart." He paused and now he was close enough for their bodies to touch. Too close. His next words came out in a husky whisper. "Someone who will love you with everything he has."

Anita swallowed hard. She could feel the heat from his body, smell his cologne. "You say you know someone like that?" She widened her eyes at him.

"I do."

The way he looked at her, that smile, the love in his eyes. "I love you. Only you." He spread his arms wide and let them drop. "I have always been yours even when I thought I wasn't. And I always will be, whether you'll have me or not." He paused and seemed to gather courage. "But I'm really hoping that you'll have me."

She reached up and kissed him, slowly at first. His response was immediate, but tentative. She relaxed and gave into her feelings for him in the same instant he kissed her with abandon. Almost as if he didn't care if she knew how intensely he loved her, because it was unchanging.

She held nothing back from him in that kiss, and neither did he.

When they parted, she lightly smacked him on the shoulder. "I knew you understood my eye communication."

He laughed. "Is that all you have to say?"

She shook her head. "I would love some chai."

"Now?" His eyes darkened and his voice thickened in anticipation of her response.

"No." She snuggled closer to him and whispered, "Tomorrow morning."

ALL THE REST OF THE DAYS—
HAPPILY EVER AFTER

Epilogue

IN LIEU OF A
FIFTH ANNIVERSARY PARTY...

Nikhil fidgeted in the groom's chair in the mandap staring at the white cloth in front of him. Two separate lives, two separate souls, becoming one.

The music cued him that Anita was on the way. Easha would walk first, then Tina. Amar was doing the puja that parents usually do. Divya would escort her down the aisle. He tried to peek around the cloth, and took a kick to the ankle from Rocky, who was holding the antarpat in front of him, his new brother-in-law Jake supporting the other side.

Her sari rustled and her anklets jingled as she entered the mandap and the music died down. Nikhil couldn't remember the last time he'd felt so at peace.

On just the other side of this cloth was a woman he loved with not just his heart, but his whole self—and who returned his love. A woman he could never be without. A woman he loved from the depths of his soul, to the ends of the universe. A woman he had once lost, but would never let go of again.

On the other side of this cloth was the rest of his life.

Rocky glanced at Jake, and then both men looked at him. Nikhil inhaled deeply and nodded. They dropped the cloth.

Anita stood before him resplendent and beautiful in her red-and-white bridal sari, unabashedly smiling at him, love emanating from her very being.

Nikhil's heart raced. He had no explanation for it, other than the knowledge that he had finally embraced his good fortune that Anita had returned to his life.

She met his gaze and silently told him she loved him. A tear in her eye told him that she missed having her parents here. He let his smile and eyes tell her that he loved her, and she smiled again.

When she was ready, she sat down across from him, her gaze never leaving his, and the rest of their lives began.

* * * * *